SHARP
SHOOTER

Also by
David Healey

Rebel Train

Rebel Fever

1812: Rediscovering Chesapeake Bay's Forgotten War

SHARP SHOOTER

DAVID HEALEY

BellaRosaBooks

BellaRosaBooks

SHARPSHOOTER
ISBN 978-1-933523-20-0
2007 Reprint Edition by Bella Rosa Books

Previously Published in the U.S.A. by Penguin Putnam Inc.
Jove Books; Mass Market Paperback; 1999; ISBN: 0-515-12693-4.

Printed in the United States of America on acid-free paper.

Book design by Bella Rosa Books

BellaRosaBooks and logo are trademarks of Bella Rosa Books

For Mary and Aidan,
and especially for Joanne, who listened and cheered.

Acknowledgments

This book would not have come around a second time without the enthusiasm of so many readers—many of whom have since become friends and acquaintances. Their kind words have encouraged me to continue writing.

I would be remiss not to thank the members of The Writers' Brigade who, in the early days after "Sharpshooter" first came out, joined me for book signings at more than one Civil War history event. Your company was always a pleasure.

Finally, a special thank you to Rod Hunter and Bella Rosa Books for giving "Sharpshooter" another shot.

"All we ask is to be left alone."
—*Jefferson Davis,*
in his inaugural address

Part I

Petersburg, Va.
November 8, 1864

Dawn.

Lucas Cole opened his eyes.

Nothing moved. The shapeless gray forms of sleeping soldiers covered the floor of the muddy trench. Some men tossed in their dirty blankets, murmuring to themselves. Others snored.

Only Cole was awake. Anyone watching would have seen only the quick, feral movement of his eyes. Once he was certain that everything was as it should be, Cole sat up. He put aside the loaded Colt Navy revolver that he had gripped in his right hand through the night in case there was any trouble as he slept among these strange men. As a sharpshooter, he roamed freely through the trenches. His Sharps rifle had also shared the blanket with him, lest anyone get notions about taking it.

Morning in the trenches was not greeted eagerly. If anything, it was better to be asleep. At least then a man wouldn't notice he was wrapped in a thin blanket, lying on some brush to keep himself out of the mud. Asleep, he could dream of mornings years ago when he would wake in a bed, with hard boards under his feet and his young wife busy around the warm stove, making a breakfast of biscuits and gravy, with the smell of coffee lingering.

Cole did not dwell on such thoughts as he woke with the first light showing on the horizon. He always rose before the sun. He had never had much use for gravy and biscuits, or even for coffee. He hated to waste that precious time when the whispery gray predawn gave enough light to move by. It was time he could use for hunting.

Cole reached for his canteen and took a drink. The water tasted muddy and gritty. His head throbbed dully from the whiskey he'd had to drink last night from a bottle shared around the fire.

He quickly made up his blanket roll and stuffed it in a depression in the trench. He slung the canteen and the Sharps over his shoulders, leaving his hands free for the difficult task of picking his way through the trenches in the poor light.

None of the sleeping men heard him go.

Cole quietly threaded his way through the earthworks. The trench where he had spent the night was one of the outermost defenses. Line after line of intertwined trenches ran back toward the city, with the trenches becoming deeper and more elaborate closer in. Some had boarded sides and bombproofs to protect against Yankee shelling. Out this far, the trenches weren't as deep, and only woven mats of saplings contained the sides.

Some trenches did not run parallel to the Yankee lines but toward them instead, gouged out of the red earth much like the grooves a dying man's hands might make as he clawed mud. It was into these shallow trenches that Cole now slipped. A sentry saw him, and Cole made sure the man got a look at the sniper's rifle slung across his back.

Deserters often tried to sneak out into the Yankee lines and give themselves up in hopes of a decent meal. They'd had enough of hunger and fighting. A man took a chance going over to the enemy, because the Yankees had lost patience with the starving Rebels. A dead Reb was less trouble to look after than a live one, after all. Cole wouldn't trust a Yankee worth a damn. He hated them with a passion that four years of war had not diminished. To Lucas Cole, anyone who wore a blue uniform would always be the enemy.

Cole slipped through the trench, moving ever closer, confident that he couldn't be seen in the semi-darkness. Still, he was cautious, for the Yankees had their pickets and sharpshooters, too. He reached the limit of the trench—where a tired soldier had simply stopped digging at the end of a day—and settled himself as low as he could into the dirt. He formed a small mound of earth to pillow the iron barrel of the Sharps and stretched himself out behind it to wait for the morning light to come up so he could shoot.

The Yankees in the trenches closest to Cole would be too wary to show themselves. Maybe a foolish boy would pop his head above the trench, but that was too much to hope for. He knew the Yankees farther back wouldn't be so careful.

As the light grew in the east, Cole spotted what he was looking for through the telescopic sight mounted on his rifle. A Yankee officer was walking along the trenches as if he thought himself perfectly safe. Ordinarily, the officer would only have to worry about ducking for cover if he heard Confederate artillery. He was nearly one thousand yards from where Lucas Cole had hidden himself.

It was an ungodly long way to shoot a rifle.

A Sharps rifle had an accurate range of four hundred and fifty yards. Beyond that it was hard to see the target, let alone hit it, and a man in plain iron sights was only a dot. But even at four hundred and fifty yards, a good marksman could put ten shots within an area four feet square.

Cole could cover his grouping at that distance with his hand.

But Cole wasn't just good. He was gifted with a rifle. He had been shooting since he was old enough to hold a musket on his own. He was one of those rare backwoods men who had only to look at a target and was able to hit it—even at a thousand yards. But long-range shooting was an uncertain proposition at best, even for the likes of Cole. A sudden tremor of the hand, an eddy of wind, even an imperfection in the bullet was enough to send the shot wildly astray.

Cole felt himself slipping into his shooter's trance. He ignored the November chill that crept into him from the ground and the frosty morning air. His body settled deeper into the trench, letting the Virginia soil hug him and steady his arms. The rifle barrel was immobile atop its pile of dirt. A shot like this required the steadiness of the earth.

All he could see was the Yankee officer walking back and forth. It was impossible at this distance to tell his rank, but Cole guessed from the way the man carried himself that he was a major, or at the very least a captain. Once a man got to be a captain he developed a certain swagger that came with rank.

I'll take you down a notch, Yank.

Cole liked to send his shots home as unseen as a lightning bolt from the hand of God. He enjoyed the idea of his rifle being a divine instrument.

Vengeance is mine, sayeth the Lord.

He had heard some preacher say that before the war, and he kept the sound of the words in his head, liked the way they went with the solid thunk of lead hitting flesh, a noise like a ripe watermelon being split with a knife. *Goddamn these Yankees.*

Hatred boiled up in him and he fought to push it back, because he must be calm to shoot. Yankees had killed his family two years ago. Cole had been off in the army. Bluebellies came to the Cole homestead to steal livestock and shot his father. His sister was in bed, sick with a fever, and the Yankees burned the house down on top of her. Cole's mother was already gone.

Don't think on it, he warned himself. *Just shoot this Yankee.* He forced his mind to go blank. Cole's breathing slowed and nearly stopped. In the last few moments before he fired, he wouldn't breathe at all. His heartbeat began to slow like the winding down of a watch, until there was scarcely a flutter in his chest.

The officer stopped and appeared to be staring right at Cole, although he knew it was impossible for the man to see him at that distance. It was a trick of the telescopic sight. In a space between his own gentle heartbeats, Cole's finger took up the last fraction of tension in the trigger.

The rifle fired.

It took a full second for the bullet to cross a thousand yards. In that time the Yankee could move or some stray gust of wind could alter the bullet's course. As Cole watched through the scope, he saw the Yankee officer flop over. The body twitched once or twice, then lay still.

One thousand yards. A clean kill.

He felt no emotion after shooting, only a sort of hollowness, much like he felt after being with a woman. He welcomed this emptiness, savored it.

Then Cole quickly reloaded, working the lever action of the Sharps. The Yankees in the works immediately in front of him would just be waking up and would wonder who was firing. Some curious, groggy soldier was bound to put his head above the works and take a look toward the Rebels.

Sure enough, a blue cap appeared. The telescope made it seem as if the Yankee was just a few feet away. The hair was tousled under the kepi, the face still creased from some rude pillow. Cole drove a bullet between the boy's eyes.

Then he was scuttling backwards like a crab out of the trench. It wouldn't be long before the Yankee sharpshooters would take up their own deadly work once again, and Cole didn't want to be their target.

He followed the trench back to the main works, where he found the same sentry on duty.

"I seen what you done," the man said, plainly awed. "That was some shootin'."

"It does work up a man's appetite for breakfast."

Some of the smile faded off the sentry's face. "That's two Yankees that won't be goin' home. And here the war's almost over. It's election day up North, you know, an' they say ol' Abe Lincoln ain't goin' to win."

"Keep your head down, boy," Cole told the sentry. "Some Yankee might blow it off and end the war right soon for you."

Heeding the warning, the sentry hunkered down behind his wall of earth and logs, watching as the lean figure of the sharpshooter disappeared into the labyrinth of muddy trenches.

"You've heard the news, General Hill?" asked General George Pickett by way of greeting the gaunt figure who entered the tent.

"It's Lincoln, then?" he asked.

"I'm afraid so. Those Yankees just don't know when they've had enough."

"It is unfortunate."

"*C'est la vie,*" Picket said. His laugh was almost girlish. "*Vive la guerre.*"

A. P. Hill glanced sharply at this fellow officer who, for all his style, often seemed not much better than a fool. His hair was pomaded and he emitted a slight odor of lilacs from some cologne he wore. And he still insisted on using the occasional French phrase.

Hill thought the war had reached a point where there was no longer any tolerance for colognes or silly platitudes spoken in French. With Lincoln's victory, the Confederacy was in desperate straits. The Northern people had shown that they were resolved to fight to the end now, and Hill feared that the end was approaching more quickly than any of them could imagine. The last few months had read like the South's obituary: the Shenandoah Valley lost to Sheridan, Atlanta fallen to Sherman. In Petersburg, the men were spread so far apart in the sixty-three miles of trenches that he doubted they could withstand a major assault. Hood's army was just hanging on at Nashville.

"Is Pete coming?" he asked.

"I don't know," Pickett said. For once, he didn't joke.

Hill was disappointed that General Longstreet wanted no part of their plan. He had told them before he found it dishonorable and the war should be won on the battlefield, not by the means that some of the officers were considering.

"Shall we begin, gentlemen?" someone said.

The crowded tent grew quiet. A single oil lamp provided light, and the faces it lit looked haggard and worn. All of them wore beards because it was impossible to keep a clean-shaven face under the conditions in which they lived. Their uniforms were shabby and dirty, but at least they still resembled uniforms. After all, these were the generals and high-ranking officers. The soldiers wore rags and had no shoes.

Hill looked from face to face before he unfolded his plan. Good men, all of them, he thought. He longed for some of the faces that were missing and would never be present again. Such was the price of war.

"You know, gentlemen, that these are desperate times. I would ask that any of you who aren't prepared for equally desperate measures would kindly leave."

No one stirred. It was as he had hoped.

"So much of the recent success of the North can be laid at the feet of its political and military leaders," he said. "Strong leadership has also led our own cause to past victories."

"It's late, General. Save your speeches. None of us needs convincing. We know what needs to be done."

"The leaders," Hill said, getting to the point. "We must eliminate the North's leaders."

"There will only be others to take their place."

Pickett laughed. "Who? Hooker, who lay drunk at Chancellorsville? Burnside, who killed all his men storming that stone wall at Fredericksburg? Up until Grant came along, the North has had no military leaders to speak of."

"But now there is Meade, Sheridan, Sherman—"

"*Grant,* gentlemen," Hill said. "We must show the North its vulnerability."

"And what would stop them from taking action against General Lee?"

"Grant will die by an assassin," Hill said. "A man acting alone. No one must know where the plan originated."

"And what of Lincoln? Should he not be eliminated as well?"

Hill considered the question. It was a problem he had turned over in his mind for some time.

"Lincoln is a political leader."

"He is also commander-in-chief of the Union's armies."

"Lincoln is a civilian." Hill had rehearsed his argument. "Grant is a military man. He is the true leader of the armies. The difference between plotting to eliminate Grant or Lincoln is the difference between war and murder."

He knew it was a weak argument, but it served to veil a greater fact, which was that Abraham Lincoln had shown himself to be a reasonable man. If the South lost, it would depend upon him to be merciful.

"How should it be done?" someone asked.

"He should be poisoned," Pickett said, affecting an English accent. "Like a character in Shakespeare."

Soft laughter filled the tent. Leave it to Pickett to be the dramatist, Hill thought.

"We have some fine sharpshooters in this army," Hill said. This, too, he had considered.

"I have a man in my regiment who can make a shot from a thousand yards," a colonel remarked.

There was a low whistle of respect.

"A bullet would be the best way," Hill agreed, glad the idea was taking hold. "Grant is surrounded at all times by his staff, and I doubt we could get close enough for some other method, like poison. Besides, a sharpshooter would show them that their leaders are never safe. Not Grant, and not whoever the Yankees find to take his place. We can reach them at any time. Now, if we agree to using one of our sharpshooters, the first question might be, 'where?'"

"Through the heart, of course," Pickett said. More laughter. Even Hill joined in.

"Our agents have had no trouble infiltrating City Point," someone said. "He would be an easy enough target."

"It could be done at City Point," Pickett said. "Grant goes out to inspect his little kindgom there—and bang!"

"I propose Washington," Hill said.

Several heads turned his way in surprise.

"City Point would be so much easier," Pickett said, being practical for a change.

"But think of it. The general-in-chief of the Yankee army being shot down in the streets of the capital. It would not be a hero's death on the battlefield. And it would show how vulnerable they are."

"And that Lincoln could be next."

Hill nodded. "They might rethink their position."

"Washington would be more difficult."

"He goes there from time to time."

"If the Washington attempt fails, there is always City Point."

Hill found it amazing that they had already decided. He had feared he would have to argue his case, let them think on it. Now it was only a matter of putting the plan in motion.

"Who will do it?" Pickett asked.

"I know a man," Hill said. He had already made inquiries among his various colonels. One name had come up several times, and Hill was intrigued that a mere private could have such a reputation as a killer.

"Who?"

"It's better, perhaps, that only I know," Hill said. "If something should go wrong . . ."

"If he's captured—"

"This man would keep his secrets, from what I hear," Hill reassured them.

"And the general?"

"Lee? He must know nothing, of course. He would never allow it."

"He would consider this treason," a general remarked.

"Perhaps," Hill said. "But there is not much hope otherwise."

There were no arguments. These men knew better than any that the Confederacy was waning. There was still hope, but it dwindled with each passing day as the Northern army grew stronger and the Southern army melted away through desertion, hunger and disease.

"Good night, gentlemen," Hill said, standing. "Morning comes early."

"You'll make the necessary arrangements, then?" Pickett asked, as if Hill were doing him the favor of having a broken carriage mended.

"I will see that it is done," he said.

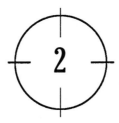

2

"Ya'll got any whiskey?"

"Nope," said Uriah Snodgrass, shaking his head wistfully. "We done drank the last of that pop skull last night."

"Goin' to be a dry week then, boy," Billy Golts drawled. "How 'bout us gettin' up a game of cards later on?"

"You got any money?" Snodgrass asked. If whiskey was scarce here in the Petersburg trenches, he knew money was even harder to come by. But it never hurt to ask. Even a second-rate gambler like Golts might have something hidden away.

Snodgrass watched as Golts, who was visiting from another mess along the lines, dug his hand into his filthy uniform blouse and came out with a handful of bills.

"I'm a rich man. I got plenty to gamble."

Snodgrass snorted. Golts knew as well as he did that the money was practically worthless. "Them's Confederate bills. Hell, with what you got there you could maybe buy a Yankee nickel."

"We got some molasses left. You interested?"

In spite of the grim prospect of everyone he knew being out of whiskey and money, Snodgrass couldn't help but smile. A little sorghum molasses was gold. At least it was worth more than the three double eagle gold pieces Snodgrass had sewn inside his belt. Sixty dollars in gold. He was probably richer than most of the officers but there wasn't a bit of food or whiskey his gold could buy.

"I got a few greenbacks," Snodgrass said slyly. "Guess you might try to win them off me. See you boys tonight."

Grinning himself, the visitor stood. Snodgrass was about to warn him to get down because the trenches through here weren't all that deep and Golts was a tall man. Just as he opened his mouth to speak, the top half of Golts's head exploded in a red mist, spattering blood, bits of skull and brains all over Snodgrass. As Snodgrass watched, his mouth still hanging open, Billy Golts's body fell in a heap on the floor of the muddy trench.

All Snodgrass and the men around him could do was stare at the body. Then Snodgrass jumped up in a rage.

"You goddamn Yankees!"

Keeping his head down, he lifted his rifle over the edge of the trench and pulled the trigger. For his trouble, Snodgrass heard an answering bullet whine overhead, uncomfortably close. No sense in two soldier boys getting killed, he thought. He cursed again, helplessly, bitterly, and leaned back against the web of woven branches that kept the earthen sides of the trench from collapsing during the torrential rains they'd had through late summer and into fall.

For days now, the Yankee sharpshooter had been pinning them down in the trench to the point where he and his messmates were scurrying and scuttling about like so many rats. No one dared take a long look over the lip of the trench for fear of catching a bullet in the eye. The couple of boys who had tried to return the Yank's fire hadn't lasted long before they had been killed. Snodgrass and the others had to satisfy themselves with wild shots toward the Union lines.

"We've been the bottom rail just about long enough," Snodgrass said angrily to everyone within hearing distance. A couple of the fellows were trying to drag poor Billy Golts's body away, but it wasn't an easy job because Golts had been a strapping farm boy. His head was a shredded mess, and as it was dragged through a mud puddle it left behind a swirl of deep red in the brown water. What would Billy Golts's mama say if she could see him now?

Snodgrass had to admit, with some guilt, that he wasn't sure what he considered the biggest loss: Golts or the possibility of winning Golts's sorghum molasses in a poker game. So many had been killed over the last three years that a man got kind of cold toward death. Then, too, Golts had only been an acquaintance, not one of Snodgrass's messmates. Each death—and to be sure, many had died—had been like the loss of a brother.

He sat there in the ditch feeling miserable, too disgusted even to clean the gore off his so-called uniform. The clothes would have better suited a scarecrow than a soldier, Snodgrass thought. The light blue pants, coated liberally with mud, had been taken off a dead Yank during the summer's fighting. His shoes, too, were from a

Yankee, this one a prisoner. The Rebels often went up to Yankee prisoners and took their shoes or coats or pants, trading them for their own battered clothes. Looking down at his feet, he could see his toes through the holes in the worn brogans. He had marched many miles in those shoes, and they wouldn't last the winter.

Snodgrass looked up and saw that the boys had made some progress dragging Billy Golts down the ditch. He noticed that one soldier hardly raised his eyes from the letter he was writing as the body went by.

Back in 1861, if someone had told Uriah Snodgrass that he would soon have no more reaction to a man's death than regretting he had missed out on some molasses, he would have said they were touched in the head. But then, there were many things he hadn't believed three years ago. He had been working as a hand on board a steamboat plying the Mississippi, and the war had seemed to be another adventure not to be missed because it surely wouldn't last more than a few months. Now, Snodgrass had more than his fill of fighting and would be glad if he never saw a trench or heard a bugle or marched twenty miles in one stretch all the rest of his days.

"You want to help me get him?"

"Huh?" Snodgrass squinted up against the sky to see who had spoken. Lost in his thoughts, he hadn't heard anyone approaching, but a man had appeared just a few feet away. "Get down, whoever you are, less you aim to get your head blowed off, too."

In one smooth motion, the man was crouching beside Snodgrass in the ditch. Snodgrass had never seen him before. He was just a boy in his twenties wearing a roughly made butternut coat. There were several thousand just like him in the trenches defending Petersburg.

What spooked Snodgrass was the soldier's eyes. They could have been made from the palest cut glass; they were that clear and expressionless. Snodgrass, who was one of the better poker players in the Army of Northern Virginia, couldn't read a damn thing in those eyes.

"I asked if you want to help me get him."

"Get who?" Snodgrass asked, momentarily unsettled by this stranger.

"That Yank sharpshooter. They done sent me down here to kill him. Do you want to help?"

It was then that Snodgrass noticed the rifle in the stranger's hands. He held a Sharps, which was rare enough in this part of the

Confederacy. But this rifle had something affixed to it that Snodgrass had heard of but never seen: a telescopic sight. He took a good look at the long tube that ran the length of the rifle's stock. It was mounted on the side of the rifle to leave room for the working of the loading mechanism in the breech.

"And who the hell might you be?" Snodgrass asked. Noting that this man also wore a Colt Navy revolver and had a rather mean-looking Bowie knife in his belt, it occurred to him briefly that this stranger might not be someone to treat roughly. But sitting there with Billy Golts's brains on him, it was hard not to be ornery. "You the angel of death or something?"

"The name's Lucas Cole," said the man, his words knobby with a hill-country accent. Those strange eyes didn't even so much as blink, and Snodgrass, in spite of himself, felt a shiver go through him. This man would be a hell of a poker player, he thought. "Now, for the last time, are you goin' to help me kill that Yankee over there or not?"

Snodgrass bristled at the cold tone of voice. Usually, he never thought twice about letting a good roundhouse punch take somebody down a notch or two when they were getting uppity. But this new boy didn't look like someone he wanted to get into a scrap with.

"Just tell me what do," Snodgrass said.

Lucas Cole hadn't waited for an answer. He was already busy studying the walls of the trench. "Find me something to dig with," he said.

"What have you got there?" the general asked.

"Pickles, sir."

"Hmm." Without another word, the general dipped his fingers into the jar an orderly carried and helped himself to a fat pickle. Major Brendan Mulholland heard it crunch as the general bit into it. Some of the pickle juice soaked into the general's thick brown beard, but he merely wiped his lips with the back of his hand and went on eating the pickle absently as he walked to the doorway and looked out over City Point.

Mulholland shook his head, thinking it was no wonder the man had such trouble with his stomach. General Ulysses S. Grant rarely ate much of anything and got most of his sustenance from cigars and coffee so bitter it could take the rust off nails. When he did eat, it was in snatches: a few pickles, a boiled egg, a plate of beans.

Mulholland thought it was an awfully nervous way for such a calm man to eat.

Of course, there hadn't been much news lately to encourage anyone's appetite. Lincoln was on the brink of defeat in the election. General Thomas had been outfoxed at every step by the Confederates in Tennessee. Here in Virginia, Robert Lee's ragged men lived on roasted rats and parched corn, but they wouldn't give up their trenches.

"Mulholland."

Lost in his own thoughts, the major had not noticed Grant turning, and now the general's soft brown eyes were peering into his own.

"Sir?" Out of habit, Mulholland began to salute, then caught himself. Grant and his fellow westerners frowned on too much formality.

"Find out where Rawlins has gone," Grant said. "He and I have to discuss the situation over there."

Mulholland didn't need the general to explain that "over there" was the city of Petersburg, where thousands of Confederate soldiers under General A. P. Hill were dug in, hungry but determined.

"Yes, sir." This time, Mulholland did salute, so smartly he could practically hear his arm cut the air, and went off in search of Grant's chief of staff. Mulholland was in charge of security at headquarters, and he was expecting the provost marshal to send him a replacement for a guard who had taken sick with fever. However, he wasn't about to tell General Grant he couldn't go look for General Rawlins because he was expecting the arrival of a private momentarily. The soldier could wait until he returned.

From headquarters Mullholland had a good view of City Point, the sprawling supply depot Grant had created on the James River, seven miles northeast of the besieged town of Petersburg. Where the southern town stood as a symbol of the ragged, failing Confederacy, City Point abounded with the plenty of the Northern war machine.

City Point had been only a sleepy town a few months ago but had since grown in size to match its name. Tremendous wharves had been built virtually overnight along an entire mile of the riverbank, and ships came and went around the clock carrying men, food, munitions and new 12-pounder Perot cannons. Railroad tracks had been laid right up to the waterfront, and the supplies were loaded directly from the ships to the railcars for transport to the Petersburg front or wherever else the materiel of war was needed.

Mulholland had no idea where to find Rawlins in this bustling camp. The nervous chief of staff sometimes scurried all around the supply depot, checking on this and that, while the calm commander appeared content to chew his cold cigar.

Major Mulholland rounded a muddy path and bumped headlong into a soldier coming the other way.

The soldier barely looked up from a scrap of paper he was holding. He adjusted his forage cap and started off again.

"Private!" Mulholland snapped at the soldier's back.

The man stopped and turned slowly, as if he wasn't quite sure he was the one being addressed.

"Yes, Private, I am talking to you! Why don't you watch—"

Mulholland was not prepared for what he saw as the soldier stopped and faced him. He fell silent in amazement. The private spoke up.

"Beggin' the Major's pardon, sir, but I was tryin' to read this bit o' paper an' didn't have me eyes in front o' me like a good soldier should."

An Irishman, of all things, thought Mulholland as he stared in disbelief. It seemed there were Irishmen everywhere, all fresh off the boat from Cobh Harbor. What astounded Mulholland was that this one had a dark brown beard, a thin build and stooped shoulders. He looked extremely familiar, right down to the mournful expression and soft brown eyes.

This Irishman could have been General Ulysses S. Grant's twin brother. He was perhaps an inch shorter than the general, but he had the same facial features and somewhat ragged appearance. As Mulholland studied the man's face, the differences between Grant and this soldier became more apparent, although at first glance or from a distance the Irishman could easily pass for the commanding general.

This fellow could have been fifty or thirty; it was hard to say exactly without seeing how many lines creased the face hidden beneath the beard. The nose was different, too, being somewhat wider than Grant's. And the Irishman wore a mournful expression, which probably had more to do with the fact that he had upset an officer than with any great military plans weighing heavily on his mind.

Mulholland blinked, thinking he would see the man differently when he opened his eyes. But this was not the case. He shook his head. There were one hundred thousand men in the Army of the Potomac. It was only to be expected that one might resemble the general, even if he did speak with a brogue.

"What does the paper say?" Mulholland demanded.

"Well, Major, sir, as I said I was tryin' to read it an' wasn't watchin' as I should be."

Mulholland bristled. "Private, I asked you what it said."

The soldier's eyes sparked with a hint of anger. Good, Mulholland thought. Now he's feeling a burr under his saddle.

"Sir, I wouldn't know exactly. But it's my understandin' that this is a note from Captain Harmon to a Major Mulholland over at his excellency the commanding general's headquarters where I am supposed to fill in as a guard for some poor lad who's been taken with fever." The soldier's look became defiant. "But I wouldn't know the exact words, now, as I'm just a poor, dumb Irishman who don't know how to read."

The last comment was offered as a challenge. These Irish were proud bastards, even when they couldn't read.

"I'm Major Mulholland," he said, taking a bit of satisfaction from the look of surprise on the soldier's face. "Now look sharp and follow me."

The soldier saluted. "Yes, sir."

Mulholland continued on his way through camp. Soldiers, officers and workmen bustled everywhere, going about the business of running an army. Some passed carrying sacks on their shoulders, some carried crates, still others were armed with axes as they made their way out to cut firewood for the coming winter. Finding General Rawlins in all this mess, Mulholland knew, might be a hopeless mission.

He headed downhill toward the wharves, barely conscious of the Irishman trailing along behind him. He noticed the private was getting odd looks from some of the men they passed. So, he thought, I'm not the only one who sees the resemblance. Captain Harmon had a sense of humor, sending this man as a replacement. Mulholland realized he had forgotten to ask the Irishman's name. No matter, he thought. When they returned to headquarters, he would get the fellow sorted out for guard duty.

"Major, sir, I would have thought headquarters was in the other direction."

"You'd be right about that, Private. Right now we're looking for someone."

"Who, sir, might I ask?"

"It really doesn't concern you, Private." Mulholland regretted his words as soon as he had spoken them. He knew he sounded like just another pompous officer, the kind of "shoulder straps" veterans such as the man behind him loved to despise, and with good reason.

"I can't read, Major, sir, but me eyes is pretty good. An' two pairs of eyes is better than one, they say."

Once again, Mulholland detected a note of challenge in the soldier's voice. These damn Irish were uppity. Nothing but trouble.

"General Rawlins," Mulholland said, thinking the private wouldn't know Grant's chief of staff.

"Sure, and I just saw the good general on me way to find you," the Irishman said. "He was walkin' up the same road as me—on his way to the headquarters, I suppose."

Mulholland kept walking toward the wharves, trying to decide if he should believe the private. Was this Irishman having a bit of fun with him? If he returned to headquarters without Rawlins, General Grant would not be pleased. On the other hand, there was no point looking for the chief of staff if he was already back with Grant.

Mulholland stopped and turned. This second time, he expected to be less impressed with the private's resemblance to General Grant, but to his surprise he found himself staring once more in disbelief. It was uncanny. "You're certain you saw General Rawlins?"

"I swear on me mother's grave."

"You realize what duty you receive is totally at my discretion," Mulholland said, lapsing again into his haughty officer's tone.

"What difference would that make as to whether or not I saw your general?" asked the private, somewhat too innocently. He knew damn well the major could set him to cleaning out privies for the rest of the war.

"All right," Mulholland said, hoping he wasn't being duped. "Back up the hill, then."

They turned and walked back the way they had come, a two-man procession of an officer and a squat private following along behind with a Springfield musket slung over his shoulder.

"Wait here," the major ordered as they came to the doorway leading to Grant's office. As he went in, Mulholland was already trying to decide upon the worst duty he could give the Irishman.

Privies? Mucking out the stables? He needed an assignment so unpleasant it would make even the boggiest peat bog in all of Ireland seem like paradise.

But there was Rawlins after all, arguing with Grant as usual. Neither man noticed him as he entered. Mulholland took one look and went back outside, where the private was standing at attention, already hard at work guarding the headquarters building.

"What's your name, Private?" Mulholland asked.

"Michael O'Malley, sir."

"I hope we didn't get off to a bad start, O'Malley."

"If I may speak plainly, sir, it was just about the worst start two men could have."

Mulholland smiled. "Ha! We're going to get along just fine, O'Malley. Now, you just keep your eyes open for any Rebs who come sneaking around."

"Aye, sir, so I will."

3

Lucas Cole took the tin plate Snodgrass found and started to dig at the muddy walls of the trench. He worked far below the lip of the trench to avoid attracting the attention of the Yankee sharpshooter, who was just opposite them, his rifle sights trained on the Rebel earthworks.

At first, Snodgrass wondered what the hell Cole was doing. There were already enough trenches around Petersburg to last until Judgment Day. But as Cole worked, it became clear that he wasn't intent on digging a new trench, but only on scooping out a shallow depression where he could lay at his full length perpendicular to the trench without being seen by anyone in the Yankee lines.

None of the Rebels in Snodgrass' mess offered to help and none bothered to ask Cole what he was doing. They only watched curiously, commenting among themselves. Snodgrass knew they were just too worn out to be enthusiastic. He went over to where Cole was working, being careful to keep his head well below the top of the trench.

"You a farmer, Cole?" he asked. From the way Cole was scooping out that trench, it was obvious the sharpshooter was a man used to hard labor.

"Yep." The plate grated against a rock. "But up until the war I never done much diggin' with a plate."

Snodgrass let loose a guffaw. Early in the war, there had been some notion that they would march into battle in neat formations. Now when they were put into a line, the first thing each soldier did was get down as low as possible and start digging with whatever was available, whether it was his plate, bayonet or hands. Even a handful of dirt in front of a man was better protection against a minié ball than nothing at all.

"I never could stand bein' on the farm myself," Snodgrass said.

"Soon as I was old enough I lit out for the river. I was workin' on a steamboat when the war broke out."

"Why ain't you in the navy, then?"

"There ain't much sailin' involved on a steamboat, Cole," Snodgrass said. "Besides, I knew it was the infantry that was goin' to see all the fun."

"If you think this is fun, find another plate and dig in," Cole said.

Snodgrass laughed again. He was quick to anger, but he was just as quick to appreciate a joke. Cole was all right, he thought, even if he was a hard case.

"Let me watch awhile and see if I can't get the hang of it," Snodgrass said.

Cole went on digging, stopping only long enough to take a drink of water from his canteen. He soon had the shallow trench completed, and he scrambled into it, sliding the Sharps rifle in front of him. The trench was deeper at the entrance and sloped upwards from there like a shoe horn, so Cole was able to slip into it unseen by the Yankees. He had dug the hole so that only the muzzle of the rifle showed, while the rest of him was safely hidden.

Cole was back in a minute.

"Can't see a damn thing," he said. "Here's where I need your help, Snodgrass. Put your hat on the end of your rifle and lift it up so it looks like someone's trying to look over the trench."

Snodgrass was ready in an instant. After days of inactivity, he was glad for some action. "Now?" he asked.

"Not now, damnit! Wait till I'm in place. I want to see where this Yankee is shooting from."

Cole's sharp tongue rankled Snodgrass, who was thinking Cole was too damn quick to give orders. The man acted like he was a goddamn officer instead of a private. But Snodgrass took his place by the trench. He would put up with Cole if it meant getting rid of the Yankee sharpshooter.

Cole picked up his Sharps, double checked to make sure everything was in working order, then wormed his way back into his hole. He took a long time getting himself settled, and Snodgrass grew fidgety.

"All right," Cole finally called, and Snodgrass slowly lifted his rifle so that his cap crept above the top of the trench like a soldier trying for a glimpse of the enemy.

Snodgrass heard the bullet sing overhead, and he flinched involuntarily, losing his grip on the musket, which fell back into the trench. The report of the Yankee's rifle rolled in after the bullet. Over in the Yankee lines three hundred yards away, someone whooped.

"Damnation!" Snodgrass picked his hat out of the mud and was stunned to find two neat holes where the bullet had passed through.

Cole still hadn't fired, and Caleb Dixon, one of the other soldiers in the trench, walked over and slapped his boot.

"You see that Yankee or what? Shoot him, why don't you."

When Cole didn't answer, Dixon gave the sharpshooter's foot a good shake. Cole kicked out, just like a cow's tail flicks at a fly, and caught Dixon in the face.

In a fit of rage, Dixon rushed back at Cole before Snodgrass could move to stop him. He grabbed both of Cole's legs and started hauling him out of the shallow hole. Snodgrass watched, somewhat amused, and was reminded of someone dragging a rabbit out of a hole by its hind legs.

"Now take it easy, there, Caleb," Snodgrass warned his messmate.

"You goddamned—" the soldier grunted, dragging on Cole's legs.

Only Cole wasn't a rabbit. He came out of the hole like a riled-up badger, ready for a fight. He got himself turned around and sprang at Dixon with fists flying.

"They're going at it now boys, *hoo-ee!*" someone yelled.

"Look at 'em scrap!"

The trench was soon filled with spectators, and the officers made no move to stop the two combatants. Nothing broke the monotony of the trench quite so well as a fight among the boys. Snodgrass knew scuffles were common enough. When somebody new came around, these farm boys liked to test him to see where he stood in the general hierarchy of who could whip whom. The end result was usually a bloody nose or a black eye, and then the fighters likely became friends.

Snodgrass wasn't so sure Cole was the kind of man who had much patience for this school-yard variety of fighting.

The other soldiers quickly gathered around, being careful to keep their heads well below the top of the trench. A few started to holler and whoop, rooting for their Caleb against the stranger, but it was almost impossible to tell which of the muddy, gray-clad bodies belonged to their messmate.

The fight was over almost before it got started. In a few seconds

Cole had Caleb pressed up against the wall of the trench, with Cole's Bowie knife held tightly against his windpipe.

Snodgrass had placed himself nearby in case of such an outcome.

"Now, Cole, ain't no sense in us killin' each other," Snodgrass said, keeping his voice light. "The Yankees will do that soon enough."

Cole's weird eyes were impossible to read. They held no spark of either anger or forgiveness, which worried Snodgrass. Hell, this boy wasn't even breathing hard, he noticed.

In contrast, Caleb's breathing came in painful jagged gasps, as if he feared a deep breath might cause his throat to expand a bit too far and cut itself on the wickedly sharp Bowie knife. His eyes were wide and white as boiled eggs.

Cole quickly took the knife away and slid it into the sheath at his belt. "No hard feelin's," he said to Caleb, gripping his shoulder. The soldier flinched at Cole's touch, as if the sharpshooter's fingers were hot.

Cole walked over to the hole he had scooped out and studied it. A knot of men hovered nearby. Although they had rooted for Caleb during the fight because he was one of their own, they were impressed by Cole's performance. He had shown he was a man who knew how to handle himself, and that was worth more in 1864 than any amount of officer's chicken guts on a man's sleeves or a fancy rifle.

As if aware of having an audience, Cole began to speak, although he might only have been thinking out loud: "The trouble with that Yankee sharpshooter over yonder is that he's dug in deep. Like a tick. When he moves, I can see just a bit of him. It's like looking through a keyhole. I'm goin' to have to shoot right through that keyhole to get him."

"He's three hundred yards off," somebody said. "Ain't nobody goin' to hit a keyhole at that distance." The men muttered their agreement.

"Oh, I'll get him, all right," Cole said. He grinned. Coldly. "Just so long as nobody goes tuggin' on my feet. Snodgrass, I want you to take a rifle and shoot over at them after I get myself settled. He'll shoot back, I reckon, and when he goes to reload he'll move enough where I can see him and put a bullet through his Yankee hide."

There he goes giving orders again, Snodgrass thought. But he didn't argue as Cole slipped back into his muddy sharpshooter's nest.

Instead, he took his musket and walked over to one of the rifle posts.

Snodgrass wasn't much of a shot, and consequently he hadn't bothered to outfit himself with much of a weapon, either. He carried an old .69 caliber smoothbore musket, accurate to just one hundred yards or so. Snodgrass figured that considering the amount of lead that flew through the air during a fight, the accuracy of his particular weapon wasn't going to have much say in the outcome of the battle.

He clambered up on the rifle step.

"Don't go gettin' killed, Snodgrass," someone called. "Keep that fool head of yours down."

"Ya'll can have my share of the beans if I do get shot," he yelled back, sparking nervous laughter.

As he settled into position, he formed a quick plan that would, Snodgrass hoped, ensure that he would in fact be around to eat his own meager ration of beans. The Yankee sharpshooter on the other side of no-man's-land had put a bullet through his hat—no sense in it being his head this time around. Keeping low, he stuck his hat at the top of the trench and flinched as a shot went past, carrying his hat with it. Snodgrass peered over the top of the trench long enough to get a shot off in the general direction of the distant puff of smoke that marked where the Yankee was hiding.

He ducked back down. All quiet. Then he heard the crack of Cole's rifle.

When Snodgrass dared to look up again, he could see Cole brazenly standing and staring toward the Union line, one hand shading his eyes. Some soldiers on the other side fired and their minié balls zipped overhead. Snodgrass could hear the faint noise of their cursing. Then Cole was safely back in the trench. Snodgrass scrambled off the rifle step to meet him.

"Well?" Snodgrass spoke for the group that was waiting.

"I got him right through the neck as he was reloading after shooting at your hat again."

"That hat's about the only part of you that's holy, Uriah," somebody said, shoving the bullet-ridden hat into Snodgrass's hands.

"God rest that Yankee's soul," said Charlie Hollis, another of Snodgrass' messmates.

The sharpshooter fixed those cut-glass eyes on him. Hollis looked away.

Snodgrass spoke up. He wondered how he had suddenly been put in the role of smoothing over the rough spots between the newcomer and his friends. He felt like he was sitting in on a poker game between two touchy players. "God rest Billy Golts's soul, you mean."

Being careful to keep his sharpshooter's rifle out of the mud, Cole picked up his blanket roll. Like most soldiers in the Rebel army, he had never been issued a haversack and probably would have discarded it anyway in favor of the blanket roll. Soldiers simply rolled their spare clothes—if they had any—and few belongings into a blanket, folded it into a horseshoe shape, tied the ends together with rope and slipped the blanket roll over one shoulder.

"Where you goin', Cole?" Snodgrass asked.

"Back to headquarters," he said. "They sent me down here to get that Yankee sharpshooter, and I got him all right."

"Hell, boy, the least we can do is feed you. We've been wallowing here in the mud for days on account of that Yankee."

Someone pushed a bottle at Cole. "Snodgrass is right, you know," the man said. "I was about tired of that Yankee pickin' us off like crows."

The light in Cole's eyes changed as he saw the bottle, Snodgrass noticed. He accepted it and took a long drink, then handed it back somewhat reluctantly. This fellow Cole had a fondness for corn liquor, Snodgrass thought, deciding he would most likely be a mean drunk.

Snodgrass stepped forward. "You been hoardin' that on us, Caleb. I thought there wasn't a drop of pop skull between here and Richmond."

Caleb laughed. It almost sounded like he was hiccupping. Poor ignorant farm boy, Snodgrass thought, wondering at the same time if Caleb had any other bottles hidden away he might like to lose in a game of poker.

"We got some salt meat," Hollis said to Cole. "You're welcome to it."

Cole looked up at the sky. He could have been alone, so completely did he appear to ignore the eager group around him. The corn liquor had set his eyes to sparkling. "I'd have a hard time getting back to headquarters before dark," he said. It was no secret how treacherous traversing the maze of trenches could be at night. His gaze wandered toward Caleb's bottle. "I'd be obliged."

Snodgrass wondered how many more times he would have to play peacemaker that night once the liquor got flowing. But the thought didn't weigh heavily on him. Whiskey. A bit of meat to go with their beans. The Yankee Cole had shot. They had all the makings of a party—and a reason for one, to boot.

"Sherman has left Atlanta!" Grant exclaimed, slapping his leg and stomping around the small office. "Ha! He promises he's going to make Georgia howl!"

Mulholland had never seen the general look so happy. But then, luck was finally with the North. Lincoln had won the election and there hadn't been a bit of bloodshed or rioting on Election Day. The nation had shown a united, democratic front, which would have a telling effect on the European powers which had expected the states remaining in the Union to tear themselves apart like so many quarreling mongrels. Now on November fifteenth, they'd had news that Sherman was leaving Atlanta with sixty thousand men with the intent of cutting a swath through the heart of Georgia.

Sherman and Grant had been plotting this march since October. With the election won, it was time to put the plan in motion. Grant had ordered Sherman to take every wagon, horse, mule and chicken within his path. He also urged Sherman to set all the slaves free and give them guns, which would give life to the South's worst nightmare: armed bands of former slaves terrorizing those who had formerly been their masters. Sherman had no stomach for that sort of mayhem and so declined to arm the blacks. It seemed he would do enough damage as it was.

"Good for General Sherman, sir," Mulholland said.

General Grant glared, and the major wondered what he had done.

"Mulholland, you don't get excited by much, do you? Here I am telling you that Sherman's army of bummers is marching through the heart of the South, and you don't so much as let out a whoop."

The major grinned. "Begging the General's pardon, sir, but I don't believe we've had much to whoop about until now, sir. I'm not in practice. But I would be happy to light your cigar."

"That's a fine idea, Mulholland. Hold on." Grant went to his desk and came back with a second cigar, which he presented to the major.

Mulholland lit them both and thick tobacco smoke curled up and hung in the peak of the tiny office, adding to the yellowish smoke stains already there.

"Thank you, sir."

Grant nodded. "There are problems elsewhere, of course. I'm

very concerned about General Thomas in Tennessee. If he doesn't move against Hood's army soon, I fear it's going to prove the worst for us."

"They do call him 'The Rock of Chicamauga,' sir."

That brought a small grin to the general's face, which Grant quickly hid. General George Thomas, while highly capable, was notoriously slow. He had been sitting in Tennessee just like his namesake—a rock.

Grant was deep in thought, puffing steadily at the cigar. "Should Lee send any part of his army after Sherman, General Meade is ready to pursue with the Army of the Potomac. I don't know what might happen. The secret is to be able to read the mind of General Lee."

"Just as he is trying to read yours," Mulholland said, releasing a mouthful of smoke toward the ceiling and enjoying himself immensely.

"Exactly," Grant said. "To be a general you must be able to guess what the enemy is thinking, like one of those clairvoyants in Washington. Maybe we could have Admiral Porter bring us a couple down here and have a séance."

Mediums and other psychics were all the rage in the wartime capital. Mulholland was surprised Grant had even noticed. He was not a man who had much use for the pastimes of Washington society. "They are all shysters, sir. Washington City is full of them."

Grant was staring at the cigar smoke that curled upward. "I suppose I'll have to be making a trip to that damned city before long, once things calm down around here. In fact, I believe I'll set December fifteenth as a tentative date. That's a month from now, I know, but there's a lot to be done here before winter settles in. You'll have to come with me to Washington City, being my head of security. Maybe I can convince Stanton to let me get rid of Thomas, and we can discuss our plans for that push in January against the Petersburg lines."

Mulholland was surprised that Grant would elect to bring him, although he was also secretly pleased. So far, there had been nothing to test Mulholland's abilities as chief of security, but he knew if Grant had no faith in him, he would have been replaced long ago. It was more likely Grant had little faith in the notion there might be assassins trying to kill him.

"They say there are constant plots against President Lincoln," Mulholland said. "Pinkerton is always discovering them."

"Don't forget it was Pinkerton who supplied McClellan with his information about Rebel troop strength. I'd say you could take whatever Mr. Pinkerton has to say with a grain of salt, or at least cut all the numbers in half."

"Still, there are enemies."

"Yes," Grant said, nodding toward Petersburg. "There's several thousand of them just over there. The only enemies we have to worry about in Washington will be those politicians on the Committee on the Conduct of the War."

"I suppose the enemies who carry guns are much easier to deal with, sir."

Grant let out a laugh. "Ha! You're right on that one, Major."

Mulholland saluted and left. The news that he would be going to Washington was welcome, for he was bored with life at City Point. The Virginia landscape had turned brown and drab with the coming of winter, and the waters of the James looked muddy and cold from the bluff where the Union headquarters was located. Mulholland would be happy to get a chance to visit Washington City.

He would also be glad to see his old friend, Anne Clark. She was a beautiful woman, and their families had known each other well. If it hadn't been for the war . . . Mulholland sighed. The war had put many things on hold, including his courtship of Miss Clark. At least he would have a chance to see her when he traveled to Washington City with General Grant.

Mulholland went back to his desk and spent the next hour writing a letter to Anne. He described life at headquarters, the dull food and the cold, how much everyone wanted the war to end. He also mentioned that he would like to see her when he came to the city with General Grant on the fifteenth. He would be staying at the Willard Hotel with Grant, so she could send one of her servants with a message.

When he was finished, he had an orderly put it in the mail bound for Washington City on that night's steamer.

4

The letter for Anne Clark arrived in Washington City the following morning. She read it in her parlor as she sat by a small fire built to keep the chill off the richly furnished room. When she was finished reading, she leaned back, reached for her cup of tea, and decided that Major Brendan Mulholland had just helped the Confederate cause enormously.

Anne Jefferson Clark was twenty-six years old and extremely beautiful. Her skin was pale, nearly the color of milk, and she had chestnut-colored hair that shimmered in the sunlight that filtered through the tall windows of the parlor. She was well dressed in a watered-silk gown with wide hoops. The pale green dress set off her skin and hair nicely, although she was rather more elegantly dressed than most women would be at that hour of the day in their own parlors.

She wanted to look her best because she would soon be out of that dress and in the arms of a man she despised, Colonel Jonathan Wilcox. On other afternoons she took a different Yankee officer into her bed. No one but the men who visited her knew she was a whore, although there were those in Washington society who had their suspicions and whispered catty comments when they saw Miss Anne Clark on the street.

No one at all suspected the fetching Miss Clark of being a Confederate spy, because in public, and in the arms of her Yankee lovers, she was patriotically outspoken for the Union cause.

Her gentlemen callers would be shocked to know the truth, which was that Anne hoped all Yankees would burn in hell. She was doing her best to see that this happened and was one of the South's most effective spies. She wasn't famous like Belle Boyd or Rose Greenhow, but her anonymity was what made her a success.

A few years ago, if anyone had suggested to Anne that she would soon be both a spy and a whore, she would have thought them mad. As a young debutante, her energies had mostly been concerned with her next social event and the latest fashions. Life had been a cycle of giddy flirtation, dances and parties. Washington was a Southern city in the heart of the Southern state of Maryland, but she met many young men from both North and South who had come to the United States' capital. That all began to change in 1858, when she was twenty years old. That was the year she met Rayford Hollander.

He was a Virginian. His family owned extensive lands south of the James River and he often came to Washington on business. Rayford was tall and handsome and moved through the world with the natural ease of a born aristocrat. The Hollanders owned slaves and several hundred acres of fertile tidewater farmland. They were not fabulously rich but had been prominent for a long time, practically since the first Hollanders came to America from England in the 1600s. They had been Cavaliers, refugees from King Charles's defeat at the hands of the Roundheads. They were cousins to George Washington and the Lees. Anne had been stunned by Rayford's graciousness, and he had found the young Washingtonian en-chanting.

Like most Southerners, Rayford could speak loudly and at great lengths about secession. He thought the best hope for the future of all states south of the Mason-Dixon line was to leave the Union and start their own country.

"We don't need any damn Yankees telling us how to live and taking away our slaves," he liked to say.

Until she met Rayford, Anne hadn't given politics much thought. She had heard the talk about secession, even the rumors of war, but had only half listened as she kept her eye on whom the other girls were flirting with around the room. She had begun paying attention for the first time when Rayford spoke. Within a month of meeting him, she believed wholeheartedly in the Cause, as it had come to be known. In Rayford's mind, it was clear that he and other Southerners were faced with a revolution much like the one the original thirteen colonies had waged against England. It would be a fight for freedom.

Their courtship was long, for Rayford's responsibilities on the family plantation often kept him in Virginia. They had formed a militia unit down there, he told her, and he was named one of the captains. He gave her a daguerreotype of him in his uniform, and she thought he was the most handsome man she had ever seen.

Her father thought Rayford was foolish. William Clark had married late in life and was white-haired and well past sixty, so perhaps age had made him cautious. "These seccessionist fools are going to destroy the country," he warned Anne. "No good will come of it."

Then the spark had suddenly been fanned into the flame of revolt. Fort Sumter fell. Virginia seceded. Rayford was busy in the new Confederate army, and with the state of war existing between the nations on each side of the Potomac had been unable to return to Washington. The two found themselves on wrong sides of that boundary river. He wrote that if she could come to Virginia, they would be married, but her father forbid her to travel to what was now enemy territory.

She had protested. "But father—"

"There's a war going on, Anne," the old man said. "It's too dangerous."

Her world quickly went to pieces after that. Her father died, and less than a week later she had a letter from a friend of Rayford's, a fellow officer in the famed Stonewall Brigade. Rayford had been killed leading his men at Sharpsburg in September of 1862. He had died bravely. There were no details.

For two months Anne did not go out but drew the curtains shut and sat in the parlor, living off tea. While her servant Hattie fretted, Anne grew ever more thin and pale. Life was meaningless, and she wished she were a man so that she could go south to die for the Cause and avenge her beloved Rayford.

And then one day she had decided what she would do. Her father had left her enough money to live well, if not extravagantly, so she did not have to worry about finding a husband to support her. Anne became outspoken about the Union cause. People assumed she had abandoned Rayford. She became popular with the flood of officers in Washington City. With liquor and the right sort of feminine attention, their tongues became well-oiled.

Anne, in her own way, had begun fighting to destroy the United States of America.

She skimmed through the major's letter once more, trying to glean any other useful information. But he had written mostly about camp life, something which did not interest Anne in the least. She only cared about the date Brendan had written that General Grant would be coming to Washington City.

Her spymaster, Thomas Nelson Conrad, had informed her recently that he needed to know the next time Grant planned a visit to Washington. Her ties to Major Mulholland had proved useful before, so the Confederate spymaster turned to her again. Of course, Anne had no idea why the mysterious Mr. Conrad wanted to know about Grant's plans, and it wasn't her place to ask.

She stood and went to a writing desk in the parlor, tore a sheet of paper in half and simply wrote "December 15" on the sheet. Then she folded it into a very small square. She put Major Mulholland's letter in the fire, where it quickly turned to ash. She would leave no evidence of her spying activities for her enemies. There was no need to encode this message, because it would be a meaningless date to most people, including Pinkerton's detectives.

"Henry!" she called, going out into the hall.

"Ma'am?" Her male servant appeared. Anne held the folded paper toward him.

"Henry, I want you to take this to Mr. Conrad's."

"Yes, ma'am."

"You have to hide it."

Henry grinned widely. "I got jest the place for it, Miss Anne. The usual secret place. Ain't nobody ever thought to look there."

He pulled an enormous watch from his pocket and sprang the lid to reveal an empty case. Henry took the message and snapped the watch shut. "I'm on my way, Miss Anne."

Anne watched him return to the kitchen, where he would go out the back door and make his way across the city to the mansion where Mr. Conrad lived.

Not for the first time, Anne wondered why it was so important to know when Grant would be in Washington.

She didn't have long to think about it. There was a knock at her door, and she heard Hattie hurrying to answer it. It must certainly be Colonel Wilcox. He was early, but that had never stopped him before.

Anne stood, straightened the rumples from her dress, and practiced a smile in the mirror over the fireplace.

The day after Anne Clark read her letter from Major Brendan

Mulholland, a message containing the date for Grant's visit to Washington was on its way to Richmond. Information traveled quickly between the Union and Confederate capitals, although couriers took great risks crossing between the two warring nations.

There were several points along the Potomac River—at Pope's Creek, Port Tobacco River and Gunston Cove, to name a few— where smugglers managed to slip across the water in spite of Union sentries and gunboats. These smugglers carried Yankee newspapers, desperately needed medicines like quinine, and reports from the Confederacy's spies. One such report on the evening of November 17 contained the information from Major Mulholland's letter. It went into a saddlebag along with a bundle of newspapers—which often proved reliable sources of information about troop movements—and a rider was soon galloping the long, muddy miles toward Richmond.

His destination was the Confederacy's Secret Service Bureau, located in a building on Richmond's Capitol Square. The building was also shared by the Confederate Army Signal Corps, which was overseen by Major William Norris. Unknown to most was that Norris was also head of the Secret Service, and it was to his desk that the packet from Washington City was carried on November 19.

And there it sat for over two weeks. Simple bureaucracy brought all the hard work of Anne Clark, Thomas Conrad and the Potomac River smugglers to a halt. Finally, just after Thanksgiving Day, which had been observed with an uneasy truce along the Virginia front, Major Norris saw fit to send the message along to General A. P. Hill outside Petersburg.

Like most high-ranking generals, Hill had his own spies and scouts, but his network fell well short of the Yankee capital. He had turned to the Confederate Secret Service for help, although he had not told Norris why he needed to know when Grant would be in Washington. The Secret Service chief had merely assumed it had some bearing on Hill's military plans.

It was the message Hill had patiently been waiting for. As soon as it arrived, he called one of his staff officers off the front porch of the farmhouse that was serving as the general's headquarters.

"Go get me that ol' boy I told you about," Hill said.

"Private Lucas Cole, sir?"

"That's the one."

"Where will I find him, sir?"

"Hell if I know, Captain. He's out in the trenches somewhere, killing Yankees. But find him. He's the best damn sharpshooter in the whole army, and I've got a job for him."

Anne's finger traced a pattern on Colonel William McDonnell's bare chest. If McDonnell had been paying attention instead of staring at the canopy over Anne's bed, lost in thought, he might have noticed her fingertip was drawing a perfect stars and bars flag—the flag of the Confederacy—on his distinctly Union chest.

McDonnell was a fool, but he was kind compared to that beast, Colonel Wilcox.

"You look tired," Anne said, giving him a gentle smile. "General Halleck has been working you too hard."

"It's been busy these last few days. Old Brains hasn't given us any rest."

"In winter? Why, I thought soldiers took the winter off. Don't they do all their fighting in the spring?"

McDonnell laughed softly. "Now what would you know about soldiering? That's a man's business."

Anne bristled at the remark, but her voice was light as she said, "Oh, I just wondered why you were so busy. You're looking thin."

"Ha! Next thing I know you'll be pumping soup into me."

Anne smiled sweetly, although inwardly she was raging. McDonnell always treated her as if she had cotton for brains. He was so pompous at times that it took all her patience not to lash out at him, and patience was not something that came easily to her. She satisfied herself by thinking that although McDonnell might believe he was awfully clever, in the end she was going to make him tell her everything she wanted to know. After all, he loved gossip the way some men loved whiskey.

"You're right, William, I don't know anything about the army," she said. "Most people don't. That's why we leave everything up to a brilliant man like General Halleck."

This elicited a hearty laugh from the colonel. "My dear, you really *don't* know anything about soldiering. Halleck brilliant? Well, the man knows quite a bit, I'll admit, but he's not much of a general. Not like Grant. That man knows how to *fight*."

General Henry Halleck was nicknamed "Old Brains" because he had been an instructor at the military academy at West Point for many years. He was a military theorist and had even written a book on tactics that had been much used early in the war, until generals learned the hard way that the days of Napoleonic-style tactics such as massed charges resulted in terrible carnage due to the long-range muskets in use by the 1860s. He had proved to be an ineffective field commander and was now stationed in Washington, where he served as Grant's chief of staff in the capital. The role fit him well, for Halleck was attuned to the politics of the city and was a good administrator.

"You say that, William, but from what I hear Grant is afraid of General Lee. Why, all Grant's been doing is sitting in those trenches down in Virginia."

Colonel McDonnell gave a superior chuckle. "Just you wait, my dear Anne. Grant will soon give Lee a prick he won't forget."

"Not till springtime—"

"You think a little cold weather will stop Grant? The Union has practically the biggest army the world has ever known! If I were General Lee, I wouldn't get my hopes up about everything being quiet on the Petersburg front until spring."

Anne was now tracing tiny stars on McDonnell's chest. The patch of gray hair there matched that on his head or, for that matter, the web of frost on the windowpane. "You mean General Grant's going to start a campaign this winter?"

Anne could hardly contain her excitement. Perhaps this was another reason Grant was coming to Washington. She would have to press Brendan Mulholland on the subject, because she couldn't let on to McDonnell that she knew Grant would be in the capital. Only ranking members of the War Department staff knew of Grant's planned visit.

Colonel McDonnell patted her hand, then grasped it in his own. "Don't trouble your pretty head about it, Anne. Let Grant do what he wants." He smiled lasciviously. "We're not planning to wait until springtime to start our own campaign, now are we?"

Hating him, Anne smiled back sweetly. "Oh, William," she said. "I wish you could stay all day." The truth was, she couldn't wait for him to leave. But for the time being, Anne would put up with being treated like a brainless child if it meant learning something useful that she could pass along to Thomas Conrad. And as soon as McDonnell left to return to General Halleck, Hattie would be carrying another message with information that Grant was planning some sort of major attack at Petersburg. With that thought in mind, Anne reached for the flaccid old body under the sheets.

"You wanted to see me, sir?"

General Hill looked up from the stack of papers on the folding camp desk. "So, you must be Private Lucas Cole."

"Yes, sir."

"I've heard a lot about you, son."

"Thank you, sir." Cole wondered what the general could possibly have heard, but he decided that would all come out in time.

Hill took a moment to study the man before him, for he knew Private Cole only by reputation. Cole was tall, lean, and rawboned as only a backwoods Southern boy could be. He didn't look much different than most of the veterans manning the Petersburg trenches. Hill didn't notice anything special about Cole until he looked into the sharpshooter's face.

The general's own eyes were intensely blue, and he had found that they disturbed some people, and often he used his own cold stare to his advantage. But the sharpshooter's eyes were colorless, pale as water, and completely unreadable. It took some effort of General Hill's considerable will not to look away. While Cole had suddenly made him uneasy, Hill was enough of a judge of men to be sure that, yes, he had found the right man.

Cole stood at attention. He was extremely curious as to why the general had sent for him. A colonel might deal directly with a private, but rarely a general. Cole's first thought was that he had done something terribly wrong to deserve the general's personal attention.

Judging by the general's sunken, feverish eyes that stared at him now, Cole thought that just might be the case. At the back of his mind there was often something nagging at him which said his killing of Yankees was little more than the murder of farm boys like himself. Sitting there behind his desk, the general looked much like Cole imagined a judge would, with a beard like Moses to boot.

"They say you're quite a shot," Hill said. "In fact, I hear you killed a Yankee officer a few days ago from a range of over one thousand yards." The general nodded appreciatively. "That's fine shooting, especially when there's a good chance they'll shoot back."

"I have a Sharps, sir. It's a good rifle."

"A good *Yankee* rifle," General Hill said. "To go along with their good Yankee horses and their good Yankee uniforms and their good

Yankee cannons. Did you know, Private, that ships come to City Point all through the day and night, unloading fresh supplies and mountains of food. I have heard that right now at the City Point docks there are fifty new caissons and fifty new cannons waiting to be sent to the field. Fifty. When was the last time our army received any new artillery?"

Cole wondered if the general planned on sending him to harass the docks at City Point. It didn't strike him as a very practical plan, considering there most likely wasn't much cover and the place was crawling with Yankees.

"I got this rifle at the Wilderness, sir, off a dead Yankee sharpshooter. He and I had been dueling all day. His rifle, the one I have now, is much better for long-range shooting, but there in the woods you couldn't see more than a hundred yards or so. My Enfield worked plenty good on him."

"So in the end you prevailed."

Cole thought back to that day. He had finally shot the Yankee. Gut shot. The worst kind of wound to have. The big lead slug had torn a hole in the Yank's belly. He had been in a tree and had tied himself to a limb to keep from falling. The Yankee had been too weak to cut himself free after being shot. He had begged Cole to finish him off—

"Private?"

"I'm sorry, sir." Cole felt his face redden. He had missed something the general said.

Hill went on, looking now at Cole somewhat suspiciously, like an irate schoolteacher.

"These are desperate times," Hill said. "They call for desperate—and patriotic—measures. Every day the Yankees produce more and more. What they call their 'war machine' is running at full steam. Our war machine has broken down, not that it ever was much. But the one thing the Yankees don't have is good soldiers." Hill paused. "Oh, they've got lots of men in uniform, I know. Conscripts, most of them. Irish. Germans. Fighting for the monthly pay the army gives them. They don't have men like you, Cole."

Cole felt the hair on the back of his neck rise in warning. Officers generally worked themselves up into giving speeches before they sent their soldiers into some hopeless fight, as if to justify it to themselves. This was just what General Hill was doing now, Cole knew. But there were no regiments of soon-to-be-dead men listening to this speech. Only him. Just one soon-to-be-dead man.

Cole lost patience.

"Who do you want me to shoot?" he demanded.

It was disrespectful to talk to a general in this manner. He watched General Hill run through several reactions, his pale, gaunt face shifting from surprise to anger to embarrassment. Cole was impressed by the general's self control, but also worried. If he was bothering to be so diplomatic with a mere private, Cole thought, there must be some terrible reason for it.

Finally, Hill sighed and spoke the name: "General Grant."

Cole was shocked. Grant! The very name was all done up in his mind with a bright blue uniform and gold buttons. Then the idea took root and began to grow rapidly. He had often wondered himself why no one thought to kill Grant or even Abe Lincoln. It made sense to Cole that if any soldier in a blue uniform was a fair target, their leaders should also be. He had even sometimes imagined himself having the strange-looking Yankee president in his rifle sights.

"It wouldn't be easy, but he could be killed, all right," Cole said, looking Hill right in the eye. "So could you. Or General Lee. Or President Davis. You see what a mess you might start, don't you, sir?"

Hill's eyes skidded away from Cole's. His gaze came to rest up in the shadowy eaves of the canvas tent. "This is why it must be done a certain way," he said.

Cole was confused. Did he want Grant knifed or drowned or kidnapped?

"What do you mean, sir?"

"Have you ever been to Washington, Cole?"

"No, sir." In fact, next to a furlough trip to Richmond, Petersburg was about the biggest town Cole had ever visited, but he didn't share this with the general.

"General Grant will be going there soon. On December fifteenth, to be exact. I'm sure of it. This is also the city where I would like to send you."

"What's wrong with City Point?" Cole asked. It was so close. Cole didn't see the sense of waiting for Grant in Washington when the general was at this moment just a few miles away.

"We must show their vulnerability," Hill said. "Imagine the general being killed on the streets of that capital city. Such an act would be a tremendous blow to the morale of the North. Of course, if your attempt in Washington fails, you are to follow Grant to City Point and complete your mission."

Cole had a hard time imagining what Washington looked like. Mostly he was wondering if there was a good stand of trees where he could take cover and get a good bead on the Yankee general.

"I could get President Lincoln while I was there, too, sir."

For a moment, Hill seemed to consider this, probably because Cole made it sound so possible. He said it as casually as if he were just going over to the woods to bring home a deer for dinner, and he might bag a turkey while he was at it.

For the first time, Hill smiled, although there was little humor in the expression. "I heard what you did at Gettysburg, Cole. And at the Wilderness. You *are* gifted with a rifle. I know you are the man to kill General Grant."

Cole's mind flashed back to the Wilderness, where wounded men crawled through the burning woods, crying for God or their mothers or something to help them. It had been hard to shoot well in those woods . . .

"Washington will be different," Cole said, coming back to the present. "Harder."

"You will have help."

"Sir?"

"We will help you enter the city. The South has many friends along the way. Once you are there, there is a place you can stay. It is all arranged."

"But where will I find the general?"

"You must create an opportunity," Hill said. "I do know that General Grant stays at the Willard Hotel when he is in Washington. I understand it is one of the city's finer establishments."

"How will I know when he's there?" Cole asked. This was all new territory to him. In the woods, he knew his way around better than most men. But a city? He imagined streets crowded with old Yankee men and their women. It did not hold promise in his mind.

"As I said, our Cause has friends everywhere. We will get word to you."

"General—"

Hill raised a hand to silence him. All sorts of questions were crashing about in Cole's head. Not the least of which was how he was supposed to flee the city once he had shot Grant. He knew soldiers would be tearing the city apart looking for the sniper. Cole didn't particularly want to be found, because the Yankees would stretch his neck at the end of a rope.

"How do you start a march, Private Cole?"

Cole sensed the general was talking down to him. Well, hell, he thought, Hill was a general. Next to God and General Robert E. Lee, there was no higher authority.

"I ain't sure I know what you mean, sir."

"Why, you start a march by taking a step, don't you? Even a march of thirty miles." Hill looked at Cole with those feverish eyes. Man must have had a touch of malaria, Cole thought. "Even a trip to Washington. First thing you do is take one step. Say you'll do it."

"I'll go to Washington, sir."

Hill nodded, as if he had expected no other answer. He reached inside his unbuttoned coat and withdrew a small leather sack. He put it on the camp desk and flicked it toward Cole with one long finger. Cole heard coins clinking inside.

"The next step is you take that bag. You'll need money. It's a little more expensive to live in Washington than it is to live in the earthworks here."

Cole slipped the sack into a pocket.

"Step three is you take that package there by the door." Cole glanced round at a parcel wrapped in a paper. "Those are new clothes. Can't send you to Washington in your, uh, uniform."

Had Hill smiled? Somewhat sadly?

"Rags is more like it, sir. You officers is the only ones with what you might call uniforms."

"Just take the package on your way out," Hill said. "And don't forget step four, which is to find yourself a place to sleep around here and be back at this tent at midnight. A scout will meet you. You'll have to travel at night to get through the Yankee lines."

"I'll be here."

"One more thing. If you're caught, you know nothing of me. You decided to do this act on your own. You are acting alone. I hope you understand why this must be so."

"Yes, sir. I understand."

"Good luck, then. You carry the hopes of the Confederacy with you."

General Hill returned the soldier's salute and watched the lean sharpshooter slip out of the room. Tomorrow would be December ninth. That gave them exactly six days to get Private Cole to

Washington City and for him to make his arrangements for the assassination. Not much time. Could the boy do it?

Hill remembered Private Cole's flinty eyes and an involuntary shudder ran through the general. The general was a devout man, and he looked upward, toward heaven, and prayed briefly for General Grant's soul, and then he prayed for his own. Cole's soul, he decided, was already lost.

5

Anne's carriage rolled through the city streets, bouncing and jarring her each time the wheels slipped into a frozen rut. The vehicle was shabby, the horse fat and swaybacked, but Anne had no money for anything better.

They jolted past the White House, and Anne looked with disdain at the muddy grounds and drab home of the Union president. The Yankees lacked taste, to be sure. The tall, gangling Abraham Lincoln was a poor substitute for the more dashing figure of Jefferson Davis.

Their destination—the mansion where Thomas Conrad lived—was just a stone's throw from the White House and practically next door to the War Department. Anne thought it wonderful that a spy lived under the very noses of the Union leaders. She had visited the mansion once two years ago. Henry had delivered her messages there many times.

She had sent Henry with another note earlier today with what that fool McDonnell had told her about Petersburg, and Conrad had sent a message back, insisting on a meeting.

As the carriage pulled up at the gated entrance, a huge, hulking man stopped to challenge them. The small eyes in his large face looked suspiciously at Anne. He kept his hand inside his coat, as if he had a pistol hidden there.

"Hullo, Mr. Messick," Henry sang out. "I done brought Miss Anne Clark to pay a visit."

A small smile crossed the tough face. "Oh, it's you, Henry. I've never seen you driving a carriage. Go right on in."

The porter unlatched the heavy iron gates and swung them open. Henry clucked to the horse and drove into the yard.

It was a magnificent place, this mansion built in the early 1800s by the wealthy and politically powerful General John Peter Van Ness. Anne was silently glad she had worn one of her best dresses for this visit. Every day she became more aware of her own disappearing wealth and the growing riches of the Yankee merchants who were making money off the war. Mr. Conrad, on the contrary, came from old money. Old Southern money, to be exact.

Henry stopped the carriage and helped her down. The door of the old mansion was open for her, and Thomas Conrad himself walked out to meet the carriage.

"Miss Clark," he said. "So good to see you! Come inside now and get warm. It's much too cold to linger outdoors."

His smooth voice marked him at once as an educated man. There was no trace of a Dixie accent. Thomas Nelson Conrad was a tall, stoutly built gentleman with thick side whiskers grown in imitation of the Union general Ambrose Burnside. It wasn't that Conrad had any special affection for Burnside or "sideburns"—as the whiskers were popularly called—but it helped to make him look all the more like a Yankee. Conrad did everything possible to hide his Southern sympathies and the effort had paid off in making him a successful spy.

Conrad took Anne's arm, and they entered the house. It was well-furnished, with expensive Persian carpets on the floors and gilt-framed mirrors in the hall. He led her into his study, where a crackling fire warmed the room. Anne sat in the horsehair chair she was offered.

"Bring us some tea," Conrad called to a servant who hovered nearby. When the woman was out of earshot, Conrad said, "You have served the Cause well, Miss Clark. I congratulate you."

"I only do my duty," Anne said. "You've done much yourself, Mr. Conrad. Perhaps it is I who should congratulate you."

Conrad inclined his head slightly in acceptance of the compliment. Anne had liked this intelligent man at her last meeting nearly two years ago, and she was glad to see her impressions confirmed. He was a very careful spymaster and had declared at their first meeting, "I was not born to be shot or hanged, Miss Clark."

"Thank you for coming tonight," Conrad said. He added, smiling, "Of course, I know this is hardly a social call. Not that I don't enjoy the company. Now, tell me more about Petersburg."

Anne detailed what Colonel McDonnell had said about General Grant's plans for a wintertime attack on the Petersburg trenches.

When she was finished, the servant entered and poured tea. Conrad waited until the servant had quietly departed, then looked up at Anne. "Very interesting, very interesting. I've been getting some information in this vein. Bits and pieces. What you've just told me supports everything we've learned so far. Your Colonel McDonnell would know. He's very close to Halleck from what I understand. Whatever he passes along comes from the very top."

"How important is all this?" Anne asked.

"I'll only say that this information will be in General Lee's hands by tomorrow night. I think Lee will have time to prepare, especially with Grant coming to Washington tomorrow. Lee will have even more time if, as you've informed me, General Grant is considering a trip to Tennessee to direct the campaign there."

"I'm glad you found my information useful," she said.

They sipped their tea. She could tell Conrad had something else to say, but he was taking his time coming around to it.

"You have been quite a help," Conrad finally began. "But there is something else I must ask. Two things, actually, that you could do for the Cause."

"Tell me," Anne said eagerly.

"There is a man coming to the city tomorrow who must be helped. We would like to send him to your house."

"Of course," she said without hesitation. "Why is he is the city?"

Conrad glanced around to make certain none of the servants was listening. He leaned toward her. "He's here to steal a map. A very important one. Will you help us?"

"You know I'll do anything for the Cause," she said.

He smiled. "I knew you would agree to help, Miss Clark. Thank you ever so much."

"What's the second thing you need done?"

"This one is harder, Miss Clark. That friend of yours will be coming to Washington tomorrow. A Major Mulholland, I believe. He's on Grant's staff. One of his 'family', as Grant likes to call it."

"Yes?"

"Whatever Mulholland tells you about Grant, repeat it to the man you'll meet tomorrow. Find out what Grant's plans are while he's in the city, where he'll be going, who he's going to see. This man might find it useful."

"That will be easy enough." Anne was thinking that this map which must be stolen was in General Grant's hands.

"Also, whatever else you can find out from Major Mulholland about these plans for an attack in Petersburg will be very useful."

"I'll send Henry or Hattie the minute I learn anything more."

"Thank you for coming, Miss Clark."

Anne wasn't sure if Conrad had brought the meeting to an end because he was busy or because he didn't want her to begin asking questions. Anne rose, and Conrad escorted her to the door. They wished each other well, and Anne climbed aboard her carriage, somewhat embarrassed by its condition, and told Henry to drive straight home.

Her head was spinning with excitement. She was to help a Confederate agent steal a map from General Grant! It was the greatest thing yet she had been asked to do for the Cause.

Lucas Cole trudged along the edge of the street, too tired to be much impressed by the sights around him. The journey through Virginia and across the Potomac River had been dangerous and exhausting. He had hardly slept these last three days as friends of the Confederacy helped spirit him into the Yankee capital.

Cole walked as if in a dream, doing his best to stay alert. This Washington City was unlike anything he had ever seen. He had given up the sidewalk because it was crowded with bustling ladies and blue-coated soldiers. The Sharps rifle, dismantled, was hanging beneath his long, loose winter coat from the harness he had rigged from scraps of rope, and the last thing he wanted was to bump into a Yankee officer who might detect the rifle hidden beneath the coat. Cole did not want to try any explanations in his Southern drawl.

Better to stick to the street, so long as he kept an eye out for carriages. The drivers were reckless and hurried.

"Beg your pardon, sir," he said, approaching a middle-aged businessman who had stopped to light a cigar. Cole forced the Southernness out of his voice, saying *your par-don* like these Northerners did instead of *yer par-din*. "Could you tell me where H Street is?"

"Why, certainly," the man said, sounding distinctly Southern to Cole's surprise. "You go down two blocks and turn left."

"Thank you, sir." Cole fought the sudden urge to salute and continued on his way.

It was now mid-afternoon on December twelfth. Cold weather had come early, and the weak sunlight offered little warmth. The people of the Northern capital were bundled against the cold, and

Cole was amazed at the prosperity evident from their winter clothes. Everywhere he saw fine suits, new hats, and overcoats with velvet collars. He saw no bare feet, except on a few of the blacks; instead, there was an abundance of fancy, well-shined shoes. The ladies wore huge, rustling dresses that looked new and radiant, unlike the careworn outfits of Southern women he had seen in Petersburg and Richmond.

He had heard that many of the patriotic women of the South had given up their fine silk dresses so that they could be sewn into observation balloons. It looked to him as if none of the Yankee women had been asked to sacrifice their finery.

His own clothes felt shabby by comparison, even though they were the best General Hill had been able to find in war-ravaged Petersburg.

The street where Cole walked was hard with frost, but the mud was not completely frozen. Here and there the sun had softened the ruts. Most of the street was solid, coated with a dry, wintry dust. Horse urine made dark stains in places, and piles of manure steamed in the cold. That didn't concern the pedestrians who hurried along the sidewalk, their fine shoes safely out of harm's way. Cole stuck to the edges of the street, feeling as if he were wading in the shallows of a raging river.

Two blocks down he turned onto H Street, just as the gentleman had directed. He found the house and stood for a moment studying the fine, stucco townhouse. On the street level there was a row of three-quarter-sized windows, but the front door was one flight up, reached by a staircase with a finely carved handrail and balustrade. He could hardly believe a Rebel spy lived here. This spy had a lot at stake, considering what he could lose if caught.

He knocked at the door.

"Yes?"

To his surprise, a black servant stood in the doorway. He had never called at a house where anyone but the owner answered. The black woman looked up at Cole expectantly, waiting for him to state his business. Cole hesitated. He had been given this address, but no name. He didn't even know who to ask for.

"I've been sent here to meet a friend of the Cause," Cole said.

"Come in," the woman said, stepping back from the doorway. "Wait here."

Cole watched the black woman disappear into one of the rooms off the front hall and waited, hat in hand, until she reappeared. "Come on in here," she said, somewhat harshly. "You bringin' trouble, I can tell."

He went down the hall and entered the room. A woman was standing by the fireplace, and she was as well-dressed as any of the ladies he had seen on the city streets. Cole guessed she was nearing thirty. Milk-white skin. An elegant lady. Her eyes were piercing as she looked him up and down.

"So, you're the one who's been sent," she said.

"I suppose so, ma'am."

Cole was aware that the servant stood behind him, just beyond his line of vision. He turned slightly until she was in view.

"Don't worry about Hattie," the woman said with a slight smile. "She's not about to put a dagger in your back, although I suppose a soldier must be cautious."

"Is it just you?" Cole was confused. He didn't understand how this woman was supposed to help him assassinate General Grant. So far, everything in Washington City was turning out to be different than he had expected.

"Aren't I enough?"

Hattie laughed. "I'll say you is, and then some."

Cole was inclined to agree. He thought this friend of the Confederacy was quite beautiful. She had green eyes and reddish-brown hair, with the pale, unlined skin that only the wives of judges and successful merchants could afford back where Cole came from. Her dress looked as new and stylish as any Cole had seen passing on the sidewalks of the city, the garment's wide hoops nearly filling the room.

He also noted the huge, gilded mirror over the fireplace and the velvet chairs and sofa. Heavy curtains framed the windows, ready to block out any winter drafts, and the floor was covered with an expensive-looking carpet. Cole realized self-consciously that his muddy boots were leaving tracks. He felt the dirt from his travels begin to itch at him and wondered what she must think of him standing here in her well-furnished parlor, smelling of horse sweat and wood smoke.

"My name is Anne Clark," she said, crossing over to him. "And whom do I have the pleasure of meeting?"

"Lucas Cole, ma'am."

She took his hands. "Oh, you are so cold! Winter has come early this year, I fear."

Cole felt the warmth of her hands and held them longer than was polite. Her skin was soft, the texture of buttermilk, the hands of a woman who had never touched a hoe or plow handle. He noticed she made no effort to break his grip.

"It is cold weather for traveling, ma'am," he said evenly.

Miss Clark turned to her servant. "Hattie, set out a bowl of hot soup for Mr. Cole. I'm sure he's hungry. And then put some water on to heat so Mr. Cole can have a bath and wash off the dust of the road."

"That would be nice, ma'am," Cole said. "Then I must attend to my business—"

She silenced him with an arching of her eyebrows, glanced to Hattie, then back at Cole. "We'll have time to talk later, Mr. Cole. Now follow Hattie here and she'll get you something to eat."

While the fancy parlor made him uncomfortable, he felt more at home in the kitchen. There were no fine carpets for his boots to muddy, only the plain kitchen floor, which was made of well-scrubbed boards. He was used to kitchens and simple homes. The cook stove was stoked, and he warmed himself as Hattie stirred a small pot.

"I always keep a little something on the back of the stove in case there's a hungry gentleman."

"Mmm," Cole said appreciatively, eyeing the stew. He hadn't had a warm meal in days, unless he could count the parched corn and ramrod biscuits Snodgrass and his bunch had scratched together back in the trenches. "That smells right good."

"There's a pump out back," Hattie said. "Go fill up a couple of buckets and I'll set them on the stove to warm for your bath."

Cole was more interested in the stew than a bath, but one thing at a time, he told himself. He found a couple of empty buckets by the back steps and pumped them full. The iron pump handle was cold, and Cole pumped with first one hand, then the other, warming the hand he wasn't using inside his coat. When the buckets were full he hauled them up the stairs, shouldered open the kitchen door, and put them on the stove to warm.

"That's some chore," he said, wondering how this thin little woman managed it.

"That's why I got you to do it," Hattie said. "Now sit yourself down and I'll get you some stew."

"All right."

Cole hesitated. The rifle was still hidden beneath his coat, and he wasn't sure it was a good idea for the servant to get a look at it. But he couldn't sit with the coat on and the rifle barrel and stock digging into him, so he shrugged off the heavy garment. Hattie gave the rifle a quick, curious look but made no comment as he slipped out of the ungainly harness. He kept his Colt revolver tucked into his belt. A Bowie knife was in a sheath over his hip. If the servant woman found his weapons unusual, she kept it to herself. Cole set the pieces of the rifle carefully on the floor along one wall, then put the coat over them to hide them from view.

"Sit down now and eat," Hattie ordered when he was done.

Hattie set the steaming bowl in front of him, along with a chunk of bread and a mug of coffee. Real coffee. He stared in amazement. After months of eating rancid salt pork or whatever else could be found in the trenches around Petersburg, even Cole could be impressed by real food.

"Don't they feed you all?" Hattie asked, sounding genuinely disgusted. "You're nothin' but skin and bones. How you goin' to fight any battles lookin' like that?"

"Ain't much to eat 'cept beans and parched corn and some captured hardtack now and then."

"Ain't no shortage of food here so long's you got money to buy it," Hattie said. "So you just eat all you want."

Cole needed no other prompting. He attacked the food in front of him. He was enjoying the soup so much that he almost didn't hear the footsteps on the stairs leading to the kitchen. At the noise, he put down his spoon. Someone was at the door, but the winter sun was behind the figure and Cole could see only a silhouette through the glass in the door. His right hand reached for the handle of his revolver.

"That you, Henry?" Hattie called.

A black man walked into the kitchen and froze at the sight of Cole.

"I didn't know you had company," he said to Hattie.

"Come on in," Hattie said. "Now I guess I've got two hungry mouths to feed. This here is Mr. Cole. This is Henry."

From where he was standing, the man could see Cole still had his hand on his revolver. His eyes also searched out the handle of the Bowie knife strapped to Cole's leg.

"Mmm, mmm. That's some knife you got there." He sat down and Hattie had a bowl of hot soup in front of him in an instant. Then she was busy refilling Cole's bowl. "You don't look like one of Miss Clark's gentleman callers," the man said.

"Hush now, Henry," Hattie said, shooting the man a warning look.

The man bent to his soup, and Cole did the same. He felt uncomfortable now with two people—two black people—in the kitchen. Where he came from, the two races did not often mix. Considering he had been sent to eat in the kitchen, Cole wondered if this Miss Clark considered him to be just another one of the servants.

Just as he was getting to the bottom of his second bowl of soup, Cole heard someone knocking loudly at the front door of the house. His hand slipped once more to the Colt.

"I best get that," Hattie said.

But before she could get her apron off, they heard a man's booming voice ringing in the hallway, followed by a woman's laughter.

"I suppose Miss Clark done let him in herself."

"A gentleman caller," Henry said, chuckling into his soup. "Sounds like that Colonel Wilcox."

Hattie rapped his knuckles with a wooden spoon. "You best mind yourself."

Cole was confused. "There's no Mr. Clark?"

"She ain't never been married. Now there was a Mr. Clark, Miss Clark's father, but he done died before the war."

Cole thought Anne Clark must be a rich woman to afford such a fine house and two servants. The thought made him uneasy. Back home, people who didn't work for their money were not to be trusted.

"Henry, go fetch me that tub from the shed out back," Hattie said, clearing away their empty bowls. "Mr. Cole here is going to take a bath. Miss Anne's orders. I'll bring you some soap and a towel, the rest is up to you."

Henry went out the kitchen door, leaving Cole alone in the kitchen with Hattie. Cole stood and faced the black woman. Up until then, their meal had been pleasant enough, but the stony face of the man in her kitchen made Hattie take a step back toward the stove, where there was a heavy frying pan handy in case she needed a weapon. He suddenly looked mean, although Hattie didn't know what could have brought it on, and she felt her legs go weak with fear. *He gonna do somethin' to me. Somethin' bad.* Even then, Hattie felt a little ashamed, because she didn't scare easily. But those cut-glass eyes of the stranger were cold and violent. *Miss Anne's done let a bad man in her house,* Hattie thought. *A real bad man.*

"Don't tell nobody about that rifle," he said, his voice low, threatening. His hand touched the handle of the big knife. Hattie imagined the razor sharp blade, felt her throat tighten. "If you do, I'll cut out your tongue. You understand me, girl?"

Hattie, her knees trembling now, could only nod.

"Now set out the soap and towel, and get out of here."

The water on the stove was sending up wisps of steam. Henry brought the washtub up the back stairs, and both he and Hattie retreated, leaving Cole alone in the kitchen.

Cole hadn't had a bath since summer. There wasn't much to wash in around Petersburg, except a few mud puddles.

He jammed chairs under the knobs of both the kitchen and back doors to prevent any surprise visitors. He positioned a third chair near the washtub and set the Colt on it within reach. He figured that in the city, a man couldn't be too careful. Then he filled the washtub, stripped down, and settled himself into the warm water.

6

As Colonel Jonathan Wilcox sat on the edge of the bed and buttoned his shirt, Anne propped herself on an elbow and looked up at him. She put on her most concerned face and said, "You look tired, Jonathan. I hope you haven't been working too hard at the War Department, now have you?"

"Oh, it's been a bit busier than usual," he said, trying to get the buttons on his shirt cuffs refastened. His fingers were fat as sausages and fumbled awkwardly with the tiny buttons. The brandy he'd had to drink didn't help. Anne reached over and finished buttoning his shirt. He sighed. Wilcox was assigned to security at the White House, and like many mid-level men, he was always eager to make himself sound important. Most of his day was spent shuttling back and forth between the War Department and the White House. A glorified errand boy. He didn't think twice about telling Anne about the day-to-day politics of either place. Considering he helped carry out much of the War Department's secret work, Anne had expected someone in his position to be more tight-lipped, but Wilcox was far too arrogant to ever think he himself might be undermining security.

Little did he know the news he told Anne often reached the Confederate high command within a few hours. "Grant's coming up here at the end of the week to meet with Stanton and Halleck. Grant wants to replace General Thomas down at Nashville, and it's not going to be easy. Thomas has many political friends in the city."

"But why replace General Thomas?" Anne asked, making her voice sound sleepy, although her mind was taut as a wire. "He's 'The Rock of Chickamauga.' "

Wilcox snorted. "He's aptly nicknamed, at that. Grant's unhappy with Thomas for not attacking General Hood's men. He's given the Rebels so much time they've dug in around Nashville like ticks. Each day that passes it will only be that much harder to dislodge them."

"So Grant is coming to Washington to campaign for General Thomas' removal?"

"That's about the size of it." Wilcox had stood and was pulling on his trousers. He rarely stayed long at her house because he usually stopped off on his way home from the War Department. It was four o'clock and there was less than an hour of daylight left. His wife and four children would be waiting for him, and so would his supper, which the fat officer made a point of never missing.

"I don't know what general they could find to replace Thomas," Anne said idly.

"Well, there's talk that Grant himself might go to Tennessee to direct the attack. Stanton's none too happy about that idea, let me tell you. But once Grant's made up his mind to do something, there's no stopping him."

Wilcox moved to a chair and began pulling on his boots. Anne smiled at him, and the colonel grinned back. "Are you sure you can't stay?" she asked. She wanted to make Wilcox feel special, but she had made a point of asking only after he was nearly finished dressing.

"Not today," he said. "Maybe next time, darling." He winked, as if by lingering in Anne's bed he would be giving her a tremendous treat.

In fact, Anne couldn't wait for him to leave so that she could pass along the information Wilcox had just given her. She already knew Grant was coming to Washington on the fifteenth and anyone could read in the papers that General Thomas was still preparing to attack at Nashville. But the fact that Grant intended to replace Thomas, and perhaps even take over the Tennessee campaign himself, was very important news. It made indulging the heavyset Colonel Wilcox worthwhile.

Having put his shiny black boots on, Wilcox tugged his coat round his corpulent body. He also buckled on his sword belt, the blade rattling dully inside the scabbard. The colonel insisted on wearing his sword wherever he went, although she doubted if he had ever drawn it in nearly four years of soldiering other than to oil the blade. She wondered if he would find it much of a weapon against the Confederate soldier who was at that very moment having supper in her kitchen.

Still, Wilcox was a far more imposing figure in his full uniform than in his longjohns. He was broad-shouldered, heavyset, and taller than most men. She had noticed that soldiers wasted no time in obeying his orders.

"Someday, Anne, I want you all to myself," he said.

"Now, Jonathan—"

He held up a hand. "I know all about the others. What will it take for you to be my mistress alone?"

"Money," Anne said flatly. It was one thing she knew Wilcox didn't have.

He frowned.

"I'd show you to the door, but you've tired me out, Colonel," Anne said, forcing a smile. "I do hope you'll be back soon."

Wilcox also smiled. "Of course I will, Anne. Now, you just lay there and rest, darling. I'll show myself out."

With that, Wilcox shut the door. Anne heard his boots clumping down the stairs, and she winced at the sound of his scabbard banging against her balusters. Swords and boots were taking an awful toll on her beautiful staircase.

Wilcox was always saying he wanted her to himself. Well, she thought, that just wouldn't be possible.

As soon as she heard the heavy front door shut, Anne leapt out of bed and dressed. She went to a writing table in her bedroom, opened a drawer, and took out a sheet of paper, a pencil, and a card on which was printed a neat block of letters. This was her cypher. At another house in the city, where the man lived who gathered information found out by Anne and other spies, there was a copy of the same cypher which was then used to decode her messages.

Taking her pencil, she wrote out:

GRANT TO GO TO TENNESSEE

Anne then consulted the cypher block. The letters A to Z were written across the top and also down the side, the A in the upper left corner being the anchor for both alphabets. The center of the block was filled with a jumble of letters. The key for that week, which was passed to her orally by a woman peddling eggs who came every Monday morning to her door, was the phrase "liberty or death."

Beneath her message Anne wrote:

GRANT TO GO TO TENNESSEE
LIBERTY OR DE ATHLIBERT

To encode her message, Anne found the letter G in the uppermost row of letters. At the left-hand side she found the letter L. She ran one finger down from the top G, and another over from the left-hand L. The letter where the two lines met was D. She repeated this encoding until her message read as a mix of letters:

DZBRK MM UF WS TXUYMTGXC

To anyone who came across this message, it would be as indecipherable as Hindu unless they had the proper cypher and key. Anne tore the paper in half, put the original message in a pocket of her dress, and neatly folded the coded message. She went downstairs to the parlor. She threw the top half of her sheet of paper into the fire, then called for Henry.

"Yes, ma'am?"

"I have a message for you to carry to Mr. Conrad." She handed her servant the paper. "Put it in your shoe."

Anne stood and watched as Henry did as he was told. Hattie was a far more reliable courier; she knew what precautions to take and hid the messages Anne entrusted to her well. But she would be needing Hattie here in the house shortly to help her with Mr. Cole. Henry would have to do.

"Go straight to Mr. Conrad's house. Don't dawdle, now. It's very important that you get their straightaway."

"I won't stop for nothin'," Henry promised.

"Now go," Anne said. "Go out the front door so you don't disturb that man in the kitchen."

Henry hesitated. He was a muscular man and served as a kind of bouncer when the occasional gentleman caller drank too much and became unruly. "He's a bad man, Miss Anne," Henry said. "You sure you want to be alone with him in this house?"

"In that case you'd better hurry back, Henry," Anne said, hoping he would be fleeter of foot than usual. "We'll be all right until then."

"Yes, ma'am."

With that, Henry headed for the front door with his message that Grant might soon be away from the Virginia front, even if temporarily. Such news might prove very useful to General Lee and his lieutenants, she thought.

• • •

Snodgrass's toes had turned the color of plums. He held them toward the smoldering fire, hoping to put some feeling back into his frozen feet.

"Goin' to have to chop 'em off," said Charlie Hollis, his face only six inches away from the blue toes. Hollis was so nearsighted he couldn't see much of anything more than a few yards away.

"What the hell do you know, Hollis?" Snodgrass snapped. "I ain't goin' to let a blind man tell me I've got to cut my toes off."

"I've seen 'em black before," offered one man. "Snodgrass's toes there ain't so bad as that."

"These might turn black yet," Hollis said hopefully.

"You best go sharpen up your knife then, Hollis, you bloodthirsty son of a bitch." Snodgrass was in no mood to joke. He had in fact seen more than one set of toes lost to the cold. If they did turn black there was nothing to do but cut them off or else the rotting flesh would spread gangrene through the body. He rubbed his feet, hoping to coax some warmth into them.

He had frozen his toes while on duty in one of the forward rifle pits. Although there wasn't much activity along the Petersburg front now that winter had arrived, it was still necessary to post men in the rifle pits forward of the trenches just in case the Yankees made any forays against the Confederate positions. Snodgrass doubted there would be any trouble because the Yankees were likely as cold and miserable as his comrades. Winter had become a mutual enemy.

If there was a hell, Snodgrass thought, it was not a place full of fire and brimstone and red devils with pitchforks. No, he would have welcomed such a hell on this bitter, December day. Hell was a hole in the Virginia mud filled with slush and water where he shivered for hours on end while equally cold Yankees not more than one hundred feet away kept their rifles pointed in his direction so that if he dared get up and stomp his feet to keep them from turning blue, he would be a dead man.

Not that he hadn't tried to strike a small truce. Rebs and Yanks were so close to one another on picket duty that if the enemy so much as sneezed or broke wind he heard it. He had wondered if the Yankees could hear his teeth chattering.

"Hey, Yank!" he had called.

"Yeah, Johnny. What do you want?"

"You cold over there?"

"Did Moses have a beard?"

"How 'bout we get up and stomp our feet some?"

There was silence as the Yank thought it over. "You first, Reb."

Snodgrass had snorted. "I ain't that cold."

He preferred to speculate on the nature of hell and the afterlife rather than experience it first hand just yet. So he had lain there in the frigid water and consequently may have lost his toes.

"Put some wood on that fire, you stingy bastards," Snodgrass said. So far he hadn't noticed any difference in his feet and it was no wonder: the fire was hardly more than a smoking heap of damp twigs. "Build it up some."

There was a small pile of wet wood beside the fire that the boys were trying to dry out. Firewood was scarce, and they had taken to pulling saplings from the woven mats securing the sides of the trenches in order to have something to burn. An actual log or plank was a rarity, although from time to time someone in their mess made a trip to the rear and lugged back as much firewood as he could.

"That's about as good as it's going to get, Uriah," Hollis said.

Snodgrass wasn't about to lose his toes. He got to his feet and stomped through the half-frozen mud, not that his extremities could feel it.

"Snodgrass—"

"You lazy jugheads are just about useless," he said. "Here I am half frozen to death and you sit there on your backsides whining about how the wood's too wet to burn. Goddamnit!"

He reached into his cartridge pouch and took out a handful of rounds.

"Oh Lord, Snodgrass, don't shoot nobody, now."

He ripped the paper tubes open with his teeth and covered a slab of wood from the firewood pile with gunpowder. As he hobbled back to the fire, the boys scattered.

"What the hell—"

"You're goin' to blow us up, boy!"

Snodgrass thought: good, we could all use a little of the biblical version of the fire and brimstone hell right now.

He put the plank on the fire and scattered twigs overtop of it.

Whoosh. The gunpowder didn't exactly explode, but the flames did leap up nicely, igniting both the plank and the twigs. Snodgrass carefully fed the fledgling flames with twigs, and in a minute the campfire was burning brightly.

"You can come back now, boys," he called, settling himself beside the healthy fire and reaching his toes toward it. "I'll keep your sorry asses from freezing to death."

One by one, the men returned, laughing. Snodgrass's bold action to get the fire burning would be the highlight of their day, if not their week. Life in the trenches consisted mainly of being cold and bored. Now that the fire was going they didn't even have anything to cook over it except a little shelled corn, which Hollis, peering intently with his myopic eyes, poured into their mess's frying pan so that it could be parched over the flames.

"Breakfast, lunch, and dinner all rolled into one," Walter Classon remarked, trying to make a joke. Nobody laughed. It was hard to find much humor in being hungry all the time. They had lost so much weight since summer that they all added notches to their belts to hold their trousers up; those whose belts were worn out had a length of rope knotted around their waist.

"I'd love a taste of whiskey to go with this," Snodgrass said hopefully, although he knew the last drop was long since gone. He was beginning to feel his toes and thought they might not have to be cut off, after all. "A new pair of shoes to keep my feet warm wouldn't be so bad, either."

His shoes were hardly recognizable as such. The leather uppers had torn away from the soles during the long summer marches when Lee and Grant had played tag, so he was obliged to hold top to bottom with strips of rags and string. Such repairs did a poor job of keeping out Petersburg's cold and mud, however, which was why his poor toes were nearly done in.

"Them Yankees has got fine shoes," Hollis said.

"Good for running," Classon said, getting a laugh from the group this time.

"I'd like to get me a pair of them shoes," Snodgrass said. He winced at the pain that was starting in his feet. "Goddamn my toes are killing me."

"That's a good sign," Hollis said. "That means they're still alive. The blood is moving again."

Snodgrass had already forgotten his toes, which were beginning to turn from a bruised sort of blue-black to a blood red color. He was dreaming about a pair of sturdy brogans to keep his feet warm through the winter.

"What we need is a poker game," Snodgrass said. "To win us some shoes."

All their eyes looked from one pair of shoes to another on the feet of the group standing around the fire. Their footgear ranged from brogans that had been patched together like Snodgrass's to mere rags wrapped around the feet to keep them somewhat warm. No one wore anything worth winning in a card game, and most of the other Rebels up and down the trenches weren't any better off.

"Maybe some of the boys back at headquarters have decent shoes," Classon said.

"Them Yankees has fine shoes," Snodgrass said. "And I wouldn't mind getting up a little game to win them."

"With the Yankees?"

Meetings with the enemy had been done before. Nighttime meetings between the two sides had taken place in order to trade. But a poker game?

"Supposin' they agree," Hollis said. "What have we got that would be worth six pair of shoes?"

The men around the fire nodded because Hollis had a point. They had some paper money issued by the Confederacy, which was nearly worthless, along with two or three Yankee greenbacks, probably not enough to interest the Yankees. Aside from their rifles, they owned nothing of value. Even then, the Yankees had superior weapons.

Snodgrass had already considered this problem, and he slipped off his belt, which was worn thin, and turned it over. As his messmates watched, Snodgrass dug his fingers into a special pouch which had been sewn onto the back of the belt and produced his three double eagle coins.

"Sixty dollars in gold, boys."

His fellow soldiers gaped. Hollis leaned in close for a look and whistled. Few of them had seen that much money at one time before the war, and in Petersburg such a fortune was unheard of.

"You could buy all the shoes you wanted with that," Classon said.

Snodgrass smiled. His toes were positively aching but he took this as a good sign and cheerfully heaped more twigs on the fire.

"I could buy the shoes." He nodded. "But I have a feeling that after the war is over, this gold may be the only hard cash between Richmond and Texas. I'd hate to part with it needlessly."

"But shoes—"

"Some food, boys," Hollis said, removing the pan of corn from the fire to cool. "Think of your bellies, too."

"Whiskey," Classon said.

Snodgrass was looking at the coins and grinning. "Maybe we could win all that for nothing," he said. "Using my money to make the pot interesting, of course."

Wrapped in a towel, Cole padded across the kitchen floor toward the door. The bath had been welcome, but the water had finally cooled, and his fingertips had puckered from soaking so long. He was glad Miss Clark was giving him a clean shirt and trousers. He would have dreaded putting his old clothes back on because they were dirty after his journey. He left them behind, thinking that the servant woman Hattie could wash them for him later.

Cole eased the chair out from under the doorknob and opened the door. He was taken aback to find Miss Clark herself standing in the hallway, holding the clothes draped over her arm.

"I thought you would never open that door," she said. Her face was stern. "Imagine, locking a woman out of her own kitchen."

"I'm sorry, ma'am." Aware that he was standing in front of this woman in nothing more than a towel, Cole felt his face begin to burn with embarrassment. His predicament did not appear to bother Miss Clark, however. She stood calmly in the hallway with a coy smile on her face. He didn't know whether to retreat into the kitchen and shut the door or stand there feeling like a fool. Instead, he kept one hand gripping tightly at the towel and reached for the clothes Miss Clark held with the other. She moved her arm away and Cole had to dance further into the hall to keep his balance.

"Come with me," she said, grabbing his free hand.

Cole had no choice but to follow her as she swept through the nearly dark house; the only sound was the rustling of her wide hoop skirt. Cole was shivering because of the cold drafts on his skin, and the bare wood floors beneath his feet felt like ice. He was glad Hattie was nowhere to be seen.

But she was there, hiding in the shadowed hallway. As soon as Cole and Miss Clark were gone, Hattie slipped into the kitchen and began going through the pockets of his clothes. Hattie made quick work of it, because she had done just this sort of thing many times before whenever Miss Anne's "gentleman callers" slept off their liquor in the big bed upstairs. Mostly she looked for papers her mistress might be interested in; Miss Anne had taught her to read well enough for Hattie to understand at once whether some document was important or not.

On the other side of the house, Cole and Anne reached the stairs, and she started up them, leading him along.

"Where are you going?" he asked. He could easily have broken free of her grasp, but by now Cole was intrigued by what was happening. She did not answer, and Cole bounded up the steps behind her, his heart beating rapidly in anticipation of her dark, perfumed *boudoir* upstairs.

At the top of the stairs they turned and went down a hallway to a bedroom. Like the downstairs parlor, it was finely decorated, with a carpet on the floor, curtains at the windows, and a dressing table with a mirror and bottles and jars of feminine potions. An oil lamp on the table gave the only light. The centerpiece of the room was the huge bed, which was topped by a lace-fringed canopy. Cole was so busy admiring the room that he hardly noticed as Miss Clark picked at the fingers that held his towel as she might undo a knot. The towel dropped to the floor.

"My, my," she said.

"What are you doing?"

He stood there for a moment, stunned. Never before had a proper woman been so bold toward him, and Cole did not know what to think. But the amazement on his face soon disappeared and his strange, colorless eyes took on a light that now made Anne Clark blush as if she were the naked one in the room.

Perhaps she had made a mistake, she thought, in thinking she could manipulate him like the other men who came to her house. For the most part, she had found men to be stupid and pliable creatures whose brains stopped functioning the moment they smelled perfume or had a taste of her lips. They could be led by their bollocks, which she, in both a figurative and literal sense, grasped firmly as she guided them into telling her things they shouldn't have.

She always managed to get the upper hand with any man, and her success in doing so had enabled her to be an effective spy for the Confederacy. But as Cole took a step toward her, she sensed this man was different. He was no soft bureaucrat or Yankee administrator. That wasn't the sort of man the South would send on a mission—even if it was only to steal a map. Looking at Cole, she only half-believed what Conrad had told her anyhow. Cole seemed far too *something* to be a mere thief. *Dangerous,* she thought. Yes, that was it. She couldn't picture him sneaking around the rooms of the

Willard Hotel.

Before the night was through, however, she intended to find out what he planned to do in the city.

He reached out and touched her cheek, and she noticed the lean arm was corded with muscle. How different he was from the soft-bodied Yankees who visited her. She put a hand to her chest as her heart fluttered.

"Mr. Cole—"

But Cole was beyond words. It had been a long time since he had been with a woman, and the tension of the last few days had left him packed tightly as a musket load. All at once he was on her, taking her into his arms and forcing her onto the bed. Anne felt herself losing control, but when she tried to push him away, Cole gathered both her hands in one of his and pinned her arms over her head and against the pillow. His free hand tore at her clothes and Miss Clark warned, "Don't rip anything! My God, Mr. Cole, you are a devil."

She helped him, and in a moment was out of her dress, their flesh sliding against each other and creating a warmth of its own on this winter's night. Cole rode her hard, driving deep into her with each thrust, and Anne heard herself giving little yips of pleasure. He gave a final lunge and arched his back, moaning, as Anne shuddered beneath him.

Oh my God! She cried out loud. Her heart was pounding.

When they both caught their breath, Cole rolled off and lay beside her.

"You are an extraordinary man," she said, still breathless. "I can understand now why they sent you. What is it you're here to do?"

"You don't know?" he murmured, his eyes half closed, barely hearing what he knew was only flattery. He was exhausted after his journey and was now completely sated from his interlude with this lovely spy.

"Tell me," she urged gently. "Maybe I can help you."

"You just did," he said.

Disappointed, Anne knew at once he wasn't going to tell her anything more. She hoped Hattie would have better luck downstairs as she searched his things.

"Why, you're hardly more than a boy," she said, regretting the words as soon as she had spoken them, although it was true that there in her bed he looked terribly young. She thought of all those young men dying in the war, her own dear Rayford among them. It was almost too sad to bear.

Cole's eyes came fully open again and fixed on hers. It was the eyes that gave him away, she thought. On a trip to Harper's Ferry before the war she had once seen a copperhead snake sunning itself on a rock, its eyes as pale and colorless as Cole's. The eyes of something deadly. Deadly and watchful.

She wondered if she had made a mistake after all, bringing him into her bed. But she had to know: what was he doing in Washington?

Cole appeared too tired to talk. His eyelids began to drift lower. The black cloud of unconsciousness was hovering.

"Sleep, Lucas," she whispered. "Sleep."

The last thing he felt were the long tendrils of her hair sliding over his chest as she bent to kiss him, and then Cole let the dark, warm cloud of sleep take him.

Anne watched him for a while to make certain he was asleep. She had dealt with many foolish men, and she knew Lucas Cole was not like them. He had a country boy's cunning. Wouldn't it be just like him to feign sleep just to fool her?

"Lucas," she crooned softly. *"Lucas Cole."*

He did not move. Satisfied, she slipped out of bed, being careful not to wake him, and dressed. It was dark now, with the only light coming from the dim oil lamp at her dressing table, and she had to feel around the room for her clothes, which were scattered and rumpled. The thought of how they had ended up that way made her smile.

Hattie met her in the hallway. She had an oil lamp and guided them down the stairs to the parlor. The gas lamps were already burning in their sconces along the walls, and a fire crackled brightly in the fireplace, keeping the damp December night at bay. Anne stood by the fireplace to warm herself after the trip through the cold house. It seemed in winter that the place was always full of drafts.

"What did you find?" she asked.

"This was all he had," Hattie said, presenting her employer with a scrap of paper, a coin pouch, and a small packet wrapped in oilcloth. "There was some other truck in his pockets. A jackknife. Matches. I reckon anybody might have them things."

"Thank you, Hattie. Do you think he will suspect you went through his clothes?"

"I don't see how he couldn't, Miss Anne," Hattie said, smiling.

"You see, I done went and washed his clothes for him. Now, wouldn't it make sense that I checked his pockets first?"

Anne smiled. "You make a good spy, Hattie."

Anne looked at the paper first. Her address was written on it in a firm hand. She guessed it had been written by whomever had sent Cole to her. She balled up the note and tossed it into the fireplace, where the paper went up in a bright flame and turned quickly to ash.

"Miss Anne—"

"If he asks, tell him you missed it and it was ruined in the washing," she said. "I can't have him carrying around a scrap of paper with my address on it if he should be caught doing whatever it is he's been sent here to do."

She opened the purse and dumped the coins onto a table. Several gold twenty-dollar pieces glittered in the firelight, as did some smaller denominations of coins.

Hattie's eyes widened at the glint of gold. "Look at all that money."

There was a little over one hundred dollars on the table. Quickly, Anne picked out a gold double eagle and put it in her own pocket. She presented Hattie with a dollar coin. Then she returned the remaining coins to the purse.

"He'll notice that, Miss Anne. I never seen a man who didn't keep track of his money."

"Mr. Cole will suspect you took it. But he won't be certain, so he'll never accuse you out loud." Anne frowned, thought of how low her funds had become. "It's twenty dollars, Hattie. We could use it."

The last item was a small, squarish package wrapped in oilcloth and bound with a leather thong. Judging by the creases in the oilcloth and the knot in the thong, the packet hadn't been opened for some time.

"That looks important," Hattie said. "Maybe it's some secret papers."

Anne was thinking just that, and she quickly unwrapped it. Inside was a daguerreotype in a cheap tin frame, like the kind a traveling portrait artist might use. The image was dark, nearly smoky, but she could make out a young woman, her cheeks retouched by the artist to give them a rosy glow.

Hattie leaned in for a look. "That must be his sweetheart," she said, looking at Anne reproachfully. Taking a few coins was one thing, but Hattie didn't approve of her employer prying when it came to something as private as a picture of a sweetheart. Anne didn't share such feelings, wise as she was to the ways of men. She wondered what Lucas Cole's sweetheart would think if she knew her man was asleep in another woman's bed.

"It might be his sister . . . or his sweetheart." Whoever it was, the girl must have been dear to Cole's heart. If he survived what lay ahead, would the girl in the photograph even know the man who returned? The war had changed more than one man—or woman, for that matter.

She carefully wrapped the package back up and retied the leather thong.

"I'll put it all back in the kitchen," Hattie said.

"That was all you found?"

"Yes, ma'am. This here, along with a pistol and a big knife you could chop wood with. You want me to fetch them?"

Thinking of that knife, Hattie hesitated, and then decided against telling Anne about Cole's strange rifle. She didn't doubt for an instant Cole would make good on his threat to hurt her. She had known cruel men down South like that, and it was better not to cross them.

"Leave them be, Hattie. We've no use for such things."

"Yes, ma'am." She supposed Miss Anne didn't want to know about the rifle, anyhow.

Hattie took the lamp and went off to the kitchen, leaving Anne alone in the parlor. She sat down in the chair closest to the fire and stared into the flames.

There had been no clues as to Cole's mission in his pockets. What was he doing in the city? Maybe he had come to steal a map, after all. Anne vowed she would keep pressing until she found out.

The morning of December 13 was a busy one for Cole. He woke before dawn, leaving Anne asleep in bed, and breakfasted on coffee and biscuits in the kitchen. Hattie worked sullenly, finding any excuse she could to run out of the kitchen. Alone, he hid his rifle on a shelf in the pantry behind some large tins and storage jars.

Hattie only spoke once, after she saw him eyeing the fresh loaves she had taken from the oven.

"Don't you touch that bread!" Hattie's sharp voice cracked like a whip. "That's for supper."

When she left the kitchen again, Cole took the bread and a cup of coffee and went out the back door. He gulped the hot black liquid as he walked the alley that led to the street, then hurled the cup away to shatter against the back of a shed.

Cole spent the morning learning the streets. Washington City, just sixty miles north of Richmond, had been a Southern city before the war, located as it was in the slave-holding border state of Maryland. Many residents considered their dear "Washtone"—as they pronounced it in Southern fashion—to be occupied now by the enemy in blue.

Yankees were everywhere. Squadrons of blue-coated cavalry passed in the street, enlisted men loitered on the corners, and officers hurried self-importantly along the sidewalks with bundles of papers under their arms. As a Confederate soldier, he found it hard to get used to the sight of so many blue uniforms. He had to keep reminding himself he wasn't wearing butternut, and so was as anonymous as anyone else on the street. Cole gave the soldiers a wide berth, nonetheless.

The streets were muddy and only the main thoroughfares were lined with wooden sidewalks. Pigs rooted in the trash tossed in the alleys, and chickens scratched at the edges of the street, out of the way of passing wagons and carts.

Cole soon discovered that like most towns and cities, the streets of Washington were laid out in a grid, the only major difference being that this grid was bisected by long diagonal avenues that connected important points. This was a unique design created by Major Pierre Charles L'Enfant, a Frenchman who in 1791 had been hired by George Washington to lay out what would become the capital city of the new United States. The circles formed by the places where the avenues intersected were intended by L'Enfant to give American artillery command of all the streets in the city against an invading enemy.

These diagonal avenues bore the names of states: Virginia, New York, Connecticut, New Hampshire, Georgia, Pennsylvania. This last avenue was the one Cole sought, and when he reached it he turned right and walked toward the heart of the Yankee capital.

After walking five blocks, Cole came to the White House. It was not nearly so grand a place as he had expected. Although the home of the Yankee president was spacious enough, the lawn was mostly mud, and as Cole stopped to take a good look, a flock of geese came around one corner of the presidential mansion, hotly pursued by a cursing gardener.

He found a group of ragged men nearby, huddled around a fire of scrap wood. The city was filled with men like these—"Wild Boys" the locals called them—Confederate veterans who had signed an oath of allegiance to the Union in order to gain their release from one of the North's prisons. They were melancholy, hungry men, cut off from their homes by the war that still raged to the South. Cole walked up and gave them the bread, which they accepted with thankful smiles.

As Cole prowled southeast down Pennsylvania Avenue, he began to scrutinize his surroundings with the practiced eye of a sniper. Trees grew at intervals along the avenue, mostly oaks, but none was especially large and their bare branches would not conceal a sharpshooter, not even at night, when the gas lamps would give the air a hazy glow.

He paid special attention to the buildings he passed. There was a mix of storefronts, most with second, third, and fourth floors above where the owners lived. He had noticed "rooms" signs in many of the houses he passed. Wartime Washington was an ideal city to make money taking in boarders. Most of the buildings were in the federal style, four stories tall, with the windows of the topmost floor tucked under the roof. Other houses had dormer windows to create living or storage space in the attic.

There was a multitude of rooftops and upper windows that would have made a perfect sniper's post, but Cole continued walking. If any of the other pedestrians noticed the lean, well-dressed man gazing at the rooftops, they didn't give him a second glance.

Cole had just two pieces of information about General Ulysses S. Grant's visit to Washington City. The first was that Grant would arrive in the capital in three days, on December 15. The second was that Grant and his entourage would make use of the best accommodations in the city, at the Willard Hotel. Cole arrived at the Willard, which was just two blocks from the White House. He ducked inside the lobby and famous bar, then left just as quickly. The interior of the hotel was too dark and cramped to be of any use.

Cole walked out and stood on the sidewalk in front of the hotel, staring across Pennsylvania Avenue. General Grant would be standing in this very spot in just three days.

On the other side of the avenue rose a row of buildings like a steep bank. Cole's eyes followed the brick and frame buildings to their rooftops and his gaze lingered for a while, judging the distance from some of the upper windows to the spot where he stood in front of the hotel.

A cold smile appeared on his face.

Cole crossed the street. He had noticed one particular group of houses across Pennsylvania Avenue located down the street in the direction of the unfinished Capitol. The houses were at the outer edge of his range for a moving shot, about three hundred yards, but they caught his eye because of the rooftops. They were all more or less four stories tall, and the smaller windows of the top floors were shadowed by the overhang of the roof. It would be hard to spot someone in one of them from in front of the hotel.

He noticed a "room for let" sign in the window of one of these houses, but walked on.

He continued down the avenue until he came to the next cross street, which was Thirteenth Street. He turned right and found the alley that ran behind the houses on the main avenue. Several homes had additions on the back. One in particular was large enough for a man to jump from the rooftop to the lower roof of the addition. A man could jump yet again to the roof of a tall outbuilding in the yard of the house next door, and from there to the ground. The effect was akin to descending a set of giant, jumbled steps, so that in the space of two or three minutes a man could escape across the rooftops and be in the alley. From there it would be easy enough to disappear into the city's streets.

A gunshot would echo in the man-made canyon formed by the buildings on both sides of Pennsylvania Avenue, making it difficult to tell where the shot had come from, and by the time soldiers went door to door, questioning residents, the sharpshooter would be headed for the Maryland countryside.

He returned to Pennsylvania Avenue to inquire at the house with the placard advertising a room. A kindly woman opened the door. She was about sixty years old, Cole guessed, with gray hair and a worn shawl clutched about her shoulders with a pudgy hand.

Cole whipped off his hat. "I come about the room, ma'am."

"Oh." The woman quickly looked him up and down, took in the polished boots and gray suit that showed beneath his greatcoat. He was dressed well enough to bring a smile to the woman's face. "Do come in," she said. "I'm Mrs. Smith."

"Barnabus Scoville," he lied smoothly.

Cole stepped into the foyer of the townhouse. It was clean and neat, although not nearly as fancy as Anne's home. The house smelled of baking bread.

She gave him a thorough tour and told him all about herself, that she was a widow and had two other boarders in the house. Cole barely noticed the heavy furnishings, the mirror in the gilt frame over the fireplace where a coal stove radiated heat into the parlor. It was what most people would have called a respectable household.

"Shall I show you the room?" she finally asked.

"Yes, ma'am."

They climbed the stairs, the widow chattering the whole time. Just as Cole had hoped, the room was on the fourth floor. It would be a hard room to rent in the winter, so far from the fires and stoves on the first floor. He understood now why the woman had spent so much time showing him the rest of the house.

She opened the door, urged him inside with her stout arms. Cole's boots made the bare floorboards creak. It was a stark space, painted white. Cole walked over to a small window and looked out.

"The view is interesting," the widow said, going to one of the windows overlooking the street. Below lay Lafayette Park, where a few hens scratched in the dirt. Busy Pennsylvania Avenue was just beyond. The house was in a district known locally as Murder Bay. "All the important people stay at the Willard Hotel over there, they say. Many other gentlemen of the city can be found imbibing there. I must say I don't approve of that. You're not a drinker, are you, Mr. Scoville?"

"No ma'am, I don't hold much with drinking."

They agreed on a price, and Cole paid her in advance, counting greenbacks into her hand.

"Thank you so much, Mr. Scoville." The poor widow sounded grateful for the money. "I'm sure you'll like it. There's always a bustle outside, although it's nice and quiet here. Why, I've seen General McClellan from my window, and even had a glimpse of that General Grant last spring."

Cole's eyes focused on the window that overlooked the Willard Hotel. Mrs. Smith found something in those eyes unsettling. They weren't warm eyes at all, not soft and brown like her late husband's had been.

Cole was still looking out the window. "I like the view, ma'am. I like it just fine."

A skinny little man darted up the street and dodged around a coal cart, startling the horse and forcing the driver to yank at the reins to keep the beast from veering onto the sidewalk and trampling someone.

"Look where you're going, you dang fool!" the driver shouted, then cursed mightily.

Sudler Dill barely heard the driver, who was muttering now into his beard and staring at the disappearing figure of the man who hurried down the street. The driver was reminded of a weasel's quick movements as the little man scurried through the morning traffic, and he thought of a final epithet.

"You dang fool *varmint!*" the driver called after him, but Dill was already gone.

Dill was hurrying on his way to the house on H Street. He was sure the news he carried was important. In fact, he had begged off work at the quartermaster's office the rest of the morning, claiming illness, so that he could get the information to Miss Anne Clark as soon as possible.

Dill enjoyed being a spy. It was the one exciting part of his life and was what had kept him going all through the war as he worked ten hours a day, six days a week, as a clerk in the army's quartermaster depot. Most of the time it was drudgery, a mere balancing of ledgers and shuffling of papers, but now and then some papers crossed his desk which caught his attention. Sometimes it seemed downright foolish to Dill that the Union would be so loose with such information, but then, they probably didn't suspect their hardest working clerk was actually a spy for the Confederacy.

Dill's heart was pounding in his chest much harder than even his brisk walk called for. He wasn't sure how much of his excitement was over the figures he had seen that morning and how much was over the chance to talk with Miss Clark, whom he considered one of the true beauties of the city. He adjusted his hat to a more rakish angle. It wasn't often that Sudler Dill was invited into the parlor of a lady such as Miss Clark. Smiling to himself as he dodged around a portly charwoman carrying a squawking chicken by the feet, he decided such meetings were simply a dividend of serving the Cause.

When Anne woke she was relieved to see that Cole had already gone. Although she was eager to learn what he was doing in the city, she knew that prying this information out of him wouldn't be easy. But there was time, and Anne allowed herself a cold smile as she thought about the ways she knew to get a man to talk. She would try them on Cole, every trick she knew, until she found out what he was up to.

She left the bed reluctantly, for the covers were warm and the room damp and chilly. Anne dressed quickly, brushed her hair, and pulled it back into a simple bun. She went downstairs with a heavy woolen shawl over her shoulders to fend off the morning's cold.

Hattie heard her on the stairs and brought coffee to the dining room.

"Good morning, Hattie."

"I don't know how good it is, Miss Anne, but at least that Mr. Cole is out of the house."

"Why, Hattie, that's not very charitable." Anne pretended to be surprised, although she knew that Hattie was always suspicious of the strangers who passed through the house. Hattie was fiercely loyal, but she had expressed concerns to Anne before that her mistress's activities and her association with unsavory people were going to bring doom on them all. "Mr. Cole is our guest."

"Well, I don't like him, Miss Anne. He's a bad man." She had finished unloading the tray of breakfast food and stood now in front of Anne, twisting up her face as if she had something else to say.

"What is it, Hattie?"

She hesitated. "Oh, it ain't nothin'. Never you mind."

Losing her patience, Anne snapped out, "There's some washing to be done when you're finished standing about."

"Yes, ma'am." At that, Hattie bowed out of the doorway.

Anne sipped her coffee, buttered a slice of bread. She appeared calm enough as she sat at the table, but her mind was reeling. She had never been so busy, and the next few days promised to be even more frantic with General Grant's arrival. She was expecting William McDonnell, a colonel on General Halleck's staff, for his usual mid-morning visit on Tuesdays. Anne hoped he could add something to this bit of news about Grant planning to take over the Tennessee campaign personally, and as she drank her coffee, she cast about for the best way to ask so that he wouldn't suspect anything. He was a nervous fellow who felt guilty about his visits to the house on H Street, so if she pointed the conversation in the right direction, the colonel would most likely say whatever came into his head. If what he told her was worthwhile, she would pass it along to Mr. Conrad.

When Brendan Mulholland arrived in Washington on the fifteenth, he would probably be her best source of information about Grant's plans. She also looked forward to Mulholland's visit because spending time in the major's company was always a pleasure. He had known her before the war and still naively believed she was a lonely single woman who was fast becoming a spinster. He had no idea she was a spy, much less what means she used to obtain her information.

Anne had just begun buttering her second piece of bread when Hattie reappeared.

"That funny little man is here to see you, Miss Anne."

"Who? Mr. Dill? Why, show him in, Hattie, show him in."

Sudler Dill was still trying to catch his breath as he followed Hattie into the dining room. He carried his hat in his hand and his ill-fitting blue uniform looked rumpled. He forced a smile, cleared his throat, wondered where his voice had gone.

"Would you care for some breakfast, Mr. Dill?" Anne asked, rising from her chair. Dill was one of her best informants: he always had reliable facts and more than once something the nervous little clerk had ferreted out found its way to the highest levels in Richmond.

Dill scarcely looked at the food on the table. Gratefully, he noticed his voice had returned from wherever it had temporarily disappeared.

"I have news, Miss Clark," he panted. "Extra ammunition has been ordered up for Grant's men down around Petersburg. *Tons* of it. And fresh horses, too, for the cavalry." He paused, caught his breath, dug a folded sheet of paper from inside his coat and thrust it at her. "I've written it all down here. The specific supplies and whose commands they're intended for. If I didn't know better, I'd say Grant's going to try a wintertime push against Lee."

As a clerk in the quartermaster department, Dill saw firsthand the reports on supplies going to various points in the Union's far-flung military operation. His information this morning excited Anne because it supported everything that old goat McDonnell had told her. A wintertime attack! These Yankees thought they were so damn sly.

"Won't you sit down, Mr. Dill?" she asked, moving closer.

"I can't stay long," he said. He never did. "If I were to be found out—"

"You would be hanged." She went closer to the small, hard-breathing man. "You are a brave man, Mr. Dill."

"It's nothing," he said. He couldn't take his eyes off Anne. She was suddenly before him, her skirts touching him. Dill knew he should move away, but he couldn't. As he stared into her witch-green eyes he felt frozen in place.

"Very brave," she said. She reached down and smoothed his rumpled hair with her fingers. Dill trembled at her touch like a shy dog. He forgot to breathe. Her hand drifted down, touched his face.

Dill jumped back as if he had been shot. Then, to hide his embarrassment, he cleared his throat.

"I must be going, Miss Clark."

Anne smiled sweetly at him.

"You'll come see me again, my brave Mr. Dill?"

"Yes, I shall. The very next time I learn something useful."

"Thank you, sir. You serve the Cause—and me—very well."

Dill reddened, mumbled something about having to get back to the quartermaster department, and backed out of the room with a hasty good-bye. Hattie showed him out.

Anne sighed, sat, looked at the paper Dill had given her. She knew he had taken a huge risk by copying these figure for shipments of weapons, munitions, and horses. She couldn't make much sense of it, but maybe Mr. Conrad could.

"Hattie?"

The servant appeared in the doorway. "That little Mr. Dill can't get enough of you."

Anne smiled. "He's a good man. He's brought me something important I need you to take to Mr. Conrad. Go get your basket."

Hattie reappeared shortly with a small wicker basket filled with eggs. Anne took out the eggs one by one, setting them on the table, then folded the paper Sudler Dill had given her as small as she could. She put this in the bottom of the basket and replaced the eggs. No one would suspect that Hattie was doing anything more than carrying a basket of eggs, Anne thought. It was one way she often sent messages to Mr. Conrad and other friends of the Confederacy.

"You want me to go right now, Miss Anne?"

"Do you think I want you to stand there dawdling, girl? Now go!"

Hattie got her coat and tied on her bonnet, and then she was down the steps and bound for Thomas Conrad's home at the old Van Ness mansion. Anne knew that if Hattie was caught, she could lose everything. The house. Her freedom. She could look forward to a cell in the Old Capitol Prison. She decided it was all a price she would gladly pay for the Cause.

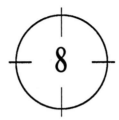

8

On December 14, Cole found a stable not far from the house where he had rented a room.

The stable owner was a stumpy, bow-legged man who looked at Cole sideways as he turned to spit a stream of tobacco juice on the straw that littered the dirt floor.

"You want a horse Thursday? Hell, mister, that's short notice, what with the soldiers and politicians snatching up every decent animal. You want a horse that quick, why, it'll cost you."

They passed several stalls with horses but stopped at the last two stalls in the long building. Both of these horses had rheumy eyes and patchy coats, and Cole doubted the animals would have made it out of Washington at a fast trot, much less a gallop.

"What do you think?" the man asked.

"They ain't fit to feed wolves. I think you'd best find a decent horse for me to hire. Like that one," Cole said, turning and pointing back at a gelding they had passed. "How much?"

"That one ain't for hire," the proprietor said. He emphasized his point by releasing a brown stream from the corner of his mouth, the tobacco juice splattering in the dirt.

"I said, how much?" Cole fixed his flat gray eyes on the man, who looked away.

The eyes disturbed the horse trader. They were utterly clear, like pools of rainwater, and he couldn't read a thing in them or in the man's stony face. He quickly struck a deal for the horse.

"I'll come for my horse early Thursday morning," Cole said. "Before dawn. See that he's fed, watered, and saddled."

"No problem, mister." The coins had disappeared into a pocket of the man's dirty clothes. He was relieved when the lean stranger left.

Cole spent the rest of the morning moving into the boarding

house. He did not tell Anne Clark, in whose bed he had spent 'the previous night.

Cole made certain Mrs. Smith suspected nothing. It wouldn't do to have a curious widow finding out he planned to do more in the room than sleep, so Cole kept his Sharps rifle hidden under his coat when he brought it into her house, in the same way he had smuggled the weapon into the Yankee capital.

Next came a small gunny sack filled with dirt, which he had taken from some men digging a cellar.

The door of his room had no lock, so there was no way to keep the widow out of the room when he was not there. Cole decided he would kill her if she did snoop.

The room itself made a perfect sniper's nest. Two dormer windows overlooked the street and the hotel entrance. One drawback was that while he could easily see the street below, he was sure he could just as easily be seen.

To avoid this, he placed a small table a few feet back from the window and set the sack atop it. He pulled up the room's other chair and now had himself a steady place from which to shoot. The angle limited his view of the street to the area immediately around the hotel entrance, but at least he wouldn't be seen if someone chanced to look up.

His window would be open, which might be unusual for December. But he counted on the fact that few people looked up as they made their way along the sidewalk or street. There was a tangle of carriages and pedestrians to negotiate on Pennsylvania Avenue and little time for looking to the rooftops, much less a reason to do so.

Cole opened the window, which squeaked up reluctantly, the sash weights thumping inside the wall. Cold air washed in, but he scarcely noticed. It would serve to keep him alert.

There was another window in the back wall which overlooked the alley behind the row of houses. Cole opened it, and then took out the coil of rope he had bought. He tied a heavy stick he'd brought especially for this purpose to one end. Leaning out the window, he threw the stick up and onto the roof. It took him several tries to get the stick beyond the chimney, which was set on the sloping part of the roof, high up near the peak. He fed out slack until the stick was lowered within reach, unfastened it, and tied the free end to the rope with a strong slipknot. He pulled until the rope was anchored securely around the chimney. The coil of rope went overhead onto the lip of the roof, where it would be within easy reach of the open window.

Cole preferred to shoot from the prone position when he was taking a particularly difficult shot, but the height of the window meant he wouldn't be able to lie down. Instead, Cole positioned himself in the chair. The makeshift sandbag held the rifle immobile, leaving him nothing to do but aim.

Cole looked through the telescopic sight and the people below suddenly sprang up larger to his eye. He drew a bead on a group of men chatting in front of the hotel entrance. The portly businessmen were all smoking cigars, and Cole thought one of the gentlemen in particular looked like General Grant. Through the telescope, Cole could see the individual buttons on the man's coat, the smoldering tip of the cigar, even the color of his eyes.

He calculated the distance. Perhaps three hundred yards. If he missed the first time, he might be able to get off another shot.

The Sharps' action was exceedingly simple, which was why it made such a reliable rifle. The trigger guard was also a lever which swung down, lowering the breech block and exposing the chamber. Cole inserted another cartridge, which was made of paper or sometimes linen. He then raised the finger lever, which also raised the breech block. The block sheared off the end of the cartridge, exposing the gun powder. Cole placed a percussion cap on the nipple, thumbed back the hammer, aimed, and fired. The entire reloading process took only seconds, and it could easily be done while keeping his head down or maintaining his balance in a tree.

On the street below, shadows were gathering as the afternoon stretched toward evening. Grant would be here in a few hours, early tomorrow morning, December fifteenth. Cole planned to go out long before dawn and get his horse, which he would tie in the alley behind the house.

He stroked the oiled barrel of the Sharps rifle. Everything was ready.

"You're sure you won't be gettin' poor me put in irons over this?" O'Malley demanded, looking uncertainly from Major Mulholland to the two other officers in Grant's office.

"No, no, it's just a joke," Mulholland insisted. He held out the general's coat. "Go ahead and put it on."

O'Malley slipped it on, admiring the heaviness of the wool dress coat. The general himself was out, and the officers were in the midst of getting ready for the trip to Washington City. They would be leaving on the steamer at dusk.

"Now for the hat."

O'Malley put that on, too, exchanging his forage cap for a wide-brimmed hat like most of the officers wore.

"And don't forget the cigar," said Colonel Joe Bowers, producing a cheroot from an inside pocket of his coat. O'Malley bit off the end and spit it on the rough board floor.

"That's the finishing touch," Mulholland said, moving to light the cigar in O'Malley's mouth.

O'Malley took a couple of puffs. "Sure, that's a fine cigar, it is. Least I'll have somethin' to smoke when I'm in irons."

"Nobody's going to be put in irons," Mulholland snapped, although the Irishman's doubts were becoming contagious. He stepped back to look at his handiwork and began to wonder if, indeed, this was a bad idea. Private Michael O'Malley, late of County Kerry, Ireland, looked so much like General Ulysses S. Grant that simply having him sit at the desk in the commanding general's office was unsettling.

Then O'Malley gave his first order in his rich Irish brogue: "Look lively, men. Jaysus! I'll not have tree officers standin' 'round. Bring me General Lee's head on a pike!"

Mulholland and the others doubled over with laughter. There was no danger of treachery, Mulholland knew, because as soon as O'Malley opened his mouth any hope of impersonating the general would seem ludicrous. The effect, too, of a man with such military bearing speaking in a brogue was so hilarious that Mulholland felt certain they could make a fortune if they put such an act on the stage.

"Look smart, here comes Rawlins," one of the officers warned.

General Grant's chief of staff clomped into the room, took in Mulholland and the other two officers with a quick sweep of his disdainful eye, and saluted Michael O'Malley. Rawlins was a big, blustery man with an ego to match. As Grant's old friend from Galena, Illinois, he had appointed himself as watchdog of the general's conduct, especially when it came to the whiskey bottle.

"General, there are some things I need to discuss with you in regard to the defenses of this outpost," said Rawlins, launching right in. "With winter coming on, I fear the men in the ranks are going to take their duties too lightly."

The man behind the desk listened calmly as General Rawlins reported. He appeared to be enjoying his cigar enormously.

"Mmm," he murmured in reply to Rawlins.

"I have prepared a report which you might like to look over," Rawlins said.

Wordlessly, O'Malley took the papers and began studying them intently.

"What do you think of that last paragraph?" Rawlins asked. "The officers might kick some, don't you think?"

O'Malley, who couldn't read a word, looked to Mulholland for help. Not that Mulholland had any ideas. Behind Rawlins's back, he answered O'Malley with a helpless shrug.

Staring down at the papers, O'Malley said, "I'm just a poor soldier, General, sir. I wouldn't know what to think of yer plan."

Rawlins couldn't have looked more stunned if O'Malley had clubbed him between the eyes. Then he turned red with rage and grabbed O'Malley by the lapels. "You fool! How could you? Damnit, damnit all! It's ten o'clock in the morning and you're drunk! Talking like an Irishman! Is that supposed to be funny?"

Letting go of O'Malley, General Rawlins spun around to face the three officers in the room. "No one is to know of this, do you hear? We'll get him to bed, and no one is to come near the general for the rest of the day. Is that understood?"

Mulholland heard his voice quaver as he started to speak, but he couldn't help it. If General Rawlins was angry now, the major couldn't imagine how he would react when he learned the truth. He looked to Bowers, but the colonel was too busy trying not to laugh to be of any help.

"Sir, that's not General Grant."

Rawlins peered into Mulholland's eyes. "Are you all drunk?" he finally asked.

Mulholland shook his head. "No, sir. Sober as priests, all of us." He winced at the Irish saying that slipped out. He had been around O'Malley too much. "The truth is, sir, that's not General Grant. That's Private O'Malley."

Rawlins went over and stood in front of the desk. "Sam?"

O'Malley leaped to his feet and whipped off his hat as he came to attention. "Me name's O'Malley, General, sir. Private Michael

O'Malley."

Mulholland braced himself, expecting Rawlins to call forth a maelstrom of martial punishment upon their heads. This had been a bad idea. A very bad idea, indeed. But Rawlins only stood a moment staring at O'Malley.

"Yes, I can see the difference now," he said slowly. "The beard is darker, and you're somewhat shorter and heavier. Your nose is different, too. Wider, I would say, than the general's."

"It's only the nose me mother and father give me, sir."

"So it is." Rawlins looked at Mulholland. "Good work, Major. There's no telling when it might be useful to have a double for the general."

"Thank you, sir."

"Now I would suggest you get Private O'Malley out of General Grant's chair before he returns. Where is the general, by the way?"

"He's over talking to General Meade, sir."

"When he returns, tell him I've been looking for him."

"Yes, sir." Mulholland saluted as General Rawlins left.

The major waited until Rawlins was out of hearing. He exhaled, realized he had been holding his breath. "Well, that was a close call." He turned to O'Malley. "You heard the general. Out of that chair and off with that coat. We have a lot to do if we're going to catch that boat to Washington tonight."

"Yes, sir." O'Malley was grinning as he obeyed the order.

O'Malley was thinking it was a stroke of luck that he resembled the great General Grant, although a nagging Irish cynicism was telling him that no good would come of it in the end.

It was time to kill a general.

Grant's carriage rattled down Pennsylvania Avenue, surrounded by a squadron of cavalry. Pedestrians stopped and stared, and at the entrance to Willard's the crowd that had been awaiting Grant began to shout and point.

High overhead, Cole hunkered down behind the rifle, which was nestled securely in the bag of earth he had lugged upstairs and placed on the table. He clicked back the hammer and double-checked to make sure a cap waited on the cone of the rifle. Two paper-wrapped cartridges sat on the table in case he was able to get off more than one shot.

The carriage drew up in front of the Willard. The knot of troopers turned their horses to face the street, the animals' breath making frosty clouds in the wintry air. People were shouting Grant's name, and a flock of small boys had appeared out of nowhere and were scrambling to see the general.

Easy, Cole warned himself. He took a deep breath, let it out. Told himself to take his time. He would have just one chance.

The carriage door opened and Cole had a glimpse of a slouched-over man with a full, brown beard and a head of brown hair beneath a wide-brimmed hat.

General Grant. There was no mistaking the brown beard and telltale cigar.

Cole sighted through the telescope, but could get no clear target as Grant made his way to the sidewalk. There were too many people surrounding him.

Easy, he told himself. *Easy.*

The general stood suddenly in the clear, and Cole made instant calculations, lowering the crosshairs slightly and moving them to the left to allow for windage. He was beginning to squeeze the trigger when a large, beefy businessman stepped in front of Grant, blocking him from view.

Cole's breath hissed out in a curse. One of those damned lobbyists. He was tempted to pull the trigger anyhow and shoot the bastard.

Grant had disappeared from view, completely surrounded now by the crowd, the businessmen's suits swirling together with the blue uniforms of the officers who had spilled out of the hotel to welcome their commanding general.

As Cole watched, the swarm of well-wishers moved en masse through the doors of the hotel, leaving him without so much as another glimpse of the lieutenant general.

A sudden knock at the door made him whirl around, the Colt already in his hand and cocked.

"Mr. Scoville! Mr. Scoville!" Mrs. Smith's excited voice called him. "General Grant is just across the street! Do you see him?"

Cole thought about shooting the damn woman through the door. "I saw him," Cole called out, trying to sound interested. "He's somethin', ain't he, ma'am?"

"Why, yes he is." He sensed the widow hovering on the other side of the door, then her footsteps faded away down the hall.

Cole looked back out the window. The carriage and troopers were already moving off. Grant would be a while at the hotel. Cole decided to check on the horse tethered in the alley, and then he would settle down to wait.

Anne had summoned Hattie to carry a message to Major Brendan Mulholland at the Willard Hotel.

She was not feeling herself this morning. Her encounter yesterday with Colonel Wilcox had been a chore. The fool kept leering at her and hinting once again that she should be his mistress, and his alone. "You'll soon be begging me," he had promised. It had taken all Anne's willpower not to throw the fat swine out on his ear.

To make matters worse, she had no idea where Cole had gone. She hadn't seen him since yesterday morning, and he had spent the night someplace other than the house on H Street. Anne tried not to worry, thinking it was likely Cole had only decided to sample one of the city's numerous whorehouses. As if she wasn't taking care of him!

Mr. Conrad had told her Cole was to steal something important from General Grant. A map. Cole seemed capable enough, but if he were caught, he might bring Yankee punishment down upon her head.

Nothing could shake Anne's resolve, however. She was going to fight the Yankees as best she could. Not for the first time, she wished she were a man so she could pick up a gun and fight them on a battlefield. Instead, her war was being fought in parlors and bedrooms, but it was a war nonetheless, and she was determined to win.

"You all right, Miss Anne?" Hattie was at the door of the parlor, her face stern with concern.

"It's nothing, Hattie," Anne said, doing her best to smile.

"Then why you been standin' there for the last hour wringin' yo' hands?"

"I'll be fine."

"It's about that Lucas Cole, ain't it?" Hattie pressed. Her look of concern had become a scowl. "You ask me, he ain't nothin' but trouble. He's a no account thief. Done stole some of that bread I baked. And dangerous, too. I don't know why you ever let a man like that in this house. He shouldn't get no further than the back door."

Anne, miffed that Hattie was questioning her judgment, bit back a harsh retort. She reminded herself that she was above arguing with the servants. Instead, she asked, "Why do you hate that man so, Hattie?"

Hattie stood silently in the doorway a moment, considering the question. Then, her mouth seemed to screw up tight, which was rare in her outspoken servant.

"Go ahead, Hattie," Anne said. "Speak your mind."

Drawing her thin frame up to its full height, Hattie said, "You know I was a girl down South."

"Yes, Hattie. I know." Anne's father had brought Hattie to Washington many years ago to help his wife with the household. She and Henry had been given their freedom at his death but stayed on; in a way, the Clarks were the only family Hattie had known.

"Down South, when I was a girl, I seen men like Lucas Cole." Hattie pronounced the name with the same venom with which she might say *Lucifer.* "Hard men. They might be the man under the foreman on a plantation, or maybe they *be* the foreman on a small plantation. Ain't no kindness in a man like that. He does what he got's to do. He don't care none who he hurts, so long as he gets done what the master tells him to do. Might be he even likes to hurt folks."

Anne was puzzled. Why was Hattie telling her this? "I don't understand."

"A man like Lucas Cole, he *gets* it done, too. Some general down South, he done told Lucas Cole to come up here and do somethin' bad, and he gonna do it. He don't care who gets hurt. He don't think for himself about what's right or wrong. You see, he's just followin' orders, just like he would back on the plantation, and don't you see how *evil* that can be, Miss Anne? He's goin' to bring that evil down on us. Then where will we be? Out in the alleys with them po' whites and beggars."

"Yes, Hattie," Anne said, suddenly feeling chilled. She moved to a chair and sat down. Anne was amazed. Although Hattie was quick to give her opinion whether Anne asked for it or not, Anne had always believed Hattie's thoughts were mostly concerned with what to cook for supper or the household chores that lay ahead.

There had been bitterness in Hattie's estimation of Cole and his kind. Anne had never suspected Hattie had resented being a slave,

and the sudden revelation in Anne's mind seemed to open a chasm
between them which had not existed before, a gap which went
beyond mistress and servant, to the greater rift between white and
black. The Yankees had put such foolish ideas in Hattie's head, Anne
decided. Maybe it was only to be expected that living in the Yankee's
capital city would poison Hattie's mind.

She held out a folded sheet of paper to Hattie.

"Take this to the Willard Hotel."

"For Major Mulholland," Hattie said, reading the name on the
outside.

Anne herself had taught Hattie her letters. For the first time since
her spying career had begun, Anne wondered how many other names
Hattie had noticed, or if she ever read any of the notes she had
carried. Anne dismissed the thought. It was too late now to grow
suspicious of Hattie.

"Deliver this to the major at the Willard Hotel, Hattie. And hurry
back."

"Yes, ma'am."

Anne thought a moment. "Hattie? Stop in the dressmakers and
get yourself some ribbon for that old hat of yours. It needs some
brightening up. Have them put it on my account."

Hattie smiled. "I'll do that, Miss Anne!"

Anne watched Hattie go, wondering why she had just told her
servant to add to her growing debt, even if it was only for a bit of
ribbon. She suspected it was because the ribbon would ease her own
conscious more than it would brighten Hattie's hat. She was good to
her servants, she told herself. She rewarded loyalty.

Hattie took her time reaching the Willard Hotel. There was always so
much going on in the city, and she liked to see as much of it as she
could. She passed through a street where trades people were selling
winter vegetables like turnips and carrots, and Hattie slowed to look
over the produce. They could do with a few things for the kitchen at
H Street, but Hattie never bought anything unless Anne gave her
permission first, even if it was just a few vegetables.

She noticed some of the white trash soldiers in the alleys giving
her a hard look, so Hattie hurried on her way. These men were not
much better than dogs, she thought. More and more, Hattie worried
she would end up just like them if Miss Anne was caught spying.

Hattie knew well enough what it was Miss Anne was up to. She just hoped this Lucas Cole wouldn't get Miss Anne in trouble. He was up to no good, if Hattie was any judge of things.

It didn't take her long to reach Pennsylvania Avenue, and the Willard Hotel wasn't far away.

She was still thinking of Cole, her small fists clenched at the thought of him stealing her bread, when to her surprise she spotted him coming out of a house on Pennsylvania Avenue. Curious, Hattie watched him walk down a ways and stop to stare across the street like he was thinking about crossing but hadn't made up his mind.

As Hattie passed the house Cole had left, curiosity overcame her. She saw the sign in the window and realized this was a boarding house. Now, what did Cole want with a boarding house? She knew how much Miss Anne would appreciate anything she found out about Cole, and after all, the man hadn't been by the house since the day before yesterday. Maybe he had moved in here.

She looked over her shoulder. Cole was nowhere in sight. Gathering her courage, Hattie knocked at the door.

A middle-aged woman answered and looked with surprise at Hattie. "Yes?"

"Hello, ma'am." Hattie hesitated. What was she going to say? And then she heard the lie roll smoothly off her tongue: "I'm to pick up some mending for Mr. Cole."

The woman looked puzzled. "Mr. Cole? There's no Mr. Cole here, just a Mr. Scoville, a Mr.—"

"Mr. Scoville, ma'am. That's the one." Hattie was taking a wild guess. "I done got the names mixed up."

"He didn't say anything about someone picking up his mending."

"Mr. Scoville said it be right on top of his bed, in a linen bag."

"I see." The woman shrugged. "Well, let's go up and look."

Hattie followed her up the stairs. "I reckon Mr. Scoville ain't been here long."

"He just moved in," the woman agreed. "He seems to be a nice man. I won't have any ruffians in my house, that I won't."

The room on the fourth floor was sparsely furnished, but Hattie saw one of Miss Anne's mugs on the table beside the bed and knew instantly it was Cole's room. Just went to prove the man was a thief.

There was a table set up in the middle of the room with a bag of dirt on it. A chair was in front of the table. The window directly in front of the table was open. Hattie noticed the window framed a view of the front of the Willard Hotel.

"My, it's cold in here!" The woman shut the window.

It sure was a funny way to set up a room, Hattie thought. What was that bag of dirt doing up here? Then Hattie noticed the tin of percussion caps on the table, just like the ones Miss Anne had for her pistol. There was also a depression in the middle of the bag, like some long object had been resting there. She looked out the window again at the gentlemen coming in and out of the hotel, and a thought came to her.

"It is peculiar," the landlady said, looking at the table.

"I don't see no mending," Hattie said.

"No," the woman said. She, too, was looking around the room, taking it all in, and Hattie realized the woman had been happy for an excuse to have a look at the room.

Hattie had seen all she needed to. "I'll come back later, ma'am," she said, and started out the door. The woman followed, chattering away, but Hattie barely heard a word.

Once outside, she hurried across the street to the Willard Hotel to deliver her message. Major Mulholland was upstairs with the general, so she left Anne's message with a porter.

Her feet quickly carried her home. Hattie went directly to the pantry and moved several large tins and jars on one of the shelves.

Lucas Cole's rifle was gone.

He had hidden it there—or so he thought, for nothing happened in Hattie's kitchen that escaped her—and must have had it now up in that room on Pennsylvania Avenue. Hattie was sure he wouldn't be using it to shoot squirrels.

Hattie stood for a moment in the kitchen, looking around at all she had. Shelves full of food, a good cook stove, a warm bed on the third floor. When Cole was caught it would all be taken away, Miss Anne would be in prison, and she and Henry would be out on the street.

Cole must be stopped.

"I know just how to do it," she announced to the empty room.

Hattie slipped into the parlor, where Miss Anne kept some writing paper in a desk. Hattie took a sheet along with a pencil and went back to the kitchen, where she sat down at the table and wrote a brief note. Miss Anne had taught her to read and write, and Hattie's handwriting was good:

> A man with a rifle will shoot General Grant in front of the Willard Hotel.
>
> —Miss Anne Clark

It didn't occur to Hattie to write any more details. She folded the paper over and addressed it to Colonel Wilcox, who knew Anne well enough from his visits to the house. He worked at the White House protecting Mr. Lincoln, so Hattie reasoned he would probably know something about protecting General Grant, too. Anne's friend Major Mulholland was with Grant, it was true, but he seemed like the type who would come running to Anne first to ask what she meant. She didn't want him going and telling Anne all about the note. It wouldn't take her long to figure out who had written it.

Hattie put her hat and wrap back on and hurried out again, bound for the White House.

When he returned to his room, Cole felt an immediate sense of alarm. The window had been closed, the chair moved. Quickly, he felt under the mattress. The rifle was just where he had hidden it.

He heard footsteps in the hall outside and turned to find Mrs. Smith looking in nervously.

"What were you doing in here?" he asked, his voice dangerously calm.

Mrs. Smith began to stammer. "This servant girl came to pick up your mending, but since you weren't here I let her in. I shut that window to keep out the wind. It's so cold up here!"

"You let someone in here?" Cole took a step toward her, and the old floorboards creaked. "What mending? Ain't nobody supposed to see what's up here."

"All I did was shut the window." Mrs. Smith's voice was pleading now, horrified, as Cole came closer, looking about as dangerous as a man could. She couldn't take her eyes off Cole's, which were colorless and cold as river ice.

Mrs. Smith started to retreat down the hall at something between a walk and a run but Cole caught her before she had gone more than a few steps. She tried to cry out, but he covered her mouth with the palm of one hand. Not that anyone else was home to hear her.

She struggled, but Cole's sinewy arms kept her pinned securely. She was old and weak, helpless; she had no business looking through his room, getting into things she shouldn't have. Goddamn the old bitch for forcing him to kill her, but she could make a lot of trouble for him.

Cole wedged her frail neck under his arm, then put one hand on the back of her head and kept the other over her mouth and chin. He twisted quickly and pulled back at the same time, and there was an audible snap as her neck broke. Her lifeless body slumped in Cole's arms. He dragged her back into his room and shoved the body under his bed, where it was hidden by the blanket that draped over the mattress and nearly touched the floor. It would do well enough as a hiding place, he thought, because by the time anyone missed her he would either be dead or high-tailing it through the Maryland countryside.

Cole sat down behind the rifle. He wasn't even breathing hard.

Come on out, General Grant, he was thinking. *I'll shoot you yet, you Yankee bastard.*

9

"You look rather dashing, Major Mulholland," said Anne, who, in spite of her disdain for Yankees, had to admit her old friend did look handsome in his officer's uniform. It was just too bad it wasn't a gray one.

Mulholland smiled and bowed slightly. "Well, you look positively enchanting, Miss Anne."

She hadn't seen Brendan in almost a year, although they had exchanged letters frequently. Seeing him here, in her parlor, made Anne wistful. He was handsome enough, wealthy, and the two of them had always gotten along well. If it hadn't been for the war . . . well, Anne didn't want to dwell on such things anymore. Men were just men, to be used accordingly. She and the major were enemies, although she was the only one who knew it.

"How have you been, Brendan?" Anne asked. As old friends, there was no point in formality. "You look well. I suppose the food must be all right at General Grant's headquarters."

Mulholland laughed. "Grant could eat sawdust and not notice. The food is pretty awful, mostly salt pork and beans and other stuff I used to turn up my nose at. But a soldier can't be too particular about what he eats."

"Considering General Grant's reputation, I would have thought there would be some awfully good parties."

The comment brought a frown from Mulholland. "He's not a drunk, if that's what you're getting at, Anne. That's just a lot of drivel in the newspapers."

"I'm glad to hear that," Anne said, not wanting to put Mulholland in a bad mood. She was hoping to learn about more than Grant's drinking habits. "General Grant has certainly done the Union proud. It's about time we had a general who could fight."

"You should see him!" Mulholland grew enthusiastic. "He's a

tiger! A regular Napoleon!"

"It must be an honor to serve on his staff," Anne heard herself lie. "That's a very important position, Major."

"Oh, it's nothing," Mulholland said, but Anne could see she had succeeded in puffing him up. Poor Brendan, she thought. He's going to melt in my hands like butter and tell me everything I want to know.

"Your grandmother seems well," Anne said. She had made a trip to see old Mrs. Mulholland in anticipation of his visit. "I saw her last week. All she did was talk about you, Brendan. She's very proud."

"She wrote me that she enjoyed your visit," Mulholland said. "It was very kind of you. She's getting on in years and appreciates the company. I saw her this afternoon, as a matter of fact." He laughed. "I've never had so much tea and cake in my life! She must have had her cook baking all week."

"You're a good grandson to her, Brendan. You're all she has in the world, really. Your parents are so far away in Chicago."

"If she ever needs anything, please let me know immediately down at City Point."

"Oh, I'd be happy to."

Her face in the gas-lit room was enchanting, and her eyes sparkled romantically as she said, "I'm so glad you're in Washington, Brendan. I hate to think of you going back to Virginia. So many of the men I knew before the war are . . . gone. At least I won't have to worry about you until springtime, when the fighting starts again. You soldiers like to keep quiet through the winter."

Mulholland took the bait. "I'm not sure how quiet we'll be this winter," he said. "There's talk of a campaign before springtime, if the weather holds out. When it's cold like this we can move on the roads because there isn't any mud. We fight the mud more than we do the Confederates!"

A dozen questions popped into Anne's mind at once. Where will the Union attack the Rebel lines? Which units? When will the attack come? Who will lead it? *Slowly,* she warned herself. *Don't seem anxious.*

"I hope you're not going to lead the attack on Petersburg yourself?"

"No! We'll leave that up to General McLaughlen or another of the brigadiers. I'll be back at City Point with General Grant, keeping warm by the stove." He sighed. "Not a very brave job, I'm afraid."

She patted his leg, leaving her hand there a moment longer than it needed to be. "You've been in battles before, Brendan, I know that. You were—are—brave."

He laughed. "Thank you, Anne. But not everyone shares your opinion of staff officers."

Mulholland had a glass of brandy, and Anne had a very small drink in her hand. Women were not supposed to take strong spirits, but Mulholland had agreed it was just the thing to warm her up on this chilly evening.

Anne splashed another inch of brandy into his glass and joined him on the sofa. The fire crackled at the hearth. The parlor door was closed against the drafty hall and Anne had given Hattie strict orders not to disturb them.

Mulholland, clearly nervous in this romantic atmosphere, drained his glass of brandy in a few quick swallows. Anne poured him another drink.

"I probably shouldn't tell you this, Brendan, but I think of you often. I remember all the good times we had before the war . . ."

"There will be good times again," he said.

"I'm not so sure." Anne sighed. When she looked up again at Mulholland, the firelight on her face made Anne look even more beautiful. "Kiss me, Brendan."

He leaned toward her for what seemed to Anne an eternity. *Hurry up and get it over with,* she thought impatiently. Finally his lips touched hers, tentatively at first, and then his kisses became searching, passionate. Anne responded and let herself be pulled deeper into his arms.

That's more like it, Anne thought.

They broke apart, sucked for breath. "Oh, Brendan. You'll have to come back and visit me. I suppose I'll have to wait until after the attack at Petersburg. Oh, I don't know if I can wait that long!"

He reached for her hands and took them in his own. "Grant will make his push at the end of January, so long as the ground stays frozen. I'll come back to you, Anne, as soon as we have the Rebels whipped."

They kissed again, and this time Mulholland, emboldened by the brandy, groped at her breasts. Anne let him feel what he wanted for a moment, then broke off the embrace.

"Oh, that's enough, Brendan." Anne tried to act flustered and moved back to her own chair by the fire. There were strict rules of society Anne would not break by bringing him upstairs. She wanted

Mulholland to think of her as a potential wife, not a mistress. For a straight-lace like the major, it would make all the difference. "We must remember ourselves. Maybe if you'll be back in January . . ."

"No later than the last week of the month," he said.

"I'll write to you," she said. "You'll have a letter every day."

"Well," he said. He reached for the decanter of brandy, hesitated, then stood. "I should be getting back to the general. There's a reception for him tonight at the White House."

Anne rose as well. "I've had a wonderful evening," she said.

The major straightened his uniform, smiled, then walked to the door. Before going out, he turned. "Anne, there are some things I've said tonight—"

"Don't you mean some things you've done tonight?"

He grinned sheepishly. "No, no. What I've said about an attack down at Petersburg. Keep that to yourself, if you would. I probably said too much about it. The brandy—"

"There's only one thing I'll remember about tonight," Anne said. "You'll write me, won't you, Brendan darling?"

"Of course I will." He smiled. "Good night, Miss Anne."

"Good night, Major Mulholland."

He went out. Anne watched him from a window, then went upstairs to encipher a message to Mr. Conrad.

Cole watched with frustration as just before dark General Grant made his way up Pennsylvania Avenue screened from view inside his carriage. There had been no chance to get off a shot as he emerged from the Willard, for the general seemed to move not as one man, but at the center of a mob of well-wishers eager to shake his hand.

As he watched the carriage disappear down the street, Cole eased the hammer down on his Sharps rifle. Nothing to do now but wait. He was beginning to wonder if he would ever get a clear shot at the general. Short of halting the carriage in the street or ambushing General Grant in the lobby at Willard's, Cole didn't know how he was going to get any closer. He considered the idea of rushing the general's entourage as Grant exited the carriage that night upon his return to the hotel, then just as quickly dismissed the thought, knowing Grant's bodyguards would cut him down before he even had a chance to get so much as a single shot off from his Colt pistol.

The shadows in the unheated room grew long as night came on.

Cold air, damp and raw off the Potomac River, washed in through the open window but Cole scarcely noticed. His hands cramped around the Sharps but he did not move, letting his fingers stiffen in the curve of the stock. It might prove to be a long, cold winter night but Cole would be vigilant. He kept his eyes on Pennsylvania Avenue, keeping watch for the general, holding still as death itself.

General Grant's entourage swung through the White House gate, joining the throng of carriages already crowding the drive.

"Here we go," Colonel Bowers said, fiddling with his collar. "Do I look all right?"

Mulholland took in the polished boots, the immaculate uniform, the gleaming hilt of the colonel's sword. "You look about as good as you ever will," he said, cracking a grin. "Just don't trip over that damn sword when you're getting out of the carriage."

They piled out of the carriages rather ingloriously, Mulholland thought, considering they were all staff officers. They stood around for a moment not knowing what to do, looking husky and somber in the greatcoats they wore against the cold. It was Grant who nimbly climbed the White House steps. His officers followed in his wake.

To Mulholland's surprise, the executive mansion was full of people. It appeared that everyone of any importance had gathered in the White House, and this crowd of dignitaries became an excited mob at the sight of Grant, flowing toward him with hands extended and cheers.

A small, animated man with unkempt white hair and a huge nose had taken Grant by the elbow and was steering him through the sea of well-wishers. The fellow was shooing people out of his way as if they were chickens, guiding Grant across the room.

"That's the secretary of state," Bowers said, leaning close to Mulholland. "James Seward."

"Not much to look at, is he?"

"Maybe not. But they say he's a bad one to cross. He's pure poison."

After a few minutes spent shaking hands, Grant and President Lincoln cloistered themselves in a separate room. They were together for an hour. When they emerged, it was obvious the meeting with Lincoln must have drained his energy, because Grant looked stoop-shouldered and tired as he continued to greet well-wishers, his smile growing thinner with each handshake.

Mulholland knew at once what he had to do. He swept up to Grant from one side just as Bowers arrived at the other, and together the two officers guided General Grant out of the room.

"I've been rescued," said Grant, once they were outside the White House. "I don't know which is more dangerous, a battlefield or a public reception."

With that, Grant climbed wearily into the first carriage and started off, with Mulholland and Bowers rumbling along behind in a second carriage.

Colonel Jonathan Wilcox scooped up the pile of reports from the captain's desk and quickly read through them, as was his habit. It seemed there was never a shortage of new and original ways assassins were plotting to kill the president. While many of these threats were purely amusing, Wilcox took them all seriously—not that there were many things in life he took lightly. His vigilance had helped keep the president safe so far. The plots that sounded chillingly plausible he passed along to Lafayette Baker and Allan Pinkerton, who headed the president's Secret Service.

Wilcox had just come from the reception, which had been an especially tiring one because of all the commotion over General Grant. The small, gruff general's stock remained high but Wilcox had observed that Lincoln gave no sign of seeing Grant as a potential political threat. If anything, the two men in some strange way seemed to thrive on each other's company. One was the master of Washington, the other the master of the massive Union army. Each relied upon the other in a way that perhaps only Grant and Lincoln could understand.

Wilcox was busy thinking about this relationship between Grant and Lincoln when his eyes came to rest on a note addressed to him. Strange, he thought, because it didn't look like an official communication. Puzzled, he opened it. He was even more surprised when he saw who had sent the note, and what it said.

All the fatigue of the evening vanished from Wilcox's hulking figure in an instant.

"My God," he said, then proceeded to scribble a hasty note to Major Brendan Mulholland, who he knew was ostensibly in charge of Grant's safety, although there hadn't been much for the young officer to do here in Washington. Wilcox folded the note in half using beefy fingers and roared out, "Fletcher!"

A sleepy-eyed orderly appeared.

"Wake up, man! Has General Grant already gone?"

"Yes, sir, just a few minutes ago."

"Damn! Well, get down the street after him. Give this note to Major Mulholland, and if you can't find him give it to General Grant himself."

"Should I take a horse, sir?"

Wilcox was in no mood for slow-witted orderlies. "There's no time for that, man! Unless you have a flying carpet handy, I suggest you run the two blocks to the Willard Hotel, which is where General Grant is staying. Run like the wind, Corporal!"

"Yes, sir." With that, the orderly was gone in a rush. Wilcox listened to the running footsteps in the hall and hoped that the man's legs would carry him to General Grant as fast as possible. A man with a rifle across the street from the Willard? How did Anne Clark know anything about that? Well, he would find that out later. If what Anne's note said was true, there was no time to waste. He shrugged his wide shoulders into his greatcoat and started off after the orderly at a brisk walk.

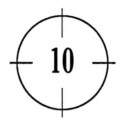

10

Horses coming.

The noise of a jangling harness broke the stillness of the night, and at this late hour Cole knew it could only be General Grant returning from the White House.

He settled the rifle into its familiar groove in the sack of earth on the table. The maple stock against his face could have been a lover's cheek as he peered through the telescopic sight at the deserted hotel entrance.

It was a good night for shooting. The sharp wind which had sliced off the Potomac all day had died to a faint breeze that barely rattled the withered leaves clinging to the pin oaks on the avenue below.

He took a deep breath, let it out, and thumbed back the hammer on the Sharps.

Mulholland tried to get comfortable on the carriage seat. He was glad it was only a short ride from the White House to the hotel. General Grant had taken the grander carriage, which was already far ahead of them on the way back to the Willard.

He was exhausted. It had been a long and tiring day. His head felt heavy, and his eyes burned with fatigue. All he wanted was a drink of whiskey and his bed.

"I finally saw the inside of the White House," he said out loud, still feeling somewhat awed.

The slumping figure of Joe Bowers on the seat across from him shifted. "Not all that impressive, is it?"

"If I didn't know better, Bowers, I'd swear you were a McClellan Democrat in disguise."

"Say that again and I'll boot you out of this carriage. I've no use for Little Mac."

"If Lincoln hadn't won the election last month, that's who would have been in the White House."

"One of these days, it might just be our General Grant in the mansion," Bowers said.

Mulholland was too tired to think about that possibility. He huddled into a corner of the carriage in an attempt to stay warm. He planned to be asleep in a few minutes, as soon as General Grant was back in his room.

Cole's body fell into the rhythm of the sniper. During years of hunting he had learned how to will his breath to stop, his heart to quiet, his very nerves to numb. Nothing must send the slightest tremor at the last instant when the rifle fired.

His heart slowed to a barely perceptible murmur. He caught a breath, held it, and did not let go of it lest it cause some faint movement along the length of the rifle. Cole did not notice the chill breeze tugging at the tendrils of his hair beneath his hat, nor did he notice how the cold had crept through the room with nightfall and stiffened all his extremities, so that his hands and fingers were little more than unfeeling clamps holding the rifle in place.

Cole let the world cease to exist, let himself float on a river of nothingness, aware only of that dim circle captured by the telescopic sight, and the tip of his trigger finger, ever ready to take up the last fraction of tension on the trigger.

Through the sight he watched the trim figure of General Grant swing down from the carriage. He was close to the shot, very close. But his line of fire remained blocked by the cavalry soldiers ringing Grant. His crosshairs danced over the general's heart. Cole's finger tightened on the trigger, but the shot did not yet feel right, did not fit together as it should like a hand into a glove.

Wait, he warned himself. *It will come.*

Mulholland was jolted from his thoughts by the sound of a soldier's hobnailed boots running beside the carriage. He could just see the blue kepi of a soldier who appeared to be chasing them.

"They must go through an awful lot of soldiers up here in Washington," Bowers remarked. "You would think they'd give these poor boys horses so they wouldn't run themselves to death."

"Message for Major Mulholland!" the runner managed to gasp.

Mulholland, instantly suspicious, put his hand to the revolver at his belt.

"Better hear what he has to say before you shoot him," Bowers advised.

Mulholland threw open the door. "Stop the carriage!" he shouted up to the driver. They lurched to a stop on the nearly deserted avenue. Unlike General Grant's carriage, they had no cavalry escort, although a couple of horsemen, seeing that they had stopped, peeled themselves away from the general's squadron and came riding toward them.

"Sir, Colonel Wilcox's compliments." Breathless as the man was, Mulholland thought he must have sprinted all the way from the White House. He thrust a piece of paper at Mulholland. "It's urgent."

"Really?" Bowers remarked from within the carriage. "Hell, boy, I thought you were running for exercise."

Mulholland struggled to read the hastily scrawled message using the light from the carriage lantern:

> Sharpshooter in window across from hotel. He will shoot Grant. Use all precautions.
> —Col. J. Wilcox

Mulholland froze.

"What's it say?" Bowers demanded.

"There's an assassin," Mulholland said. He banged on the carriage door to get the driver's attention. "Move, man, move! Catch up to General Grant's carriage."

But Mulholland could see at once that they would never reach Grant's carriage before it arrived in front of the hotel. He leaped from the carriage, stumbled, then ran as fast as he could toward the general's entourage, which was no more than one hundred feet ahead.

One of the horsemen attempted to block his path, but Mulholland dodged around him, causing the horse to shy.

"What in hell—"

Ignoring the rider, Mulholland dashed forward. It was not easy running in the rutted street in his dress boots while trying to keep his sword from tripping him, but he still covered the distance faster than the carriage he had left behind.

To his horror, he saw Grant's carriage halt and the general hop nimbly down. Mulholland was up on the sidewalk in the next instant, pounding toward Grant, who had stopped beneath a streetlight, fully exposed, to light one of his cigars.

Several horsemen, sensing that something was amiss, drew their revolvers and swung them toward Mulholland as he sprinted toward the general.

"Don't shoot him!" Bowers shouted as he leaned out the door of the second carriage, which was racing up the avenue, making an awful clattering as it banged across the frozen ruts. "Hold your fire, boys!"

The sights drifted across the general's chest. *Not quite.*

Another step, general, Cole silently urged. *Take another step.*

Grant walked clear of his escort and paused beneath a gas lamp to light a cigar. In that instant, Cole settled the crosshairs on a point in space slightly above and to the left of Grant.

Cole began to think the bullet home, imagined it striking the general slightly off center in the chest, heard the satisfying *whunk* of the bullet hitting flesh. The crosshairs drifted, and Cole's fingertip anticipated them, waiting for them to cross that place again just above and to the right of the general.

In the next instant, Cole fired.

Mulholland dove.

As Lieutenant General Ulysses S. Grant lifted a flaming match toward his cigar, Mulholland plowed into him, sending general and cigar flying.

Out of the corner of his eye, Mulholland saw a stab of flame across the street and heard a minié ball zip past them. Mulholland never heard the crack of the rifle because it was drowned out by the tremendous grunt Grant made as he hit the ground with Mulholland on top of him.

All hell broke loose.

The night was filled with shouts and whinnying horses. Some troopers unsheathed their swords, others waved pistols at the rooftops. A few pointed to where they had seen the flame of the rifle's muzzle.

Mulholland leaped to his feet and grabbed two of the closest soldiers who had dismounted.

"You two, get the general inside," he ordered.

Grant, still shaken from being tackled, had to be helped to his feet by the troopers. Joe Bowers ran up, his pistol drawn. "Was he shot?"

"Knocked the wind out of him," Mulholland panted, breathless himself. "You take care of the general, Colonel. I'm going after the sharpshooter."

Bowers took command of the nervous horsemen, shouting them into control, while Mulholland swung into the saddle of a spare horse. Taking two troopers with him, they galloped pell-mell across the wide avenue and through Lafayette Park.

"He's in that building to the left, sir," one of the troopers shouted. "I seen the muzzle flash." The cavalryman waved a gloved hand, and the three riders wheeled in that direction.

At first, Mulholland was not able to pinpoint which building the sharpshooter had fired from. In the nighttime gloom the shabby boarding houses and storefronts of Murder Bay all looked the same. Mulholland had a passing thought that if whoever had fired from the window was still at his post, he would have a clear shot at his pursuers. He only hoped the rifleman was too busy trying to escape.

The riders reined up short of the buildings as Mulholland tried to determine which one hid the sniper. His eyes strained against the dark faces of the buildings.

"Major, that one there's got an open window on the top floor."

Mulholland spotted it as soon as the trooper pointed. "In we go," he ordered.

They quickly dismounted, dropped their reins, and dashed up the steps of the small townhouse. Without stopping to knock, the burliest of the troopers threw his weight against the door and it burst open. All three men hurried inside to find a white-haired man trembling in the hall, clearly scared out of his wits.

"God in heaven, what's going on? Are the Rebels here?"

"Who's on the top floor?" Mulholland demanded.

"Why, that's Mr. Scoville, one of the other boarders. What's wrong? I thought I heard a gunshot."

"Anyone else up there?"

"No, no," the man said, sounding even more alarmed. "What's going on? It's just Mr. Scoville upstairs. Don't know where Mrs.

Smith is. She's been gone—"

Ignoring the old man, Mulholland nodded toward the stairs and the troopers went bounding up them.

Cole watched them come.

There was no time for a second shot. Grant was already safely inside the hotel, out of sight. Whoever tackled the general had saved his life.

Another instant and the bullet would have bored into Grant's heart. Instead, the shot cut the air just above Grant's head.

Bitterly, Cole levered open the breech and loaded another round.

And now the Yankees were after him. He saw the riders start toward the row of houses where he was hidden and knew he could have dropped two of them, maybe all three, with the Sharps. But there would only be others following them, and he would have revealed his position, making it that much easier for his pursuers to find him.

If Cole felt nothing while he was shooting, he felt even less afterwards. That numbness took a while to shake, and his mind worked in a fog.

Already he heard the Yankees' boots on the front stairs, listened to one of the boarders shout about Mr. Scoville upstairs.

The two troopers ran up ahead of him, and Mulholland followed. They flew up all four flights of steps, their revolvers drawn, expecting at any time to meet the sniper coming down.

"He must have gone out a window," Mulholland said in disbelief when they met no one else in the house. At the top of the stairs, the first trooper edged around the corner into the hall, in case anyone was waiting for them. The three of them were out of breath after running up four flights.

"All clear," the trooper panted, and together they advanced, revolvers at the ready.

There were three doors. Two led to rooms that didn't overlook the street.

"Check those other rooms," Mulholland said.

Mulholland stood guard at the third door as the troopers made a quick search of the other rooms. They were back in a few moments.

"Nobody there, sir."

Mulholland dropped his voice to a whisper. "If he's anywhere, it's in this room. At the count of three we'll rush him." He jerked his chin at the big cavalryman. "You hit that door good now, you hear?"

"Yes, sir."

"One, two, three—"

Cole forced himself to think. He looked around the room, damned himself for not having a better plan. He should have a lock on the door or nailed it shut, but he hadn't counted on the Yankees finding him so quickly.

The window on the back wall was the only way out. The rope was there, ready, but he would have to buy himself some time if he was to escape.

His joints were stiff with cold as he stood. Strange he had not noticed before. Cole had to work his hands a few times to get some feeling back into them.

Beneath his feet, he felt the floorboards shake as the Yankees stormed up the stairs.

Cole did not hurry. He slipped the rifle sling over his shoulder so that the Sharps hung across his back. In the pause before they broke down the door, Cole picked his Colt off the table and swung it toward the doorway.

The darkness exploded.

Mulholland heard the man to his left cry out before he himself went down. His pistol flew from his hand as he hit the floor. The man to his right fired, but was cut down in the next instant. Mulholland lay there, wondering how badly he was hit. He knew a man often didn't feel his wound at first, even though it had enough force to knock him down.

Frantically, his hands searched the floor in front of him for his revolver. He tried to move, but the weight of one of the dead troopers was pressing down on him, pinning him to the spot. He felt helpless, half expecting the assassin to fire again and finish him off.

Mulholland heard a noise, looked up. Framed against the starlight from the winter sky, he saw the sharpshooter slip out the window.

Mulholland managed to pull himself free. He got up, tested his legs, and decided he felt all right, although he wished he had some light so he could see inside the cramped room. He was not wounded, but thought he must have tripped over the chair which had been jammed under the doorknob. In any case, falling had probably saved his life, or he would have been shot down like the other two men.

He found his revolver, which had not been fired, and hurried to the window. There was no porch below, and not so much as a ledge the man could have stepped onto. Although it seemed impossible, the sniper must have taken to the roof.

Mulholland ran to the other window. Across the dark expanse of Pennsylvania Avenue, he could see a knot of soldiers approaching. Most likely, Joe Bowers had sent them. He saw no commotion in the street, as he had expected after the assassination attempt.

The thought that someone had tried to murder General Grant suddenly enraged Mulholland. It was his duty to protect the general, and although the assassination had failed at the last instant, it had come dangerously close to succeeding.

Rage propelled him back to the window where the assassin had gone out, and he tried to ignore that he was forty dizzying feet above the ground. Above and to his right, he heard the sound of feet sliding on slate, and looked up in time to see the soles of the assassin's boots disappear over the ridge of the roof.

Mulholland shoved the Colt into his belt, got one foot out the window, then eased himself out, hind-end first, trying to find a handhold. His right hand found nothing but the slate shingles, but he tried to dig his fingers into the crevices, while with his left hand he took hold of the side of the dormer, spreading his hand and trying to grip the wood siding through sheer friction. His gaze slipped to the alley below, and he was nearly overwhelmed by a sudden, nauseating fit of vertigo. Ignoring it, Mulholland forced himself up the roof, his boots scrambling on the shingles. A slate broke loose and shattered far below.

Cole slipped and started to fall. As soon as he lost his balance, he threw his hands out on either side of him, clawing at the slates. His hands caught, held. He crossed the peak in a four-legged crawl, then jumped down to the roof of the house next door. Below him, he could hear shouts and hoof beats as Yankees spread through the area, searching for him. Up on the cold rooftops, his footing was treacherous and uncertain, but he had no choice but to run. The Yankees had found him too quickly. But if he could only get to the horse in time, he might still be able to get away.

He heard a noise on the roof behind him and knew he must have missed one of the soldiers in the room. Damn! Someone on the rooftop would give him away. Quickly, he stepped out of sight behind a chimney, unshouldered the Sharps, and held the rifle butt like a club in front of him.

Mulholland shoved himself up until he was straddling the ridge of the steep roof. He had a glimpse of the running figure of the sniper on the flat roof of the three-story house below. He would have risked a shot, but the man presented a poor target in the darkness, and Mulholland didn't want to waste his rounds. He might need his ammunition later, if the sniper had another pistol.

It was only a few feet to the surface of the flat roof below, and Mulholland lowered himself until he was hanging his full length off the gable, then dropped to the next roof.

He rolled as he hit to break his fall, then sprang to his feet and started to chase the assassin.

Although it was dark, it was easy running on the flat roofs of the houses on this stretch of the street, and Mulholland forgot his caution as he hurried to narrow the gap between himself and the sharpshooter. He was running full speed when the man stepped out from behind a chimney. In one sickening instant Mulholland saw the rifle butt loom toward him and knew there was nothing he could do.

He caught the blow full in the face and fell backward, stunned.

The sharpshooter walked out of the shadows and stepped on Mulholland's wrist, pinning the hand that held his revolver.

Mulholland knew he was going to die. There was nothing he could do. *My God,* he thought. *Not like this.*

He saw the flash of a knife and closed his eyes.

Cole knelt and put one hand over the Yankee officer's mouth. He let the Yank see the Bowie knife he took from a sheath at his belt, then held it at the soldier's throat. At the touch of cold steel, he felt the man's body grow tense and start to squirm.

"You're like an old rabbit dog, ain't you, Yank? Got my scent in your nose and you won't let go." The point of Cole's knife found the juncture where the underside of the chin joined the throat. "Well, I'm sorry about this, Yank."

The man tried to scream through Cole's steely fingers.

Cole hesitated. He hated to kill a brave man. The old woman had been weak and meddlesome, but here was a soldier doing his duty. If he didn't kill him, the Yankee would follow him for sure and give him away. He pressed the point of the knife against the soft flesh of the officer's throat and felt the man grow limp, saw eyes open and roll back in fear.

Then Cole moved the knife away from the man's throat and instead drove the blade deep into the thick muscle of the Yankee's thigh. He felt the man heave in pain beneath him. His hand sealed in the man's scream.

Cole had spared the man's life. But with the wound in his leg, the Yankee wouldn't be chasing him anymore.

Cole got to his feet and leveled the Colt at the major.

"Make a noise and I'll shoot you, Yank." He backed away and disappeared into the darkness.

The Yankee, writhing in agony, started to shout, remembered the revolver pointed at him, and instead hissed after Cole, "I'll run you into the ground, you Rebel bastard!" Blood was gushing from between his fingers and darkening the slates with a black slick.

As soon as he was out of sight, Cole heard the Yankee shout, "Over here!"

Fast as Cole was on the rooftops, the Yankees were faster. A squadron of cavalry had swarmed into the alley behind the row of houses and snatched up Cole's horse. He crouched on a rooftop behind a chimney and watched.

He had to take a chance or they'd catch him in a few minutes.

The soldiers spread out to search the alley, and Cole jumped down from the low roof. There was a shout, the crack of a carbine, and Cole ducked through a gap between two houses too narrow for a horse.

He started running, and the shouts and hoof beats faded behind him.

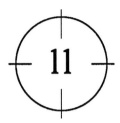

11

"Yankees, Miss Anne!" Hattie screamed, running into the parlor, where Anne was reading a smuggled copy of the Richmond *Whig*. "There's Yankees at the door!"

"Lock the back door," she said to Hattie, surprised at how calm she felt now that the moment she had feared for years had finally arrived. The Yankees must have finally figured out she was a spy. Well, she wouldn't go without a fight.

Anne went to the table in the front hall and took out a loaded pistol. She started toward the front door, vowing to herself that the first soldier across the threshold would be a dead man.

She heard knocking at the door. A pause. More knocking, more insistent this time.

"They're in the back yard!" Hattie called from the kitchen, and came running up the hall. "What are we going to do?"

"Open the door," Anne said.

Hattie instantly collected herself. "They've come for you, haven't they, Miss Anne?"

"Yes," she said, standing in the hall, a few feet back from the door. By now, the Yankees were hammering at the door. "Go ahead and open it."

"Best put that pistol away, Miss Anne," Hattie said. "They'll shoot you, sure."

"Just open the door," Anne quietly ordered.

Hattie did as she was told, then stepped aside. Colonel Wilcox was on the front step and did not appear at all surprised at the sight of Anne Clark leveling a pistol at him through the open door. Behind him, several soldiers raised their rifles, and the hallway of the house echoed with the click of hammers being cocked.

"Hold your fire," Wilcox said sharply to the men behind him. He took a step into the house and whispered harshly to Anne, "Don't be a fool, woman. Give me that pistol. What are you doing?"

"You won't take me off to prison alive," she said. "I may not get all of you, but I will get some of you Yankees."

Wilcox took another step forward. He lowered his voice so that the soldiers couldn't hear. "What on earth are you talking about? We haven't come to take you to prison, Anne. We've come to protect you."

Anne held the pistol steady. "What are you saying, Colonel Wilcox?"

Wilcox appeared puzzled.

"Why, your note, Anne. Your information proved very useful. It saved General Grant's life." He took another step toward Anne and reached out his hand. "We've only come to watch for the assassin, in case he should return here." The smile changed to a leer. "I can only assume he's a *friend* of yours. I didn't suppose I was the only one, you know."

Anne felt as if a cannonball had exploded in her hallway, and she actually reeled. What information had she given the Yankees, for God's sake? Who was the assassin?

And then Anne knew as Cole's expressionless eyes flashed in her mind. Cole wasn't a thief, as Mr. Conrad had said. He was a killer. She felt stupid for not realizing sooner. Wilcox had said Grant had been spared, so she deduced that Cole had tried to kill the general. The enormity of the realization took her breath away.

"You mean he's not . . ." Anne let the question trail off. Cole had survived. God help her if he found out she was the one who had betrayed him, although she wasn't sure yet how she had managed it.

"Dead? Oh, no. The assassin just missed him, thank God. It could have cost us the war."

Before Anne knew what was happening, Wilcox had his hand around the pistol. She let him take it, then turned and walked into the parlor.

"I'm sorry about the gun," she said, her mind already racing, trying to come out on top of whatever had happened tonight. "You startled me. Men pounding on my door so late."

"I understand," Wilcox said. "Women aren't used to this sort of excitement."

The comment was like cold water on her face. Damn these men, they always thought they were so superior! Anne sat in a chair in the parlor and struggled to control herself until she learned more about the situation.

Wilcox brought his men inside the house and began giving orders. He posted guards in the kitchen by the back door as well as the front door. Their orders were to let Cole into the house if he returned, then to take him prisoner. Even in her dazed state, Anne thought the orders were hopelessly optimistic. Cole wasn't going to let anyone take him prisoner, she knew.

Once his men were in place, Colonel Wilcox entered the parlor. Anne saw her chance to learn more about what was happening.

"Do you really think he'll come back here?" Anne asked.

"The assassin? I don't know. I just came here—well, I wasn't certain of the connection. When I got your note, I thought it might be wise to guard your house."

What note? Anne wanted to scream the question at him. "I'm glad you got it in time."

"How did you know someone was planning to assassinate General Grant?"

Anne wished she *did* know. She managed a faint smile. "It's amazing what some men will say, Colonel Wilcox, under the right circumstances."

"I'm sure you would know, Anne." He sighed. "It will probably be hard to get near you now."

For a moment, Anne thought he was implying she would be imprisoned. "Whatever do you mean?" she stammered.

"Why, you'll have more than your share of callers, Anne. Washington is a rewarding city for beautiful women loyal to the Union cause."

Anne wondered if it wasn't too late to get her pistol back, so she could shoot him after all. She wished again that she was a man, so that she could at least die in battle like her beloved Rayford, fighting for the Cause.

The house rang with the sound of Yankee boots on her floorboards, and she could hear the enemy speaking to each other in low, guttural voices that sounded terribly sinister to her ears.

How had this happened? There was so much she didn't know: Cole being an assassin, a note warning Wilcox about him. Who had sent it? In the meantime, she would play the part of loyal Yankee hostess, no matter how much she detested the role.

"I'll have Hattie put on some coffee. Your men may have a long night." Anne got to her feet, smiled at Wilcox. "It's so very kind of you to bring your men here to protect me, Jonathan. That assassin is a beast. When I found out . . . well . . ."

"How did you ever come across him, Anne?"

"As you said, Jonathan, I've met my share of men." She hated him for saying it, too.

Anne went past the soldiers who had crowded nervously into her townhouse. Two were at the back door in the kitchen, the bayonets on their rifles gleaming in the lamplight.

"I'm making coffee for you men and Colonel Wilcox," she announced, and went about putting on some water on the stove to boil. Hattie should be doing this, she thought.

"Much obliged, ma'am," one of the soldiers said.

Just then, her servant entered the kitchen. Her eyes were wide with apprehension as she watched Anne working at the stove. At first, Anne thought Hattie was simply nervous about the soldiers. "Maybe these men could do with a plate of biscuits," Anne suggested, thinking that work would calm her servant.

Hattie was jumpy as a rabbit as she went about mixing the flour, water, and lard on the wooden table. She kept casting sideways glances at Anne.

And then Anne understood. *The note.* Of course! Hattie had written it. It was all Anne could do not to launch herself across the kitchen and attack her servant, and only the presence of the two guards by the door made her stay in control of herself.

Hattie approached the stove to slide the tray of biscuits in. Anne chose that moment to lift the pot of hot coffee off the stove top, and she brushed Hattie's hand with the hot metal pot.

Hattie snatched her hand away with a stifled cry, and the two soldiers spun around in alarm.

"Oh, did I burn you?" Anne's voice was syrupy with concern. "I'm sorry, dear."

Anne's smile was sweet, but her eyes were cruel and sharp as daggers as she met Hattie's frightened stare.

Cole was running for his life.

At first, he didn't know what to do. His horse was gone and there was no escaping the city on foot. He couldn't go back to Anne Clark's house because it was too much of a risk.

Then he thought of the river.

Keeping to the alleys and unlit side streets, he hurried toward the Potomac without encountering another soul. Cole thought of the thugs he had seen lurking in the alleys by day and never let his hand stray far from his revolver. Anyone who blocked his way would be a dead man.

Finally, he reached the wharves. The wind here was sharp and wet, although Cole could see nothing of the mighty Potomac except a great black void which was even darker than the night. The water appeared to absorb all light.

He had no plan beyond knowing that where there was water, there were boats. And a boat was his best way out of the Yankee capital.

The only thing to stop him were the sentries. He could see at least two, blue-coated, their rifles slung over their shoulders.

Crates of cargo were stacked all around the wharf. Cole slipped from one to another as he made his way closer to the river. Above the wind off the river, Cole was close enough to hear the men talking. He couldn't make out the individual words.

Cole glanced toward the blackness of the Potomac. He could see nothing of the water, but he could hear the current rippling around the pilings at the waterfront. Cole had never been around the water much, the wet sound of the current lapping at the shore set his nerves jangling. He tried to recall just how wide the river was at this point. It was well over a mile to the Virginia shore, and it would not be an easy voyage on a dark winter's night.

The thought of pushing off into the pitch-black Potomac wasn't pleasant, but he saw little other choice.

He found a tiny rowboat tied up at the pier. There was a little water in the bottom of the leaky boat, but it would probably make it to the other side. If any Yankee patrols stopped him, he'd just tell them he'd gone fishing for catfish. They'd either shoot him or dump him in the river.

Cole, checking first to make sure no guards were walking the wharf, slipped through the bales of goods and headed for the river. The boat was tied carelessly, and the wooden craft looked piteously small as it rose and fell on the chop at the river's edge.

He climbed into the boat and untied it. Cole had been around boats some as a boy and knew how to work the oars well enough to get him to the other side. He had used stars to find his way through the woods at night, and those same stars might prove useful if the current carried him out into Chesapeake Bay; otherwise, he simply planned on keeping the lights of Washington off the stern as he rowed toward Virginia.

He had failed in Washington City. But he knew there was another place where he could find Grant.

City Point.

"No one is to hear of this," General Grant said. "If news of this—" he sought for a word "—*attempt* gets out, it will undermine the confidence of the public in our leadership."

"Should I notify the president?" Bowers asked.

"No. Someone else might tell him, but he won't hear it from me."

Mulholland lay on a couch in Grant's office, watching the general pace the floor. A doctor had bandaged his wound, which, while painful, was a clean cut and had quickly stopped bleeding. The Rebel sharpshooter had obviously meant only to disable him, not kill him.

Mulholland found this strange, considering the sharpshooter had no qualms about killing. It had been very close with General Grant. But the Rebel was also a murderer. They had found the body of the woman who kept the boarding house under the bed in the Rebel's room. Her neck was broken.

Although Mulholland was thankful the Rebel had spared his life, he hoped that one day he would have an opportunity to repay the man for the stab wound. Mulholland still subscribed to the idea that soldiers abided by certain rules of duty and honor, and the thought that the Rebel had killed the old woman made him outraged. This wasn't a soldier they were dealing with, it was a criminal.

He was in an expansive mood, despite his wound, and he felt less and less pain, thanks to Colonel Bowers keeping Mulholland's glass topped off with the Willard Hotel's best whiskey. He wasn't the only one drinking, for it was long after midnight, and the thought of what might have happened had Mulholland been a little slower in tackling the general left an uneasiness that only whiskey could keep at bay. Even General Grant had helped himself to one small glass of whiskey. After all, they were behind locked doors, with guards out front. He had sipped the amber liquid, savored it, then put the empty glass aside.

As Mulholland lay on the couch in a thickening alcoholic fog, he had to admire the way General Grant was handling the situation.

Grant did not scare easily. In fact, he did not appear shaken by the incident at all, although he was extremely concerned with what might happen if word got out that a sniper had taken a shot at him in downtown Washington, just down the street from the White House. Already there were rumors going around the bar downstairs that Grant was drunk and his men had helped carry him in because he was too intoxicated to walk.

"Let them think what they want," Grant said. "If the newspapers don't have me dead, then they will have me drunk. There is no getting at the truth for these journalists. They print only what they hear second-hand from those whose only vantage point has been from a bar stool."

"Sounds like some of our generals," Bowers said.

Grant smiled. "Well, at least General Thomas can't be included in that last remark. He has done very well at Nashville, even if he took his time going about it."

"In General Thomas's case, maybe some drinking would have helped," Bowers remarked.

The general smiled thinly, and Mulholland wondered if Grant was having a hard time resisting the urge to have another drink. It was a conversation awash in whiskey.

Mulholland would have needed more than one, had he been the one the sharpshooter had targeted. As it was, he found being stabbed a good excuse for medicinal doses of whiskey.

"How's that leg, Major?" Grant asked.

"Fine, sir," he managed thickly. In fact, he had drunk so much whiskey he could barely feel his legs at all.

"You'll stay here in Washington until you're well enough to travel," Grant said.

Alarmed, Mulholland swung himself to a sitting position, ignoring the pain. His place was in City Point, especially considering he was sure the man he had chased tonight was not the only sharpshooter the South would send for Grant.

"No!" he nearly shouted. "I mean, with all due respect, General, I'll be fine for traveling."

"Headquarters is no place for a wounded man and we're leaving first thing in the morning."

"I'll be up and about in a few days, sir." Mulholland could hardly believe he was arguing with the general. "Besides, it's not over."

Looking puzzled, Grant asked, "What do you mean?"

"They will be sending others, sir. The Rebels are growing desperate."

Grant nodded, and he suddenly looked immensely tired. "Yes, I suppose they will." He sighed. "Come along then, Major, if you feel up to it. I may need your help yet at City Point."

Part II

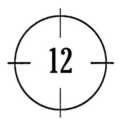

12

Cole kept the lights of Washington beyond the skiff's stern as he rowed with all his strength against the vicious currents of the Potomac River. The bone-chilling wind on the open water whipped up whitecaps that drenched him with an icy spray. Soon Cole could no longer feel his hands. They were only frozen hooks around the oars, but his sinewy arms pulled and pulled as he forced the rowboat across the river.

Waves caught the boat and rocked it dangerously. Cole ignored the wild bucking and concentrated on digging his oars into the water. If his small craft capsized, Cole knew he would drown in the cold river because he was too far out to swim to shore.

The current swept him far downriver. He soon sensed a difference in the night behind him, a quietness beyond the agitated waves, and when he looked over his shoulder Cole spotted the Virginia shore. He paused briefly in his rowing to study the dark riverbank. There were no lights, no voices of sentries. It seemed safe enough. Another few minutes of rowing and the bow of the little rowboat ran up on the sandy shore.

Cole leapt out, then crouched in the darkness. His hand was so cold he could barely hold the pistol he had pulled from his belt. But there was no sound, no stirring.

Satisfied, he shoved the rowboat back out into the river, letting the current take it and sweep it farther toward Chesapeake Bay. If the Yankees did figure out how he had escaped, he didn't want them to have any clues as to where he had landed.

This was a flat and marshy place, so different from the hill country he had called home. Cole headed away from the river, moving south. It was a moonless night, and he slipped cautiously through the marsh for fear of stumbling into one of those mud pits that could swallow a man up to his waist in thick, black ooze. The surface was mostly frozen, although in places he sank through the skim of ice and the heavy mud sucked at his boots. He was soon on dry land, and Cole struck out across the countryside.

He was tempted to leave this whole damn war behind. He could easily have followed the Potomac up through the Appalachian Mountains to Ohio on the other side and then struck out across the country for the west.

He knew he had tried his best. It was all that could be asked of a soldier.

But Lucas Cole was not ready to give up. He hated these damn Yankees who had invaded his own beloved home, killed his father, killed his sister. So many good hill country boys had died.

The Yankees thought they were safe, having chased him off from Washington City. Well, they could think again. If anyone had been with Cole, they might have seen the smile on his face and felt even colder than the December night should have made them feel.

Cole walked south. He was going to City Point.

If he had failed to kill the general in the Union capital, he would kill him at the big Yankee supply base where the Appomattox and James rivers converge.

He still wasn't sure how that Yankee major had known he was about to shoot General Grant. There was no way the Yankee officer could have seen Cole taking aim across the street. Well, it wouldn't have been the first time some instinct had saved a man. He promised himself General Grant wouldn't be so lucky again. He'd show those damn Yankees yet.

Vengeance is mine, sayeth the Lord.

Cole found a road and swung along it, trying to put as much distance between himself and the river as possible. His trip across the marsh had soaked whatever parts of him had stayed dry while crossing the river, but as long as he kept moving, he would be all right. The moment he stopped, though, the cold would sink its teeth into him.

He heard horses ahead and in seconds had dodged off the road into the trees. He crouched there, his pistol ready, as two horsemen rode past, heading north.

"We're gettin' a damn early start, Bill," one said to the other, his voice ringing in the still night.

"You want to get a good price on them hogs or don't you?" Bill said, sounding irritated. "You have to get there right early."

Satisfied that the men weren't soldiers but only farmers going to a Saturday market, Cole relaxed. They were soon gone down the road. Cole kept moving. He was hungry, but he had to cover some miles before morning. Just in case anyone figured out he had slipped across the river, he didn't want to give any patrols an easy job of finding him.

When a pale, pink light showed on the eastern horizon, Cole halted. It was false dawn, he knew, but the light would be up soon enough.

He had worked up a sweat swinging down the dark road with long strides, but as soon as he stopped moving the cold hit him like a club. All his clothes were wet, and his feet, too.

Cole moved far off the road to a dense thicket of tangled mulberry and multiflora rose. There was a dank, musky scent of rabbits and deer in the sheltered spaces under the huge briers, and it was here that Cole built a small fire using some of the waterproof matches he kept in a coat pocket. The heads of the lucifers were dipped in wax, and they flared into life when Cole swept one down the rough inner fabric of his coat. Once the fire was burning, Cole stripped off his clothes and stretched them like animal skins to dry near the flames. He kept himself wrapped in his coat.

In the growing light he found a rabbit trail, set a snare, then returned to the fire. He'd be having rabbit for breakfast before he set out again.

Once his clothes were dry, Cole kicked out the fire then rolled himself in his coat on top of the warmed earth. He kept his pistol in his hand and his rifle nearby.

Cole was asleep as soon as he closed his eyes.

Snodgrass tugged his jacket more tightly around himself but the cold still found every unbuttoned gap and threadbare hole, chilling him to the bone. The wind blew in out of the west from the Shenandoah Mountains, knife-edged and wet, smelling of snow. Not a star was visible in the sky and the band of Rebels Snodgrass led stumbled toward the meeting place in pitch darkness.

"You reckon we can trust them Yankees?" Charlie Hollis asked.

Snodgrass snorted. "You know them Yankees is askin' themselves right now, 'You reckon we can trust them Rebs?' "

"I wish I'd brung me a gun along."

"Hollis, if you're so all-fired scared of them Yanks, why don't you go back?"

The Confederate trenches lay just a few hundred feet away, but it might as well have been a few hundred miles across the frozen mud. The ground had been torn up by shells until it resembled a roughly plowed field, with the water in the furrows frozen into slicks of ice. No man wanted to cross it alone in darkness, especially with nervous pickets posted along the way. They had put out the word along their section of trench that there would be a meeting of the two sides in no-man's-land, but a nervous Southern farm boy on picket duty might forget all about that as he listened to someone approach in the darkness. Better to stay with the group.

As if in answer, Hollis tripped and went sprawling. The frozen ground was hard as rock, and he cursed as he went down.

"Careful now, Charlie, you'll get dirty."

The men laughed in spite of the cold and the dark. The thought of any of them getting any dirtier was indeed hilarious.

"Don't spoil yer nice uniform now, Charlie," someone said.

More laughter.

A voice hailed them from the darkness. "What do you Rebs think is so all-fired funny?"

Snodgrass peered toward where he thought the voice had come from and could just make out the light of a veiled lantern.

"That you, Billy Yank?"

"I reckon it is, Johnny Reb."

"Well, we're here to play some cards if you boys are ready."

Snodgrass's booming voice seemed to dispel any suspicion between the two sides. The lantern was unveiled, and the men in blue uniforms quickly joined those in dirty, ragged butternut.

A tall fellow with a red beard held the lantern. "Snodgrass?" he asked.

"I'm here," Snodgrass said, stepping into the thin ring of light.

The Yankee grinned, white teeth flashing behind his beard. "Snodgrass, it's about time I had a chance to win back some of that money you took off me last month."

"You can only try, Colburn," Snodgrass said. He and Colburn had played cards before and had set up this meeting tonight. None of the other faces was familiar. "Where's all your friends from last time? They lose all their money?"

Colburn's smile faded. "Why, three of the four is dead in a

month's time, Snodgrass. Fever got two and one of your goddamn sharpshooters got the third."

Snodgrass wondered if Lucas Cole was to blame for killing one of his former poker partners. "What about the fourth?"

Colburn grew serious. "Why, he done had the worst fate of all, Snodgrass. He got religion and decided poker was the Devil's game."

The handful of men, Yanks and Rebs alike, roared with laughter. When they quieted down, Colburn said, "This lantern don't exactly warm the bones on a night such as this. Anyone handy at building a fire?"

Charlie Hollis had brought along a pocket full of kindling for such a purpose. Clumsy as he was, Hollis was adept at building fires and cooking. The poker players from both sides had carried as much firewood as they could, and Charlie quickly had a roaring campfire going. They rigged blankets to create a windbreak, and soon the whole group was gathered around the fire, warming their toes and fingers.

"This is downright homey," Colburn said.

"I wouldn't get used to it if I were you," Snodgrass said. "We'll soon be pushing you boys all the way back to the James."

Colburn snorted. "You been drinkin' that Virginia swamp water again, Snodgrass? Soon as spring comes the war will be over. I wish the officers on both sides would just decide to quit making us shoot at each other until then."

Snodgrass was about to tell Colburn he was wrong about the war being nearly over, then thought better of it. He himself had said as much often enough. He just didn't like to hear a Yankee say it. But there was no denying that the war was drawing to a close. Briefly, Snodgrass thought how easy it would be to go back tonight with these Yankees and give himself up. He would sit out the war in some prison camp, probably no colder than he was now but perhaps better fed.

He had only to look around the fire to see where the war was going. The Yankees looked like they had been roughing it for a week in the woods. Most of their faces were nearly clean shaven, their uniforms were new-looking, and they all wore greatcoats to keep out winter's chill. Snodgrass also noticed the shoes on their feet. All of the Yankees wore shoes, while some of his fellow Confederate poker players made do with strips of rags tied around their toes, even in this bitter weather.

Looking around the fire at his own comrades, Snodgrass nearly felt his heart breaking. What had happened to the boys of '61? The soldiers had turned into shabby, derelict men. They didn't look like they were coming off a week-long hunting trip in the woods, but that they had lived in the woods all their lives, like goats. Their clothes were muddy and torn, their hair long, stringy, and dirty. All of them had beards, and the teeth that shone through them in the firelight were stained yellow from tobacco juice. More like a pack of beggars than soldiers, thought Snodgrass.

He eyed the Yankees' shoes covetously. With a fine pair of brogans on his feet he would be able to walk away from Petersburg and leave this misery behind. It would all end soon enough without him, anyway. The war could certainly go on without Uriah Snodgrass, he thought.

Colburn produced a deck of playing cards and shuffled them expertly in his long fingers. Snodgrass admired the newness of the deck. His own cards were thin as leaves.

"What'll it be, boys?" Colburn asked, his eyes sparkling. "A little poker?"

"Maybe you could teach us how to play?" Snodgrass said innocently.

"Ha! Don't let him fool you, boys," Colburn said to the other Yankees who hadn't played cards with Snodgrass before. "This man was a riverboat gambler before the war."

Wariness flashed in the faces of the other Yankees.

"Actually, I was a deckhand," Snodgrass said. "I did watch a lot of card games, though. Solitaire, Old Maid."

"Old Maid like hell."

In truth, Snodgrass had spent about half his time playing poker and the rest coiling ropes and doing chores aboard the steamboats. There were always passengers who wanted to play a hand, and at the one-horse towns along the Mississippi, there was always a game to be had in a waterfront warehouse. These games often turned dangerous, but Snodgrass had learned that quick thinking was usually a better weapon than a derringer. Losing a few dollars was better than having some character lose his temper and start shooting. Playing cards was mostly about learning how to read people.

Colburn dealt the cards. They used a blanket spread near the fire as their table. One of the Yankees produced a bottle, and Snodgrass took a careful sip, just enough to warm himself. He longed to pour a long drink of the whiskey down his throat, but he wanted to keep a clear head.

The first pot was for a few coins. Snodgrass let the Yanks win.

"He's just buildin' up your confidence, boys," Colburn warned his fellow soldiers. "Now he's goin' to rob you blind."

Snodgrass laughed, fumbled the cards when it came his turn to deal. "Cold hands," he said apologetically, hoping the novice Yankee gamblers thought he was just plain inexperienced. Colburn sat quietly with a grin frozen on his face, apparently enjoying the performance.

The pot quickly went from coins to paper money, and by the third hand there was a pile of greenbacks on the blanket, mostly one-dollar bills bearing the likeness of Treasury Secretary Salmon P. Chase. The Rebels had a harder time matching this pot because they didn't have much Union currency. Their Confederate bills were worthless, except for their value to the Yankees as souvenirs. Snodgrass played carefully and was thankful when Colburn folded, leaving just a milk-faced farm boy from Massachusetts and himself to battle over the pile of money.

"I'll see your bet and raise you two," the boy said. He had that curious New England accent.

Snodgrass looked around the circle at his fellow Rebs. All of them had folded. Snodgrass tossed his last greenback on the blanket, hoping the boy wouldn't go higher.

"What have you got, Johnny Reb?" the boy said, his face flushed with excitement at the thought of winning that pile of money.

"You first."

The boy laid down the cards on the blanket. "Three queens," he said.

"Full house," Snodgrass grunted, plunking down his cards. He scooped up the money, noticing Colburn had never revealed his hand. Snodgrass thought Colburn had probably dropped out so the Rebs could win some playing money. Snodgrass was thankful. Otherwise, the poker game would have been over in two hands.

The whiskey bottle went around again. Snodgrass held it in his hands for a moment, imagining the warmth of the liquid through the glass, then passed it on after taking only the smallest sip.

"What's the matter, Snodgrass, you become a deacon recently?"

"I swore to my mother I wouldn't drink so much."

The soldiers laughed. Almost all the younger ones had made similar promises to their mothers, while the older men had made such promises to their wives. None of them kept them, of course. Being a soldier was hard enough; being a moral soldier would be unbearable.

"This is how they ought to settle this here war," Hollis said when it came his turn to deal the cards. He handled them in the same nimble way he had started the fire that kept the cold night at bay. "Let General Lee and General Grant sit down and play a few hands."

"What about Jeff Davis and Abe Lincoln?"

"Them, too, if they want."

"I don't know about that," Colburn said. "I can't see Honest Abe bein' much of a poker player. Now Grant, on the other hand, might just be a match for General Lee."

"He might be a match in more than a poker game," said the fresh-faced Massachusetts farm boy, who was still smarting from losing that pile of money to Snodgrass.

"I wish they *would* just play poker," Snodgrass said, wanting to keep things light. He wasn't going to let this game break up before he had won new shoes for his messmates. "It would save a lot of us from getting killed, that's for damned sure."

"Amen," Colburn said. "Hell, I'll even loan those boys my cards if they want to play."

The game ebbed and flowed. Snodgrass had quickly loaned his greenbacks out to his messmates to keep them in the game, and the money went around from one person to another. Snodgrass made a point of losing steadily until he was down to a few greenbacks.

The whiskey bottle was mostly empty by now, and the group of poker players was distinctly louder and more jovial than it had been in the beginning.

"Keep it down, boys," Colburn warned his own comrades. "We don't want some officer getting nosy about what we're doing out here. They don't take kindly to us associating with the enemy."

While the pickets on both sides were aware of the poker game in no-man's-land, there was no point in pushing their luck. Officers frowned upon meetings between the enlisted men in the opposing trenches.

Just as the whiskey had made the men louder, it also made them more daring in their bets. The pots on the blanket became larger and larger. Finally, one rose to a dizzying amount—there must have been one hundred dollars sitting there. Only Colburn, Snodgrass and the farm boy were still in.

"I'll see your five and raise you five," Colburn said, looking steadily at Snodgrass over his cards. The Yankee must have had a good hand, Snodgrass decided, because he wasn't much for bluffing. But then, Snodgrass had been dealt some good cards. Powerfully good cards. He did his best to look dour. Meanwhile, the farm boy tossed another five dollars on the pile. The two men then turned to Snodgrass.

He grimaced. He let his brow wrinkle. Snodgrass had never been one to believe in a stony "poker face." "Goddamn, boys, but I'm out of money."

"Get your friends there to loan you some," Colburn said. Snodgrass could see the Yankee could almost taste the money, and if he could get five dollars more, all the better. But the enormous pot had already cleaned out most everyone around the campfire.

Snodgrass did his best to look desperate. Inside, though, he was grinning to himself with a wizened smile.

He dug into his pockets and produced one of his treasured double eagles. All eyes were on the twenty dollar gold piece as it glittered in the firelight. Such a coin was a rarity indeed, and few men—Yankee or Confederate—had ever seen one in civilian life.

"You are a wealthy man," Colburn said. "And here I thought you was just a poor secessionist."

Satisfied that the coin had inspired the necessary greed in both Colburn and the young farmer, Snodgrass tossed it onto the blanket, where it lay heavily atop the greenbacks.

"I'll see your five and raise you fifteen," Snodgrass said. He knew his hand was that good. How good was Colburn's? He doubted the farm boy had anything worth worrying about. Mentally he ticked off the combinations that could beat him. Was Colburn holding one of these?

It seemed to take Colburn a while to catch his breath. The boy was simply staring wide-eyed.

Colburn looked around the fire at the Yankee faces, and Snodgrass noted with satisfaction the same sign Colburn saw—none of them had fifteen dollars. Not even together.

"I ain't got it, Snodgrass," Colburn said. He put his cards face down on the blanket, and Snodgrass's breath stopped at the thought that he had dropped out. But then Colburn's hand patted a pocket of his uniform blouse and came out with a silver watch. "It's worth five dollars, at least."

Snodgrass shook his head. "I already got one of them."

"Who says you're going to win this one?"

"These cards in my hand do, boy."

"Come on, Snodgrass. I'll send the money over to you."

"Like hell you will."

Colburn eyed the paper money and the double eagle like a child might ogle a candy jar. "Well, then—"

"There's maybe one thing I'd consider of value," Snodgrass said, immediately getting the attention of the two Yankees. "Your shoes."

Colburn snorted. "These things ain't worth fifteen dollars, Snodgrass."

"Not just yours, you damn fool Yank." Snodgrass looked around the fire. "All of your shoes."

Colburn thought a second. Then his hands were busy undoing the laces. "Off they go, boys," he ordered. "Every last one of your shoes into the pot."

It was done in a minute. Six pairs of Yankee brogans shared the blanket with the money.

Snodgrass's hands were sweating despite the cold. Before the war he had seen far more money in a single pot, but never before had he wanted anything so badly as those shoes. He looked back at the cards in his hand. There were only a few hands that could beat him. Colburn must have been awfully damn confident if he was willing to risk walking barefoot back to the Yankee trenches. "You first," he said to the farm boy.

"Three kings," the boy said, putting the cards down.

Colburn's wolfish face showed he had easily beaten that. He put his cards on the blanket. "Full house, Snodgrass. What have you got?"

Snodgrass had forgotten all about the chill of the night air and the wind sifting under his collar. All he saw were Colburn's eyes watching him across the fire. His hand shook a little as he spread his cards on the blanket.

"Royal flush."

Suddenly everyone was thumping him on the back.

Even Colburn was smiling.

"You don't give a damn about that money," he said, seeing now what Snodgrass had been planning all along. "You just wanted our damn shoes."

Snodgrass shrugged. "The money ain't too bad, either."

"I guess not."

The game had tapped out the Yankees. They were broke and so there would be no chance for them to win back their money. Even the whiskey was gone. The Yankees watched wistfully as the Rebs traded the shoes between themselves to find the pairs that fit them best.

Colburn reached for Snodgrass's hand. The two men shook over the flames. "Colburn, it's been a pleasure, as usual."

The Yankee grinned. "See you in hell, Johnny Reb."

"See you in hell, Billy Yank."

"Goddamn you both, be careful!" Mulholland cried out as Colonel Bowers and Private O'Malley helped him aboard the steamer. His wounded leg had stiffened during the night, and his aching head was paying the debt for the whiskey that had helped ease the pain of the stab wound.

"Hush now, Major sir, or the good general might be sendin' you to a hospital bed where you belong instead of lettin' you come aboard this damn boat." O'Malley locked one of the major's arms in a powerful grip as they started across the gangway. Bowers helped him on the other side.

"The private has a point," Bowers said, chuckling. "Now shut up or we'll drop you in the water."

Although he knew Bowers wasn't serious, Mulholland couldn't resist a look at the river, the water still dark as coffee in the dusky early morning. He shivered and felt sick with whiskey and pain. But he had to go on to City Point.

"Just get me in a bunk," Mulholland said.

Grant was already on board. The general was in an upbeat mood after the news from Nashville. General Thomas had crushed Hood's army. They had attacked at 6 A.M. yesterday morning as rain and snow fell and pushed all day until the Confederate army was in full retreat toward Franklin, Tennessee. Thomas had lost over 3,000 men, Hood about 1,500. But Hood's army was in such disarray, and he had lost so many as prisoners and so much artillery, it was doubtful the Confederate's Army of the Tennessee would ever be a fighting force again.

Grant was returning to City Point thinking he might be able to try a similar wintertime push against the Rebel trenches at Petersburg and bring a rapid end to the Confederacy. These secret plans had been much on the minds of the staff, and it was assumed this was what Grant and President Lincoln had discussed during their private meeting last night at the White House.

"Here we are," Bowers said, helping Mulholland onto the deck of the steamer. "Grant's already below, so you can hobble and carry on as much as you like."

"Damn you," Mulholland said, but he managed to smile.

Bowers produced a flask of whiskey from a pocket. "Have a good drink of that and it'll cure what ails you."

Mulholland emptied half the flask. Bowers offered it to O'Malley, and the Irishman smiled gratefully, then drank. The warm rush of liquor felt wonderful, and by the time Mulholland reached his bunk his head no longer ached and he could almost ignore the pain in his leg.

"Now sleep sweetly, Brendan," Bowers said. "We'll be back at City Point by dark."

"I don't plan on dancing around the deck, believe me."

"Take this," Bowers said, pushing the flask into his hands. "A nip now and then might do you good."

"Yes, sir, Colonel."

Bowers and O'Malley left him alone. He tried to get comfortable in the slab-bottomed bunk, but the pain in his leg was intense. He hoped it wasn't getting infected, or else some doctor would have to take it off.

Damn that Reb!

Mulholland cradled the whiskey flask in the crook of his elbow and tried to decide what he would do first to prevent any more sniper attacks once he got to City Point.

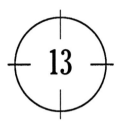

Snodgrass went to bed early that night in order to get a few hours of sleep before he undertook his dangerous journey. He slept fitfully, shivering in his blankets. One by one his messmates dropped off to sleep. There wasn't much to keep them up on these long winter evenings. No cards, no liquor, not much food. They had all been together so long that there wasn't even any point in swapping stories because they knew all there was to know about each other and had retold anecdotes so many times that the tales had all the appeal of cold beans.

Night sounds came to Snodgrass as he lay in his blanket. Men snored nearby, and he could hear the crackling made by the coals of their dying fire. Behind their own lines in Petersburg a dog barked. It must have been some distance away, but such a noise carried far on the winter air. These were all soothing, if lonely, sounds, and for a while he was tempted simply to close his eyes and sleep.

But he had made up his mind. It would be a long, hard winter in the trenches, and for what? They would shiver and starve until spring, then fall away under the first Yankee attack. The end of the Confederacy would soon follow.

One of their messmates had already disappeared in the night. The boys hadn't talked much about it. All up and down the trenches the same thing was happening. Hundreds were deserting each week. General Lee's army was melting away.

While Snodgrass didn't like the thought of being a deserter, he didn't see much point in remaining a soldier, either. The adventure was over as far as he was concerned. Springtime would bring defeat and possibly death in one of the last desperate battles that was as certain as April rain. Being a gambler by nature, Snodgrass knew a bit about odds. He thought his chances of survival would be much better if he hoofed it out of the Confederate army as soon as possible.

He rolled out of the blanket, trying his best to ignore the cold that immediately enveloped him. He was already fully dressed, with Colburn's good Yankee brogans on his feet. Walking shoes. Quickly, and as quietly as possible, Snodgrass made up his blanket roll. He had already decided to leave his rifle behind. It wouldn't be much use to him anyhow, only a hindrance.

"You too, Uriah?"

He nearly jumped at the raspy whisper. Snodgrass turned to see Charlie Hollis propped up on one elbow in his blanket.

"I'm afraid so, Charlie. Ain't much sense in waiting for the end that I can see."

"You're probably right. Where you headed? South?"

"Nah. Too many damn provost guards. I'm goin' north. I'll try to get past the Yankee lines and cross the Potomac into Maryland. I'm headed for Washington. I hear there's already a bunch of ol' Southern boys in the city, and nobody bothers much with 'em."

"Sounds like a good plan. Long as the Yankees don't shoot you."

"Well, I'll take my chances." Snodgrass slipped the blanket roll over his shoulder. "Why don't you come with me, boy?"

Hollis thought it over. "I signed on to fight for my country, Uriah. I aim to finish the job."

Snodgrass bent down and touched Hollis's shoulder. "You're a good man, Charlie. Now, you ain't goin' to raise no noise about my leavin', are you?"

"Hell, Snodgrass, you ought to know me better than that."

"Good luck to you, Charlie."

"Be careful now, boy."

Snodgrass stood and took one last look at the section of trench that had been his home the past few weeks. He felt no sentimentality about leaving such a place. It was the very pit of hell. But he would miss the boys. They were as brothers to him, and if they would have listened, he would have taken them along.

With that final thought, Snodgrass started out. He had to take his time, picking his way around the sleeping forms of men, piles of equipment, smoldering fires, and the assorted trash that littered the floor of the trenches. He had picked a dark, starless night, which would make him a difficult target for any alert sentry, but which also slowed his movements.

Snodgrass went to a rifle step, climbed it, and slipped over the top of the trench. He lay still for a moment to see if he had attracted anyone's attention. But there was only quiet. He rose to a half-crouch and began making his way through the line of rifle pits that ran forward of the trench. Depending on the individual soldier on duty, passing through his own lines might be easy or deadly. Some soldiers might be sympathetic toward a man going over to the Yankees; some might shoot him.

He worked his way forward over the rough ground, thankful for the new shoes on his feet. Without them, such a journey would have been foolhardy.

In the darkness he couldn't see the Confederate sentries. But then, they couldn't see him, either. As quietly as he could, he crept forward. The ground was rough as a plowed field, and his foot slipped into a crevice between two shell-torn hummocks of dirt, cracking the skim of ice that lay atop the mud puddle in the depression.

"Who goes there?"

Snodgrass debated whether or not he should answer. He waited. Just when he was about to start moving again, he froze at the sound of a musket hammer being cocked.

In spite of the cold, he felt his forehead break out in a sweat beneath the band of his hat.

The sentry's voice had come from the darkness maybe thirty feet away. Snodgrass couldn't see the other soldier because he was probably hidden in a rifle pit gouged from the Virginia mud. But could the sentry see him outlined against the dark sky? Maybe he should just yell out that he was surrendering to the Yanks and see what happened.

"I ain't goin' to ask agin," the Southern voice said. "If yer a Yank, I'll shoot. If yer a yellowbelly deserter, I'll shoot ye twice."

That was all the prompting Snodgrass needed. He took off running, fleeing pell-mell toward no-man's-land. Despite the rough footing, Snodgrass flew over the ground, wanting to put as much distance as possible between him and the sentry. He kept expecting at any moment to feel a hot chunk of lead between his shoulder blades.

Behind him, the sentry's rifle cracked. The minié ball whined harmlessly past him into the night. Snodgrass nearly whooped for joy. By the time that boy reloaded, Snodgrass planned to be lost in the darkness. He kept running flat out for another couple hundred feet, then plunked himself down and gasped for breath.

He supposed the gunshot had wakened the sleepy sentries of both sides and made them more alert, so he decided to sit for a spell and let the night settle down again. From where he sat, he couldn't see anything of either the Confederate or the Yankee works, so he felt safe enough. He was smack dab in the middle of no-man's-land, which was just where he wanted to be.

Crossing over to the Yankees and surrendering did not appeal to Snodgrass. Neither did trying to slip behind the Confederate lines to take his chances with the provost guard. There were rumors that patrols were hanging deserters as they caught them, or shooting them on sight. So Snodgrass had decided to use the narrow strip of land between the opposing trenches as his highway to freedom.

The other option, which he had not considered before, was that he could simply return. He would be back with his company before dawn, and no one but Charlie Hollis would ever know that he had tried to desert. Just as quickly as it had come, Snodgrass dismissed this thought. He had already made his choice, and it would be more cowardly now to return than to push on toward freedom.

His mind made up, and satisfied that all was quiet again, Snodgrass stood and started walking north.

Anne woke earlier than usual on December 16. It had not been a good night for sleeping. Colonel Wilcox and his men had stayed until two o'clock in the morning, and Anne had been forced to endure the man's company. He had made liberal use of her brandy as he directed the guarding of her house from his chair by the fire. She had dreaded that he might insist on a trip upstairs, but fortunately the presence of his own soldiers had forced Wilcox to keep his amorous feelings in check.

Cole had not appeared. Not that she had expected him. He would have been a fool to return to her house after the assassination attempt on General Grant was thwarted. Wilcox had finally gone early that morning, leaving just one guard in the front hallway and another in the kitchen. It had been somewhat unclear whether the guards were to keep the assassin out or Anne in. She had settled the question this morning by having Hattie feed them coffee and biscuits before sending them on their way.

Hattie.

There was no doubt it was Hattie who had written the note to Colonel Wilcox, warning him of the assassination attempt. The idea of Hattie sending messages and forging Anne's signature enraged her.

She had other reasons to be angry. After all, how could it be that Hattie had found out what Cole was up to in the city without ever telling her? How had Hattie learned this? It stung Anne's pride that her servant had found out what she could not.

What angered Anne more than anything and made her breath quicken with rage was that she had been credited with preventing General Ulysses S. Grant from being killed. For her own purposes she had always tried to appear patriotic and pro-Union, while of course she did everything she could to undermine the Yankees. But this last bit, that Wilcox had praised her for saving Grant's life, was really too much. Grant should by all rights be dead, and he probably would have been without Hattie.

Anne slipped down the hallway to the kitchen and glided through the door. Hattie was busy arranging things on a shelf and didn't notice. She gave a little cry when she turned around to find Anne in the kitchen. As a rule, Anne rarely entered.

"Jumpy, aren't you, Hattie?" Anne asked. Her smile was sweet, but something in her face made Hattie start to tremble.

"It ain't nothin', Miss Anne. Them soldiers made me tired, is all."

"Is that right?"

Anne walked to the stove. There was a small barrel there filled with kindling sticks for the stove. Each piece of wood was roughly two inches square and two feet long. These pieces of oak were hard as iron and nearly sharp as a knife along the seam where they had split away from the larger log. She picked one from the barrel, hefted it in her hand to test its weight. As she looked at the stick, she could hear Hattie's feet shuffling across the floorboards, trying to get away. But there wasn't anyplace to go.

"Miss Anne—"

"You brought those soldiers here, Hattie. Why did you write that note to Colonel Wilcox?"

"I didn't write no—"

"Hattie." Anne smacked the oak stick against the open palm of her left hand. She found the slight pain it caused satisfying. "I know you did it. Now tell me all about it."

Hattie broke down in tears. "I seen what he was goin' to do, Miss

Anne! I seen it! Yesterday I took that message to Major Mulholland like you said, and I seen Mr. Cole come out of a house there, by the Willard Hotel. It was a boarding house, and when I talked to the lady what run it she brought me up to his room. I knew somethin' was wrong by the way it was set up. He was goin' to shoot General Grant. If that happened, he would of got caught and then where would we be, Miss Anne? Out on the street in the cold with them dirty beggars is where. Them Yankees would of found out you was helping him."

Anne couldn't believe what she was hearing. She took a step toward Hattie. Without thinking, she raised the stick high overhead and swung it down as hard as she could with an unladylike grunt. The wood caught Hattie across the face and she fell, screaming, as she put a hand to the bloody gash on her cheek.

Her own brutality shocked Anne. The worst of the anger broke and died away like a wave on a beach. Otherwise, she might have beaten Hattie to death in a rage. Instead, she took a step toward the whimpering figure on the floor and deliberately hit her across the back. And again. The thump of wood on Hattie's bones and flesh reminded Anne of how the coal cart drivers beat their horses to discipline them. She struck at Hattie's hands, held up to fend off the blows, and gashed the knuckles. Hattie screamed again.

Anne was aware of the kitchen door opening. Suddenly, Henry was there.

"Miss Anne!" he cried out. Henry held out his arms as if to stop her, but he would not touch her. He *could not* touch a white woman. But he did move around until he was between Anne and Hattie. "Why you doin' this?" he asked.

"Ask her," Anne said, pointing the stick at the sobbing woman on the floor.

At that, Anne opened the lid on top of the cook stove and tossed in the bloody stick. She turned. "You best not write any more notes, Hattie."

As she walked out of the kitchen, Anne didn't see the eyes of her servant, angry as her own, and full of hate as they had never been before.

Henry noticed and was alarmed. He saw the rage and pain and put a hand on Hattie's shoulder. "Bide your time," he said, looking down at Hattie's bloody face.

In the hallway, Anne was still breathing heavily. *Damn Hattie!*

Upsetting everything. It was all Anne could do not to march back into the kitchen and give her servant another beating.

She might have, too, if at that moment there hadn't been a knock at the front door.

"Now what?" Anne wondered aloud. She hoped the Yankee guards hadn't changed their minds and come back. Before she opened the door, she paused in front of the hall mirror to smooth her hair and dress, erasing any signs of her angry outburst in the kitchen.

A porter from the Willard Hotel was waiting on the step.

"Message for you, Miss Clark, ma'am," the porter said awkwardly. She wondered if he had been at the door long enough to hear Hattie's screams.

"Thank you." She gave him a coin and sent him on his way.

The note was from Brendan:

Dearest Anne,
As this finds you, we are already on Chesapeake Bay, bound again for City Point. While I look forward to fulfilling my duties at headquarters, I am not looking forward to the dullness of life in winter camp. A few more days in Washington City would have been welcome. General Grant is not happy except when he is in the field and, of course, I must go with him.

We had some excitement here last night and I got a scratch that has put me off my feet, otherwise I would have delivered this myself before we set sail.

Do write me and, also, let me know of my grandmother's health. I fear she grows more feeble all the time.

Your servant,
Brendan

She read the note, and sighed. *Damn you, Brendan*, Anne thought. *Damn you for being a Yankee.*

Snodgrass woke abruptly from a deep sleep. Just before daybreak on the morning of December 17 he had found a large oak tree off the road and curled himself in his blanket beneath it, huddling against the huge trunk for shelter from the wind. This was one of the main roads to Washington. The Potomac River crossing was just ahead, and as soon as it was dark he planned to move on toward the city.

Snodgrass hugged the blanket more tightly against his body. Bone-tired as he was, he wondered what in the world could have awakened him. He tended to sleep soundly as a bear.

Something jabbed at his side, and Snodgrass, immediately tense with dread, saw that it was a boot. Through eyes still bleary with sleep he saw three hard-looking characters looking down at him. Not farmers, and not soldiers, either, from the look of them. Two were holding rifles in their hands and the third had a revolver in his belt with his jacket pulled back so Snodgrass could see it. He had thought he would be safe enough here in the northern Virginia countryside, but now Snodgrass wished he had made his camp a little farther off the road.

"That's right, soldier boy, it's time to get up."

"What do you want?" Snodgrass asked groggily.

"We don't want nothin'," said the man who had been prodding Snodgrass with his boot. He had an unshaven face and yellow teeth, and his clothes were a patchwork of uniforms and civilian clothes. He wore sky blue Union trousers, a short butternut shell jacket, and a striped linen shirt. The other two were dressed similarly. All three had roundish pig faces that seemed shadows of each other, as if the men were related somehow, perhaps even brothers or cousins. Their heavy faces also showed they were well fed, which meant they hadn't recently come from the trenches around Petersburg, no matter which side they were on.

"We was jest afraid you done overslept, seein' how late it is," the one pig face said. "Sun's been up three hours."

"Unless, of course, you was travelin' at night and sleepin' by day, like a yallerbelly deserter," said another man.

"I reckon I overslept," Snodgrass said, getting creakily to his feet. "Not that ya'll look like the provost guard."

"See?" said the second man, turning to the other pig faces. "I done told you, boys. He's one of them yallerbellies."

"Ain't many deserters headin' north," the first man said. "Lessen' they was Yankees."

"Well, I ain't no Yankee." Snodgrass was feeling increasingly uncomfortable. It was like he had three mean old dogs circling him, and it was just a matter of time before one of them decided to bite. He wondered if maybe he should have carried a gun after all; not that it would have done much good with these men, who already had the drop on him.

"Then you must be runnin' out. That's a hangin' offense, boy."

"I'm on leave," he said. "I'm goin' to see my relations in Maryland."

"Where's your papers?"

"I ain't got any papers."

The man turned to his companions with an evil grin. "He ain't got no papers."

"Hell, you couldn't read 'em anyhow if I did."

Too late, Snodgrass realized he had said the wrong thing.

One of the pig faces stepped forward, and if it hadn't been for the tree behind him, Snodgrass would have reeled back on account of the stink of the man's breath. He exhaled a vapor that smelled of rotting teeth and tobacco juice and half an onion all rolled into one. Snodgrass's eyes watered. He fought the urge to shove the man away, which would only provoke these fools.

"He's right uppity for a deserter, ain't he, boys? Let's see how he acts when we stretch his neck some."

"Why waste the time?" The leader of the little trio guffawed. "Let's jest shoot him. Folks will be comin' along this road, now that the day's gettin' on."

"Fine by me," said the one who had been for hanging. He lifted his rifle and brought the muzzle to within a few inches of Snodgrass's heart. Snodgrass was surprised that some detached part of his mind noticed the weapon was an Enfield, which meant these men were most likely Southern deserters. Yankee or Southern, they seemed intent on shooting him, and his heart began to flutter wildly in his chest. It wasn't supposed to end this way, he thought. This was a damn fool way to die after all he'd been through.

"Guess you won't be goin' to Maryland after all," said the leader, grinning. "Go ahead and shoot— "

Pig face never finished his sentence.

A neat black hole appeared on the front of his striped shirt. He moved his lips a few times but no sound came out.

The report of a rifle crashed through the silence.

The wounded man took a few faltering steps backward. Blood was running out of his mouth, and his eyes had glazed over. He went down to his knees, then slumped over into the thick carpet of oak leaves, his mouth still moving.

"What in hell?"

The second man was pointing his rifle toward the woods, moving it from one spot to another as he searched for a target. There was no smoke to be seen, and the echo of the gunshot made it impossible to tell where the shot had come from. He was still keeping his rifle trained on the woods when Snodgrass watched the man's head explode. The outlaw, now with only half a skull, went crashing off into the underbrush to die.

One man remained, and he forgot all about Snodgrass as he turned and ran. He had only gone a few steps when a third shot rang out and the bullet shoved him off his feet as it hit him square between the shoulder blades.

Stunned, Snodgrass figured he was next. He dove for the ground and hunkered down at the base of the oak tree. One of the dead men had dropped his rifle within reach, and Snodgrass grabbed it and lay behind the oak with the gun in his hands, ready for whoever was out there. It could have been some farmer fed up with outlaws, or a home guard patrol so nervous it opened fire without warning.

The shots had come awfully fast, so it was either one man with a breech loader or three men with rifles. Judging by the time that had elapsed between when the bullets struck and the rifle reported, the shots had been made from some distance, and whoever it was knew how to shoot. Snodgrass wished again that he had unrolled his blanket in some spot deeper in the woods so he could have avoided all this trouble, but in the darkness just before dawn he had misjudged his proximity to the road.

He waited behind the rifle sights, expecting at any moment to see movement between the trees.

Nothing.

A minute went by. Then another. Snodgrass felt himself going from scared to impatient. In a card game, it would have been the equivalent of waiting for a man to show his hand when there was an awfully big pot riding on the cards.

"Show yourself," he finally shouted at the trees. In the morning light the gray trunks stood out like so many soldiers. Ranks of men like they'd had back at Gettysburg and Fredericksburg. Where had they all gone?

"You ain't goin' to shoot me now, are you?" a voice called back from the woods. Something familiar in its sound.

"I don't know yet," Snodgrass yelled back.

Then, he saw him. One man. A figure moving easily through the underbrush, his feet barely making a sound as he crossed the thick brown leaves on the woods floor. A lean man who crept through the woods like a gray fox.

Lucas Cole.

Snodgrass would have been no less surprised to see General Lee himself, but there was no mistaking the sharpshooter from the trenches back in Petersburg. Cole had simply disappeared one night after the staff officer had come for him, and although Snodgrass had done some asking around, no one remembered seeing Cole. Snodgrass had just figured the man had moved on or else had been killed as he worked his way into one of the sniper pits forward of the line.

When Cole was close enough, Snodgrass could make out those strange, depthless eyes. They had a light all their own on this gray morning. Snodgrass felt a chill go through him.

Cole's gaze flicked over the bodies of the three dead men, then turned to Snodgrass.

"Well, I'll be," Snodgrass said. "If it ain't the sharpshooter."

"Snodgrass, I can't believe you let them boys get the drop on you."

Aside from that one half-joking comment, Cole appeared in no mood to talk. He quickly plucked the revolver from the belt of one of the dead men, then handed it to Snodgrass.

"We best get going," Cole said. "Take this, and bring that rifle along, too. No telling who might turn up now after them gunshots."

"You mind telling me what you're doing here?" Snodgrass asked.

"Later," Cole said, busily scanning the road for any friends the outlaws may have had. "Let's get a move on before somebody else comes along."

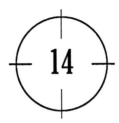

14

Someone was following him.

Sudler Dill spotted the man in the dark coat as soon as he left the War Department. Just to be sure, he turned down an alley, popped back out on the street, and looked behind him.

There was the man again. He stopped when he saw Dill looking and pretended to be interested in a display of hats in a shop window. When Dill began walking, so did the man.

Dill felt a chill go through him, and it wasn't because of the crisp December air. Dill had good reason to be afraid. In his coat pocket he carried highly incriminating papers just now stolen from the War Department. The paperwork detailed supplies destined for various units around Petersburg. Any Rebel commander worth his salt would be able to tell at once where Grant's wintertime push against the Confederate fortifications would come from upon seeing which units were being resupplied with ammunition and food. The Confederate defenses were stretched so thin that this information was vital if they wished to withstand an attack. A Union hammer blow against a particular point in the line could not be withstood with the troops on hand. The Confederates would have to concentrate their men in order to halt a Yankee attack and perhaps fool the enemy into thinking the Rebels had more men in the trenches than they actually did.

It was the sort of information that could fend off a military catastrophe. All in Sudler Dill's pocket. And he was being followed.

He found his feet still carried him toward Anne Clark's house on H Street. Dill didn't know who else to pass the information to, because she had been his spy contact for as long as he had been in the War Department. Well, it looked as if he had passed too many secrets to Anne, because he must have come under suspicion, or there wouldn't now be a man in a long, dark coat following him through the city streets.

Dill knew he had to get these papers to Anne, but he didn't wish to put her in danger. Dill's mind worked desperately as he hurried down the street, and he quickly came up with a plan that, with luck, would see that the information he had stolen at such risk would do some good.

He rounded a corner, and then broke into a run for most of the block while his pursuer was still out of view. Then Dill approached one of the trades people in this section of the street. There was a woman selling jams and pickles from a cart, and Dill went up and handed her a thick packet. The woman stared at him with a blank expression on her round face.

"What's that, mister? You want to buy something?"

Dill poured it all out at once, amazing himself by how smoothly he lied: "I've just had some bad news from someone who found me here on the street. My cousin is gravely ill, and I must go see him. I've no time, you see. Will you give these to my sister? She'll be along shortly. A tall woman, brown hair, very pretty." He slipped her a five-dollar bill and watched her eyes go round with amazement. "There's a good woman. Thank you."

Then Dill was gone, leaving the flabbergasted woman staring at the packet in her hand. He had kept two sheets of paper tucked into his breast pocket because the Union men would expect to find something on him, and he wanted to make certain they would not be disappointed. As long as they found something incriminating, they would never suspect he had given the bulk of his stolen papers to the street vendor. Taking a stub of pencil from his pocket, he wrote a simple message on the back of one of the papers, then balled the sheet tightly in his fist.

Dill walked on. There were now two men following him, both in long, dark overcoats. Pinkerton men, or maybe Lafayette Baker's. Baker was the War Department officer responsible for catching spies and he had a reputation for ruthlessness. Dill decided it was likely that the men behind him carried pistols. The pair quickened their pace and narrowed the gap between themselves and Dill.

Not quite sure how to proceed, he moved on until he came to H Street and turned down it. The men were right behind him. He walked faster but soon heard swift footsteps on the sidewalk behind him.

"You there, Mr. Dill. You'd better stop," a gruff voice growled not ten feet away. Dill stopped and turned. To his surprise he felt very calm and was able to say in an even voice, "Yes?"

"Don't play stupid with us, now," one man said. "You're a spy, Mr. Dill. That's the long and short of it. Hand over the papers."

"What papers?"

One of the men stepped forward, grabbed Dill roughly by the arm, and thrust his hand into Dill's coat pockets one by one. He pulled out the single paper Dill had kept.

"What's this, then?" the man asked, a vicious sneer on his face. "You can't play dumb now."

The detective had not noticed the tight fists at the small man's sides.

Dill shrugged. "Nothing. I don't even know how it got there."

The first detective was busy reading the sheet, which Dill knew contained information about artillery supplies. He looked up. "Where were you taking this?"

"Why, to Mr. Walter's house."

"Point it out to us, and be quick about it."

Dill led them to Miss Clark's house. Maybe this was foolish, but he had an idea Miss Clark would know just what to do. The three climbed the steps, with Dill between them, held captive by his arms. He looked like a boy pressed between his two large captors. They knocked, and Anne Clark herself answered the door. Dill thought she looked as beautiful as ever.

Both detectives, who had been expecting Mr. Walter, were taken aback at the sight of Miss Clark. No one looked more surprised than she did. Her face did not betray a trace of recognition as she looked first at Dill, then at the burly detectives who held his arms.

"What's going on here?" she asked. "Who are you?"

"Don't you know this man, Mrs. Walter?" The detective sounded doubtful.

"Mrs. Walter? What? My name is Anne Clark. Who is this man?"

"There's no Mr. Walter here?"

"Certainly not." Miss Clark's look was indignant. "I'm not married."

"You've never seen him before?" the detective gave a tug on Dill's arm, making him bounce like a puppet. No one noticed one of Dill's fists open and release a tiny ball of paper, which fell to the wooden landing.

"Of course I've never seen him," Miss Clark said. "Who are you, anyhow?"

"It doesn't matter, ma'am. Sorry to bother you," the detective said. He turned to Dill and said in a low voice. "Enough of your tricks, Mr. Dill. We'll see how well you like Old Capitol Prison! After a few days of the rats chewing on you at night, you'll be glad enough to tell us who you were going to see."

They turned around on the small landing, savagely twisting Dill, and started back down the steps to the sidewalk. For the first time, Dill opened his mouth and shouted. "You won't stop us! Others will follow in my footsteps!" He looked directly at Anne. "In my footsteps!"

The detective silenced him with a cuff on the ear. "Shut up, you damn Rebel!"

Anne managed to keep her composure until the three men had moved down the street. Then she stepped inside and shut the door, allowing herself to slump against the heavy wood. They had caught poor Mr. Dill! She dreaded to think of what the Yankees would do to him. A thin little man like him wouldn't last long in prison, considering it was only December and the worst of winter still lay ahead with Old Capitol Prison damp and full of drafts. He would catch a fever and shiver himself to death. It would be kinder, she thought, simply to shoot him. But the Yankees had never been known for kindness, she thought bitterly.

A more chilling thought came to her. While the Yankees weren't kind, they also had no scruples about locking women up in that dreadful place. Hadn't Belle Boyd and Rose Greenhow been kept in Old Capitol Prison for spying? Anne glanced at the hall table where a loaded pistol was kept in a drawer. If the Yankees ever came to arrest her, she vowed to kill a few first.

Anne was puzzled. Why had Dill come to her house? He wouldn't have done it without good reason, not if he'd known he was being followed. Wracking her brain, she opened the door and looked back down the street, but Dill and his two captors were already gone. That's when the ball of paper on the landing caught her eye. Quickly, she snatched it up. Safe once again behind the heavy door, she unfolded the paper and read the short message scrawled in pencil: Virginia & E.

Now what on earth was that supposed to mean? The front of the sheet contained some information about cases of hardtack biscuits sent to various units. It hardly seemed something Dill would have taken such risks to deliver. *Virginia & E.* She tried to remember if Sudler Dill had given her some sign as he stood captive on her front steps. Why, he hadn't spoken at all, except when the two men had hauled him away. Then it came to her. Footsteps! He had looked right at her and shouted something about others following in his footsteps.

"Hattie!" Anne shouted excitedly. She reached for her heavy shawl and hat where they hung in the hallway.

Hattie came from the kitchen at a trot, drying her hands on her apron. An ugly bruise showed on her cheek from the beating Anne had given her. Hattie had been walking on eggshells around her mistress, trying to get back in her good graces. "Yes, ma'am?"

"Get your coat on and come with me. We'll go out the back door."

Hattie ran and got her coat, and the two of them left the house and crossed through the back yard to the alley that ran behind H Street. It was possible one of the detectives had stayed to watch her house, and Anne didn't want to take any chances.

Knowing the fastidious Mr. Dill, Anne was sure he had taken the most direct route from the War Department to her house, which meant he would have taken Virginia Avenue to Twenty-second Street. This was the route Anne and Hattie now retraced.

"Keep your eyes open, Hattie."

"For what, Miss Anne? You lose somethin'?"

"No, but Mr. Dill did, and we must find it."

"You've got to tell me what it looks like so I'll know it when I see it."

Unfortunately, Anne had no idea what they were looking for. Was it an envelope? A box? A bundle of papers?

"Oh, I don't know, Hattie!" Anne said sharply. "We'll know it when we see it."

They hurried down Twenty-second Street, their eyes going in every direction, searching the ground, the front steps of houses, even the trees.

"I never did go lookin' for somethin' unless I knew what it was," Hattie complained.

"Hush up and keep your eyes open."

They came out on Virginia Avenue. This was a more commercial street, and the sidewalk and muddy avenue were alive with traffic. In all this hustle and bustle, Anne wondered how they would ever find whatever it was Sudler Dill had hidden along his route, if he had even come this way. There were several ways to reach her house from the War Department, Anne thought, her hopes fading, and who was to say Mr. Dill had taken this one?

She continued along, fairly dragging Hattie by the arm. They soon reached the corner of Virginia Avenue and E Street. The muddy streets converged at an angle, forming a plaza that was filled with the carts of vendors.

"Ma'am!"

The shout brought Anne up short. A woman was waving at them from a cart a few feet away. Anne didn't know her, as she seldom shopped on this street.

"Come on, Hattie!" Anne caught her servant's arm and pulled her toward the jam seller.

"This must be for you, ma'am," the woman said. "A gentleman left it a short while ago and said his sister would be along to claim it. I seen you was the one by the way you was looking everywheres like you done lost something."

"Yes?" Anne said expectantly.

The woman held up a packet of papers but kept them close to her body. Her eyes were sly and greedy. "The gentleman said you'd give me something for watching it, ma'am."

"Oh?" Anne said, knowing the woman was probably lying. But all she cared about was getting those papers. For a brief, panicked instant, she realized she had no money. She was tempted to grab the packet and run, but it wouldn't do to make a ruckus on the street.

"He said you'd have something for me, ma'am," the woman repeated, a hardness creeping into her voice.

Hattie spoke up angrily. "She's tryin' to gouge you—"

Anne raised a hand to silence Hattie's irate outburst. The woman waited expectantly.

"I don't have any money with me," Anne said. She tugged the heavy shawl from her shoulders.

"Don't give her your shawl!" Hattie protested. "You'll catch your death."

"Hush, now, Hattie," Anne said, then turned to the woman. "Will you take this? It will help keep you warm."

The woman felt the material of the shawl between thick fingers. With a satisfied grin, she threw the shawl around her heavy shoulders. The fine garment contrasted sharply with her worn clothes. She tossed the packet to Anne. "Here's your dern papers."

"Come, Hattie," Anne said. As they walked away, Hattie took off her own coat and laid it over Anne's shoulders. "I don't want you catchin' cold, Miss Anne. Who am I gonna work for if you die of some fever?"

"I'm glad you're so concerned about me," Anne said wryly. "Now hurry up, so we'll both be too warm to catch cold."

They rushed back to the house, where Anne sat down in a chair by the fireplace in the parlor and read through the papers Sudler Dill had risked—and lost—everything to steal. What she saw proved that his sacrifice had been worthwhile, for if Anne understood these papers, it proved the Union was planning to bring a swift end to the Confederacy long before General Lee had a chance to launch his springtime campaign.

She hid the papers in a drawer and returned to her chair. In the morning she would deliver them to Mr. Conrad herself, for this information was too important to trust to Hattie or Henry. She would have left immediately, but she was expecting Colonel McDonnell to pay his respects at any moment, and maybe he would let slip something more about what General "Old Brains" Halleck was up to in preparation for the attack on Petersburg.

Mulholland climbed down from the bluff the morning of December 23 to meet the night boat from Washington. He was still limping from the stab wound he had received in the capital, although it was healing well enough. He would be in fine shape by the time the spring campaign began.

It was a gray, dismal morning, cold enough for the mud to freeze into hard ridges. Clouds rose with every breath of the damp, raw air that washed off the James and Appomattox rivers. The vessel—a side wheeled steamboat—cracked the thin ice that had formed overnight as it drew alongside the dock.

Mulholland spotted the man as soon as he came down the gangplank. Unlike the other groggy soldiers and officers who lumbered onto the dock, this one crossed nimbly from ship to shore, his eyes alert, darting here and there like a wary crow's. Strapped across his back was a long bundle wrapped in oilskin and tied with twine. He carried nothing else. He was black-bearded and his long hair fell down over the shoulders of his green tunic. No regular enlisted man would have been allowed to keep his hair that long. As if looking like a frontiersman wasn't enough, the man also wore the forest green uniform of Berdan's Sharpshooters. Although Colonel Hiram Berdan's famous regiment of marksmen had been disbanded and its soldiers sent to various other units, from time to time a man would be spotted wearing one of the distinctive coats.

Mulholland stood on shore, waiting for him. As the man approached, Mulholland had the feeling the fellow in the green coat was well aware he was standing there but was pointedly ignoring him.

"Corporal Bayliss?" Mulholland spoke up, annoyance creeping into his voice.

"Who might be asking?"

The man stood before Mulholland, thin as a gun barrel and reeking of stale whiskey. Must have been a card game on the night boat, Mulholland thought.

"I'm Major Mulholland. If you aren't Bayliss, be on your way. If you are Bayliss, you'd better salute damn quick before I take away that gun strapped to your back and put you to work driving a mule wagon."

That made the dark eyes smolder. But Bayliss saluted just well enough that Mulholland couldn't justifiably send him off to work with the mule skinners. Besides, he wanted a sharpshooter badly.

"Yes, sir."

"Come with me, corporal. We have work to do."

They made their way up the hill from the river. Corporal Bayliss's eyes flicked everywhere as he took in City Point.

"You really think some Reb is going to work his way in here, find some tree to hide behind, and pick off General Grant? There's not much in the way of cover."

Mulholland tried to place the accent. New England? It was possible, even though most of the sharpshooters he had known were from one of the border states or else the Midwest. He had supposed New Englanders no longer had much use for rifles and so were not very good marksmen.

"Oh, they'll find a way, Bayliss." He stopped short of telling this New England sharpshooter how General Grant had almost been assassinated at the capital. "Believe me, they will find a way."

"So you sent for me to be a guard dog, sir?"

"Not you in particular," Mulholland said. This man could stand to be taken down a notch or two, he thought. Arrogant men rankled

him. While arrogant officers sometimes had to be endured, he had
no patience whatsoever for arrogant enlisted men. "But someone like
you. One guard dog is about as good as another."

The New Englander grunted. "You might try asking the guard
dog what he thinks about that idea."

They hiked up to the headquarters building on the bluff without
speaking another word. Mulholland's limp became more pronounced
because he hadn't been getting much exercise around headquarters
and the walk was fairly steep. Lately, too, he had been drinking more
than his share of whiskey and smoking almost as many cigars as
General Grant. His liver ached dully. The cold robbed him of breath
as they hiked, and he was soon breathing loudly. *Damn.* He would get
his marching legs back come springtime.

Bayliss followed along quietly. Mulholland had to look over his
shoulder to make sure the man was still there. He noticed with some
annoyance that Bayliss wasn't even breathing hard.

"What do you think?" Mulholland panted once they had reached
the promontory where headquarters stood. To the north were the
wharves they had just come from and the river. But to the south and
west was a gray blur of wintry trees.

Bayliss studied the distant trees with a practiced eye, squinting
toward the woods.

"Those trees are over one thousand yards away," he said. "He'd
have to be one hell of a shot to hit the general from out there."

"Could you do it?"

In answer, Bayliss unslung the bundle across his back and began
unwrapping it. He soon revealed a rifle with a heavy, octagonal
barrel. The stock was checked so that a man with sweaty hands could
better grip it. A telescopic sight ran all the way from the point of
comb to the end of the forestock.

"I've never seen anything like that," Mulholland said, admiring the
rifle. But then, he was a staff officer, not much given to noticing the
details of rifles. This one appeared to have a unique design that
hinted at a special purpose. "New issue?"

Bayliss grunted, which Mulholland now understood was a laugh.
A taciturn New England sharpshooter's way of laughing.

"No, sir, these rifles have been around since before the war.
Imported from England. Not too many of them about."

Bayliss went on to explain. It was a Whitworth rifle, he said. In a
.455 caliber. At one hundred yards it shot a pattern so tight you could

cover it with your hand and not even stretch the fingers. At one thousand, a decent marksman could drop a man every time."

"Lord," Mulholland said. "It's a wonder the whole army doesn't have those."

"That's because like most any purebred, it's temperamental. Hard to load because the bullet is seated tightly in the barrel. Tends to foul after only a few shots, which is fine for the kind of work I do with it, but not very practical for the ranks." He grinned crookedly. "But for all its faults, Mother of God is it accurate."

Bayliss's knobby thumb stroked the rifle tenderly.

"I'll have a man show you your quarters," Mulholland said, anxious to be away from this strange soldier.

Bayliss did not appear to be listening. He was studying the terrain, one hand raised to shade his eyes. "I could do it," he said. "I could shoot the general. But I'd want to be closer in, or else find out when the general was riding out to make an inspection of the lines. I'd get in a tree so I could shoot over whatever escort was riding with him."

Mulholland nodded, glad he had brought the man despite his rough manner. What he wanted was a sharpshooter's perspective on how to defend against another sharpshooter. He had made inquiries and found that Corporal Bayliss was one of the best. Certainly, he had done his share of sniping. If anyone could get inside the head of a Rebel sharpshooter, Mulholland believed Bayliss could.

"Keep that rifle handy and stay within sight of the general at all times," Mulholland said. "I'm afraid someone's going to make an attempt on General Grant sooner rather than later."

Bayliss grinned. "I'll be ready," he said.

From that morning on, the sharpshooter seldom left his post. He did not associate much with the other guards, however, because he appeared to consider himself to be above mere sentries. O'Malley could be overheard referring to Bayliss as "the stuck-up Eagle-eyed bastard." But never within earshot of Bayliss, of course.

General Grant gave grudging approval to Mulholland's use of someone like Bayliss, if only because he was concerned about the safety of his wife, Julia, while she was in City Point. Grant had other problems to occupy his mind, for there was always a stream of couriers coming and going, as well as visitors.

In the days just after the trip to Washington, one of the main topics of gossip around headquarters had been that Robert Lincoln, the president's son, was going to join the staff. Mulholland had seen a copy of the telegram from President Lincoln:

> Please read and answer this letter as though I was not President, but only a friend. My son, now in his twenty-second year, having graduated at Harvard, wishes to see something of the war before it ends. I do not wish to put him in the ranks, nor yet to give him a commission to which those who have already served long are better entitled and better qualified to hold. Could he, without embarrassment to you, or detriment to the service, go into your Military family with some nominal rank, I, and not the public, furnishing his necessary means? If no, say so without the least hesitation, because I am as anxious, and as deeply interested, that you shall not be encumbered as you yourself can be.

Robert Lincoln arrived soon afterward. Grant had decided the president's son should be a captain. His position? Assistant adjutant general of volunteers. Which meant that he fetched coffee and ran messages all over City Point. Grant had read between the lines of Lincoln's telegram, and he wouldn't let the president's son anywhere near the fighting.

None of the staff had ever seen Lincoln's son before, aside from likenesses in the illustrated newspapers. He had the nickname of "The Prince of Rails," from his father's campaign days when Robert had toured the country by rail car with the presidential candidate.

He looked nothing like his father. While Lincoln was a tall, emaciated, strange-looking fellow, Robert was a stylish young man. He wore a small mustache and a nicely tailored uniform. He got along well enough with everyone but was not especially popular with the staff, although he carried out his duties to the letter. He rarely mentioned his father, and it soon became obvious that the great man and his son were not very close.

"He's a nice fellow," said Adam Badeau, another one of the headquarters officers, as he, Mulholland, and some others stood talking. "Bright, manly, gentlemanly."

"He's annoying as a puppy dog," Mulholland said. He was in a foul mood, for some malady was causing his bowels to run like water. Daily, he felt himself growing thinner. "That Lincoln is always jumping into everything."

"He's young," Badeau agreed. "But I like him. He says he wanted to be in the service long ago, but his father would not allow it."

"More like his mother wouldn't allow it," Bowers said. "They said when their son Willie died that she almost went mad. She wasn't going to send her oldest off to the war."

"He could be worse," Mulholland said. Indeed, most of them admired the fact that Robert, for all his occasional pomposity, was only trying to do his best. He was working hard to make his own mark rather than to rely on his father's reputation.

As Mulholland left with Joe Bowers, they passed the sharpshooter Bayliss, who was lurking near the headquarters building.

"Keep an eye out, Bayliss," he said.

The sharpshooter answered with his habitual crooked grin. "I am, Major, I am. He's here, you know."

"Who?" Bowers asked.

"Ask the Major," Bayliss answered.

They walked off, the marksman's comments putting Mulholland's teeth on edge. Even the devil-may-care Bowers had taken notice.

"That man you brought in is a strange one," Bowers said. "What's he talking about, 'He's here.' Who's *he*?"

"Remember what happened in Washington?"

"Hell, Brendan, who could forget that? I think back on it as a nightmare."

"They're going to try it again."

"Who?"

Mulholland shrugged. "The Confederate Secret Service, a group of radical officers. I don't know who's behind it. Maybe even a man working alone, some Yankee hater."

Bowers nodded. "I could see where that might happen. Do you think there's a chance they might . . . well . . ."

"Anything is possible. That's why I brought in that man Bayliss. He was one of Berdan's Sharpshooters. He's one of the best."

"Fight fire with fire," Bowers said. "Maybe we ought to tell Bayliss to go shoot General Lee for us."

Mulholland laughed. "If only that would work! The war would be over soon enough."

"If the Rebs don't surrender by June, I think the general might agree to such a plan. Especially if they're sending sharpshooters to get *him*."

They paused for a moment and took in the teeming camp that City Point had become. Everywhere they looked there were tents, shanties, workmen, wagons, soldiers. For a single, fearful moment, Mulholland let himself imagine a man in that tangle of men with a gun under his coat, a fellow with beady Southern eyes, marching up to headquarters with a deadly purpose.

As if reading his thoughts, Bowers said, "Maybe you should double the guard."

"The general won't hear of it."

"I may put a word in with a higher power."

"Who? Are you going to ask Robert Lincoln to send word to his father?"

Bowers laughed. "Higher than that, even! I may mention the need for more guards to Mrs. Grant."

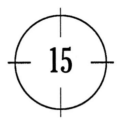

15

Sudler Dill was taken straight to Old Capitol Prison. As the tall, faded red sides of the prison came into sight at the corner of First and A Streets, Dill felt his legs give way beneath him.

"Stand up and walk like a man," one of his captors growled, and the two men shoved him upright between them.

"What's going to happen?" Dill managed to ask, although he thought he knew the answer all too well. That which he had dreaded for so long had finally occurred; he had been arrested for spying, and there would only be one end for him now.

"We're going to lock you up tight with the rest of that Rebel scum," the detective said. "Then I imagine Colonel Baker is going to have a little talk with you."

Dill felt the hairs stiffen at the back of his neck. Everyone had heard of the ruthless Union spycatcher, Lafayette Baker. He had a reputation for cruelty, and Dill was not looking forward to the encounter.

The prison was a rambling building, with additions that wandered off in several directions. It had housed Congress after the British burned Washington during the War of 1812, and later became a boarding house. Although it was huge, the building had never been intended for a prison. It looked decidedly makeshift, with boards nailed over some of the windows and bars on others. That it served its purpose well, however, there could be no doubt, because dozens of pale faces stared out, watching with interest as another Rebel was brought to the Old Capitol.

My God, Dill thought. *What is to become of me?*

They passed through what had once been a grand arched entryway. Inside, the place had been cut up like a rabbit's warren, and Dill was half-shoved, half-carried down various hallways and up short flights of steps. Crumbling walls and scraps of wood and trash were everywhere. Filthy, stinking clothing lay in piles, and the dark corners seemed to move . . . which they did, Dill realized, because of the swarms of rats.

"Put him in there," ordered a hulking guard with traces of a German accent. The man was at least twice Dill's size. "Number eight."

The men threw Dill into a room, and he found himself lying in a clutter on the floor. "You just sit tight till the colonel gets here," one of them said.

"He won't be going nowhere," the guard said. He shook his head. "Look at that, a traitor if I ever saw one. What will they do with him?"

"Shoot him." The men sneered at him and then were gone. The big guard gave him a wicked look, then shut the door.

In those first few moments after the door shut, Dill thought he would go insane. *Imprisoned!* He took a few deep breaths to calm himself and inspected his surroundings. There was a single, barred window in the room that overlooked the city's broad streets. The room was furnished with an iron bed, battered wooden table, and slop jar. The jar was half full of someone else's waste and stank terribly. Dill tried to ignore it; the odor was the least of his worries.

He had hardly looked around the room when the door opened and a tall, heavyset officer walked in. Two dangerous-looking young men were with him, wearing civilian clothes, and Dill wondered what was coming next.

"Don't you know to salute an officer when he comes into a room?" the man asked lazily. He nodded at one of the men, who stepped forward, grabbed Dill's arm, and forced it into a salute.

"Who are you?" Dill stammered.

"Colonel Jonathan Wilcox, deputy special provost marshal for the War Department."

"You're not Lafayette Baker."

"No, I'm not." Wilcox sighed. "But Lafe Baker is a busy man. Besides, you'll find I do just fine in his place."

Dill noted the colonel's flinty gray eyes and wide shoulders and wondered why he had bothered to bring the other two men with him. He started to introduce himself, "I'm Sudler—"

A fist cracked against Dill's jaw, and his world exploded in black and red. He went down on the floor and hung his head, shaking it to clear his double vision.

There were rules about the treatment of prisoners. But all such rules were dispensed with at the Old Capitol, the Union's vilest prison. Many prisoners had been killed trying to "escape," and Dill wondered if that was what was about to happen to him.

"As of now, your name is Horseshit," Wilcox said. "Now tell me, Mr. Horseshit, what you were doing on H Street? Who were you going to see?"

The detectives had already told Wilcox what had happened. Dill had led the detectives to the home of Anne Clark, whom Wilcox knew well enough from his frequent visits to her *boudoir*. The news had astonished Wilcox. Was she a spy like this fool here? Or had Dill simply picked a house on that street to avoid giving away the one he was truly there to visit? Dill had claimed he was going to see a man named Walter, but Wilcox's men had quickly determined there was no such person in that neighborhood.

"I was going to see Mr. Walter." Dill's voice quavered.

Wilcox shook his head in disgust, and the two bully boys moved in.

Dill raised his weak arms to protect himself, but it did no good. One of the thugs kicked Dill in the ribs, and he felt them give. The pain was excruciating, and he gasped for air.

They hauled him to his feet and shoved him against a wall of the room. While one man held him up, the other went to work with his fists, punching Dill first in the face, then in his damaged ribs. He tried to cry out but didn't have the breath for it.

"All right, all right," the colonel said. "Have you had enough, Mr. Horseshit? There is no Mr. Walter. Now, tell me who you were going to see on H Street."

Dill summoned all his breath and managed to stammer through lacerated lips, "Go to hell, you damn Yankee."

Wilcox laughed out loud, then stepped forward and slapped Dill so hard the sound echoed down the hall. Dill's face stung like it was on fire. "Give him another go, boys."

A fist slammed into Dill's jawbone, and, mercifully, he blacked out. The two men continued to kick and beat him even after he had slumped to the floor.

Wilcox went out into the hallway, perplexed by the news that Dill had led the detectives right to Miss Clark's house. They had told him she appeared not to know Sudler Dill in the least, and as tempted as he was to believe that, Wilcox had his doubts.

Could it be possible his sweet Anne had been playing him for a fool this whole time? She was the most outspoken woman for the Union cause in the capital, it seemed, but Wilcox realized now that might have been a ruse. Mentally, he recounted what he had told Anne upstairs in her *boudoir*. Maybe he had let slip some War Department gossip, but nothing that could be of much interest to a Rebel spy.

But the idea that she might have tricked him! Wilcox thought briefly of going to the house on H Street and whipping the truth out of her, much as his men had beaten that miserable wretch Dill.

He had no intentions, however, of dragging Anne Clark to the Old Capitol. If she was a spy, he could muzzle her easily enough. It would be disastrous to his career if word got out that his mistress was a Rebel spy. Besides, there was no sense in putting her in prison when he could have her all to himself. With a smile on his face, Wilcox made his way back out of the stinking corridors and headed for his office in the War Department.

After Wilcox and his henchmen left, Dill slowly regained consciousness. His whole body throbbed with pain, and his face wore a mask of blood. He still managed a weak curse, which he directed at the closed door of his prison cell.

"Damn you Yankees. Damn you all."

He lay there, gathering his strength. Dill hoped he had not given Anne Clark away. It had seemed so important to get the information he had stolen to her that he had been willing to take any chance. Maybe it had been a mistake. Or maybe they believed him.

One thing was certain: Wilcox and his thugs would be back, and next time they might succeed in beating the truth out of him. Dill couldn't see himself begging for mercy from the Yankees and trading an end to the pain for information of his spy work.

Dill managed to pull himself to his feet. Everything hurt. His ribs were probably broken, because each breath was a fiery agony. He forced himself upright and looked around the room. The door to the hallway was still closed, so the big German guard out there couldn't see him and probably assumed he was still passed out.

Sudler Dill then undertook the bravest act of his life.

He took off his coat and slipped his suspenders from his shoulders. Then he unbuttoned them from the band of his trousers.

He stretched them between his hands and considered their length, hoping they would be sturdy enough.

Dill went to the window. It was not terribly high, but the bars across the windows were at a good height. He kicked over the slop jar, and its stinking contents ran over the floorboards in a spreading pool. Dill couldn't smell it because his nose was broken and still streaming blood. He maneuvered the slop jar under the window, upended it, and used it as a step. He was just high enough to reach the top of the window bars. His side ached considerably when he raised his hands over his head, and Dill had to stop twice to catch his breath before one end of his suspenders was tied to the window bars.

He pulled on the knot as hard as he could to test it, but the strap didn't budge. Resolutely, he tied the free end of his suspenders around his neck and secured it with another double knot.

Dill felt strangely calm, now that it had come to this. The Yankees would trouble him no more, and he felt a sense of elation—of victory—in having cheated them out of the pleasure of killing him or making him reveal his secrets.

He took a deep breath and stepped off the slop jar, kicking it across the room in the process.

The strap stretched but wouldn't let his feet touch the floor. Dill kicked his legs wildly. Without thinking, he found some final surge of strength and clawed at the strap strangling him, but his arms were too weak to pull himself back up.

Be still, some dying part of his brain urged him. *Let it take you.* His dancing legs and flailing arms moved more slowly and finally hung limp.

It was an hour before the guard opened the door. Dill's face was purple, and his swollen tongue protruded from his mouth. His dead eyes bugged from their sockets and the air was putrid from the contents of the slop jar soaking into the floorboards and the unmistakable stink of Dill's own bowels.

"Mother of God," the big German gasped, and he made the sign of the cross.

Cole and Snodgrass slithered down the steep cliff that formed the western bank of the James River.

"It's damn cold down here by the water," Snodgrass complained.

"But nobody will ever find us here," Cole explained. "If we hide out on top of the cliff, our chances of running into a Yankee patrol are pretty good. We'll be all right down here."

Snodgrass grunted grudgingly and looked out across the flat, brown water. The mighty James. Nearly a mile distant he could see the wharves at City Point and the ships riding at anchor in the river at the Yankee supply base. A few big houses sprang from the bluff overlooking the river, and he wondered if one of them might be General Grant's headquarters.

It was December 26, the day after Christmas. It hadn't been much of a holiday, and Snodgrass remembered some of the fine Christmas dinners he'd had in days gone by. The memory of them was enough to make his mouth water.

He glanced again at the skiff that would carry them to the opposite shore once darkness fell. It was a rotten, leaky old thing they had untied from a wharf downriver. He wasn't looking forward to a voyage in that unsteady craft. Snodgrass preferred his boats much bigger, with a paddle wheel and a steam engine.

"Tell me again why we have to cross that river," Snodgrass said. "I'm still waiting for you to make sense."

"I have some unfinished business with the Yankees," Cole said in a cold tone that made Snodgrass reluctant to ask anything else.

"Hell, Cole, the war will be over come spring. Ain't no sense quarreling with the Yankees at this point. In a few weeks we won't even be enemies anymore."

"You ain't got to come," Cole said. "Stay right here if you want."

Cole squatted on his haunches by the water's edge and took a hunk of bread from his pocket. It was hard, crusty, and stale, and Cole's jaw worked as he chewed, a hard knot of muscle flexing along his jawbone.

Snodgrass looked behind him at the steep cliff, then out again at the water. His options were limited. The countryside was crawling with Yankee patrols, and he knew they had survived this long mainly due to Cole's woods sense. He could smell things in the air just like an animal, including Yankee cavalry.

"We're still going to join up with one of them work camps?" Snodgrass asked.

"Hell, yes."

"I reckon they'll feed us, all right," Snodgrass said. "I reckon I can wait out the war there just as well as anywhere."

"Then you're in." Cole nodded. "We'll set out as soon as it gets dark."

"You really think we can get by all the sentries over there?"

"We'll find out," Cole said.

"Despite all our victories elsewhere, all anyone can see is the Army of Northern Virginia," Grant said as he sat in his chair by the stove. "General Lee is about where's he's been all along, holding us off."

"Their army is nothing but skeletons and corn husks, sir," Adam Badeau answered. "We'll blow them away this spring like a strong wind."

"Mmm," muttered Grant. "I only hope those in Washington see fit to keep me in command until then. Lincoln's behind me. But Congress is impatient for action."

"Politicians," Bowers said, derision in his voice. "I'd like to see them out here, freezing their arses off."

Grant gave him a sharp look, and Bowers reddened, turning to Mrs. Grant. "Pardon me, Mrs. Grant. It's this soldier's life that's ruined my manners. For a moment I forgot there was a lady present."

Julia Grant smiled to show she had taken no offense. She kept her head tilted to one side because she was cross-eyed and rarely looked at anyone directly. "You were ruined a long time before you joined this army, Joe Bowers."

Her comment brought laughter, which was scarce enough at headquarters. Yesterday's Christmas celebration had been enjoyable, but winter's dreariness had settled over them once more.

Julia Grant rose from her chair by the stove, her wide dress expanding and filling the cramped living quarters with the rustle of crinoline. "Come dear, let's turn in," she said, as if the room wasn't full of soldiers.

General Grant yawned prodigiously. "Yes, it's getting late."

He turned to Adam Badeau. "Alert me if anything arises."

"Of course, sir."

There had been some fairly reliable intelligence that the Confederate fleet upriver in the part of the James River that Southern forces controlled was going to make a raid on City Point. When the Confederate gunboats planned to make this foray wasn't known for certain, but no one was particularly worried as the river was well defended and obstructions had been planted upstream to prevent the passage of enemy boats.

Grant turned to Mulholland. "Keep an eye out, Major."

"Yes, sir."

The general and his wife said their good nights and went off to bed.

Mulholland was amazed at how the presence of his wife had changed the general. Grant hardly cared a whit for his own safety. But now that his wife had come to City Point, he had suddenly become interested in the measures Mulholland was taking to secure headquarters. He heartily approved of the sharpshooter who was on almost constant duty outside, although that strange New Englander made many on the staff uneasy.

With the general safely in his room, Bowers produced a whiskey bottle and poured the few staff officers present a generous cupful.

"Nothing like it to warm the bones," Bowers said.

"Some decent brandy would be better," Badeau complained. "This stump whiskey you've got here could take the hair off a dog."

No one argued with that. And no one refused a second splash of whiskey when Bowers made the rounds of the room. Indeed, Mulholland thought it was the perfect way to drive off the damp, clinging cold that had settled over the army encampment along the riverbank.

Then the door opened and a courier came in, causing some of that chilly dampness to wash in. Mulholland shivered and backed toward the stove.

"Captain Terry's compliments, sir," the young officer said to Badeau. "He wanted me to inform you that the Reb gunboats have got loose on the river."

"What?"

"Yes, sir. All six of those ironclads they've had upriver slipped past the obstructions and the boats are headed for City Point."

The courier's news stunned them all into silence. But only for a moment, and then the staff sprang into action.

"I'll wake the general," Badeau said. "He should know this."

Bowers hid the whiskey bottle. The rest of them quickly drained their cups or stepped to the door to fling the stuff out into the night.

Mulholland heard O'Malley curse as the liquid splashed on the hard mud. " 'Tis a terrible sin. Merciful Mary, to throw good whiskey on the ground is a thing not to be forgiven!"

Sin or not, no one wanted to be caught with a cup of whiskey in hand should Mrs. Grant come out of the back room. She knew her husband's weakness well enough and would not want him tempted by his subordinates.

Grant appeared, looking groggy and even more rumpled than usual, if that was possible. He was still pulling on his coat.

"What's going on?"

Badeau quickly outlined the situation.

"How long ago did they get past the obstructions?"

"I don't know, General. But we may be in trouble."

Six Confederate gunboats were capable of doing serious harm to the immense supply base at City Point. If they came close enough, they could lob shell after shell into the densely packed wharves at this point where the James and Appomattox rivers merged and cause a great deal of destruction. It was a precarious situation.

Grant knew it. Mulholland could tell the normally calm general was ill at ease when he immediately lit up a cigar, sat down at his makeshift desk and began writing out orders as quickly as his pencil could scribble across a page.

The commotion soon brought Julia Grant into the office. She had thrown on some clothes, and her head was covered by a nightcap. She slipped among the knot of men, although she hardly went unnoticed. Some were embarrassed to be caught up in a fight with a woman present. Many of the staff officers agreed that war was not for a woman, especially if she happened to be the commanding general's wife.

"Are the Rebel gunboats likely to fire on our little household here?" she asked lightly, trying to make it sound like a joke.

"They'll never get this far," said Grant, puffing ferociously on his cigar and sending out great gouts of tobacco smoke. His pencil scratched across yet more sheets of paper as he wrote out orders to reinforce the shore batteries. "Besides, we have the *Onondaga* on patrol. She's one of our biggest ironclads. Any of the Rebel gunboats that tangle with her would be like the canary taking on the cat."

"Well," said Julia Grant. "I knew there wasn't anything to worry about."

Mulholland left the hubbub in the office behind and went out to the front of the headquarters building to check on his guards. He knew O'Malley was one of the men on duty and was glad of it, for the Irishman had a watchful eye and knew most of the couriers by sight. Anyone suspicious would be stopped and questioned at bayonet point. To his surprise, he also found the sharpshooter Bayliss in the shadows.

"What's happening, Major?" Bayliss asked.

"Some of the Reb gunboats are loose on the river. There's some fear they may try to shell the camp here."

"Confusion like this can be a dangerous time," Bayliss said quietly. "Men scurrying about in the dark, no telling if one of them's an assassin."

"O'Malley knows most of the couriers by sight. He'll stop anyone else."

"You might ask them to draw the curtains, too, sir. You can see right into the damn office."

As Mulholland walked around the building, he was horrified to find he could look right in among the staff from outside. There was the general sitting at his desk, his wife beside him. As he watched officers walk to and fro, he was reminded of a play on a stage, only there was no dialogue. He hurried back inside and pulled the curtains across the windows.

Grant read the latest dispatch and scowled. "The *Onondaga* has lost her head of steam and the skipper has taken her downriver, out of range of the gunboats. Of all times!"

Suddenly the thumping of guns began, the noise carrying up the bluff to headquarters.

"Here they come," someone said.

Mrs. Grant pulled her chair closer to her husband's desk and asked in a low voice which all of them nonetheless could hear, "Ulyss, what had I better do?"

"Well, the fact is, Julia, you oughtn't to be here." Grant attempted a laugh, but it came out choked on cigar smoke.

"Sir, I could get an ambulance up here to carry Mrs. Grant out of range," Mulholland said.

"Should I go, Ulyss?" she asked.

Grant chewed his cigar and hunched over in his chair. Mulholland thought the general looked a good ten years older than he actually was.

"Let's not run out into the night just yet," he said. "We'll concentrate for the moment on halting those gunboats. Send word to the batteries along the shore that they'll have to make a fight of it."

"Yes, sir."

"Now, Mulholland, bring up that ambulance, just in case. We'll have plenty of time for Mrs. Grant to get away should the need arise. The firing on the river will tell us how close they've come."

On the other side of the James River, a leaky wooden skiff had started out from the base of the cliff. It was a dark and moonless night, and the muzzle flashes of the shore batteries upriver were blinding as they fired at the oncoming Rebel gunboats.

"We picked one hell of a night to cross the river," Snodgrass said. "If any of those batteries get sight of us, they'll blow us out of the water."

"They ain't goin' to spot us," Cole said as he leaned into the oars, pulling the skiff easily across the black water. "Them Yanks is lookin' for gunboats, not a little ol' boat like we're in."

The Confederate gunboats were visible only when a round would explode over the river. The gunboats weren't wasting their time firing at the shore batteries, except for an occasional shot. They had better targets, because if they came in range of the huge wharves and warehouses at the Union supply base, not to mention the scores of vessels anchored in the James, there would be hell to pay. Even two or three gunboats could do terrible damage if they were able to shell City Point for any length of time. The pandemonium made it a perfect night to slip across the James River in a skiff.

There was a high-pitched whistling sound, and suddenly a round shot slashed into the river, sending up a fountain of spray.

"Oh Lordy!" Snodgrass hissed. "Somebody's done seen us."

Another cannonball hit the water, so close that the splash soaked them in the boat.

"Get down," Cole ordered. "We're making too good of a target. Get down flat in the boat."

Snodgrass ground his teeth as he heard the next shot whistle toward them. But the cannonball went wide. "Why the hell are we goin' to the Yankee side of the river, anyhow?" he demanded.

"I have to shoot General Grant," Cole answered.

Snodgrass would have thought anyone else was joking, but not Cole. "Ain't that somethin'," was all he said, wondering to himself what he had gotten into.

In the distance, Mulholland could hear the guns along the river. He went outside, saw bright stabs of flame from a battery on the shore. Answering pinpricks of light out on the water. It reminded him of fireflies on a June night. Only the thud of the guns indicated a fight was taking place, the noise rolling downriver long after the flash of the cannons.

"Looks like there's a bit of a scrap going on," O'Malley said, not sounding too concerned. "It's sure got headquarters stirred up like a nest of hornets."

"There'll be hell to pay if those Reb gunboats make it down here."

"With all those guns going at them, the only place they'll be going, Major sir, is to a watery grave. Now isn't that a cold thought, men going into the black river on a January night such as this? It almost makes a man sorry for them Rebs."

"You just keep your eyes open for those same Rebs in case not all of them do go down in the river."

"Yes, Major sir." O'Malley saluted.

Mulholland hurried to see about the horses for Mrs. Grant's escape. Until his eyes became accustomed to the darkness, he went carefully along the muddy avenue leading to the stables. Several soldiers were up, stirred to restlessness by the bombardment.

"Are the Rebs tryin' to break out of Petersburg?" a voice asked.

"No, that's just them comin' down the river to give us what fer," another answered. "Didn't even know they still had it in them."

Mulholland found the stable, more by smell than sight. The odor of straw and horses was powerful, and he slipped inside the shed, grateful for the warmth. Horses whinnied softly. No wonder the Savior was born in a stable, he thought. It was a gentle place on a winter's night.

A ring of men were playing cards around a lantern. They all looked up, surprised to see a staff officer in their midst and soon hitched a horse onto an ambulance. Because an army did not have much use for carriages, the ambulance wagons were the next best thing. They were often used to transport dignitaries visiting the troops, or officers too indisposed to ride a horse.

Mulholland took a lantern and led the horse toward headquarters while one of the stable hands drove.

"What's going on, sir?" the man asked, raising his voice over the distant thunder of river batteries. "Are we under attack?"

"Yes, some Reb gunboats are on the river. We'll have to get Mrs.

Grant to safety if the firing comes much closer."

"Hell, Major," the driver said. "What's a woman doing here? The general ought to know better than that. This ain't no place for a woman."

Mulholland didn't answer, but he was beginning to think the same thing.

Headquarters was only a short distance away, and they pulled up to find a milling knot of officers who had come up to find out what was happening. He frowned, for these men should have been with their units in case there were orders to move. Couriers rode back and forth at breakneck speed into the night. One passed too close and their horse shied, rearing back in its traces. Mulholland put his hand on the mare's flank, soothing her. "Whoa, girl. Whoa, now."

When they reached headquarters, pandemonium still reigned. Mulholland left the driver and ambulance outside and squeezed back into the cramped headquarters office, which was by now full of officers awaiting orders.

The general was busy, so Mulholland said to Mrs. Grant, "The ambulance is ready should you need it, ma'am."

"Thank you, Major," she said, sighing. "I suppose I shouldn't even be here, at the front. It's easy to forget there's a war going on."

"The Rebels have been hoping to catch us off guard for some time now," he replied. "Their only hope is a surprise attack."

Grant held up a hand for silence in the room. "This dispatch just came in from one of our posts upriver. Only one of the Rebel gunboats has made it down the James," he said. "Just four of their boats started out, not six. Two ran aground and one was destroyed by our river batteries. That leaves just one vessel."

"Where the hell did they get six boats from, that's what I'd like to know," Bowers fairly shouted. "Some of these damn people can't count."

"Four or six, it ain't exactly the Spanish Armada," someone said.

"I suppose I won't be needing that ambulance, after all," Mrs. Grant said.

"There's still one Rebel gunboat on the river," Mulholland said. "With the munitions we have stored along the water, a few shells could still be terribly destructive."

Another courier came in, and Grant smiled when he read the dispatch.

"Well, I wouldn't worry much about that Rebel gunboat. She's going to have her hands full. The *Onondaga* has gotten back into action, after all." Indeed, the *Onondaga* was a powerful ironclad, and a lone Rebel gunboat that tangled with her would not fare well. The general stood, stretched. "Maybe now we can all get a good night's sleep. Come, Mrs. Grant, let's to bed."

The staff said their polite good nights, and the general and his wife disappeared into their private rooms. Mulholland went out and sent the ambulance back to the stable. By the time he came back into the office, the whiskey bottle had reappeared.

"I'll take a drop," he said, finding a tin cup. "Just the thing after all that excitement."

"I wish those Rebs would just give up," someone said. "I guess they don't know any better. It's like when you chop off a snake's head and the body keeps squirming."

"We'll see what happens in spring," Bowers said, his face firmly set. "We'll chop up them snakes into little pieces."

16

Anne should have known there was going to be trouble as soon as she saw Colonel Wilcox. His pig like eyes were bloodshot, and his breath reeked of whiskey.

"Hello, Anne," he said and leered.

They were in the parlor. It was the day after Christmas, and Wilcox had come at six o'clock, which was late for one of his visits. Wilcox always made a point of getting home in time for supper with his family, although Anne wondered if he was more concerned about missing a meal than with seeing his wife and children.

No dinner with the family tonight, she thought, looking at the ugliness in his eyes. He had been drinking to work himself up to something, and she doubted any good would come of it.

"How nice to see you, Jonathan," she smiled, hoping to soften him. He would be a dangerous bully, she thought. "You haven't brought any of your soldiers along tonight, I see. You're on a lone mission?"

"You could say that."

"Won't Mrs. Wilcox be worried about you?"

He waved a hand in dismissal. "She has her hands full. One of the ladies in her hospital commission is ill, and she's seeing to the woman's children. She'll be out late."

"I see," Anne said. She attempted another smile, much less warm this time. "So you've come to pay me a visit?"

"We have something we must discuss," he said. He crossed to the table where she kept the decanter of brandy and poured himself a large glass.

"I could use a drop of that myself," she said.

Wilcox nodded, poured in a finger of brandy for her. Neither of them sat down, but stood with their glasses by the fire.

"What a pleasant way to spend a winter evening," he said. "A fire, brandy, the company of a beautiful woman. It can't be more than twenty degrees outside. I do feel sorry for those poor Rebels locked up in Old Capitol Prison. There's not a spark of heat in the place. I imagine some of the weaker ones will freeze to death this night."

Anne immediately thought of poor Sudler Dill. There had been no news of him. She still considered it her fault that he had been captured, because he had been coming to bring her information.

"Let's talk of more pleasant subjects, Jonathan," she said.

He smiled wickedly and slurped his brandy. "You don't find the thought of prison pleasant?"

"Why, no."

"Then perhaps you should listen closely to my proposition."

Anne stared at him. His drunken eyes were set far back in his fat face. She struggled against an overwhelming feeling of revulsion. Wilcox had never been one of her favorites. Even old Colonel McDonnell was preferable. He was pompous and dull, but kind enough in his own way. Anne really didn't want to hear what Wilcox was about to say, but she knew she had no choice.

"What on earth are you scheming?" she asked. Her patience dangled by a thread.

"It seems that *you're* the one who's been scheming," he said. "You're the one who's a spy."

She tried to laugh but didn't do a very good job of it. It came out as a strangled noise. She felt cold all over, and the glass nearly slipped from her fingers. She took a sip of brandy to brace herself. "I don't know what you're talking about."

"Come off it, Anne. I know all about you. That note you sent me about the assassination attempt. How did you know about it unless you were a party to the sharpshooter's plans? You sent me a warning, I'm not sure why. Maybe because you were afraid your precious Major Mulholland might get hurt? Well, he did, anyhow. Your sharpshooter friend put a knife in him."

"Stabbed?" Brendan's note had only mentioned a scratch.

"He'll live," Wilcox said bitterly. He took another gulp of brandy. "I have other proof. That War Department clerk who was spying . . . Sudler Dill. He was carrying information to your house, Anne. How do you explain that?"

"I don't know what you're talking about."

Wilcox laughed. "I knew you would deny everything. You're smart. Every whore has to be smart."

Anne moved to slap him, but he caught her hand easily in his own and squeezed it so hard she cried out. He let go, laughing even harder. "You are a feisty spying whore, at that."

"You bastard."

"How you Rebels curse! That's exactly what you friend Mr. Dill called me before he hung himself."

"What?"

"Oh, you didn't know?" Wilcox smiled cruelly. "It seems he couldn't bear the thought of being in a Yankee prison. I talked to him first to find out what he knew. That's one of my duties as deputy special provost marshal, to interrogate certain prisoners. Your Mr. Dill told me everything, Anne. Everything."

Wilcox was lying, but there was no way Anne could know. He went on: "Maybe Mr. Dill had an attack of conscience. No sooner did we leave his cell than he used his suspenders to hang himself. It must have taken him a while to die, from the looks of him. It wasn't neat and quick like it would have been with a rope."

Anne slumped into her chair, her eyes staring blankly ahead. She hadn't felt this way since she'd had the news of her beloved Rayford Hollander dying at Sharpsburg. She had not loved Mr. Dill, of course, but she had admired him. He had more courage than a hundred Jonathan Wilcoxes. He had served the Cause. Now he was dead, thanks to the Yankees.

"What do you want?" Anne asked.

The blank look gone, her eyes took on a sharp focus that startled Wilcox even through his liquor-fogged brain. He realized, as he never had before, that this could be a dangerous woman. After all, she had fooled him for so long that if it hadn't been for recent events, he would have never guessed she was a Rebel spy. But the brandy had made him bold.

"Two things," he said, looking down at her from where he stood by the fireplace.

"Go on."

"The first is that you'll see only me. You may be a whore, but I want you to be my whore and nobody else's."

"Your mistress?"

"Yes," Wilcox said. He smiled. "I like the sound of that. It should also keep whatever fact-gathering you're doing in check. Unlike some other loose-lipped fools—your precious Major Mulholland for one— I've never let slip anything useful."

"I'll need money," Anne said. "I can't live on nothing."

Wilcox shrugged. "That's not unreasonable. I'll give you a few dollars a month to keep yourself up. I can't have my woman looking like one of those whores that you see hanging around the barrack's gate."

"You truly are a bastard," Anne said.

Wilcox laughed. "Save your praise. You haven't heard my second rule."

"Which is?"

"I want you to spy for me."

Anne grabbed the arms of her chair and hissed at him. "Never!"

"You haven't much choice, Anne. You'll see. Now, I know there are people in the city you pass information to. I want their names. Anyone who brings you information—like the late Mr. Dill—I want their names as well."

"I'll never be a traitor," she said.

"You already are! A traitor to the Union. Treason, Anne. Think of it." He slapped his hands together and rubbed them for warmth. "I have a nice little cell in Old Capitol Prison picked out just for you, unless you agree to cooperate."

Anne smiled at him coldly. "Aren't you forgetting something?"

"What might that be, Anne?"

"All I have to do is make sure word gets to the right people, *Colonel*, and your career will be ruined. Isn't it your job to catch spies? You were too arrogant to ever think I might be one. Imagine the scandal it would cause in Washington when word gets out that one of Lafayette Baker's underlings was bedding with a Confederate spy and telling her all his secrets."

"Don't think I haven't thought about that," Wilcox said. "I suppose you could ruin me—my marriage, my family, too, for that matter. But if you do, I promise you I'll have you locked away in prison. That might not be enough, so I would arrange for you to be shot while trying to escape. Certain guards are happy to perform such services for a few dollars. Do we understand each other?"

Anne knew he wasn't bluffing. She had heard the stories about Old Capitol Prison, of the Southerners murdered by Yankees.

"Yes," she said. "We do."

"Good. Now let's seal our agreement the same way we would a marriage." Wilcox swept a heavy arm elegantly toward the doorway. "To your *boudoir*, madame."

She had no choice but to obey. Anne climbed the stairs to her room, stripped, and got under the covers. The unheated room was icy, and she shivered.

"We'll soon be warm enough," Wilcox said. His uniform was off and he slipped in beside her, still wearing his long underwear.

Anne was hardly aware of what her body was doing. If she was not enthusiastic, Wilcox didn't notice. He was too drunk.

It was over in a few minutes. Anne had never felt so dirty and used, like a ripe sow brought in so a boar could rut. She had never felt so blue. Had it all come to this? She barely noticed when the colonel's fat lips nuzzled her neck and slipped down to kiss her breasts.

He cursed at her lack of enthusiasm.

"Go get me something to eat," he growled. "I missed my supper coming here, you know."

"Hattie's not well."

"Is there something wrong with your own legs?" he asked.

The floor felt like ice under her feet. Anne pulled on a robe and went down to the kitchen. She looked around, wondering what in the world she could feed him. It wasn't enough that the man had blackmailed his way into her bed, but now he had made her into his servant. Damn him! The man was a leech. How was she ever going to pry him loose?

She took stock of the food. There was a loaf of bread, some cold beef. He would want something to drink. Hattie had filled a pitcher with buttermilk, which was the only thing to drink besides water and brandy. Wilcox wouldn't want water, and he'd already had enough brandy.

Anne cut some slices of bread and meat. She poured a glass of buttermilk, noticing how thick and rich it was. That's when she had an idea of how to get rid of Wilcox.

There was a small, empty bottle on a shelf which had contained some kind of patent medicine Hattie had taken. Anne retrieved it, wrapped the clear bottle in some rags, laid the bundle on the table, and smashed it with a heavy skillet. She struck it again and again until the bottle was flattened, then unwrapped the cloth to reveal the broken pieces of glass.

These weren't nearly small enough. Anne plucked out a few shards, and ground them with a mortar and pestle until she had a handful of glass slivers. These she put into the buttermilk and let them settle.

She held the glass up. It was impossible to detect anything in the buttermilk.

Anne put the food on a tray and carried it up to her bedroom, where she found Wilcox nearly asleep. The brandy had made him drowsy.

"Where have you been, woman?"

"I don't normally spend much time in the kitchen," she said, in a haughty voice. "Eat this, and damn you."

He laughed. "You should be thanking me, Anne. Another man would see you hanging from the gallows."

Wilcox sat up. She put the tray on the bed, within his reach.

"Are you planning to stay the night?" she asked.

"Why? Do you charge extra for that?"

"Don't forget your wife," Anne said bitterly.

"She's a darling woman. But she doesn't know how to keep a man warm at night, like you do."

Wilcox rolled a slice of bread around some meat and ate it. He chewed noisily, breathing heavily through his nose. It took all Anne's willpower not to look at the glass of buttermilk.

He paused, took another bite, chewed. "I never understood you damn secessionists," he said. "Wanting to start your own country. It doesn't make any sense."

"Maybe not to you Yankees. But it makes sense to us."

Wilcox reached for the glass of buttermilk, brought it to his lips, but didn't drink. "You're going to lose. Why not give up? There's no sense putting yourselves through all this misery. Look at you. What you've become. For what?" He laughed. "Of course, maybe you're just enjoying yourself."

With that, Wilcox took a sip of buttermilk. He took another bite of the meat and bread. If that was how he was going to drink the milk, Anne thought, he'd find the glass in the bottom. If that happened, he might just take her to prison and shoot her himself.

"The war isn't over yet," Anne said.

"It will be, come spring, if not sooner."

"Once General Lee gets moving—"

"General Lee, General Lee! I'm sick of hearing about General Lee. He's not a Greek god, you know. His soldiers don't have shoes or food. How can they fight?"

Wilcox tilted back his head and gulped down the buttermilk in one long swallow. A cold smile came to Anne's lips as she watched his throat pump, and she imagined the glass splinters flowing down to fill his belly.

He belched. "Just the thing to settle a man's stomach," he said. "A glass of buttermilk."

"Oh, yes," Anne said dumbly. She watched him expectantly, but nothing happened.

It took an hour for the glass to do its work. Wilcox groaned, rolled over, rubbed his belly.

"That meat you gave me wasn't spoiled, was it?" he asked.

"Hattie just cooked it," Anne said.

"Something's playing hell with my innards," he said.

Wilcox got out of bed, went over to the chamber pot. She heard him gasp as the first of his piss streamed into the porcelain bowl.

"My God," he howled. "It's red. I'm pissing blood."

"Oh, I've seen that before," Anne lied. "Sometimes when men overexert themselves—"

Wilcox groaned. "God. The sight of it's enough to make a man sick."

"Come back to bed," Anne said. "I'll get you some more brandy. You'll feel better."

The colonel got back under the blankets, moaning the whole time. "Maybe a doctor—"

"It's nothing. Let me get you some brandy."

Anne left him there and went downstairs to the parlor to retrieve the brandy bottle. Wilcox had already made a good dent in it, she thought bitterly, remembering the cost.

When she returned, Wilcox was a lump under the blankets. She wouldn't even have known he was alive except for the groaning noises he made.

"Drink this," she said, pouring him a bit of brandy. "It will make you feel better."

Wilcox forced himself up on one elbow and gulped the liquor down just as he had polished off the buttermilk. "That's better," he said.

Anne got back into bed. It was very strange crawling under the covers with a man she knew was going to die.

The glass was working faster than she thought it would, carving his innards to ribbons, gouging holes in his intestines. Wilcox groaned.

"Send for a doctor—"

"It will pass—"

"For God's sake, Anne—"

"Shhh. Have some more brandy."

Wilcox could hardly get the liquor down. He gagged, clutched his belly, and started from the bed. "I must see a doctor," he said. "There's something wrong with my innards. My God." The pain set him whimpering.

Anne put a hand on his chest and pushed him gently into the sheets. "It's nothing," she insisted. "You'll be fine."

The colonel batted her hand away. "I'm sick, I tell you. I feel like I'm dying."

"Perhaps you are." For the first time, Anne allowed herself a smile. Wilcox saw it and his eyes grew wide as he realized what had happened.

"You bitch! You've poisoned me, haven't you?"

Wilcox lurched out of bed. For a moment, Anne didn't know what to do to stop him, short of tackling him. But Wilcox never made it to the door. He fell to his knees, his fingers clawing at his fat belly.

"Louise!" he cried, shouting his wife's name. "Louise!" Then Wilcox slumped over and began writhing on the floor. Pink spittle colored the edges of his mouth. Anne watched him as she finished the last of the brandy in his glass.

His eyes were liquidly glowing and hateful. "You've killed me, woman. Goddamn you! I don't know what you've done to me, but you've killed me."

Anne lifted the glass of brandy in a mock toast. "Rot in hell, Yankee."

He died with a few final agonized twistings on her bedroom floor as he bled to death internally from the scores of tiny cuts the glass had inflicted. When he stopped moving, Anne got out of bed and brought the oil lamp closer to get a good look at him.

There wasn't a mark on his fat body, no sign at all of how he had died.

Satisfied, Anne got back into bed and screamed for all she was worth. She soon heard Hattie and Henry banging down the stairs from their room on the third floor. Their eyes went wide at the sight of Colonel Wilcox face down on the floor, wearing only his long underwear.

Henry bent down and put an ear close to the colonel's mouth. He looked up at Anne.

"He's dead, Miss Anne. Ain't no breath at all."

"How horrible! I woke up, and he was grabbing his chest. The next thing I knew there he was on the floor. You best go fetch the doctor, Henry."

"He don't need no doctor, ma'am. He be needin' an undertaker."

"Go!" she commanded.

Hattie had been nervous as an alley cat around her mistress since Anne had given her a beating. All that was forgotten in the current crisis.

"Hattie, I want you to empty the chamber pot," Anne said.

"Why for?"

"Don't quibble. Just do as I say."

Hattie carried the covered pot out. While Hattie was gone, Anne did her best to make herself fit to be seen. There was no time to dress, but she managed to put on her best robe. Her hands flew to her hair and put it in some kind of order. She wanted to look at least somewhat respectable for the doctor when he arrived, although that seemed ludicrous under the circumstances.

Hattie came back. "That pot was full of blood, Miss Anne."

"You can rest assured it wasn't mine, Hattie."

They heard voices in the hall. Henry was leading the doctor upstairs. "Now Hattie, you just keep quiet," Anne said.

The doctor came in. He was an old, kindly looking fellow, considering he had been rousted out at such a late hour. Old Dr. Crimmons had treated the late Mr. Clark, and he greeted Anne by name.

"Thank you for coming, doctor."

Crimmons got down on his hands and knees to examine Wilcox. He shook his head and stood back up. Crimmons took one look around the room and quickly assessed the situation.

"Not much I can do for that fellow. I would imagine he had a heart attack. It's common enough in someone of his age and weight."

"He had a wife and family," Anne said, even managing to bring a few tears to her eyes. "They must not know about this."

Crimmons nodded. A younger man might have called for the authorities, and there would have been a scandal. A married man dying of a heart attack in a semi-clothed state in a single woman's bedroom late at night . . . but Crimmons had seen a great deal in his years of doctoring. Little shocked him anymore, and he didn't feel the need to shock anyone else. The dead were dead. It was the living who needed the most help.

"You there," Crimmons said, turning to Henry. "Help me get his clothes back on him."

Wilcox was heavy, and it took all four of them to dress him even down to his sword belt and boots. The boots gave them the most trouble, and it was only with considerable tugging that they got them back on his feet. They all grabbed hold and half-carried, half-dragged his dead body downstairs. Anne couldn't help thinking she could have saved them all a lot of trouble by making sure he died downstairs.

"Oh, Lord," Hattie said. "I can't be touching a dead man!"

"Shut up and get his feet," Anne ordered.

With much grunting and straining, they got him downstairs. Crimmons went out to make sure the street was empty.

"All clear," he said. He and Henry managed to carry Wilcox out to the doctor's carriage. He hurried back to the front door.

"Thank you, doctor—"

He interrupted her. "Not a word of this, Miss Anne. Not a word. I do this as a favor for your late father, who was a gentleman. Now, I'll take Henry with me and we'll leave this fellow on a corner somewhere when no one's looking."

"He worked at the War Department."

"Very good, very good. We'll take him out now. He died of a heart attack. For the sake of honor, wouldn't it be better if he died on the street, on his way home from work?"

With that, the doctor went out, taking Henry with him. She soon heard the doctor's carriage rattling away down the dark street.

Anne smiled. Colonel Jonathan Wilcox would trouble her no more, and the death of Sudler Dill, that nervous little man who had been so loyal to the Cause, had been avenged.

17

The morning after the Rebel gunboats had been turned back, two men appeared at the laborers' camp in City Point, looking for work. The foreman could see at once that both men had seen some hard living lately. They looked dirty, tired, and a little wet. He guessed a dunking in the river might have done that.

"You men got any skills?" the foreman asked.

"Just two hands and strong backs," Cole said. He supposed being able to shoot a man off a horse at a thousand yards was not an ability the foreman was seeking. Neither was playing poker, as in Snodgrass's case.

Beside him, Snodgrass grinned affably. "We ain't afraid of hard work, if that's what you mean."

"Where you boys from?" the man asked. "I hear a little butternut in the way you talk. You ain't Reb deserters, are you now?"

From the way in which the foreman asked the question, it sounded as if he didn't really care about the answer. But he had to ask.

"We're from Maryland, up around Frederick. Lots of folks up that way is loyal to the Union. There's no work up there this winter. We figured there'd be plenty down here with the army."

"Well," the foreman said, stroking his salt-and-pepper beard and appearing satisfied with Cole's answer. He was a short plug of a man, squat as a boulder and mean-looking as a bulldog. Had to be mean to run a work camp, Cole thought. "What I need is someone with skills. Carpentry. Blacksmithing."

"I know all about river boats," Snodgrass spoke up. "I used to work aboard steamboats before the war."

"Marylanders who know about river boats," the foreman said, a knowing grin on his face. "Ain't that somethin'? Next it'll be Massachusetts boys who can hoe cotton." He laughed at his own joke. "But hell, we can always use hands on the wharves, Marylanders or not. Git your truck an' foller me, boys."

As soon as the foreman turned his back, Cole and Snodgrass looked at each other and shrugged. They were hired, even if the foreman had his suspicions.

He led them to a large tent in a corner of the workers' camp. Obviously an army hand-me-down, the once-white canvas was dirty and patched, and Cole doubted it was much good in the way of keeping out rain. But considering he and Snodgrass had been outdoors these last few days, traveling at night again after their close call with the Virginia Home Guard and then being extra cautious as they neared the Yankee lines, a tent would be welcome shelter.

Inside there was an old stove and several cots. The tent was empty because all the men assigned to it were out working.

"This here'll be your tent," the foreman said. "Looks like there ain't enough cots, so you'll have to sleep on the ground. But if we get some more flu through here like we had in December, there'll be plenty of extra cots for you."

"I'd hate to profit off another man's misfortune," Snodgrass said.

The foreman scowled. "I won't abide no smart talk."

Cole shot Snodgrass a warning glance. His eyes were hard enough to drive nails.

"This suits us fine," Cole said. "Who should we see at the wharves?"

"Ask for Mr. Harrington." Another wicked little grin told them the dock boss would be a hard man. "He'll put you right."

After the foreman left, they unloaded their gear, which consisted of a blanket roll thrown across their shoulders. Their revolvers were rolled inside the blanket because it wouldn't do to show up at the Union army with guns in their belts. Cole had hidden his rifle just as he had in Washington, by dismantling it and hanging the various parts by slings beneath his long winter coat. He quickly shucked off his coat and stowed the pieces of the Sharps in his blanket roll.

"I hope nobody goes through that," Cole said. "They'll get suspicious, finding all those guns. But I don't know what else to do."

"Nobody will touch it," Snodgrass reassured him. "In a place like this, a man knows he'd best respect what belongs to another. This is a rough bunch."

"The man that takes my rifle dies," Cole said quietly. Simply stating a fact.

Snodgrass looked Cole over. He saw a firm set to the jaw, the lean face of a backwoods hunter. The sort of man who considered laughter to be wasted energy. Anyone who wasn't a fool would give him a wide berth.

"Not to worry, Cole," he said. "Ain't nobody goin' to fool with your truck. Now let's get down to the wharves and find ourselves some work."

It was Tuesday morning, December 27.

Anne's old carriage rolled through the gate of the Van Ness mansion. She had been summoned to Thomas Conrad's house on urgent business. A messenger had come to the house on H Street, and she had left immediately, but not before giving Hattie strict orders that any gentleman callers could wait in the parlor for her return. It was a Friday night, which meant she would be busy. Anne felt the war effort was growing desperate, and she hated the thought of missing the least bit of information that might help the Cause.

Conrad himself was waiting for her at the door, just as he had been during her two other visits.

"Good evening, Miss Clark. Thank you for coming on such short notice."

"It is my pleasure, sir," Anne said.

Conrad looked somehow different than he had last month. Thinner. He also appeared to have lost more of his hair, unless it was only a trick of the feeble gas lamps in their sconces along the hall.

They sat in his library, as they had on those two other occasions. As before, a servant served tea. Conrad seemed to have abandoned his easy manner. He rushed headlong into his explanation.

"We're losing the war," he said. "There's no doubt about it now. Huge numbers of General Lee's men are deserting every day, and the ones that are left haven't enough food to eat or even enough clothes to keep them warm."

"But in the spring—"

Conrad sipped tea and shook his head. "Grant will sweep them out with a broom. It's a shame . . ."

Anne knew what he was thinking. *Cole.* There had been nothing in the newspapers, except some drivel about Grant being carried into the Willard Hotel in a drunken fit. They both knew he had come close to killing the general. Anne knew why he had failed—Hattie's note—but she volunteered nothing about that to Mr. Conrad.

"You must have a plan to shore up the Confederacy," Anne said.

"As a matter of fact, I do." Conrad shrugged. "It might work. I've been in contact with our friends in Richmond about it. But this plan depends largely on you."

"Oh?" Anne was both stunned and thrilled.

"I need you . . ." Conrad paused, started over. "The *Cause* needs you to go to City Point. You know that officer on Grant's staff, don't you? A Major Mulholland, I believe? Find an excuse to visit him. When you do, you must find out as much as you can about Grant's plans for a winter attack on Petersburg. We have reason to believe— mainly from what you've been able to discover already, Miss Clark— that the attack will come within two weeks. General Lee *must* know the exact date, and the details of the plan. If he can thwart the Yankees, it will give new morale to our troops, especially after Hood's loss at Nashville."

Anne hardly knew what to think. "How can I go to City Point? A woman would not be welcome in camp."

"Women go there all the time. Even General Grant's wife is there. It's only a day's trip from Washington on a steamer. Most take the night boat, so that they haven't lost a day."

"I'll go," Anne heard herself say. What other choice did she have? The Cause needed her.

Conrad smiled. "I knew you would, Miss Clark."

They talked briefly of gossip in the city about various generals and politicians. None of it was very useful. Conrad once again showed her to the door himself.

"This is very important, Miss Clark," he said gravely as he opened the carriage door for her. "Hurry back to me as soon as you can."

Anne climbed into her carriage. Henry clucked to the horse, and they started for home.

Go to City Point! To spy! Anne was both excited and afraid. This was far different from prying a few secrets from men who visited her bedroom. She knew if she was caught spying in City Point, she would be hanged.

Bitterly, Anne wished she had at least thought of asking Mr. Conrad for the money to buy passage on the steamer.

Snodgrass fit right in with the work camp rowdies, a far rougher bunch than the soldiers. Where the troops had officers and rules to keep order, the workmen had fists and threats. These men used language so blue it would have made the toughest old sergeant cringe, and when they came in from their ten or twelve hours of work, all they wanted to do was eat, drink whiskey, and play cards until they passed out from exhaustion. In the morning, they roused themselves to do it all over again. It reminded Snodgrass of his riverboat days.

"If we stay here long enough I'll be a rich man from playing poker," Snodgrass confided in Cole. "These boys ain't got much money, but what they do have I'm doing a fair job of taking away from them."

"See that you don't take too much of their money," Cole said. He didn't want to attract undue attention to themselves.

"I let them win some," Snodgrass said. "You have to, with such a violent bunch."

Bloodthirsty might have been a more apt description. Fistfights broke out every few minutes in the tent camp, and there was quick money to be made on the bets over who would win the fight. Despite the best efforts of the army's provost marshal, who oversaw law and order in the workmen's camp, liquor flowed in rivers, and it was a rare night that drunken men weren't seen stumbling from one tent to another, or staggering toward the sinks beyond the tents. The drunker ones simply relieved themselves outside the tents, and on warmer days the whole camp stank of sweat and urine.

At first, Cole had wondered why these seemingly fit men weren't in uniform. He soon learned that many already had been, and when the term of their enlistment ended, they decided that while army life wasn't for them, being away from home had its attractions. Others were considered physically unfit for military duty but sound enough to unload steamboats at the wharves for ten hours a day. Not every man could be in the army.

Besides, fighting was only one aspect of the largest military machine the world had yet known. The United States army also required wheelwrights to repair its thousands of ambulances and supply wagons, carpenters to build warehouses, butchers to slaughter the cattle that would feed the army. Men like those in the work camp had the inglorious task of making sure the military machine kept its belly full and its wheels rolling and a roof over its head.

Indeed, Snodgrass might have made his fortune in a place such as this with nothing more than a deck of cards and a small pistol handy in case tempers became unruly.

Cole had more on his mind than card games. He and Snodgrass spent that first day in City Point working at the wharves. He was bone tired when they returned to the worker's camp. But as soon as it was dark, he slipped out of camp.

He needed to know where Grant's headquarters was located. In Cole's mind, Lieutenant General Ulysses S. Grant, the Yankee responsible for this teeming tent city known as City Point, was a marked man.

You got away in Washington, he thought. *You ain't goin' to be so lucky this time.*

Cole had not forgotten his orders, given by General Hill, who was just a few miles away to the west. *Grant must die.* If anything, the huge military base surrounding him only reinforced the necessity of assassinating General Grant. For Cole knew well enough that the South had nothing to match this splendid supply base. What the Confederacy did have was wonderful generals. Until Grant, the North had lacked leadership.

If the Confederacy had any hope of at least fighting the war to a draw, it must remove Grant. Or Lincoln. For in the end, Cole believed it was men who would win the war, good generals and presidents and soldiers, not bags of grain or warehouses full of blankets.

As Cole wandered the camp on Tuesday night, he discovered how simple it was to move around the huge base unchallenged.

Headquarters was easy enough to find. All he had to do was ask. He soon reached the bluff overlooking the Appomattox and James Rivers but was not impressed. Grant had not taken over one of the grand houses but had claimed a rough little building as his own. Cole noted the sentries outside the door, including a Yankee in a green uniform. One of Berdan's sharpshooters. Tough bastards, they were.

Cole didn't hang around headquarters for long because it was too risky. There were many officers rushing about, and they didn't think twice about stopping a man and asking his business. Briefly, Cole considered simply walking up to the headquarters building with a Colt revolver in his belt and seeing if he could get at Grant. He decided against this for the same reasons he had not tried to get at Grant inside the Willard Hotel back in Washington City. He would not be a martyr. Escape must be possible.

As he watched headquarters from a safe distance, he spotted an officer come out of the office to light a cigar. The sudden flare of the match lit his face. Cole's eyes narrowed. It was the same officer he had stabbed on the rooftop back in Washington City. The major turned and went back inside, but not before Cole noticed the man's limp. *Must have gotten him good with that knife . . .*

Cole made his way back to camp and turned in for the night.

The next night Cole was back again. This time he struck up a conversation with a soldier who was working to free a wagon that had bogged down in a muddy section of road. Cole put his shoulder to the wheel to help get the wagon free.

"Virginia makes some sticky mud," the Yankee said. Cole had never heard an accent like the soldier's. The words were harsh and nasal.

"The Rebs can have it, far as I'm concerned," Cole said.

"The general over there don't look too eager to give it up," the soldier said, nodding toward the headquarters building.

"You ever seen him?" Cole asked.

"General Grant? Why, sure. He takes a walk just about every day in that field yonder." The soldier jerked his head toward what was now lost in darkness. "You can look at him all you want then. 'Course, he don't look like much. Not like a general, at least."

Cole gave one last mighty push, and the wagon was freed from the mud. The Yankee wagon driver thanked him and was on his way.

Cole skirted headquarters in a wide loop and came out at the edge of the field. Even in the darkness he could sense it was very wide, with trees nearly a thousand yards distant. Satisfied, he went back to the workers' camp.

At lunchtime the next day, he approached one of the workers, who was wearing a blue soldier's uniform blouse.

"I'll give you two dollars for that shirt you're wearing," Cole said.

"Hell, yes," the man said. Two dollars was a fortune for an old shirt.

He walked along the wharves until he found a young soldier. "I'll give you a dollar for that hat," Cole said.

"Two dollars," the boy said fiercely.

Cole paid and walked off with the hat.

That night, Cole put on the shirt and hat, so that he could pass for a Yankee. He took his rifle from its hiding place beneath his blanket and headed for the field just beyond headquarters where the general liked to walk.

The woodcutters hadn't yet reached the trees ringing the field, and there was solitude to be found with the only sound being the winter wind stirring the bare branches overhead. Now and then he might hear a distant shout from camp.

Cole sat down with his back against a tree and the rifle across his legs. He had brought along a small flask of whiskey to keep off the winter night's chill, and he took it out and had a sip. It clawed at his throat going down, but the liquid's warmth radiated out from his belly. It was cold, so he put his work coat on over the soldier's uniform. He had his floppy hat stuffed into a pocket, and he put it on. It was much warmer than the Yankee forage cap.

The moon was up, and it didn't take him long to determine that this field was just what he wanted. The range would be long depending upon how close General Grant came to these trees. But the trees also made the perfect cover. He felt far more at home in this kind of sniper's post than he had in the boarding house back in Washington.

Out here, it was easy to imagine he was simply up before dawn for a deer hunt, or spending the night in the woods during a long hunt, as he used to do when he was a boy. Nothing more to shoot than deer. No men. Shooting a deer didn't keep you up nights wondering if what you were doing was a sin. A deer was hide and antlers and meat. There was a reason for killing it, for before the war Cole had never killed anything he didn't eat. But why did you kill a man?

He had never held much with religion or the Bible, but he knew enough to realize that killing a man was a mortal sin. Cole supposed there were circumstances under which you could kill a man and it wasn't a sin. In the Bible, those people from olden times were always slaughtering each other in one war or another. But those had been holy men and holy wars. It was hard not to believe he had done the sinful kind of killing and thus had blood on his hands.

He recalled the old woman in Washington City. She would have given him away. Cole had broken her neck with no more thought than he might give to killing a chicken.

Sinful.

He told himself that the Yankees had been the ones to start it, killing his family the way they had. Cole was only trying to avenge their deaths.

He took another sip of whiskey, slipped the flask into the pocket of the Yankee tunic. *Don't think on this business of it being a sin to kill others in a war,* he told himself. He knew it might make him hesitate. *And the one time I wait too long to pull the trigger is when some other man will kill me. It's a damn sight better to sit out in the woods sipping whiskey and feeling bad about shooting men and be alive than it is to be dead and in a hole in the ground. If I even got that instead of most likely my body getting all bloated on the battlefield and finally bursting and my putrid innards running out like I seen too many times. It's a terrible thing to see a man rotting in the sun.*

He tilted the flask up, emptying it.

My time will come for dying, maybe tomorrow or next week or maybe I'll be an old man fifty years from now and die in my bed. Almost twice as long as I've been alive now.

Or maybe he only had a few hours to live. In that case there was no sense in complicating life with worrying about whether or not it's right or wrong to shoot a Yankee. When the war was over he knew he'd never kill another man.

Cole put his head back against the rough trunk of the tree and closed his eyes. If he had brought a blanket he could have slept out here, instead of surrounded by snoring drunks in that tent that stank of bean farts.

When the war was over he was going out West where the land was pure and he could start all over again. Like the way the Earth was in the beginning of the Bible. Before men had come and brought sin to the world. Cain killing his brother, Abel. What was Cole doing if not killing his brother? Do not think on that, he warned himself.

Somewhere in the darkness a twig snapped and Cole heard another sound like a briar's barbs snagging on woolen trousers, then pulling free.

His eyes were the only part of him that moved, trying to pinpoint the source of the noise.

Footsteps in the leaves came closer. There was no stealth to the walk, so it wasn't someone out looking for him. *Damn,* he thought. *This whole big woods and some fool Yankee has to walk right by here.* Then again, there were several thousand soldiers within just a few hundred yards, and it was likely one or two would wander out this far from time to time in search of scarce kindling or maybe some sassafras root for tea.

Cole rested the rifle on his knees, pointing the muzzle out toward the woods. The metallic snick of him pulling back the hammer sounded loud as cannon fire to his ears.

A dark form barged into the tiny clearing where Cole sat. He heard the man gasp as he spotted Cole, the moonlight gleaming on the Sharps and the long telescopic sight. The man was so close Cole didn't even have to aim. The muzzle was pointing up at the Yankee's chest.

"My Gawd," the man whined. "Don't shoot."

Thinking of the sin of killing a man, Cole hesitated.

And the Yankee spun and went crashing away through the woods, howling like a pack of banshees was after him.

Cole cursed himself for not pulling the trigger. Then he was on his feet and running nimbly in the man's wake, rifle in one hand, knife in the other. If he could kill the man with the knife it would attract far less attention than a rifle shot.

Chasing someone through the woods at night was not easy. Cole did not want to bang his rifle against a tree, so he held it in tight to his body and tried to fend off the branches that slapped at his face with the other hand. Countless roots and debris tried to trip him at every step, and he ran blindly for the most part, smashing his way through clumps of mountain laurel and deadfalls.

Fear had given the other man fleet feet, for he was already out of the woods and into the clearing where Grant liked to walk, high-tailing it back to camp, still screaming like the devil himself was biting at his heels. Shooting the man now would have brought the whole camp running, so Cole let him go. He did not want to be seen in the open, even at night, so he stopped at the edge of the field and turned back into the woods.

Cole knew he must make his move soon. His nighttime scouting was risky, but it had been necessary in order to determine the best way to get at General Grant. But the longer he waited, the more likely incidents like the one tonight were going to happen. Besides, back at the workmen's camp, it had been impossible to completely hide his rifle and pistols in such cramped living quarters. Not a few men had weapons, but Cole's rifle obviously had a special purpose and must have raised some eyebrows. Fortunately, the labor camp was a place where a man was best off minding his own business, and if anyone had found Cole's rifle unusual, they hadn't said a word about it.

Not worried now about catching anyone, he went soundlessly as a forest animal, disappearing into the woods without so much as a broken sapling in his wake. If that fool who had nearly tripped over him brought any sentries back to look for him, they would find nothing but trees and moonlight.

On the morning of December 28, O'Malley went into the headquarters office and found Major Mulholland lounging in a chair with Colonel Bowers and Captain Lincoln. He saluted all three at once, noting that only Captain Lincoln didn't bother to nod acknowledgement.

O'Malley had noticed that, unlike Mulholland or Bowers or even Grant, Captain Lincoln tended to look down his nose at poor Irishmen such as himself. This might be America, O'Malley thought, but in spite of all the ballyhooing about democracy, there was gentry all the same, the snooty Captain Lincoln being a member of that class.

"Major Mulholland, sir. There's someone here who I think you should see. He has quite a little tale to tell about a man lurking in the woods with a fancy rifle, and if I'm any judge, he's telling the plain truth."

"I'll go out to him," Mulholland said. He was no longer lounging, but on his feet and full of excitement.

"Sounds like your sharpshooter has arrived," Bowers said. "Like they say, be careful what you wish for on account of you just might get it."

"It was bound to happen, Joe," Mulholland said. "They tried it in Washington, and it was only a matter of time before they tried it here."

"Tried what?" Captain Lincoln asked.

Exchanging a look, Mulholland and Bowers went out to hear the soldier's tale while Captain Lincoln set to work copying some papers Bowers had given him so that they could be sent up to Washington City on the night boat.

"It's best he doesn't hear," Bowers said, leaning toward Mulholland and keeping his voice low. "He is the president's son, after all."

The soldier they found waiting for them was a boy from New Jersey who was clearly in awe of being at headquarters. Mulholland noticed the boy kept looking past he and Bowers, as if hoping for a glimpse of General Grant within the building.

"Tell us what you saw, Private," Mulholland said, folding his arms impatiently on his chest.

"I was out in the woods just beyond here—" he flailed toward the distant trees with one hand.

"What were you doing in the woods, Private? Your duty is to be with your unit."

The soldier looked sheepish. "To be honest, sir, I was looking for a place to set up a still."

Bowers guffawed.

"You know that making spirits is not allowed, Private."

"I know it, sir, and so does our company commander, Captain Archer. He won't abide none of that, not like some of these officers, which is why I was out in the woods looking for a place to set up a still."

"Go on," Mulholland said.

"Well, I walked out into a clearing and there he was."

"Who?" Mulholland demanded. He thought the boy seemed to enjoy keeping him in suspense, and he was growing more impatient.

"I saw a Johnny Reb out there with a fancy rifle. Had one of them sights on top that's a long tube."

"A telescopic sight."

"I don't know the name for it," the boy said. "He was just settin' there. When I came across him he jumped up and came after me, but I guess I lost him in the woods."

"This was last night?"

"Yes, sir."

"How do you know he was a Reb, and not just one of our men. It was dark, after all."

"If he wasn't a Reb, sir, then why did he chase me with a knife?"

Mulholland gave the boy the hardest look he could summon. "Who else have you told this to?" he asked.

"Nobody, sir," the private hurried to answer. "Well, just a few of my messmates. They're the ones who told me to come on up here."

"Mmm." Mulholland was sure the soldier was telling the truth. Whomever he had run across in those woods had left quite an impression. "That will be all."

"Yes, sir."

The soldier turned to go. "And Private?"

"Sir?"

"Tell no one of else of what you saw. Leave it at your friends.

That's where it stops."

"Yes, sir."

The soldier gave a smart salute, turned on his heel, and headed back to his unit.

"Interesting," Mulholland said.

"I'd say that boy's lucky to be alive. Sounds like there's a Johnny Reb sharpshooter out there, all right. The question is, what are you going to do about it, Mr. Chief of Security?"

Mulholland thought a minute. For all the time he'd had since returning from Washington, he realized he really hadn't made any plans. He had brought in Bayliss, of course, but other than having him guard headquarters, he didn't know how else to put the sharpshooter to work.

They returned to the office, which was empty except for Captain Lincoln at his copying, and Mulholland began pacing the floor inside the cramped room. Robert Lincoln glanced up, clearly looking annoyed as the floorboards creaked under Mulholland's feet.

"We have to go from being the hunted to being the hunters," Mulholland finally said. "It's the only way out of this."

"It was mighty lucky, that boy finding the sharpshooter out in the woods. I'd wager it won't happen again."

Mulholland stopped pacing, and a slow grin transformed the worry lines on his face. "I know where he's hiding," he said.

Part III

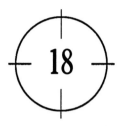

Mulholland searched the workers' camp for the sharpshooter just after sunrise. He took along Bowers, O'Malley, Bayliss, and a huge guard named Simpson—a good man to have if there was trouble.

"We aren't harboring any deserters, Major," the camp foreman said when they met him at his tent. Mulholland detected a note of hostility in the man's voice, probably because civilians of his fiber did not think much of officers. "These are all honest, working men."

Behind him, Mulholland heard O'Malley guffaw, and he shot a glance at the Irishman to silence him.

Honest men or not, it was common knowledge what went on in the camp once those working men had finished their day's labors. "Do you think I'm a fool?" Mulholland demanded. "For one thing, this camp is full of men who should be in uniform."

"Maybe," the foreman said with a shrug. "But then who would the army find to tote its supplies and fix its wagons and unload its ships? There's a better use for some men than cannon fodder."

Mulholland bridled at the comment but managed to keep his temper in check. The foreman was a surly man, but unfortunately Mulholland knew he had little authority over this short fellow who was shaped like a feed sack. "I did not come here to debate with you, sir. I believe you may be harboring a fugitive."

"Must be an important one," the foreman said, eyeing the group that had come to search for the sharpshooter. Although there were only five of them, they were heavily armed. Both officers had traded their swords for revolvers, and all three enlisted men carried Henry repeating rifles. There was a hard look to the soldier in the green coat, the foreman noted, and he quickly averted his eyes when the man met his curious stare.

"Why we're looking for the man doesn't concern you," Mulholland stated matter-of-factly. "But maybe you can help us find him, nonetheless."

"You expect me to remember one man out of all the ones in this camp?" The foreman snorted. "That's a mighty tall order to fill."

"If I were you, I'd think about filling it, then," Bowers chimed in. "Or maybe a visit from some of the provost marshal general's men would help refresh your memory?"

The foreman winced as if he had been struck. Bowers' threat had real teeth, for the provost marshal had the ability to put an abrupt end to all the gaming, whiskey-selling, and pleasures of the flesh that were readily available in camp. That could also put an end to whatever cut the foreman was getting for turning a blind eye to illegal activities.

"Well?" the man asked gruffly. "What's his name?"

"We haven't got a name," Mulholland said, feeling some of the wind go out of him.

"What's he look like then, this man?"

"We're not sure."

The foreman looked exasperated. "You're asking me to help you find a man when you don't even know anything about him? God help me!"

"He's Southern," Mulholland said, already feeling his hopes dying. Hearing the foreman's reaction brought home the fact that they had little information to use in finding the sharpshooter. "That much we do know. Also, he would have come to the camp within the last few days, certainly within the last three weeks."

"We've had a lot of men come and go," the foreman said, no longer looking overly concerned, now that he knew he could hardly be expected to identify the man they were seeking. Find a man without a name or a description? This officer must be crazy.

"Come now, it can't be that many men," Mulholland said, trying hard not to sound like he was pleading. He offered the only other clue he had: "The man is a former Confederate sharpshooter and he may have arrived here from Maryland."

A glimmer of recognition crossed the foreman's face. He thought of the two men he had put to work on the wharves. They claimed to have come from Maryland, which was a lie, considering one of them had worked around steamboats. And the other fellow had a look about him—not the sort of man you'd want to tangle with. As for being a Reb sharpshooter, who knew? But he was a better candidate than the immigrant workmen who streamed into camp or the broken-down veterans looking for work after being chewed up and spit out again by army life.

"There may have been someone," the foreman said. "Two men. They came in here last week. They had Southern accents, all right, but that's not such a rare thing. Follow me and I'll show you their tent, although I'd imagine they're still out working."

Mulholland had no way of knowing if the man had simply concocted this story to satisfy him or if this was a genuine lead, so he had no choice but to follow the squat foreman. Their small contingent traipsed through the camp, drawing curious stares from the few men who lurked around their tents.

Mulholland had only seen the place from a distance, and he was both fascinated and disgusted by its squalor. Sibley tents sprouted everywhere, and the dirty, torn canvas was an indicator that the tents were worn cast-offs from the army—like many of the workmen themselves. Trash littered the muddy avenues between the rows of tents and the broken glass of whiskey bottles was strewn about, glittering dully.

From time-to-time a feverish, hollow-eyed man would look out from between the flaps of a tent.

"Too sick to work," the foreman complained. "But still eating plenty of our damned food."

"Why don't they report to hospital?" Mulholland asked.

The foreman laughed. "Most men would just as soon take their chances nursing themselves than risk their lives with those drunken sawbones who call themselves doctors. A man can go in there with a cold and come out in a coffin, most likely. Don't forget that a lot of them have already seen the inside of a hospital in their army days, which was enough for one lifetime."

It was true that the hospitals did not have a good reputation, although they had improved remarkably since the early days of the war. Still, Mulholland wondered how such sick-looking men survived out here in the unheated tents.

They walked for what seemed to Mulholland like a long time. There were no signs marking any of the haphazard alleys in the sprawling camp, yet the foreman appeared to know the place as well as the back of his hand. He led them up to a tent where a grizzled, scrawny little man was whittling.

"Here's another one living off the government's bounty," the foreman said, glowering over the man sitting on the ground. "Bill

Yates, one of the laziest sons of bitches ever born."

If Yates took offense, he didn't show it, but Mulholland thought it was probably lucky for the foreman that the man was only carving with a tiny jackknife.

"What's wrong with you?" Mulholland asked.

"I got me a bad knee," the man said without enthusiasm, as if he were tired of explaining. "A ball clipped it at Chancellorsville, and it ain't been right since."

"Where are those other rascals staying in this tent?" the foreman asked.

Yates squinted up at the group of men as if noticing them for the first time. "What's going on?" he asked, setting aside his whittling. "Is this some kind of inquiry? You want me to try to dance a bit on my knee to prove its bad?"

"That won't be necessary," Mulholland said, asserting himself. He turned to the foreman. "What business do we have with this man?"

"We're looking for a couple of your tent mates, Yates. Those two fellows who started bunking here last week."

Yates got to his feet, although it obviously pained him to put any weight on his leg. "You mean Snodgrass and Cole?"

Mulholland's heart began to beat more quickly. They had a name! He couldn't believe it was going to be this easy to catch the sharpshooter. All they would have to do was wait for him to return from the work detail.

"That's them," the foreman said. "We'll be waiting for them when they get back from the wharves this evening."

Yates grinned. "Why, you can wait all you want, but you ain't goin' to see them."

"What not?" Mulholland demanded.

" 'Cuz they're gone. Cleared out of here this mornin'. Before first light."

"Did they say where they were going?" Bowers asked.

"Nope. Left without a word. Doesn't surprise me a bit with Cole. He was an odd bird. A tough one. Wouldn't want to cross him. But Snodgrass was all right. He would have been one to say good-bye, though."

Mulholland hardly knew what to think. To have just missed the opportunity to catch these men before they could do any harm was almost more than he could bear. Of course, there wasn't any proof that they were anything more than drifters from Maryland, but that they had suddenly disappeared earlier in the day was not a mark in their favor.

"Did one of them have a rifle?" Bayliss asked.

All eyes turned to Bayliss, but he was looking intently at Bill Yates.

"Snodgrass maybe had a derringer," Yates said. "But Cole had a rifle. It was a Sharps, with one of those fancy telescope sights on it. He kept it rolled in his blanket during the day, but at night he would take it out to clean it or go wandering off somewhere with it." The small man shook his head in disgust. "The way he held that rifle in his arms you would have thought it was a woman."

Mulholland caught Bowers's eye, watched the colonel's eyebrows rise in an arch. There was little doubt now they had narrowly missed catching the Confederate assassin.

"His rifle was safe here?" Bowers asked. "Everyone must have known he had a rifle like that right in his blanket roll."

Yates snorted. "You never saw this Lucas Cole, Colonel. A body knows better than to go foolin' with something that belongs to somebody like Cole. Like I said, he was a hard man."

"What did this Cole look like?" Mulholland asked.

"He was a lean fellow, about average height. Brown hair and spooky eyes."

"Young or old?"

"Fairly young."

Mulholland could hardly believe what he was hearing. This fellow Cole sounded a lot like the sharpshooter he had seen in Washington.

"Well," the foreman said. "I guess you found who you was lookin' for."

All the foreman's bluster was gone, because he realized something important was going on. After all, majors and colonels with armed guards in tow didn't usually come looking for one of his laborers. He could only guess at the importance of Cole having what to him sounded like a sniper's rifle. The two officers looked mighty disappointed that Cole had disappeared.

Mulholland considered what to do next. Comb the roads looking for the two men? He doubted they would be traveling where any cavalry patrol could pick them up; most likely they had taken to the woods, where a cagey Southern boy could stay hidden as long as he wanted, no matter how many soldiers Mulholland sent to search for him.

No, his only choice now was to enact the plan he had been formulating for the last couple of days. It was risky, but it just might work.

Frowning, he turned to the scrawny laborer who stood before them, waiting to be dismissed so he could return to his whittling. "Thank you, Mr. Yates. That will be all."

Without so much as nodding at the foreman, Mulholland turned around and started heading back to headquarters. "Come on," he said, and his small knot of men followed him back the way they had come through the squalid camp.

"I'm sure going to miss eating regular," Snodgrass said. "But I won't mind not having to work at the wharves. All that lifting and fetching can wear a man down after a while."

"It was for the best that you left there," Cole said. "If those Yanks ever came sniffin' 'round, they'd catch you sure."

Snodgrass knew that was true enough, and he had no desire to have his neck stretched or serve as target practice for a firing squad of Yankees. The open road again was just fine with him, given the alternative.

"You sure you want to go through with this, Cole?" he asked. "You and me make a pretty good team. We could leave this whole damn war behind us and go out west somewhere and have some adventures with all them Injuns."

"I would like to shoot some buffalo," Cole admitted. "I ain't never seen one, but I hear they're somethin'. And I hear tell there's still all kind of game out there to the far west—antelope, elk, even grizzly bear."

Snodgrass shook his head. "You're about the only man I know who would want to tangle with a grizzly."

"I hear some of them are nigh on twelve feet tall when then stand on their hind legs." There was awe in Cole's voice. Years ago an old trapper visiting family in the area had told him stories about the game out west, and it had taken hold of Cole's imagination like nothing else. "Just picture such a creature, Snodgrass. All claws and teeth. And there's herds of buffalo so big you can't see the end of 'em."

"Well, come out west with me and you can hunt all you want," Snodgrass said, not pointing out that Cole had left out the Indians, who from what he had heard weren't too keen on sharing their game with white men. He waved a hand toward the western horizon. "All we've got to do is ride across them mountains out there. We can leave this damn tidewater Virginia behind us. Nothin' here but scrub pine and Yankees, anyway."

They had made their way out into the countryside beyond City Point through stealth. Traveling without being detected had become an old game for both of them, so they knew to keep near the hedgerows and woods in case a cavalry patrol came along. Moving at night would have been even better, but Cole had insisted they clear out that morning. Reluctantly, Snodgrass had agreed.

In an isolated windswept field, the two men halted. The winter chill made Snodgrass shiver, and he was already missing the tent and meals back at City Point. Funny how a man could come to love cold beans! But at least they filled his belly.

"I reckon this is it, Cole. I head out from here. I'll try to get out of this hornet's nest of Yankees and around our own boys, too. I don't fancy being put back in a trench for the rest of the winter."

"Or worse," Cole said. "I'd say you're what's called a deserter."

Snodgrass made a face of mock astonishment. "Hell, that's an ugly name. I was just seeing the sights, is all."

"Good luck to you, Uriah."

"It ain't too late to drop this whole thing, Cole. Think on it, now."

"No need to think. I set out to do this, and I will."

Snodgrass admired Cole's stubbornness, even though he thought it foolish. Sometimes a man had to cut his losses, and if he didn't like a hand, he folded. Even so, Snodgrass felt tempted to stay and help Cole. Wouldn't shooting General Grant rile those Yankees! But he knew Cole was a man who worked alone, so he didn't bother to offer.

He stuck out his hand, and Cole gripped it. A powerful hand, Snodgrass thought. He hated to think about Cole getting himself killed over some foolish mission, but he knew all too well there was no changing his mind.

"Good luck to you, Cole," he said.

"Keep your good luck, gambler. You might need some yourself."

"Hattie, don't drag that along the ground!" Anne snapped.

Hattie's face was stony as she obeyed her mistress and lifted the portmanteau higher. It wasn't until Anne had turned her back and was hurrying on toward the steamer that Hattie's eyes gleamed with hatred.

It was Monday evening, and they were catching the night steamer to City Point as Mr. Conrad had suggested. Taking Hattie along was costing extra, but Anne couldn't travel alone with propriety. Besides, she needed someone to carry her luggage. A proper Southern lady didn't do such things.

Anne briefly considered that Hattie might be tired. She had walked all the way over to old Mrs. Mulholland's house to deliver a special pecan pie Anne had baked. Then, this afternoon, she had returned to make sure the pie had the desired effect on the old woman.

Mixed in with all the molasses in the pie filling had been an entire bottle of laudanum, which probably wouldn't kill the old woman, but it had put her out of her head. Anne knew well enough that the old woman had a weakness for pecan pie and would eat more than a slice or two. The molasses had disguised the taste of the opiate. The old woman's sudden "illness" was giving her an excuse to bring Brendan Mulholland the news firsthand.

Once on board, they hurried toward their cabin. The wind off the Chesapeake Bay was too cold and biting to making staying on deck pleasant.

They would be in City Point by morning. Wouldn't Brendan be surprised to see her! She had just the excuse, however, thanks to old Mrs. Mulholland.

19

It never failed to amaze Snodgrass how much life was like a game of cards. As he crossed the brown Virginia fields, he thought: a man never knows what hand he's going to be dealt, and then he has to give some of the cards up in hopes of getting some new ones that would give him the advantage—or at least cut his losses.

He would have been happy enough to finish out the war in City Point, even if it meant a few months of backbreaking work unloading ships at the wharves. Snodgrass had never had any real convictions about fighting for the Confederacy. It had simply been another adventure. To him, going off to war was just like signing onto a bigger steamboat that might be going up different rivers. Just as he had gone off to work on the riverboats when he was a boy, he had gone off to war when the time came. But as far as he was concerned, the time for fighting was over. The adventure had petered out. He was more interested in self-preservation.

Lucas Cole, on the other hand, was one of those men who would never give up. He was a Yankee-hater through and through. He had mentioned before how some Yankee soldiers had done something awful to his family. Well, he could understand why Cole might hold a grudge, but to him it made more sense to punish those individuals responsible rather than take on the whole damn Union army.

Cole was a stubborn one, Snodgrass thought. But not a particularly lucky man. He got of out of scrapes through sheer determination, whereas Snodgrass preferred to avoid scrapes altogether.

While picking off a few Yankees in the trenches was one thing, assassinating General Grant was something else altogether. Snodgrass just hoped Cole hadn't bitten off more than he could chew.

The dry winter grass swished around his ankles as he walked.

Where are these ol' feet carrying me, he wondered? He really didn't have any plans. Snodgrass guessed he would head south, trying all the while to duck whatever home guard or provost units were on patrol. His belly rumbled a bit as he walked, and he wistfully thought of how he had missed his noontime beans and would miss supper as well, even if it was only some old salt horse—beef pickled in brine—that the workmen like as not ended up with. Something was better than nothing, at least.

He was so caught up in thinking about food that he didn't notice the cavalry patrol riding up until too late. They were riding hard, and they swept into the field he was crossing with no warning.

"Good Lord!" he sang out, then started running for the tangle of brambles at the field's edge.

A trooper beat him there, cutting off his escape route. The cavalryman trained a carbine on him one-handed as the other hand held the reins of the stave-sided horse. Only Confederate horses could be that ill-fed and still go tearing around the countryside, he found himself thinking, even as he stared up into the barrel of the Sharps carbine.

Behind him he heard someone shout, "Hold it right there, you yellowbelly deserter!" There followed the unmistakable sound of a revolver's hammer snicking back.

Knowing there was no way he could outrun a horse, let alone a bullet, Snodgrass stood there helplessly with his hands at his sides. He cursed himself for turning his luck sour by thinking about it a few minutes ago.

A cavalryman rode up whom Snodgrass took to be the leader of the patrol, although he looked awfully young and had no uniform or insignia. He wore brown homespun trousers, a shapeless hat and a filthy farmer's work coat.

"Throw down your arms!"

"I would but they're attached to my shoulders."

The officer lashed out with his boot and caught Snodgrass a good one in the chest, sending him tumbling in the grass.

"I won't take no foolishness from a goddamn yellowbelly."

Slowly, Snodgrass got up and brushed himself off. "Sorry, sir, but I ain't got no *arms* to speak of. Just a jack knife and a blanket roll."

"What unit you with?"

"The Sixth Maryland."

Passing himself off as a Marylander had worked well enough with the Yankees, so he figured he would try it with the Confederates.

Snodgrass saw the officer glance around at his men, then finally fix his eyes once more on Snodgrass. They were hard-looking eyes, Snodgrass thought, for such a young man. Goddamn this war, he thought, it's turning everyone savage.

"That's a Yankee unit," the boy-officer said.

"Yes, sir."

"You're tellin' us you're a Yankee deserter?"

"That's right. I figure General Grant can win the war without me. I'm going home to Frederick."

"Where's your uniform?"

"I guess if I wore that, all the farmers on my way home would peg me for a deserter right off. I got some ol' clothes off a sutler."

Once more, the officer looked around at his men. "All right," he finally said. "I reckon we'll take you prisoner, Yank, deserter or not. Good thing you ain't a deserter from our army, 'cuz we would've strung you right up from the nearest tree. Hell, we still might."

Snodgrass didn't doubt for a moment that this young officer would have stretched his neck at the first opportunity. Of course, he wasn't ruling out the possibility that the cavalrymen might do that yet, especially if they figured out he wasn't a Yankee after all.

"Get on with you, Yank," one of the cavalrymen ordered, prodding Snodgrass with the muzzle of his carbine. Snodgrass started walking at a quick pace to keep up with the horses. He figured they must have been close to the Confederate lines or they wouldn't have wasted time walking. They made no attempt to tie his hands, and he couldn't help but wonder if they were hoping he would make a run for it so they could shoot him down.

"You boys is mighty close to our lines, ain't you?" Snodgrass asked.

"Shut up now, Yank. Save your breath for walkin'. If you cain't keep up we'll shoot you."

Snodgrass didn't fancy being anybody's prisoner. These Rebs were an untalkative bunch, too, and they thwarted his considerable efforts to start a conversation. This made him feel uneasy, for he knew that once they started talking with him, it would be that much harder for the cavalrymen to shoot him.

"Ya'll have got some mighty skinny horses," Snodgrass said, trying again. "You ought to see the animals they've got over at City Point. Fine, big horses."

"Shut up, Yank."

"Would ya'll mind stopping a minute? I find myself caught short in all the excitement of being captured."

The officer rode back and glowered down at him. "What do you think you're up to, Yank?" he demanded.

One of the men called out, "Hell, lieutenant, I could take a shit myself."

Unable to argue with that, the officer simply nodded toward some bushes at the edge of the field they were crossing. "You just keep shakin' them bushes, Yank, the whole time you're over there. The minute you stop, we'll pump that bush full of lead."

"Yes, sir," Snodgrass said, trying to appear wide-eyed with fear. He trotted over to the bushes and started shaking them.

"Shake them bushes, Yank!" somebody called, and he heard the troopers laughing. "Shake 'em!"

"Don't shoot!" he cried as pitifully as possible.

What had he been thinking to himself about luck? Maybe his streak hadn't run out yet, after all. He had an idea about how to get away from this bunch that just might work. Snodgrass had a length of string in his pocket, and he quickly tied it to the bush. Yanking on the string for all he was worth, he kept the bush dancing at a lively rate as he backed deeper into the undergrowth at the edge of the woods.

"I'm shakin' it!" he called. "Don't shoot."

It was a good thirty feet of twine. When he got to the end he turned and ran like hell into the trees.

He heard shouting, but they gave him maybe half a minute before they poured bullets into the bush.

"The bastard's in the woods!" he heard one of the troopers shout.

Snodgrass ran like a rabbit for the deepest part of the woods. Thank God there was something in Virginia besides scrub, he thought, as the trees closed in around him. Branches slashed at his face and briars ripped at his skin, but he kept running, dodging trees and clumps of undergrowth.

Behind him, he heard the cavalrymen crashing through the woods. But just as quickly, the noise stopped. The trees were too thick to ride through, and they weren't about to dismount to chase a lone deserter, not when they were so close to the Yankee lines.

He ran until his lungs felt as if they were on fire, and then he slowed to a trot. His face stung from where branches had whipped across his cheeks and his hands were torn by thorns, but at least he had given those cavalrymen the slip. By and by the woods thinned out and Snodgrass popped out onto a country road heading, it appeared, to nowhere. With a shrug, he started walking. From what he could tell, the road ran east, back toward the Yankee camp.

Let's see where *this* hand takes me, he thought. He hoped Cole had made it through the patrols. Knowing Cole, he had slipped around any more cavalry, blue or gray, that was scouting the area.

He had gone maybe a quarter of a mile when a soldier in blue stepped out from behind a tree and pointed a musket with a nasty-looking bayonet at his belly.

"Halt, Reb!"

"Aw, hell," Snodgrass said, putting his hands up.

"I seen you coming, Reb," the soldier said, and Snodgrass saw now he was merely a boy, old enough only for peach fuzz on his face and wearing a uniform so big for him it hung off his thin frame like a sack and he'd had to roll back the sleeves and the cuffs of the trousers.

"I'm starting to feel like an old man," said Snodgrass, who was still short of thirty. "How old are you, boy?"

"Sixteen."

Snodgrass's hands were still up over his head. He'd be damned if he'd go back to the Yankee camp as a prisoner. This boy was young and possibly foolish. He sighed, looked down at the road.

"I'll be damned," he said. "Somebody done dropped a silver dollar."

The boy's eyes flicked downward, unable to resist. Snodgrass jerked the Springfield's muzzle skyward and then punched the young soldier so hard on the chin he was sure the boy's mother felt it. He fell like a sack of potatoes, and Snodgrass dragged him off the road. The young Yankee would be fine when he came to, though he might have a headache.

Snodgrass quickly stripped the uniform off the boy and changed into it. Big as it had been on the youth, it fit him well enough, and he was soon swinging down the road back toward City Point.

To hell with it, he thought. He was through pushing his luck. He planned on getting his old job back and eating his share of beans and salt horse in relative safety until the war was over.

• • •

Cole was hunting again.

He sought out the place he had scouted during his nighttime trip through the woods. Just beyond where the trees ended was the field where General Grant liked to walk. There was a towering pine tree at the edge of the woods that seemed made especially for a sniper. Unlike the deciduous trees surrounding it, the pine's green boughs would camouflage him well, and the branches were sturdy enough to support his weight.

There was a round in the chamber of the Sharps, and he had the Colt within easy reach, tucked into his belt, in case he came across any Yankees. Since leaving camp this morning, he no longer felt like a fugitive or a man on the run.

Behind him, the woods were deep enough that he could disappear into them after he shot the general. The trees and underbrush were too dense for cavalry, so any pursuers would have to chase him on foot. With luck and a head start, Cole doubted there was any man who could catch him once he was into those trees. Beyond that, he didn't have much of a plan for escape, but once he had gotten away he would see what was next. He was confident the woods would hide him.

The tree he had chosen was so big that no limbs grew within reach of the ground. He would have to pull himself up and had already hidden a length of rope nearby for just such a purpose. Quickly, he took the coil of rope from its hiding place beneath a clump of multiflora rose, tied a stick to one end, and threw it over the lowest branch of the pine. Then he gave it slack until the end of the rope was within reach. He tied the end to the main length of rope with a slipknot and pulled until the knot was tight against the tree branch. Just like sending a flag up a pole, he thought. He shimmied up the rope, untied it, and began his ascent into the dark web of branches.

A sniper's best post was up high, where curious eyes seldom pried and there were few obstructions to send the bullet astray. During the Battle of the Wilderness, Cole had climbed from one tree to the next as the lines wavered back and forth. Sometimes he'd had to stay put because the ebb and tide of battle had suddenly put his tree behind Yankee lines. Fortunately, the soldiers were usually too busy blazing away at the Rebs in front of them to notice Cole just a few feet over their heads.

Cole climbed until he found a place where a strong limb branched out from the trunk. He straddled the limb, resting his back against the tree trunk. A fork in the limb made a natural rifle rest, and he had an eagle's eye view of the field.

He had brought the rope along for a dual purpose. First, to get himself into the tree, and second, to keep himself *in* the tree. He planned to spend the night in the pine if necessary, and he didn't want to go crashing to the ground if he should fall asleep. He lashed himself to the tree trunk, just as a sailor might lash himself to the mast in preparation for a storm. He made a few loose loops around the Sharps rifle as well. With his big Bowie knife he could cut himself free in an instant.

Cole had brought along two canteens and plenty of food. There was even a pint bottle of whiskey to keep him warm, for it would be a long, cold wait in the tree. At least the thick branches helped break the winter wind, he told himself.

It was just as well Snodgrass had gone on, because the man would not have lasted an hour in the tree, and he would not have been much use on the ground. Besides, Snodgrass would have been the first to admit he couldn't have hit anything farther than the length of a card table. Cole didn't plan on needing to take more than one shot, and it would be much easier for one man rather than two to give the Yankees the slip afterwards.

He felt enormously happy, no matter that he was already cold and uncomfortable. Cole's mind and body readily ignored physical discomforts. He was doing what he loved to do, what he had been born to do. *A killer of men?* he wondered. *No,* he told himself. *You're only a hunter, even if the prey this time happens to be Lieutenant General Ulysses S. Grant.*

"Put this on," Mulholland ordered, handing O'Malley an officer's coat. They were in Grant's outer office, but the general was out making an inspection of the camp, as he often did on Tuesday mornings. After coming up empty during their visit to the workmen's camp this morning, Mulholland had decided to put his other plan for thwarting the sharpshooter into action.

"I'll not be getting into trouble for this, will I, Major sir?"

"Just do as you're told, Private."

O'Malley shrugged, then took off his dark blue soldier's blouse and pulled on the officer's coat. It was very plain, considering the only ornament on it was the four stars on the shoulder straps.

"You'll have me impersonating General Grant again, will you?" O'Malley asked. His eyes sparkled with amusement. "The general must be needing a stand-in for a dress parade."

Mulholland exchanged a look with Bowers. He had debated with himself over whether he should tell O'Malley what he was planning to do. After all, his plan could easily get O'Malley killed.

"Something like a dress parade," Bowers offered. "But you'll be parading for one person in particular."

"You must mean Abraham Lincoln!" O'Malley laughed.

"Now for the hat," Mulholland said, deciding he could explain the particulars of the plan to O'Malley in the morning. No sense in having the Irishman fret over it all night. He clapped a broad-brimmed hat much like Grant's on O'Malley's head, and the transformation was complete.

"A double measure of whiskey for all the lads!" O'Malley sang out in his brogue. "That's an order."

"Put a cigar in his mouth and you can hardly tell the difference between them," Bowers said. "Until you hear that brogue."

"Aye, and an Irishman never loses his brogue," O'Malley said sadly. "It is our curse."

Bowers stood a few feet away, admiring their handiwork. He shook his head in astonishment. Clean-shaven, it would have been easy enough to tell the general apart from O'Malley. But because they both wore beards, their similar heights and builds made the two men virtually indistinguishable, especially from a distance. "If I didn't know better I would say you were his twin brother," Bowers said. "Anyone who knows Grant well enough wouldn't be fooled—"

Mulholland broke in, "But from a distance—"

"Their own mothers couldn't tell them apart."

"What are you two gentlemen planning?" O'Malley asked, that twinkle in his eye sparkling. "A wee bit o' mischief, is it? Some joke on the general?"

His smile faded as Bayliss walked into the room. The sharp-shooter's sudden appearance actually seemed to make the temperature dip a few degrees. That man is the devil himself, Mulholland thought.

Stoic as Bayliss was, his mouth opened in amazement when he saw the costumed O'Malley. He said nothing, just stood there working the wad of tobacco in his mouth, then leaned out the door to spit a long stream of brown juice onto the frozen ground. "That Reb sharpshooter will never be able to tell the difference," he announced at last.

O'Malley's eyes took on a wary expression. "What's this about a Reb sharpshooter? I thought you gentlemen were going to play a wee practical joke on someone."

"We are," Mulholland said. "It's just that he'll be wearing butternut."

O'Malley took the hat off. "I don't know that I want to be doing this, Major sir. It sounds dangerous."

"Don't worry, O'Malley," Bayliss offered, a wicked grin on his face. "If this Reb is any good, you won't feel a thing when he kills you. It'll be just like closing your eyes. Only you'll never be opening them again."

"That's enough, Bayliss!" Mulholland's eyes blazed at him, but Bayliss appeared not to notice. He turned to O'Malley. "The plan isn't for you to be shot, but only for you to draw out the enemy sharpshooter. All you're required to do is walk in that field where the general likes to stroll occasionally."

"But sir," O'Malley said. "How will you know where this Reb is until he fires?"

Mulholland ignored the question. "Bayliss here will pick him off once the sharpshooter has given his position away."

O'Malley shook his head. "I don't know that I want to be doing this."

Mulholland was torn. He knew he could very well be sending O'Malley to his death. Yet desperate times called for desperate measures. If the Rebel sharpshooter wasn't rooted out, there could be terrible consequences for the Union if he should be successful in assassinating General Grant. They must do what they could to stop him.

Mulholland did not attempt to explain all of this to Private O'Malley. He liked the jovial Irishman and felt terrible enough as it was, but saw no other path to take. Besides, there was no easy way to explain to a man that his life was expendable in the service of his country, while the life of another—such as General Grant's—was infinitely more valuable.

"You will do your duty, Private O'Malley," Mulholland said quietly. "It is all that is asked of a soldier."

A scuffling of feet broke the silence that followed. Mulholland turned. The sentry he had left on duty outside was standing in the doorway. He saluted.

"You have a visitor, sir."

"Just a minute." Mulholland wondered who it could be. With a jerk of his head, he directed O'Malley to get out of sight. "Show him in."

"*Her,* sir," the guard said.

"What are you talking about?"

The doorway suddenly filled with a wide hoop skirt as Anne Clark walked into the office. Mulholland was stunned.

"Anne?"

"Oh, Brendan—I mean, Major Mulholland." She wore a look of concern on her face. "I'm so glad I found you."

"But Anne, I don't understand—"

"It's your grandmother, major. She's very ill. I had to come and tell you myself."

"Is she dying?"

"No, but she's very ill." Anne Clark looked around at the staring soldiers, the colonel, and the sentry. They acted as if they hadn't seen a woman in ages. Well, she thought, they probably *hadn't* in this place. During her short walk up from the wharves, the camp had impressed her as a godforsaken, bleak, and cold place. "*Very* ill."

Mulholland wasn't sure how to take the news. "Should I go to Washington, Anne?" he asked. "Does she need me?"

Anne came up close to him, and the office filled with her perfume. She noted that she had the undivided attention of the three men in the room, which pleased her. "Tomorrow," Anne said. "It can wait until tomorrow."

Mulholland turned to Bowers. "We'll give our plan a try tomorrow morning," he said. "Then I'll catch the night boat for Washington."

20

The problem of what to do with Anne Clark was quickly settled by Mrs. Grant. An unchaperoned young lady's sudden arrival at the military camp created a small crisis, because there were certain rules of propriety which had to be followed.

Mrs. Grant stepped in and made arrangements for Anne to stay at the house nearby which had been taken over by the quartermaster. Several wives occupied the house, and it was arranged that Anne would spend the night in the room of a woman whose husband was in Washington on Army business. Hattie would sleep on the kitchen floor with the other servants.

First there was dinner, beefsteak and potatoes, and the conversation was lively thanks to Anne's presence. After dinner, Mulholland was able to get a few minutes alone with her to ask about his grandmother.

"It's a strange ailment," Anne explained. "She's out of her head, but she doesn't have a fever. That's why I came. I thought that perhaps, considering her age, she is no longer herself."

Mulholland nodded gravely, but he realized with some guilt that his thoughts were more on Anne than his aging grandmother. Anne was a beautiful woman, and during dinner the other staff officers had flirted relentlessly, if politely. They understood Anne had come to see Major Mulholland and none of them.

"It was kind of you to come, Anne," he said, noticing how the candlelight made the red highlights in her hair shine. "I thought I wouldn't see you again until the war was over."

"From what I understand, Brendan, it may be over very soon if General Grant orders the attack—"

"Anne." He put a hand on her elbow and leaned close to whisper. Mulholland felt a cold tingling in the pit of his stomach as he realized he had told her too much during his trip to Washington City. "You shouldn't know anything about that attack. Don't mention it again . . . to anyone."

"Don't worry, Brendan. Your secrets are safe with me. I was only wondering—"

"No more." He shook his head with finality. "We can't discuss it."

Anne hid her disappointment with a smile. If Brendan wouldn't tell her anything, maybe someone else would. That Colonel Bowers seemed the sort who would talk freely after enough whiskey and some feminine company. Of course, she might have to stay a few days in City Point. It was January 3, and with the holidays over, she might be able to extend her visit even if Brendan returned to Washington to see to his ailing grandmother.

General Grant entered the room with his wife, followed by some of the staff officers. They took up chairs around the stove, and Anne's chances of learning more about the Union attack on Petersburg were ended for the evening.

Cole was chilled to the bone when he woke up Wednesday morning. He had spent Tuesday night in the pine tree, dozing as the wind sighed through the soft-needled branches, and the winter chill had crept through him as soon as the last of the daylight faded from the sky.

Maybe it had been foolish to spend the night. He could have risen long before dawn and been in position, but at least he had been safe from detection up in the tree. Not like the other night when that fool Yankee had nearly tripped over him in the dark.

His vigil in the tree cleansed his mind and left him ready for what lay ahead. Cole believed a hunter had to earn his prey, especially if it was a great trophy. Along with every success, there must be some suffering, he thought.

Somewhere in the night, in the strange way that dreams have of becoming tangled up with waking reality, he had imagined he was hunting a huge buck named General Grant. In his dream, the buck had a rack of antlers that even old timers had never seen the like of, while his prey this particular morning had nothing more on his head than a broad-brimmed hat.

He'd heard tell that ol' Mosby had a Union brigadier general's dress coat that he kept as a prize. *These Yankees ought to be thankful we don't take scalps like the Indians.*

When he woke from his strange dreams, Cole was so stiff with cold he could barely move. It took much flexing and unflexing of his fingers to get them working properly. He unbuttoned his trousers and pissed out into space, watching the stream of urine steam in the cold morning air as it arced toward the forest floor. Then after a hunk of bread and a few sips of warmth-giving whiskey for breakfast, he settled down to wait.

Anne had breakfast with the ladies in the big house on the bluff and then went off in search of Brendan at Grant's headquarters. She found him working in the outer office.

"Good morning, Major."

Brendan looked up and smiled. "I trust they took good care of you at the quartermaster general's?"

"They were very kind to me. It's a comfortable house. I couldn't help wondering why General Grant didn't make it his headquarters."

Brendan shrugged. "All he cares about is work, not entertaining. In fact, he's already out this morning, having a look at the wharves. I'll bet the quartermaster is just finishing his coffee."

They were interrupted by a soldier with an Irish accent.

"Excuse me, Major sir, but you said to report to you first thing this morning."

Brendan held up a hand to keep him from coming any farther into the office. "Let's talk outside. I'll be right back, Anne."

The major limped out with the Irishman, and Anne found herself alone in the office.

She wasted no time. Anne went to Brendan's desk first. She took a quick look at the papers there but saw nothing important. The same held true for the other desks in the room. Much of what she saw appeared to be routine military paperwork.

Anne glanced toward the door. She could hear Brendan's voice talking in muffled tones outside. How much time did she have?

There was one desk left to search, that of General Grant himself. His office was just beyond that of his staff, and Anne quickly stepped through the doorway.

It looked like the office of a frontiersman. Rough pine boards, a small stove, a window with cracked panes of glass, obviously salvaged from some old house. The only finishing touch was a braided rug under the desk. The rug was coated with the black mud of City Point.

His desk was surprisingly empty. Not a paper was to be seen. There was a notebook on the desk, with a pencil laid on top. Anne stopped to listen, could still hear Brendan's voice outside. If she was caught . . . Her heart pounding, Anne pushed the pencil aside and flipped open the notebook.

Most of the pages contained "General Orders" pertaining to routine camp activities. The final page, however, caught her eye. Curious, she glanced at a few of the lines:

> . . . **General McLaughlen will lead his 3rd Brigade, 1st Division, IX Corps out from the trenches at first light on Jan. 10th. That force will concentrate at Colquitt's Salient and hit the Confederate force directly adjacent under Gordon. The attack will be supported by Gen. Hartranft's 3rd Division . . .**

Anne didn't need to read further. McLaughlen! She remembered Brendan had mentioned the general's name back in Washington. It would now be possible for the Confederates across from the Yankee general to prepare for an attack. She took the sheet from the notebook, folded it up, and tucked the paper up her sleeve. Then she closed the notebook and replaced the pencil atop it.

She heard footsteps and rushed out of Grant's office to meet Brendan headlong.

"Anne, for heaven's sake. What are you doing in the general's office?"

"Oh, I just wanted to see it," she lied smoothly and smiled. "He's such an intriguing man."

"His office is off limits," Brendan snapped. "Now don't go telling people you were in there. The general would have me for lunch, considering you're my guest."

"Really, Brendan. I won't tell a soul. I'm sorry." The paper in her sleeve felt like a hot coal, and she expected at any second for him to grab her arm and call for the guards. But he had already forgotten.

"Anne, if you'll excuse me, I have some things to see to. I'll see you later today, and we can catch the steamer together this evening for Washington."

"Oh, that's why I came to see you this morning, Brendan. I'm leaving sooner. I have to get back to Washington. In fact, I'm taking the first steamer that leaves today."

He looked disappointed. "I thought you would . . . well, I'll call on you in Washington." He smiled. "It was very kind of you to bring me this news in person."

She smiled back. "My pleasure, Brendan. Do come see me when you get to the city."

Anne nearly ran from the headquarters building to the quartermaster's house. She found Hattie in the kitchen, helping the other servants clean up.

"Hattie, we're leaving. Come with me and help me pack."

"Leaving, Miss Anne?"

"Yes, now come on."

They climbed the stairs to the room where Anne had spent the night. It took only minutes to pack, with Anne rushing Hattie on.

"I don't know why you in such a hurry."

Anne undid her sleeve and took out the paper. "Because of *this*," she said, waving the folded sheet in Hattie's face. Anne quickly found a more secure hiding place for the paper in a pocket of her traveling coat. "Now let's get going."

They hurried out of the house. Anne didn't even bother to look for the ladies who had played hostess to her; there was no time, and besides, she wouldn't be coming back.

The house on the bluff overlooked the wharves, and they made their way down the steep wooden stairs that had been built across the face of the cliff. Anne attracted not a little attention from the men working at the wharves. But they quickly noticed she was well dressed and had a servant in tow. Such a lady deserved respect, and no one dared make any catcalls.

She found the wharf where the steamer had let them off yesterday morning. A different ship was now tied up there. Anne approached a young lieutenant who seemed to be in charge of the gangway.

"Excuse me, Lieutenant. But is this ship going back to Washington City?"

"It is, ma'am, in about fifteen minutes."

"Do you think they can take me?"

"Why, ma'am, there should be plenty of room."

Anne smiled brightly at him. "Thank you, Lieutenant. Hattie——"

"Miss Anne, I done forgot your portmanteau."

Anne felt her temper flash and might even have sworn at Hattie if the lieutenant hadn't been standing there. She took a deep breath and tried to calm herself. *Damn Hattie.* There wasn't time for this. If General Grant opened his notebook and found his orders missing . . .

"Go back and get it," Anne said. One of her best dresses was in the portmanteau, and Anne's funds were such that she couldn't afford to leave the dress behind. The boat would soon be gone, she and Hattie would be aboard, and she would be beyond the reach of these Yankees, if they even suspected her. "I'll wait here with the lieutenant."

"You'd best hurry," the young officer said to Hattie. "This ship's leaving in fifteen minutes. I don't know if they'll wait for you."

"You heard the Lieutenant," Anne said, anger edging into her voice. "Now *run.*"

Hattie scooted away across the wharves, back toward the stairs that climbed the bluff.

"Where the hell is Bayliss?" Mulholland demanded.

"I don't know, Major sir. I ain't seen him since last night."

"Damn that arrogant bastard."

"What should we do, sir?"

"Get that coat and hat on, O'Malley. I'm leaving for Washington City on tonight's steamer, but I want to catch that damned sharpshooter before I go."

"Yes, sir."

"If that damned Bayliss isn't around, I'll back you up. There's a rifle in my quarters."

Headquarters was still empty, so O'Malley shucked off his private's coat and hat. He was soon dressed in an officer's coat with stars on the shoulder straps. He put on a wide-brimmed hat with a gold tassel, just like General Grant wore.

"All right, O'Malley, let's get out to that field. We're going to catch that damned Reb."

As they started out the door, Mulholland was surprised to see Hattie come running up. He was alarmed, thinking that something must have happened to Anne.

"Major, Major Mulholland—"

"Hattie, what is it?"

"I got to talk to you." She was breathing hard and Mulholland thought she must have run all the way from the waterfront. "In private."

"O'Malley, go on ahead to the field. I'll catch up."

"What about Bayliss, sir?" O'Malley looked nervous. "He's supposed to back me up."

"Damn Bayliss! I'll back you up. Now go. And put on my damned overcoat until you get to the field. I don't want anyone arresting you for impersonating an officer on your way there."

"Yes, sir."

Once O'Malley had started off, the general's uniform covered, he turned to Hattie. "Come in," he said. "What's so important that you've run all the way from the waterfront to tell me?"

Hattie blurted it out: "Miss Anne is a spy!"

"What on earth are you talking about?"

"Your grandmother ain't sick. Miss Anne baked a pie and put somethin' in it to make her that way so's she'd have an excuse to come down here. She really come to find out about that attack on the Rebels."

Mulholland felt his belly clench into a cold fist. "Go on."

"That ain't all. You know in Washington how that man tried to shoot General Grant—"

Mulholland's mouth fell open. "How in the world do you know about that, Hattie?"

"The man that tried to shoot him was named Lucas Cole. He done stayed with us. Miss Anne helped him."

Cole? He couldn't believe what he was hearing. That was the name of the man who had disappeared from the workmen's camp. Hattie must be lying! Anne couldn't be a spy.

"These are very serious charges, Hattie. How am I supposed to believe you?"

"She got a paper with her she stole from here," Hattie said. "It's in her coat pocket. You just look there, and you'll know."

He remembered finding Anne in General Grant's office that morning. Could she have taken something from his desk? The coldness in his belly expanded, grabbed at his chest. He didn't want to believe what he was hearing.

"Where is she?"

"Miss Anne down at the boat, waiting to go aboard."

"Come with me," he said, and started out the door. They walked quickly, but Mulholland's injured leg hampered him. The wound hadn't healed completely, and descending the staircase to the wharves was painful. Once on the waterfront, he could see Anne in the distance, waiting by the gangway of a ship.

He quickened his pace. Hattie's news had planted a seed of anger. He realized he had told Anne too much about Grant's plans for an attack on Petersburg. It hadn't seemed to matter. But if Anne had come to City Point to learn more and had stolen valuable papers while she was his guest, it would be a terrible betrayal of their friendship. He felt his rage growing.

Anne spotted him approaching. She had been talking to an officer stationed at the foot of the gangway, and now she turned and started up the narrow walkway toward the waiting steamer.

"Stop that woman!" Mulholland shouted. The startled officer at the gangway stared at him. "Stop her!"

Several heads had turned to see what was going on. The young lieutenant started up the gangway after Anne. She stopped and headed back to shore.

"Brendan," she said as he approached. She smiled warmly. "You didn't bring my portmanteau? Hattie went to fetch it."

"I need to talk to you, Anne."

"The ship leaves in a few minutes—"

"Come down off the gangway, Anne." His voice was low and icy.

The lieutenant had recognized Mulholland as a member of the headquarters staff and he stood dumbly to one side, wondering what was going on. "Sir?"

"Search that woman's coat pockets, Lieutenant."

"Brendan, this is ridiculous. What's going on?"

"Sir, you want me to search her?"

"That's what I said, Lieutenant."

Anne flashed an angry look at Hattie, then took a step back, toward the gangway. The lieutenant followed with a puzzled look on his face.

"Ma'am?"

She dug her hand into her pocket, came out with the paper. In a fury she crumpled it and turned to throw it into the river.

Mulholland caught her wrist in an iron grip. "Give me that," he said.

"I don't know where it came from. Hattie must have put it there."

"Miss Anne, I seen you—"

"Shut up, both of you," Mulholland said. He smoothed out the crumpled sheet and blanched at what he read. *The orders for the attack on Petersburg.* She must have stolen it right off Grant's desk.

"I just thought I'd take it as a souvenir," Anne said. "I didn't even notice what it said."

"Lieutenant, place this woman under arrest."

"Yes, sir."

The young officer stepped forward and put a firm grip on Anne's arm.

"Hattie, you stay close," he added. "I don't want you running off. I've got some more questions."

At that, they started down the waterfront toward the steps that led up the bluff.

"All this can be explained, Brendan," Anne was saying. He noticed she had become very pale. "This is a misunderstanding."

"You knew about the sharpshooter in Washington?"

"What has Hattie been telling you?"

Mulholland's leg pained him considerably as they climbed the steep stairway. When they reached the top, he turned to the lieutenant. "Thank you, Lieutenant, that will be all."

The other officer saluted uncertainly, still wondering what all this was about, and headed back down the stairs. Mulholland took Anne's arm.

"Where are you taking me?" she asked. "Back to the quarter-master's house?"

"I'm afraid not, Anne. I'm going to have you locked up in a guardhouse."

"Then what?"

He stopped and stared at her. Anne had never seen his eyes look so hard. "I suppose you'll be hanged."

Without another word, he led her toward the group of huts where prisoners were kept.

O'Malley walked out into the open space beyond the headquarters buildings feeling as if he had a large target pinned to his chest.

He wasn't wearing a target, of course, just an officer's uniform and the shoulder straps with four stars. He also wore a broad-brimmed hat with gold braid and had a cigar in his mouth that tasted far better than the crude stuff an ordinary enlisted man got to smoke now and then. Didn't he look to be the grand General Grant himself! But the thought was no consolation for O'Malley, who couldn't help nervously eyeing the trees in the distance.

"You're a fool for doing this, Michael O'Malley," he warned himself out loud, for there was no one nearby. The guards Major Mulholland had posted stood some distance away, as if to leave him to his thoughts.

Although he didn't want to be out in this field in some sharpshooter's rifle sights, what other choice did he have? Major Mulholland had ordered him out here, and there was no refusing a direct order. Guard duty at headquarters was soft enough, and if he didn't do as the major told him it might just be back to the trenches for him, where a man was more likely to catch his death of cold than by a bullet.

Bullet. He tried not to think about the fact that he might very well be in the sniper's rifle sights at that very moment. With luck, he told himself, there wouldn't be anyone out there at all, for the major was known to be a wee bit overcautious. Besides, the trees where the sharpshooter might be hiding were so distant, O'Malley didn't see how anyone could hit him from that far off. What was it, he wondered? Half a mile away? God himself couldn't shoot a rifle that well.

Aye, O'Malley, and this is not the time to blaspheme the Lord.

He took a long pull on the cigar, savoring the rich tobacco, then blew a great gout of bluish smoke toward the gray winter sky.

"Ha!" he said aloud, trying to make himself feel braver. Laughing at death. It didn't quite work.

He hoped Bayliss, that man with a pall of evil on him, was hidden somewhere in the trees, searching for the Rebel sharpshooter. He wished the major would hurry back, just in case Bayliss wasn't in position.

The Irish were always getting the dirty jobs, even in America.

O'Malley reminded himself that he was supposed to be imitating General Grant. So O'Malley clasped his hands behind his back, clamped the cigar between his teeth, then strolled along absently, much as he had often seen General Grant doing in this very field.

Mulholland's nerves were strung as tightly as piano wire as he started back toward headquarters. He could scarcely believe he had just put Anne under arrest for spying. Anne a spy! He had been serious when he told her the penalty was hanging.

The way he felt at the moment, he would have been glad to play hangman. Anne had made him look like a fool. She had been welcomed to City Point because she was a friend of his and she had taken advantage of their friendship by stealing orders for the Petersburg attack off Grant's desk.

He intended to stop at headquarters to return the orders Anne had stolen, as well as make an explanation to General Grant. Then he had to hurry out to the field, where O'Malley was serving as bait for the Rebel sharpshooter.

While Mulholland had told Grant about the threat from the sharpshooter, he hadn't made the general aware of the plan to lure the marksman from hiding. Grant generally didn't want to be troubled about such details. He had more important things to worry about as commander in chief.

The only person in the office was Robert Lincoln, who was busy copying some papers.

"Hello, Robert. Where's General Grant?"

"He's gone out for a walk," Lincoln said. "He said something about having to stretch his legs."

Mulholland thought at once of the sharpshooter lurking in the woods. "Did he say where he was going for a walk?"

"He didn't say." Lincoln gazed back at Mulholland quizzically. "Why? Is something wrong?"

"I hope to God not," Mulholland said.

He took off at a run from headquarters, cursing the pain in his leg that slowed him down. In an army where few men ran unless they were being chased by screaming Rebs waving bayonets, Mulholland drew more than a little attention. Not that he noticed. He was too busy racing toward the field beyond the headquarters buildings.

It was mid-morning when the blue-clad figure of an officer appeared in the field.

Cole's heart speeded up slightly, until he willed it to slow down. By the time he was ready to pull the trigger, his heart would be beating as quietly as the footfalls of a stalking tomcat.

He eased the Sharps into position. The fork in the tree limb made a natural rifle rest. He put a fresh primer on the nipple of the rifle and eased back the hammer. Cole moved slowly. No sense rushing now. He was sure the general would be in the field for a while.

Once the rifle was ready, Cole put his eye to the telescopic sight. Everything suddenly jumped closer—individual clumps of grass, a single whip of a sumac sapling that had gotten itself started in the field, and General Grant himself. Cole had never seen him up close, but there was no mistaking the commander of the Union armies with his plain, blue uniform and brown beard. A cigar jutted from his mouth and Cole watched the general tilt his head back and blow smoke skyward, as if he was enjoying the cigar immensely. The most telltale sign of all that it was Grant was the shoulder straps, each with four gold stars.

Cole's body and mind began to slip into its shooting rhythm. Slowly, he willed his heartbeat to soften. The thumping in his chest wound down to a mere murmur. His breathing quieted until he was only taking sips of air. Both eyes were open, his shooting eye focused on the target in the telescope's field of vision.

Nothing must stir the rifle by the smallest fraction if the shot was to be true. He sensed the tree that held him reaching down to spread its roots in the Virginia soil. Cole was anchored in earth and rock. He found it best when he was making a difficult shot like this to let his mind wander. While his thoughts drifted, another part of his mind would set up the shot, calculate the height at which he should aim above Grant's head to compensate for the bullet's trajectory. Then the crosshairs found that spot, and Cole's finger tightened ever so slightly on the trigger, beginning to take up the slack. The trick was to get the rifle to fire so that it was a surprise and his body would not flinch in anticipation of the recoil, for even the smallest twitch could send the bullet wildly astray.

Most important, Cole began to think the bullet home. He imagined where the shot would strike, creating a neat, round hole, then the sound following—*thunk*—of lead rending flesh and bone. If he imagined it happening, it took only a bit of pressure from his finger to make it reality.

In the rifle scope, Cole could see General Grant strolling along enjoying his cigar, oblivious to the fact that he was just seconds from death. Grant stood still, and the pad of Cole's finger felt electric as he eased the last bit of pressure from the trigger.

As Cole aimed, a second figure entered the telescope's field of vision and stood face to face with the general.

Blue coat. Broad-brimmed hat. Brown beard. Cigar in his mouth. Four stars on his shoulder straps.

Cole let up on the trigger. Blinked his eyes. There was not one General Grant out there, but *two*.

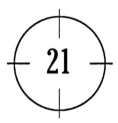

21

At first, General Grant looked amused. He had something of a smile on his face as he chewed his cigar and looked O'Malley over from head to toe. A few staff members and guards were some distance away, looking on curiously.

"That's good, very good," Grant said. "Why, I don't believe our own mothers could tell us apart."

O'Malley found himself at an uncustomary loss for words and only managed to mutter, "Thank you, General sir."

Then General Grant's disposition changed. He chomped his unlit cigar more furiously, and his face took on a bull-headed expression.

O'Malley noticed a change in himself, as well. He began to quake. *I'm a poor fool,* he thought. *What have I gotten myself into?* General Grant looked about as friendly as a thundercloud.

"Now would you mind telling me, *Private,* what in blazes you're doing impersonating me?"

The shaking that had started in O'Malley's fingertips had by now spread to his toes. Normally he could talk his way out of most anything, but his tongue now felt all tied up.

"Well?" General Grant demanded. "You have about ten seconds to explain yourself before I have you locked in the guardhouse."

"Uh, you see, General sir, I'm only following orders."

"Whose orders?" he demanded.

"Why, it was Major Mulholland and Colonel Bowers that got me outfitted like this."

"Is there a reason?" Grant's eyes were hard and dark as chunks of coal. "By the way, that looks like *my* good coat you've got on there, Private. You sure as hell better not get it dirty. Now tell me what you're doing here."

"I'm supposed to be dressed up as you because there's a Johnny Reb sharpshooter out to assassinate you, sir. Some soldier saw him lurking about. He's got a fancy rifle and a dead eye, they say."

"Oh?" The angry look on Grant's face began to fade, and O'Malley felt his own tongue begin to loosen.

"The idea is that I'll draw this sharpshooter into the open, where Corporal Bayliss will shoot him."

"I don't see Bayliss."

"He's hidden away in a treetop somewhere around here. He was out before dawn."

"You mean he's watching us now?"

"Yes, sir."

"Where is this sharpshooter, then?"

"Well, general sir, he's supposed to be way over there in those trees."

General Grant stared curiously toward the distant tree line where the axmen had not yet reached. "Why, he'd have to be one hell of a shot to hit me—or should I say *one* of me—from that distance."

"With all respect, sir, let's hope he's not that good a shot."

O'Malley saw a new expression cross General Grant's face, and it made him uneasy. In General Ulysses S. Grant's eyes, O'Malley was surprised to see a flicker of fear.

Cole stared in disbelief at the two men in the round circle of the telescopic sight. They couldn't *both* be General Grant. But he couldn't tell them apart. Maybe up close the difference would have been apparent, but at this distance the men looked exactly alike. Same build, same height, same uniform.

What were these Yankees up to? He wondered briefly if the men were twin brothers, which enabled the general to be in two places at once. If this was the case, it was no wonder General Grant had turned the Union army around.

He would have time for only one shot. Cole figured he had an even chance of killing the right man. He wondered how Snodgrass would have liked those odds and decided they really weren't that bad. No worse than flipping a coin.

Cole let the rifle sight waver from one man to the other, his finger all the while taking up tension on the trigger. In the instant before the hammer swung down, one of the generals turned and stared in his direction, as if searching for him among the trees.

The Sharps fired and one of the generals pitched over backwards into the field.

Mulholland was running as fast as his feet would carry him when he heard first one shot, then another. He stopped, listened for more gunfire, took off again. The second rifle would be Bayliss's, he thought, glad that the sharpshooter must have posted himself in the field after all.

His heart was racing, and it wasn't all from the effort of running. Fear had made a knot in his chest, for he knew the first shot must have been the enemy rifleman. Who had the Rebel sniper shot? He prayed to God General Grant hadn't been in the field.

Mulholland's lungs felt like they were on fire. His injured leg felt as if it were being stabbed again and again each time his foot hit the ground. He cursed his uniform, which was not made for speed, because as he ran his long coat managed to bind around his legs, and his heavy boots were better suited for stirrups than a footrace. By the time he reached the field, he was nearly winded, and the sight which greeted him took the rest of his breath away.

He could see Bayliss loping toward the trees, dragging out a revolver as he ran. Mulholland took that as a sign that Bayliss must have at least winged the enemy sharpshooter.

It was then that he spotted the figure in the brown winter grass. General Grant had indeed reached the field, because several of his guards were sprinting toward the fallen man. One soldier was already at the wounded officer's side, and all Mulholland could tell was that he had a general's shoulder straps and a cigar in his mouth.

Was it O'Malley or Grant himself who lay in the grass? Mulholland half-ran, half-limped across the field, gritting his teeth against the pain. He prayed it wasn't the general, while at the same time he hated to think that the sharpshooter had shot the Irishman. Whoever it was looked to be dead, considering the knot of men already gathered around were only staring down at him without bothering to offer any assistance or comfort.

Mulholland reached them, looking first at the living general. The man chewed on his cigar as he looked down at the dead man in the officer's coat. He spoke: "This has to be one of the most hare-brained schemes I've ever seen, Major," General Grant said quietly. "I suppose it worked, but it cost this man here his life."

Mulholland noticed this general spoke without a brogue, but he studied the face just to be certain. Brown beard, gray eyes with crow's feet at the corners, a heavy brow that hinted at a stubborn nature.

"Yes, it's me," Grant said, noticing Mulholland's stare. "It's the other fellow that sharpshooter has shot."

Mulholland looked down at the figure in the grass. The face was similar to Grant's, even down to the eyes, which stared blankly at the sky. There was an ugly, purple and black hole just beneath the left eye where the sharpshooter's bullet had entered.

"Best roll him over, boys, and have a look," one of the guards suggested.

Mulholland had seen many gruesome wounds, but he grimaced all the same when he saw the back of O'Malley's head, which was shattered and gory where the bullet had exploded his skull. He turned away, feeling a wave of nausea roll over him. He had seen worse sights in this war, but it never got much easier.

"That's enough," Grant snapped at the guards. "Turn him over. Let the man have some peace."

"Good Lord," Mulholland muttered, still feeling slightly sick to his stomach. He stood up straight and tried not to look at O'Malley's body. "Sir, I'd suggest you get back to headquarters, just in case Corporal Bayliss did not disable the enemy sharpshooter."

Grant appeared not to have heard. He was still looking down at the Irishman. "Find out who his people are, Major, and I'll write them a letter, although I'm sure it will be small comfort." He turned toward the trees where the sharpshooter had been hidden. "I believe I'll put the woodcutters to work tomorrow chopping down every tree between here and Petersburg."

"Yes, sir," Mulholland said, not knowing what else to say. He reached down and picked up the broad-brimmed hat O'Malley had been wearing and used it to cover the private's face.

"If you bring this sharpshooter in, Major, hang him tomorrow morning," Grant said. With that, he walked off, his guards forming a cordon around him in case Bayliss's bullet hadn't done its work.

Mulholland suddenly found himself almost alone in the field and looked toward the trees with an uneasy feeling. What if Bayliss hadn't hit that Rebel? The sharpshooter might very well have Mulholland in his sights at that moment.

Shoving the thought aside, he looked down at O'Malley. At least it had been quick. O'Malley's life had been snuffed out as quickly as a candle flame is blown out. He probably hadn't felt a thing. This realization was no consolation to Mulholland, who felt responsible for his death. O'Malley had been reluctant to serve as General Grant's decoy, but Mulholland had, through a combination of direct orders and an appeal to the man's sense of duty, finally gotten him out on the field in the general's uniform.

Some men liked to know the end was coming so that they could make peace with God and prepare themselves. O'Malley had not had such a chance. Although he had been a Catholic, O'Malley had never struck him as being religious, but no man wanted to be unprepared for the afterlife. He hoped O'Malley had already made his peace with God before this morning. Most soldiers who had been on a battlefield had done so.

He took a final look at the body. *Forgive me, Private O'Malley. May you rest in peace.*

Mulholland unholstered his revolver and started toward the woods. It was time to settle up with the Rebel sharpshooter.

Cole thought he might have time to reload and shoot the second officer, who was standing over the crumpled figure of the dead general and making no attempt to get away. He worked the lever of the Sharps and was just reaching for a fresh cartridge to feed into the breech when he felt a bullet rip down his side.

The shock of the impact made him drop the rifle, which knocked against the branches on its way down before spinning toward the ground. Only the fact that Cole had lashed himself to the tree trunk kept him from falling after it.

There was no pain, although Cole knew there would be, soon enough. He found he was more worried about his rifle than anything. But he forced himself to inspect his wound, and what he saw made him wince.

Just before the bullet struck, he had turned slightly to get a cartridge from the box on his belt. Otherwise the bullet would have hit him clean in the chest and Cole would have drowned in his own frothing blood as it filled his lungs. The bullet had raked him the length of his ribs, passed under his pectoral muscle, and come out beneath his collarbone, just missing his shoulder and head. If he had moved his head another inch back as he looked into his cartridge box, the ball would have entered at the soft underbelly of his chin and blown off the top of his head.

He knew it was not a fatal wound, but it would be a painful one once his nerves lost their numbness. The bullet had sliced through the flesh along his side much like a farmer's plow cuts a furrow in a field, and in the depths of the gouge Cole would see the whiteness of his own rib bones, some of which were surely cracked by the bullet's impact.

Grudgingly, he had to admire whoever had shot him. That was some shot to make through all those tree branches, and it looked as if it had been taken at some distance. The smoke from the Sharps must have given him away, he thought.

Looking out into the field, he could see the commotion he had caused. A knot of men was running for the fallen man, and here came another officer tearing onto the field like a pack of hounds was at his heels. He also saw a man in a green coat loping toward the trees where he was hiding. One of Berdan's sharpshooters, he'd wager. He had heard about those men, that they were the best shots in the whole damn Yankee army. Well, he thought bitterly, one of Berdan's men had lived up to his reputation today.

He knew if he was to avoid capture that he must move quickly before the pain of his wound set in and immobilized him. Just as with wounded deer, he had seen badly shot men do things that later appeared impossible, simply because in the aftermath of being wounded they had not yet gone into shock and had not yet felt the terrible bite of pain because their nerve endings were still too stunned to register.

Cole knew he would not have long before this happened to him. He only hoped to be on the ground, where he at least had some chance of escape. But if he didn't hurry, that Berdan's sharpshooter in the green coat was going to find him up here in the pine, and he'd be no better off than a treed coon.

Taking out his Bowie knife, he cut away the rope that held him to the tree trunk. The finely honed steel cut easily through the strands of hemp. Free of the rope's grip, Cole had to steady himself because he was beginning to feel dizzy. It wouldn't be long before the wound took effect. He had to get out of the tree as fast as he could.

He started down, slipping from one branch to another. It was always easier to climb up a tree than down, but Cole descended as quickly as his body would allow. His hands and feet were so numb with cold that they did not move easily, and once or twice when he bumped his ribs the pain was excruciating, and he fought the dizziness that made the forest floor below spin madly.

He wasn't more than halfway toward the ground when he heard the green-coated sniper call out, "I guess I got you, didn't I, Reb? I'm comin' to finish the job!"

Like hell you will, Cole thought. *I might be wounded, but I'm still a mean Yankee-hating son of a bitch.*

He pulled the Colt revolver out and gripped it in his right hand. He knew if the Yankee caught him in the tree he wouldn't have a prayer. There would be nothing to do but let the Yank shoot him out of the branches or else climb down and surrender.

There would be none of that, Cole thought. He looked down at the ground. How far? Fifteen feet? It would take him too long to climb down. Already he could hear the Yankee crashing toward him through the brush. The bastard must have picked out the tree where Cole had stationed himself and made a beeline for it.

Cole turned around and looked down. The forest floor was thick with leaves, pine needles, and spongy soil, which might serve to cushion his fall just enough so he wouldn't break any bones. Jumping wouldn't do his wound any good, but he wasn't about to be caught in the tree.

No choice but to take his chances.

Getting a good grip on the pistol, Cole leapt into space.

He had tried to jump away from the tree so that the heavy limbs that studded the trunk would not punish him as he fell. Even so, it was like running a gauntlet as branch after branch beat against his body. He had hoped to land on his feet and roll, but the branches turned him so that he landed off balance, the spongy ground gripping one ankle and twisting it. He slammed against the ground and lay there gasping like a fish thrown up on shore. The revolver had been knocked out of his hand and lay a few feet away. Nearby was the Sharps. He could see at once the fall had made a mess of the rifle, bending the lever action and twisting the telescopic sight.

Cole got his breath back and scrambled toward the Colt. Every movement made his body scream with pain, and his twisted ankle would not take any weight. He cursed.

"Hold it right there, Reb."

Cole froze. The revolver was just a couple of feet away. He debated making a grab for it. He might just be able to get off a shot—if the shock of the fall hadn't jammed the action and if debris hadn't clogged the barrel.

He glanced over his shoulder. The Yankee sharpshooter was only a dozen feet away, and if he was as good with the revolver in his hand as he was with a rifle, Cole knew he would never reach his own weapon.

"Don't even think about it," the Yankee said, as if reading Cole's mind. "I won't miss."

Helpless, Cole did not move. His body ached, and he was unable to stand upright. Each lungful of air was like breathing broken glass. Something was dripping into his eyes, and he swiped at his face with the back of his hand. It came away bloody, and he realized a tree branch must have gashed his face as he fell.

The Yankee stood there grinning while he held the revolver easily on Cole. For the first time in his life, Cole understood how a wounded, cornered animal must feel. Full of rage and yet powerless. Waiting to be killed.

Cole was determined to fight rather than be dragged back to some jail hole back in City Point, where they would hang him.

"Bastard," he hissed. "You goddamn blue-bellied Yankee son of a bitch."

Something in Cole's face must have rattled the Yankee, because he took a step back and the grin was wiped from his face. He held the revolver more carefully.

Even though Cole knew the man would gun him down before he took two steps, he didn't care. Better to die fighting than be taken prisoner.

With a scream of pure animal rage, Cole lunged at the Yankee. He still had his Bowie knife in a sheath at his belt, and it flashed out as Cole tried to plunge the blade into the Yankee's heart.

If he hadn't been so sorely injured, he might have had a chance. But his wounds had slowed him. As Cole attacked, the Yankee dodged to one side like a matador and swung the revolver down, clipping Cole on the temple.

The blow knocked him off his feet. He was struggling to get up when the Yank kicked him in his damaged ribs. The pain was so intense that Cole's mind balanced on the rim of consciousness as the Yank stood over him. The grin had returned to his face.

"Hurts some, don't it?" he asked. "You goddamn Reb, I ought to kill you right now."

Smiling maliciously, the Yankee drew back his foot and kicked

Cole again with his boot. Helpless, Cole rolled himself into a ball, trying to protect his ribcage, but the boot found his injured side again. And again.

"You are a mean one, ain't you Reb?" the Yankee said. "You killed somebody, all right, Reb. Only I don't know if it was General Grant or that Irishman."

Irishman? Cole was in too much pain to unravel what the green-coated sharpshooter was saying. He was floating in a state of semi-consciousness, dots swimming across his vision like dappled sunlight on a summer's day. He heard someone moaning, realized to his horror that he was making the noise, and willed himself to stop. He opened his eyes and glared up at the Yankee.

"Madder than a trapped possum, you are," the Yank said. He kicked Cole again.

Cole heard someone shouting in the distance. What was that? Then a wave of pain washed over him and carried him far out into a sea of blackness.

"That's enough," Mulholland said, running up to the clearing beneath the pine tree where Bayliss was standing over the Confederate sharpshooter.

"He's just getting what he deserves," Bayliss said. He hawked, spat into the thick leaves. "Who did he shoot? Grant or the Irishman?"

"O'Malley is dead," Mulholland said. "I don't think he ever knew what hit him. This fellow here got him right through the head."

"The son of a bitch can shoot, all right," Bayliss said. "You're just damn lucky he picked O'Malley. If he'd gotten Grant, there would be hell to pay."

Mulholland didn't like to be reminded that his plan, instead of working smoothly, had almost turned disastrous.

At their feet, the prisoner stirred slightly. Bayliss kicked him sharply and the man cried out, then lay still.

"*I said that's enough!*" Mulholland felt his face turning red as he struggled not to let his anger at the morning's disasters bubble over. He lowered his voice. "If you kick him again, Private Bayliss, I'll see you put in the guardhouse for a week."

"What's this?" Bayliss sneered, surly as ever. "Are you worried about damaging him? By all rights, he should be dead anyway, but I guess he moved just in time so my bullet only grazed him."

"He's a prisoner now," Mulholland said, although the explanation sounded hollow even to his own ears. "I won't have him mistreated."

As he looked down at the Rebel's bloody and powder-grimed face, he recognized the same man he had encountered in Washington. While the man's persistence was unnerving, Mulholland felt relieved that there probably wouldn't be other sharpshooters. Whatever the man's motives or orders, he had obviously been the best the Confederates had.

Bayliss was staring at him. Finally, a malevolent grin crossed his face. "It's just you and me out here, Major. How 'bout if I finish him off? He's just going to hang, anyway. That's what happens to spies and traitors. This will save us all a lot of trouble. You can just claim he was trying to escape. Nobody is going to question one of Grant's staff officers if you tell it like that, especially not General Grant."

Mulholland was one step ahead of Bayliss because the thought had already crossed his mind. He owed this Rebel soldier nothing. After all, wasn't this the man who had stabbed him on the rooftop in Washington and who had just murdered Private O'Malley, whom he had rather liked? Bayliss was right; no one would have questioned them if they brought this man in dead. It would have been understood that Bayliss's bullet was merely swift justice for a man who was destined to swing from a rope.

Just as quickly, he had decided against it. Shooting the Confederate, even if he did deserve to die, went against everything Mulholland believed in. Simply put, it was wrong. He holstered his revolver.

"Come on, let's bring him in," Mulholland said, ignoring Bayliss's suggestion. "I'll take his shoulders, you take his legs."

Bayliss was slow to respond. Testily he jammed his own revolver in his belt and stooped to pick up the wounded Reb's feet.

"What about his rifle?" Bayliss asked.

"Leave it. I'll send someone back to get it."

At that, they lifted the Rebel. Mulholland had expected him to at least groan in pain, but the man was out cold.

"Maybe he's already dead," Mulholland said.

"He's just playing possum, most likely."

It wasn't easy carrying the soldier through the woods. Every briar and sapling they passed grabbed at their ankles and tried to trip them. Once Mulholland stumbled and very nearly dropped the Rebel, but he regained his balance just in time.

When they came out of the woods into the field, Mulholland signaled for some of the men standing around O'Malley's body to help them. With their assistance they soon had the sharpshooter stretched out beside the man his bullet had killed.

Mulholland sent one of the men for an ambulance to carry O'Malley's body and the Rebel back to camp.

"There's a cargo, all right," one of the soldiers said. "A dead man and the one who killed him, side by side."

"Just as long as it's not General Grant dead," another soldier said. "That was mighty close."

Bayliss caught Mulholland's eye and for a moment he thought the sharpshooter was going to give him a malevolent wink, as if to let him know he knew how badly his plan had gone wrong. Mulholland glared back until Bayliss looked away. Uppity bastard, he thought. But then, maybe Bayliss figured it was safe enough to confront him because Mulholland might not be on the general's staff much longer. It was possible Grant might dismiss him because of the morning's events.

Mulholland was dreading his return to headquarters. General Grant had dealt with the situation calmly enough, but Mulholland was sure that once the general had time to let what had happened settle in, he was going to come down like hail and lightning on his head.

"Get these men loaded up," Mulholland ordered once the ambulance arrived. "Take Private O'Malley to the hospital, where they can prepare him for burial."

As they lifted O'Malley's body, one of the men asked, "Should we leave the Rebel at the hospital, sir?"

"No," Mulholland said. "Take him to the guardhouse. No sense patching him up. We're just going to hang him tomorrow."

22

Cole came to his senses, not sure if he was alive or dead. He couldn't see a thing, only darkness, and cold had crept into his aching bones. Thinking he might already be in a grave, buried alive, he put his hand in front of his face. His fingers touched nothing but air, not the rough-sided boards of a coffin as he had expected. He winced at the pain brought on by moving his arm and knew he wasn't dreaming. Or dead.

His mind was still addled after passing out. Cole felt no shame for losing consciousness. He knew it was simply the body's way of helping him survive too much pain. Otherwise, a man would go out of his head.

If he wasn't dead and in a grave, then where in hell was he?

He blinked as his eyes tried to adjust to the darkness. He stood, groaning with pain, and felt his way along until he reached a log wall. The only light in the room was seeping through the chinks between the logs. Plenty of cold air washed in, too, so it was no wonder his body felt so stiff.

The realization of where he was struck Cole almost as hard as the Yankee's bullet had. He was a prisoner, locked up like a dog in a Yankee guardhouse.

The thought put Cole close to panic. He had never liked being in small places for very long, not even the warm kitchen of a house. Being confined against his will in this Yankee cell was enough to set his heart racing. His hands groped along the walls, searching for a door to pound on, until he got control of himself.

Don't be a fool, he warned himself. Don't let them see you weak.

Cole took a deep breath and began to explore the cell. It was empty enough, with only his makeshift bed, while the odor coming from one corner of the cell told him there was also a bucket where he could relieve himself. He returned to the spot where he had awakened. There seemed to be some straw on the floor, and a foul-smelling blanket. At least they had given him that much, although the thin blanket was hardly enough to keep him warm. But then what did the Yankees care whether or not he was comfortable? They were just going to hang him.

Sitting there with the blanket over his shoulders, he felt as dismal and blue as he ever had. Never in his wildest imaginings had he thought he would finish the war this way. Hanging from a rope. Cole had planned on surviving the war, or at the very worst to be shot and die on the battlefield like so many others had. But the thought that he had been taken prisoner so that he could be hanged was nearly overwhelming.

The walls of the cell felt like they were closing in on him. If it hadn't been for the gaps between the logs, he wouldn't have been able to tell if it was day or night outside. Once again, he fought down the urge to pound on the door, which would have been a futile effort because he knew damn well they wouldn't be letting him out just because he was asking.

It might have been worth it, he thought, if he had at least shot General Grant. But evidently these Yanks had outsmarted him and used a decoy to lure him out, where they could get him in their sights. *They sure lured you to the bait, boy.*

Seething with an anger as pitch black as his prison cell, Cole was still brooding when he heard someone opening the door.

He was on his feet in an instant, ready to make a charge for the door as soon as it opened a crack. But the Yankees had once again anticipated him, for when the door swung open there were two guards outside with bayonets fixed on their muskets, and the muskets pointed into the doorway. No chance of escape.

A third Yankee was holding a lantern, even though it was daylight behind him. It was the green-coated Berdan's sharpshooter who had shot Cole, and he stepped into the cell holding the lantern high and lighting all the corners.

"This place stinks bad as a shithouse," the Yankee said. "But it's good enough for the likes of you, Reb."

"Go to hell, Yank."

"From the looks of it, you're going to beat me there." The Yankee laughed viciously. "They're going to hang you tomorrow morning. They'll stretch that scrawny neck of yours right out."

"Don't come here to tell me things I already know," Cole said, struggling to keep himself from tackling this Yankee bastard.

"Since you put it that way, Reb, I guess I'll tell you about your friend, the lady spy."

Cole stared at him. "What are you talking about?"

"That woman they got locked up in the next guardhouse. I overheard Major Mulholland talking with some of the other officers at headquarters. Some woman named Anne. She helped you back in Washington City, when you tried to kill the general there."

"What's going to happen to her?"

"I reckon there might be a double hanging tomorrow morning."

Cole couldn't believe what he was hearing. Anne had come to City Point and been captured? If she had, she was a fool. He took a step toward the Yankee sharpshooter.

One of the guards swung his rifle up and prodded Cole's chest with a bayonet. The Yank sharpshooter laughed.

"He's a mean one, this Rebel is," he said, half turning to address the guards. "You can't trust a man with eyes like his because you can't read anything in them. A snake has got eyes like that."

Cole grabbed at the muzzle of the rifle, to shove it away. The guard clicked back the hammer of the Springfield.

"Steady there, Reb." The Yankee grinned wickedly. "Don't want to cheat the hangman, now do you?"

Cole let his hands hang loose at his side. If he ever got free of this mess, he vowed he was going to make this man pay.

As if reading his mind, the Yankee said quietly, "You'll never get the chance, Reb. There's no escaping this place."

In answer, Cole shrugged. "What's to be is to be," he said.

"That's a good way to look at it. I reckon you won't mind then that I picked up your rifle out in the woods. It's banged up some, but I can fix it. And then tomorrow, after you're swinging in the wind, I'm going out to the front lines to shoot a few Rebels with your rifle. Think about it, your Sharps killing your own kind."

The Yankee made it sound obscene. "I hope she blows up in your face, Yank."

He laughed. "I'm going to carve notches in that stock for every worthless Johnny Reb I shoot with it."

Still grinning, the Yankee sharpshooter backed out of the room and shut the door behind him. Cole heard the sound of a heavy bar being slid into place. Darkness thick as a wet blanket once more filled the cell. At a loss for anything better to do, Cole began to pace the cell like a caged animal, back and forth, back and forth, as he mulled over in his mind that he was going to die in the morning.

Snodgrass had spent most of the night playing poker with some mule skinners. They didn't have much money, but there had been whiskey, and he had been good and drunk by the time he burrowed into a pile of straw in one of the mule sheds. One of the damn stupid beasts had almost killed him during the night by stepping on him, and for most of the day Wednesday his head ached from the effects of John Barleycorn and his side ached because of the damn mule.

"I hope your goin' to give us a chance tonight to win back some of our money," one of the mule skinners said.

"You can try," Snodgrass said.

He had fallen in with these men and was busy mucking out the stables and fixing harnesses. It had been simple enough lying to the sergeant about being assigned to drive a wagon. Most of the men had volunteered from many different units, and nobody thought to question Snodgrass. He had already made up his mind that it would be too risky to return to the workmen's camp.

"I ain't stayin' up half the night again," the soldier said. "I want to get up in time to see them hang that Reb sharpshooter."

"What sharpshooter?" Snodgrass kept working at shoveling out the mule stall, not wanting to appear too interested.

"The one they caught this morning trying to shoot General Grant." A soldier was always glad to pass on some news, and it made the man puff up a bit to tell Snodgrass something he didn't know. "This Johnny Reb was up in a treetop trying to shoot the general, and one of our own sharpshooters got him. Winged him, I guess, because he's still alive enough to hang."

"Is that right?"

"Yep. Got him locked up in the guardhouse, along with that lady spy they caught this mornin'."

"You know about as much as this mule here," Snodgrass said.

The other soldier fumed. "To hell if I don't."

Snodgrass laughed and kept working as if the news didn't mean anything to him. He knew without a doubt who the Reb sharpshooter was. *Cole, what the hell have you got yourself into?*

• • •

"Come in, Major Mulholland," General Grant said.

"Yes, sir."

Mulholland had been dreading this moment. He knew he had made a mess of this whole sharpshooter business. His plan had cost Private O'Malley his life and very nearly gotten General Grant killed.

"Colonel Badeau, would you please leave us?" Grant asked. Mulholland noticed Badeau looked everywhere but his face to avoid meeting his eyes. This, coupled with the fact that Grant wanted them to be left alone, was not a good sign.

"About this sharpshooter business, sir—"

Grant held up a hand to silence him. "When you're in a hole, Major, the best thing to do is to stop digging."

"Yes, sir."

"You should have informed me of your plan. Not to do so was foolish. As it was, Private O'Malley lost his life, and I think his death is as much on your hands as on the hands of that Rebel sharpshooter."

"Yes, sir."

"Things don't always go according to plan. I should know that better than anyone." Grant paused, looking very stern. "From now on, however, you will tell me when you have some plan designed to protect me. Perhaps then I won't be in *danger* next time."

"It won't happen again, sir."

"If you hadn't saved my life in Washington, I might not be so lenient. Make certain that O'Malley gets a decent burial with a priest present, being as he was a Catholic. Now as for that Rebel, you will see to it that he is hanged before breakfast tomorrow morning."

"Yes, sir."

"Now, what about that woman?"

"Anne Clark? She's a spy, sir. I caught her with a copy of your orders for the Petersburg attack. She's locked up in one of the guardhouses."

"She's a friend of yours, of course."

"She was. But no traitor can be a friend of mine, sir. I think you should hang her."

Grant nodded. "I'm sure she is aware of the penalty for spying."

"Yes, sir, she is."

"I don't particularly want to hang a woman." Grant sighed. "Let me think on it."

Grant turned back to the papers on his desk, signaling that the meeting was over. Mulholland saluted crisply and left Grant's office, feeling somewhat relieved. He knew he had gotten off lightly with Grant, although he had at the same time been charged with seeing that the general's dirty work was carried out. Fair enough, he thought.

Badeau, Bowers, and Captain Lincoln were waiting in the front room. All three eyed him with expectant looks.

"When's the court martial?" Bowers asked.

"There's not to be one," Mulholland said. "Just a hanging."

Young Robert Lincoln blanched. "My God, you don't mean the general's going to have you hanged—"

"Nothing like that," he said. "I'm to make sure the Rebel sharpshooter is strung up properly."

"Sounds like a pleasant job," Bowers said. "Nothing gets a man's appetite up for breakfast quite like a good hanging."

Captain Lincoln stared at Bowers as if he were insane.

"For heaven's sake, Mulholland," Badeau said. "Use your head next time. You should tell the general about this sort of thing. And that woman—"

"Had us all fooled," Bowers pointed out. "You can't blame Brendan for her."

Mulholland sighed. "Damn her. Well, I've got to see to poor O'Malley's burial."

"Sure, and you're the one who put him in his grave, Major sir," Bowers said, mimicking O'Malley's brogue.

Bowers was always joking, Mulholland thought as he stepped out into the chill, gray day. But whether Bowers intended it or not, there had been a great deal of truth in that last remark.

Anne was cold and miserable. The one thing she had feared more than anything else—imprisonment—had finally happened to her.

There was no way out. She had already pushed at the doors and walls. It was dark inside the log hut, even though it was still daylight, and she could barely see. Maybe it was just as well, for the place stank to high heaven, and there were furtive scurrying noises in the black corners. Rats.

Damn Hattie and damn Brendan Mulholland! Hattie must have made

Brendan wise to her spying, and he had wasted no time in stopping her from catching the steamer. Another few minutes and she would have been on her way back to Washington.

Not sure what else to do, she made her way across the dark cell to the door and banged on it gently.

"What do you want?" came a rough voice from the other side.

"I was just wonderin' your name," she said, trying to make her voice sweet and syrupy.

"Why?"

"I like to know who my jailers are. If I need something, I can call you by name. And if you need something . . ."

The man outside laughed, and she heard another soldier guffaw. "Listen to the Reb whore talk, Jimmy," the man said. "She wants to give us all a little Dixie and then let her go, I guess."

"They say them Southern women is lively." The soldier thumped on the door. "You lively in there, ma'am?"

Anne slunk away from the door and lay down on the pile of rags that served as a bed. Although the old blankets stank, the floor of the cell was dirt, and the bedding wasn't quite as damp and cold as the rest of the place.

She thought of her fine house in Washington, of the way the sunlight streamed in on winter days through the tall windows and how at night the fire in the parlor kept the chill at bay. There would be no more of that. Yet she didn't regret it. Everything she had done was for the Cause.

A rat thrashed in the corner, and Anne drew her knees up under her chin to keep her toes out of the growing darkness as the daylight faded. In a way, she hoped Brendan had been right about the Yankees hanging her. She didn't want to die, but it was better than wasting away in a pitch-black cell with rats for company.

Snodgrass worked with the mule skinners until nearly three o'clock that afternoon, then slipped away to find out where Cole was being held.

The City Point guardhouses had a famous reputation. There were so many soldiers in camp that the base was literally a small city. A few guardhouses could not keep pace with the cases of drunkenness, brawling, and other infractions, so the provost marshal had built a large stockade for soldiers. It was big as a warehouse, cold and dark, full of the army's riffraff.

Individual guardhouses were reserved for special prisoners: officers, civilians, and spies awaiting hanging or a firing squad. Each was guarded by two sentries who had bayonets on their muskets.

The odds for escape, thought Snodgrass, were not good. Not with so many soldiers around.

There were several huts, and Snodgrass was at a loss as to which one held Cole. His luck changed when he saw a Yankee in a green uniform march up to one of the log huts and a sentry open the door. Snodgrass had heard about those Yankee sharpshooters in green. And he had seen how the sentry kept his rifle at the ready. That would be where Cole was being held.

He had to come up with a plan to break Cole out. Why am I doing this? he wondered. They had about as much chance of escaping as a three-legged horse did of winning a race.

Cole saved my life back with them highwaymen, Snodgrass thought. *He got captured doing his duty, trying to help the Confederacy.*

"Aw, hell," he said out loud, heading back toward the stables. "I must be a damn fool to even think about it."

Cole surprised himself by being able to sleep. When he woke up, it was impossible to tell the time except to guess it by the waning daylight coming through the chinks in the logs. He slept again, and when he woke this time the cell was dark as a tomb.

After what seemed a lifetime in the cold, reeking cell, he heard the bar being removed once again. He didn't even bother to make a run for freedom, which was just as well, because the guards were ready once more with the muskets and bayonets. A gritty looking sergeant practically threw a tin plate of food into the cell.

"That there's yer last meal, Johnny Reb," he said. "Hope you enjoy it."

Then the door slammed shut, and the heavy bar was in place once more. Cole was a captive without possibility of escape.

On the plate was a mess of cold, greasy slop. In the darkness he couldn't tell what it was, but it must have been edible, for in the blackness he could hear rats scurrying along the walls at the scent of food. He just hoped the vermin weren't hungry enough to nip at him during the night. At least, he reminded himself, it was only going to be one night.

Cole ate the food, disgusting as it was. He did it to keep his strength up. He had to remind himself again that he was going to hang soon. Even so, he wolfed the plate of rancid slop, trying not to smell it. The guard had also set a cup of muddy water by the door, and he drank it down. He tossed the empty plate by the door and soon heard the rats nosing at it.

His meal finished, Cole lay down on the straw, wrapping himself tightly in the blanket to keep the rats off. There was nothing left to do now but sleep. Lord knows, he was weary. His rest last night in the tree had been fitful at best and, after his ordeal today, he felt exhausted. His injured side ached and flamed so much, though, that he didn't think he would be able to sleep. Cole longed for a little whiskey to take the edge off the pain and perhaps dull his mind as well, so that he could get some sleep.

To his surprise, he found himself dozing off. He supposed some men might spend their last night on Earth in contemplation, but Cole saw only torment in that. He wasn't much for religion, and he figured he was about as good in the eyes of God as the next soldier. He didn't much believe in heaven and hell, anyhow. Besides, he didn't want to spend his last hours dwelling on something which he hadn't been able to decide on in all his years so far.

Cole had considered telling the Yankees that he had been following orders given to him by none other than General A.P. Hill, but he doubted they would believe him. It wouldn't have done much good, other than to let the Yankees know he hadn't been acting alone. Such a thought might keep them from sleeping too easy at night, but it would not spare him from the hangman's noose.

What bothered him the most was that the Yankees were going to get all three of the Coles: his father, sister, and now himself.

"Goddamn them," he said aloud to the walls.

Well, even if he hadn't been able to kill General Grant, he had cut short his share of Yankee lives. He found some comfort in that thought.

His hanging would go unnoticed by most. It wasn't like he had anyone waiting for him at home. They were all gone now, thanks to the Yankees. He wondered if Anne ever thought of him. There had been no time to see her before he'd had to flee Washington.

Cole slept. He woke hours later to the sound of the bar being slid back from the door. For a moment, he didn't know where he was and thought in his confusion that he was a boy again, back home in his own bed. Then he remembered he was in a Yankee guardhouse, waiting to die. They must be coming for him. He was to be hanged at dawn, and no light came through the chinks in the log walls, so he guessed it was very early in the morning.

The door opened. Darkness outside. No soldiers entered, and Cole had the uneasy feeling that whoever stood in the doorway was trying to see him in the darkness.

"Well, are you coming to hang me or not?" Cole called out.

"Is that you, Lucas Cole?"

Snodgrass! Cole could hardly believe his ears. "Did they capture you?"

"Hell, no. I came to get you out of here. I'm on a secret mission."

"If they catch us, they'll hang you, too."

"That's why we'd better not get caught. Now, I'm not going to light a lantern. But can you see well enough to navigate out of that there box you're in?"

"I reckon I can."

Cole rolled out of his blanket and to his feet. He was aching and sore from sleeping on the cold bed, and his wounds made him feel like a pair of wet leather boots that had been left to dry too close to a fire and were now stiff and brittle. But he groped through the blackness until he found the door.

Outside, it was brighter, and he could make out a few other guardhouses scattered around. On the ground nearby was a soldier, neatly bound and gagged. The whites of his eyes popped furiously at Snodgrass, whom Cole was surprised to see was wearing a Yankee uniform.

"I showed up saying I was here to relieve his partner and after he left I got the jump on this fellow," Snodgrass explained. "He was terrible ornery, let me tell you, but I had my hand clamped so tight over his mouth he couldn't make a sound."

"Good. We'll do them other sentries just like him," Cole said.

"What other sentries? We have a clear road—"

Cole grabbed him by the arm. "We have to get her out, Uriah. Come with me."

"Get who out?"

"Her name's Anne Clark. You ain't goin' to let them Yankees hang a woman, are you?"

Snodgrass had no choice but to follow. He remembered that the mule skinner who had told him about Cole being captured had mentioned something about a woman spy. He didn't know why Cole was interested in her, but he didn't have time to ask.

Cole snatched the sentry's rifle and handed it to Snodgrass. He kept the bayonet for himself.

"Where are we goin'?" Snodgrass asked in a harsh whisper.

"This next hut. She's locked up in there. You go around one side, and I'll go around the other."

They moved on silent feet. Snodgrass slipped around the far corner and stepped out with the rifle just as Cole put the bayonet against the other sentry's neck.

"Make a sound and I'll cut your throat," Cole hissed.

Snodgrass had the muzzle of his rifle right up under the nose of his man. The Yank looked afraid to breathe.

"Open that door, Yank," Snodgrass ordered.

The guard did as he was told. They hustled the two soldiers inside and, while Snodgrass covered them with the musket, Cole grabbed the woman off the foul-smelling old blankets. She started to scream, and Cole clamped a hand over her mouth.

They slipped back out, shut the door, and locked the guards inside.

"Anne, it's me, Cole. I'm going to take my hand away. Now don't scream."

The woman stared at them, stunned. "Lucas? What are you doing here?"

"I was going to ask you the same thing," he said. "We'll have time to talk later. Now, let's go."

"That's a fine idea," Snodgrass said. "Follow me."

Cole had only a vague notion of where they were, but Snodgrass appeared to know the way. They carried the three rifles they had taken from the sentries with them, along with a handful of cartridges and percussion caps. No sooner were they out of sight of the prison area than they came to a wagon and mule team waiting in a roadway. Snodgrass pulled a blue uniform blouse from the back.

"Put this on," he said to Cole. "We can't have you wearing those bloody rags. How is that wound, anyhow?"

"Tolerable," Cole said, wincing as he took off his old shirt because the cloth stuck to dried blood in places. He had to pull it free, and it came away with a tearing sound that made Cole grunt in pain.

"Coming from you, Cole, that means it probably feels like the devil's got his pitchfork it your side. Well, up on the wagon with you."

Cole looked uncertainly at the wagon and mule team. It did not look promising for a fast escape. On the rough roads around City Point, they wouldn't be able to outride an infantry company, much less a cavalry squadron.

"You could at least have found us some horses, Snodgrass."

"Hah! They'd stop us in a minute on horseback. But no one will ever question a couple of mule skinners. We'll ride out of here without any trouble, even if it ain't long on style."

"What about her?"

Snodgrass looked at the woman they had just rescued. "Get in the back, under that piece of canvas. Ain't nobody goin' to look."

Cole knew he wasn't in any position to argue, so he started to climb toward the wagon seat. He was stiffer than he thought because his sore body balked at the effort until Snodgrass gave him a shove from below so that Cole landed on the hard wagon seat like a sack of potatoes.

"Much obliged, Snodgrass," he said, gritting his teeth in pain.

"My pleasure. Giddyap, mules!"

They started rolling. The wagon made a tremendous racket as the rickety wheels squealed and rattled at every bump in the road. Cole was sure every Yankee for a mile around was going to come running to see what all the ruckus was about.

Anne looked out from under the tarp. "They'll catch us," she said. "We have to move faster."

"This is as fast as these ol' mules will go," he said. "Who are you, anyhow? I heard someone say you were a spy."

"She is," Cole said.

"How did you two come to know each other, then?"

"She helped me in Washington."

"What was you doing there, Cole? You never did tell me."

"Trying to shoot General Grant. Then I came here to try."

"So that's why you're here," Anne said.

"That's right. And you?"

"I came to see what I could find out about a Yankee attack on Petersburg."

Snodgrass shook his head. "You two lead excitin' lives, I must say."

"You think to bring along any weapons, Snodgrass? A revolver, at least?"

"Mule skinners don't carry much in the way of guns. And it's against regulations for enlisted men such as ourselves to carry sidearms."

"Lord help us," Cole said.

"We have the rifles off the sentries."

"There ain't but a dozen rounds total."

"It might be enough."

"My, Gambler, but you do believe in good luck."

In spite of their situation, he felt strangely elated. Snodgrass was a good man in a tight spot, which was exactly where they were. If he and Snodgrass couldn't escape the Yankees, nobody could.

"The Lord's about the only one who can help us, to be sure. Now when we come to any pickets posted on the road, you just let me do the jawing."

Cole glanced over at Snodgrass, who was intent on trying to see the roadway in the darkness. "Don't think I ain't glad you're here, Snodgrass, but I kind of figured I'd seen the last of you."

"Turns out some of our own cavalry picked me up for a deserter."

"Which you are."

"Yep, which is why when they started talking about ropes and firing squads, I gave them the slip and come back here."

As they went bumping and rattling over the dark road through the Yankee camp, he heard Anne curse.

"Not too comfortable back there, is it?"

"It's better than where I was," she answered.

They rolled on toward the Confederate lines, trying to put City Point behind them.

23

Mulholland was not looking forward to hanging the Rebel sharpshooter, but General Grant had ordered him to oversee the execution personally. There was no disobeying a direct order from Grant, so Mulholland had risen just before sunrise on this cold winter's morning to see that the death sentence was carried out.

Anne's fate had yet to be decided. Only the fact that she was a woman had kept her from swinging on a rope beside the sharpshooter this morning.

During the night, the muddy ruts of the camp roads had frozen and there was a skim of ice on the mud puddles that invariably dotted the roads. By noon, Mulholland knew the roads would be churned to mud again, spattering horses, men, and equipment alike with the black Virginia soil.

It had been into the same soil that the major had committed Private O'Malley's remains yesterday. During a short, windswept ceremony attended only by himself, a gravedigging detail, and a priest, Mulholland and the gravediggers had stood hatless in the cold while the priest muttered nearly unintelligible Latin over the Irishman's grave. Once the priest had finished, the gravediggers went to work, and all night Mulholland's dreams had echoed with the hollow sound of dirt thudding on O'Malley's plain pine coffin. Austere though the ceremony had been, he knew it was a much better burial than many soldiers had received.

At that moment, Mulholland despised the war so much he could taste his hate as a bitter bile in his mouth. *Damn these Southerners!* They may have been gallant men—and women, he added to himself, thinking of Anne—but they were fighting for one of the worst causes in history, as far as Mulholland was concerned. The freedom of the states was one thing, but how could men so protective of their own rights also support the enslavement of the whole African race? It seemed a hypocrisy which must fail in God's eyes, although it had taken four long years to fight the Confederate States of America to its knees.

Lost in thought, Mulholland was nearly at the guardhouse where Cole had been secured when he noticed the commotion outside.

Thinking the guards had rousted the sharpshooter out early for the hanging, Mulholland quickened his pace. He just wanted to get this whole terrible event over with as quickly as possible.

"All right, where's the prisoner?" Mulholland demanded, striding up, one hand on the hilt of his sword, which he had worn for the occasion.

"Sir?" one of the men asked. Behind the group of soldiers, the guardhouse door stood open.

"The prisoner," Mulholland said impatiently. "Bring him out. Let's get this over with."

"He's gone, sir."

Stunned, Mulholland stared at the man. Only then did he notice that one of the guards was rubbing his wrists, and that there was some rope lying on the ground.

"What do you mean?" Mulholland asked quietly.

"They jumped me last night, Major, and tied me up," the soldier with the sore wrists explained. "Some big galoot of a Southerner got the best of me. He let the prisoner out. That was before daylight, so I suppose they've been gone a couple of hours."

"The woman's gone, too," a corporal added. "They took her and locked the sentries in the guardhouse."

The major cursed so mightily the soldiers were left staring. He felt a sudden rage that nearly blinded him. *Be calm,* he ordered himself. He swore again. *Cole and Anne both gone?* Just as Mulholland had feared, the Confederacy must have had agents in their camp.

He fired off questions at the guard: "Just one man helped him escape?"

"That's all I saw, sir," said the soldier who was rubbing his raw wrists.

"Did they have horses?"

"Nobody saw any horses, sir," the guard spoke up. "All I heard was a wagon."

Someone guffawed. "Nobody would escape in a wagon!"

"Shut up and let the man speak," Mulholland said. He turned back to the guard. "A wagon, you say?"

"Yes, sir. Leastways, I reckon it was them. I heard a wagon start out right after they left."

"Which way did they go?"

"Sounded to me like they were heading west out of camp."

Mulholland nodded. If he had been trying to escape, the last mode of transportation he would have chosen would be a wagon. Horses would be much faster. But then, the Rebel sharpshooter had been wounded. Besides, he thought, who would ever question a wagon on the roads out of City Point? They came and went at all hours of the day and night, hauling supplies to the various positions up and down the James River and over toward Petersburg.

"Good Lord," Mulholland said, thinking out loud. "They can't have gone too far in a wagon."

He left the guards and hurried back to headquarters, where he would get men and horses to go after them.

It looked as if the hanging would have to wait.

Cole would have preferred to walk. It was a rough, bumpy ride aboard the wagon, which had no springs and lurched wildly in every frozen rut.

"To hell with this contraption," Cole growled, gritting his teeth at the pain in his side. "We can make better time on foot, even with my ribs laid open."

"Trust me, Cole," Snodgrass said, winking in the growing daylight. "I know how to play my cards."

"They'll be on the roads looking for us as soon as they find out we're gone."

"Then I'd better persuade these mules to move along. Giddyap, mules!" He gave the reins a shake and yelled fiercely at the mules, but the dumb brutes did not quicken their pace. Snodgrass seemed not to notice. "Not bad for a riverboat man, eh?" he said, grinning.

Cole had no choice but to hang on and hope for the best. Snodgrass appeared not a bit worried about their chances for escape, although he was a man given to facing long odds. But their situation had gone far beyond a hand of poker, Cole thought, and with each minute it grew lighter and their chances of escape diminished, for he was sure the Yankees would soon have cavalry squadrons scouring the roads for them.

They came to a checkpoint where a picket stepped from beside the road to stop them. Anne had hidden herself in the back.

"Getting an early start, are you?" he asked.

"That's right. We have some supplies for the boys up front."

"I'll bet it's god-awful cold in them trenches this morning," the picket said, stomping his feet.

"Better them than me," Snodgrass said. "I'd rather drive a wagon than have Reb sharpshooters trying to serve me lead for breakfast."

"Ain't that the truth." The picket waved them on with a grin. "Get out of here, you damn mule skinners!"

Once they were out of earshot of the picket, Cole snapped out, "What the hell is wrong with you, Snodgrass? You ain't got to hold us up jawing with the enemy, now do you?"

"You just ain't sociable, Cole. Besides, that picket won't think anything of us, whereas he might if I was all quiet and nervous."

Cole knew it was as pointless to argue with Snodgrass as it was to argue with the wind. He shut his mouth and hung on to the bare wooden seat as they rumbled along the road.

Leaning low over the mare's neck, Mulholland urged her along the road at a gallop. Ten cavalry troopers trailed behind him, with Corporal Bayliss bringing up the rear, his Whitworth rifle slung in a saddle holster.

Even in a wagon, the Rebel sharpshooter, Anne, and the accomplice who had helped them escape had nearly made a clean getaway. The couple of hours' head start they had on the nearly empty roads had given them a good lead on the troopers. Mulholland had no way of knowing in which direction they had gone or what road they had taken.

But a sentry had remembered seeing a wagon pass before sunup with two men riding the seat. That sighting had set them on the right road, and now all they had to do was catch up.

They rode pell-mell down the road, forcing men and wagons out of the way and leaving cursing soldiers in their wake. Traffic had increased after first light with the flow of troops and supplies between City Point and the Petersburg trenches. But Mulholland refused to let the business of the road slow their pursuit any more than necessary. He was determined to catch Anne and that Rebel sharpshooter and return them to the guardhouse. They weren't going to make a fool out of him.

His spurs dug into the mare's flanks. Clods of frozen mud flew up from her hooves as she raced along. Mulholland was no great horseman, but he rode well enough. Some of the troopers behind him were better than circus performers at doing tricks in the saddle. *Where had these men been in 1861?* he wondered. The cavalry had been a laughingstock then. Most likely they were the same men, just accomplished horsemen now after four years of sleeping and eating in the saddle.

An old mule wagon didn't stand a chance of outrunning them.

Mulholland came to a halt at the next picket outpost. The mare was snorting, and her lathered flanks steamed in the cold January air.

"You there!" Mulholland shouted at a picket. "Did a wagon pass this way early this morning?"

"Yes, sir, two men in a wagon." The young sentry looked alarmed at all the horses stamping about in the road, his eyes as big as saucers as he stared. "Said they were on their way to Petersburg."

Mulholland held up a gloved hand and waved the squadron on.

Even over the terrible creaking of the wagon, Cole sensed they were coming. Hooves pounding along a frozen road can be heard from a long way off.

"They're right behind us," he shouted at Snodgrass, who was trying to urge the mules on a little faster. But mules had just two speeds. Slow and slower.

Snodgrass cursed. "I thought we'd have more time."

"What's your plan now?"

"I don't know, Cole. I just figured we'd get as far away as we could and see what happened next."

"God help us," Anne said. "We'll never outride them in this contraption."

"I say forget the wagon and take your chances on foot."

"If they have horses, they'll ride us down in a minute."

Cole looked at the road ahead of them. The ground rose, and the road was cut into the hill, so that the banks of the road climbed three or four feet above the surface. For most of its length, the road was bordered either by stone walls or thick brush. If they stopped the wagon at the top of the road any Yankees coming at them would have to dismount, because horses couldn't ride through the close-growing trees and underbrush.

"This is as good a place as any," Snodgrass said.

Snodgrass drove on to the rise. They halted, but not before Snodgrass had pulled the wagon sideways to block the road. The sudden silence now that the wagon was no longer creaking and groaning was unnerving, like the quiet before a storm.

On the north side of the road was the Appomattox River. It was an overcast morning, and the river looked cold and gray. It was much too wide to cross at that point; they had hoped to make it farther west, where the river became more shallow and narrow and they could possibly have unhitched the mules and hung on as the animals swam across. A small gunboat steamed up the center of the river, drawing some fire from a Union battery on the other side of the river near Dutch Gap.

"That's one of ours," Snodgrass said.

"It's probably scouting to see if the Yanks have set up any more batteries over on the north side of the river," Cole said.

"Can you swim, Miss Clark?" Snodgrass asked.

"I can do whatever I have to do to escape," Anne said.

"You reckon you could swim that river, Cole?"

The effort of the escape and wagon ride had taken a lot out of him. His side felt as if some animal was gnawing at it, and he wondered if maybe the Yank sharpshooter's bullet had cracked a rib or two when it grazed him. He had done something to his leg when he fell out of the tree yesterday, and he couldn't put his full weight on it. He was bruised, battered, and sore. Cole didn't give up easily, but he knew his limitations. He would have a hard time walking to the river, much less swimming it.

He leaned over the side of the wagon and spat. "No way in hell."

Snodgrass exchanged an anxious glance with Anne. He was beginning to think the river was their only way out. But if Cole couldn't make it . . .

"I aim to fight," Cole said. He reached back into the wagon and picked up one of the Springfields they had taken from the guardhouse sentries.

"We ain't got a chance," Snodgrass said. "Let's unhitch the mules and ride the hell out of here."

"We'll have to ride double of one of the mules. How far do you think we'll get before their horses catch us?"

"Listen to him," Anne said, grabbing Cole's arm. "There's no other way."

"Sure there is," Cole replied. "Anne, you and Snodgrass have to make a run for the river. Follow right along the water's edge, fast as you can, up toward Petersburg. Horses won't be able to follow you. If you hit any Yank sentries, swim for the other side. You might not even hit any if you're lucky."

"What about you?" Anne asked. "You can't come with us?"

Cole fixed his frightening, colorless eyes on her. She let go of his arm. "I've got a rifle," he said. "It's all I ever wanted."

Anne nodded. It was the best plan they had.

But it was already too late. A group of blue-coated cavalry came riding around a bend in the road behind them. The galloping hooves on the frozen road shattered the morning quiet.

"Aw, hell," Snodgrass said.

Mulholland saw the wagon in the road and knew it must be the one they were pursuing.

I've got you now, he thought.

He could see three people on board. One had a rifle, but Mulholland wasn't about to halt and deploy his men in a skirmish line. He had ten men on horseback, and they were facing a mule wagon carrying a wounded man and a woman. One charge and they would be overwhelmed.

He drew his revolver and rode up the road toward the wagon. Firing from horseback wasn't easy, not if you wanted to hit anything, but Mulholland aimed as best he could. He remembered for an instant that Anne was up there, that if there was shooting she might be killed.

Mulholland didn't give a damn anymore. Anne had made a fool of him. She was a lying Reb, and if he brought her back to City Point alive, they were just going to hang her.

He pulled the trigger.

A bullet snicked into the wagon, sending bright splinters of wood flying.

"Brendan," Anne hissed, recognizing the lead rider who had fired. "You Yankee bastard."

More shots followed, and the air was soon full of whining lead.

"Best get under the wagon," Cole said. "Snodgrass, bring the other rifles."

"What do you want me to do?" Anne asked, sliding under the wagon next to Snodgrass. He was busy pulling back the hammer on the Springfield and taking aim.

"Keep your head down," he said, and Anne's ears seemed to split as the rifle fired.

"Pour it into 'em, Snodgrass!" Cole shouted as he reloaded. He ripped open a cartridge with his teeth.

With a whoop, Snodgrass grabbed the other loaded rifle and fired. His shots seemed to be doing little damage to the charging Yankees. In his excitement, he had forgotten about the natural tendency to aim too high when shooting downhill.

"Here they come, boy!" he shouted.

"You've got to aim lower, Snodgrass. Aim for their knees and you'll put those shots right where you want them."

Snodgrass reloaded and fired again. A rider tumbled from his saddle.

"You got one," Anne shouted. "Now shoot the major. Shoot him dead."

They fired as fast as they could, and the shots were telling among the massed riders. The riders were some distance away, and Snodgrass and Cole had them in rifle range long before the troopers' revolvers could do much harm. Two more troopers fell before they saw the major turn his horse and wave the men back.

One bullet had struck a horse, and the screaming animal was on its knees. The trooper had been thrown but wasn't hurt. He put the muzzle of his revolver behind the horse's ear and put the animal out of its misery.

The Yankees also did their share of damage. The troopers were all armed with Colt revolvers, and they sent a hail of lead at the wagon, even if the shots weren't accurate. The two mules were slumped in their traces, riddled with bullets.

A wounded trooper got up and tried to run back toward his companions, who had taken shelter behind the stone wall. Cole took careful aim and shot him.

"You could have let the man go," Snodgrass said.

"No," Anne said. "Kill all the Yankees you can. Kill every last one of them."

Cole rolled over and sat up to reload.

"Cole."

Snodgrass's warning came just in time. Cole ducked, and a bullet smashed into the spokes of the wagon wheel where he had been peering just a moment before.

"I saw him get his rifle out and take aim," Snodgrass explained.

"It's that sharpshooter," Cole said, glaring at the distant soldier in the green uniform. "I'll get that son of a bitch."

"What are we going to do?" Anne asked.

Cole looked at Snodgrass. "How many rounds you got left?"

"Just three."

"I've got five."

"We can't hold them off if they make another charge."

"No," Cole said. "We can't. Give me that ammunition."

Snodgrass handed it over. He still had one round in the rifle. "What are you planning to do, Lucas?"

"I'm going to stay right here and wait for the Yankees. You and Anne are going to make a run for the river."

Snodgrass shook his head. "We ain't leavin' you here, Cole."

"You said yourself it was the only way out of this."

"He's right," Anne said. "Lucas can't run. But we can."

"The lady knows what she's talking about," Cole said. "Now go on before they come at us again. Go straight through the woods and don't stop till you come to the river."

In his heart, Snodgrass knew Cole was right. He and the woman might just have a chance if they could slip down toward the river. Snodgrass also knew the Yankees would never capture Cole alive, and if they ran, he would be leaving Cole to his death.

"I don't like this hand," Snodgrass said.

"It's what we've been dealt. Now get."

Snodgrass looked at Anne. She nodded. He turned to Cole, trying to think of something to say. "Hell, Lucas—"

"Go on."

Snodgrass put a hand on Cole's shoulder, but the sharpshooter didn't seem to notice. His attention was fixed on the Yankees down the road.

"We're goin' to jump out from under this wagon and run like hell," Snodgrass said to Anne.

"Wait a minute," she said. "Give me your knife, Lucas."

Cole unsheathed his Bowie knife and gave it to her. Anne deftly hacked a foot of fabric from the hem of her dress. "Now I can run," she said, handing Cole his knife. She looked into his eyes for a moment. Anne, too, knew what would happen when they left Cole. She saw no fear in his copperhead's eyes, only a deadly paleness. "God keep you, Lucas."

In answer, Cole peered down the rifle sight at the Yankees.

"Let's go," Anne said.

She rolled out from under the wagon and started running for the trees. Snodgrass followed.

Mulholland sat in the saddle, wondering what to do next. He had expected to quickly capture the wagon. Instead, he had lost two men. The trooper who had been forced to shoot his horse mounted one of the dead men's animals.

He flinched as a rifle went off nearby. It was Bayliss, who had dismounted and taken that fancy Whitworth of his from the saddle holster, trying to pick off the Rebels.

"Goddamn. Missed him."

"Reload and try again," Mulholland ordered.

"Yes, sir." Bayliss's voice dripped sarcasm.

"I will not have that!" Mulholland spun his horse around and almost rode Bayliss down. For the first time, he thought he saw a flicker of panic in Bayliss's face before he pulled back on the reins. *Steady,* he warned himself. *Keep a cool head. It's Anne and that Reb sharpshooter you're mad at, not Bayliss.* "Take your goddamn fancy rifle and try to shoot them."

Wordlessly, Bayliss fell to reloading.

"We ought to try again, Major," a trooper suggested. "They won't hold us a second time."

Mulholland was thinking the same thing. Ride right up there and shoot them down. That was the thing to do.

"Form up, men. We're going to try again."

As they were getting ready, Mulholland saw Anne and one of the men dash from under the wagon and head for the trees.

"There they go!" a trooper yelled.

Mulholland made up his mind in an instant. "You and you stay with me," he said, pointing out two of the cavalrymen. "The rest of you go after them. Go!"

The troopers wheeled their horses and galloped for the trees. They would have to dismount because the horses couldn't ride through the thick woods. Still, he doubted Anne and the other Rebel would get far before his men caught them.

Mulholland was left with Bayliss and the two troopers. There was just one man under the wagon. The Reb sharpshooter. As Mulholland stared out at the distant wagon, he realized he wasn't in any hurry to ride out there. That Reb was one hell of a shot, and if he had a couple of loaded rifles ready and some spare ammunition, he might shoot two or three of them before they could reach the wagon.

Bayliss was watching him. "It don't seem so easy when you think on it, does it?" he said. He nodded toward the field in front of them. "I think I can slip closer and get a good shot at him. If I can get out to where that dead horse is, it'll give me some shelter. The ground's higher, and I'll have a better chance of hitting him."

"All right," Mulholland said. "We'll put some fire on that wagon to make things hot for him."

One of the troopers had a Spencer repeating rifle in his saddle scabbard, the other had a Sharps carbine. One of the riderless horses had wandered over, and Mulholland took another carbine from the scabbard.

"Whenever you're ready," Bayliss said.

"Let's make him keep his head down, boys!"

They opened fire on the wagon. The trooper with the Spencer kept up a steady fire, while Mulholland and the other cavalryman were able to fire rapidly with their carbines.

No answering shots came from the Reb sharpshooter.

"Maybe he's dead," one of the troopers said. "He didn't run with them other two."

Bayliss slipped over the stone wall and ran crouched over for the dead mare about a hundred feet out from the stone wall. He had almost made it when a puff of smoke showed from under the wagon and Bayliss was suddenly spun around and flung headlong into the brown grass. The Reb sharpshooter had shot him in the leg.

Bayliss struggled to his knees, and, dragging his ruined leg along behind him, he began crawling toward the shelter of the stone wall.

Another shot rang out, and Bayliss tumbled forward, hit in the elbow. Somehow, he still propelled himself toward safety. He was maybe twenty feet away from the wall.

"He's picking me apart," Bayliss shouted, his normally gruff voice shrill with fear and pain. He fell down and reached out his one good arm to Mulholland. His blood shown bright red against the dry winter grass.

Much as he detested Bayliss, Mulholland couldn't leave him out in the open. He put the carbine down and vaulted over the wall. His ran as best he could, half dragging the leg the sharpshooter had stabbed back in Washington. It hurt terribly, but Mulholland barely noticed, because he was expecting at any moment to feel one of the sharpshooter's bullets knock him off his feet. He reached Bayliss, got a hand under each arm, and started dragging him back toward the wall.

A rifle fired. Mulholland heard the ball hit Bayliss full in the chest with a sound like a mallet pounding a peg into the ground.

Mulholland kept dragging him and one of the troopers ran out to help. They managed to get over the wall before the Rebel fired again.

"He got me good that time," Bayliss coughed out, his eyes wide and white with the shock of being shot. By the time one of the troopers uncapped his canteen to give Bayliss a drink of water, his sightless eyes were staring up at the gray winter sky. Mulholland let go of the body, and it slumped to the frozen ground.

"Let him have it," Mulholland said, reaching for the carbine.

They had plenty of ammunition. He watched as splinters of wood flew from the wagon wheels. A shot cracked a spoke. No answering fire came from the wagon. After a few minutes, he ordered the two troopers to stop firing.

"He's got to be dead," one of the cavalrymen said.

Mulholland agreed. He stood up, climbed over the stone wall, and started walking toward the wagon.

"Sir!"

The major ignored him. They had riddled the wagon with gunfire. He was sure the sharpshooter was dead. Behind him, he heard the cavalrymen curse and start out after him.

They passed the dead mare and the bodies of the two dead soldiers.

"Sweet Jesus," one of the troopers said, looking down at the soldier who lay facedown in the grass, shot in the back while trying to run for the stone wall.

"Poor Jimmy," said the other soldier. "That Reb's a son of a bitch, all right."

As they walked closer, Mulholland saw that the wagon looked as if someone had attacked it with an ax. Chunks of wood were missing, and many of the boards had been splintered. Mulholland had his revolver out in front of him, his finger on the trigger. Behind him, the troopers had their carbines ready.

The Reb was sitting up under the wagon, propped against one of the wheels. At first, Mulholland couldn't tell whether he was alive or dead. He walked closer, and saw a flicker of movement as the Reb tried to raise a long Springfield rifle with one arm. His other arm was a bloody mess where a bullet had struck it just below the shoulder. The whiteness of bone was visible through all the gore. Mulholland could also see a bloody hole in the Reb's chest, and there was pink froth at the corners of his mouth.

"Drop that rifle," Mulholland said. He knew he should have shot him, but he felt a glimmer of pity for the man.

The Reb smiled. His eyes were cold and hard as clear flint. There was no fear of death in them, like there had been in Bayliss's eyes. In fact, he could see nothing at all in those eyes. Mulholland tightened his grip on the pistol.

"You can go to hell, Major." The muzzle swung up.

Mulholland shot him. The bullet caught him in the chest, and the Reb jerked back against the wagon wheel, the rifle slipping from his grip.

The Reb's eyes were still staring at him with a pale glare.

Mulholland heard shooting down by the river and turned in that direction. Anne and the other Rebel were getting away.

24

"Run as hard as you can!" Snodgrass shouted.

At the sound of the first shot, he grabbed Anne's hand and together they stormed through the woods. Branches whipped at their faces and briars slashed at their legs, but they didn't care. If the Yankees caught them, they'd get worse.

More shots cracked the winter air, but the Yankees were still too far behind them to do any harm. A bullet buzzed past like a fat wasp, clipping the branches, but Snodgrass barely noticed the sound over the gasping of his own breath. It had been a long time since he'd run anywhere.

He saw Anne chance a look over her shoulder.

"Don't worry about what's behind us," Snodgrass panted. "Keep your eyes on what's ahead."

Anne fell, and Snodgrass pulled her back to her feet.

"All right?"

"Go, damn you, go!"

From much farther behind them, Snodgrass heard more shooting. That would be Cole, he thought. He wondered how long the sharpshooter would last. Cole was a tough bastard.

They burst out of the trees onto the shore of the Appomattox. Instead of finding escape at the river, they saw that they were trapped by the swift-moving water. Erosion had cut the bank, so it was a good eight feet above the muddy river. There was no sandy shore, not that they could have used it as a trail with several Yankees on foot right behind them.

They both stood on the steep bank, gasping for breath, and looked out at the gray-brown water. The current sucked at the edges of the bank below, swirling beneath the thin ice that had formed in the branches of a tree that had once stood on the bank until the river undercut it. The water made a sinister gurgling as it passed through the dead limbs. Far out in the river, the Confederate gunboat they had seen earlier churned upriver under a stream of black smoke that poured from its engine.

"Dear God," Anne said. "We can't swim this."

"Looks damn cold," Snodgrass agreed.

He looked up and down the bank. If they ran in either direction, fallen trees and thick underbrush would slow them down. There was no sandy beach at all that would have made for easy running—for them and the Yankees.

Behind them, there was shouting. A carbine cracked, then another. They heard the bullets hiss past.

"Looks like they ain't goin' to give us a chance to surrender," Snodgrass said.

"I'll never surrender." Anne's face was savage. "I'll throw rocks at them if I have to, but I won't surrender. They're only going to hang us if they take us back to City Point."

More gunfire came from the trees. Someone shouted, "There they are!"

Snodgrass looked again at the Appomattox. He had seen his share of rivers in his days aboard steamboats, and this one was cold and uninviting, the current swift and muddy. He knew if they tried to swim across, they would likely drown. He glanced at the trees behind them, expecting to see a blue uniform at any moment. If they stayed, they would be shot, or as the woman had said, taken back to City Point for a proper hanging.

"Take my hand," he said.

Anne did so, looking up at his face. He had expected to see fear and uncertainty in her eyes, but her expression was one of fierce determination. She was a tough one, he thought, just like Cole. *Damn but the South had some good ones.*

From the corner of his eye, he saw a blue blur in the brush.

"Go!" He took a few running steps, his hand in Anne's, and the two of them lept off the bank and plunged feet-first into the river.

The shock of the cold water gripped them in an icy fist. They both came up spluttering, spitting out water so muddy they felt the grit in their teeth. On the bank overhead a Yankee had appeared, and Snodgrass saw the soldier raise his carbine.

He reached out and shoved Anne's head under, then ducked himself.

The bullet left a white trail as it slashed underwater. There was another white trail, and another. They bobbed up again for air.

"Swim out," Snodgrass managed to shout to Anne. She struck out for the middle of the river with awkward strokes, the heavy fabric of her dress weighing her down. More soldiers appeared on the riverbank, and they ducked beneath the surface and swam underwater for as long as they could. They came up again, and Snodgrass realized he could no longer feel his hands or feet. Damn, but that water was cold.

"I'm freezing," Anne complained.

"We have to stick together," he said. "Swim as hard as you can. Use your legs, kick. We'll have to move fast if we want to cross the river before the cold gets us."

The current carried them steadily downstream, back toward City Point, but they worked their numb arms and legs hard so that the shore became more distant all the time. The soldiers were still firing at them, running after them along the riverbank. But fallen trees and heavy brush prevented them from keeping up.

Even when the soldiers' rifles were no longer an immediate danger, Snodgrass knew they were still in trouble. The river was their new enemy. Beside him, Anne was gasping for every breath, and his own swimming had slowed, no matter how hard he tried to kick his legs and move his arms. The icy water was sapping their strength.

"Come on," he tried to shout encouragement to Anne, but his words came out feebly. They had left the riverbank far behind them, but it was a long way to the other side. Snodgrass thought they might do better to swing back toward shore and hope to land downriver far from the pursuing Yankees. But cold and wet, how could they possibly escape once on shore again?

Anne was swimming hard, cursing the cold, cursing the Yankees. It would have been comical if they hadn't been facing death.

She gagged on a mouthful of water. The weight of her dress pulled her under. Snodgrass got a hand under her and yanked her back to the surface.

"Back to shore," he said. "We can't make it."

Together, they turned.

Snodgrass hadn't counted on the current. It streamed down on them, carrying them ever farther from shore. They couldn't swim against it.

He knew they were losing time. The cold would still their arms and legs, and they would slip below the surface.

He put a hand out, pulled Anne close to him. Together they kicked for the other side. It was now their only hope.

Despite all her spunk, the run through the woods and the cold river had taken much out of Anne. She was able to do little more than flail at the water. Snodgrass pulled her along, but he knew they would never make it across. The muddy water surrounded him, and Snodgrass wondered at the strangeness of it. He had left the riverboat life to join the army. All those dusty miles of marching, all those battlefields where men around him had caught minié balls, and here he was about to drown. On a river again.

At least it was a peaceful way to die. His legs and arms had no feeling, and he was barely able to keep Anne's head above the surface. He sucked in a mouthful of water, choked, gagged on more water as he tried to get air.

Snodgrass never felt a thing. He was breathing in as much water as air, trying to keep Anne's head above the surface. His arms and legs barely moved. Something touched his shoulders. He felt it again. Whatever it was had hold of his collar and was pulling at him. He held on to Anne for all he was worth, then felt himself slip under the river. His eyes were open, and the world disappeared in a swirl of muddy water.

He never expected to see the surface again, but suddenly he was being jerked out of the water.

"Hold him now!" a voice shouted. "He's a heavy bastard."

Strong hands grabbed at him. He held Anne in his arms.

"We've got her now, son," a voice said. He was lifted, felt hard boards under him.

"Get them in the wheelhouse," someone ordered. "They're half drowned and most likely frozen."

Someone put a bottle to his lips and Snodgrass tasted brandy. He turned over on his side and vomited a bellyful of river water on the deck.

He heard laughter. "Look at you wastin' all that good water," someone said. "You'll be all right now."

Snodgrass found himself inside the gunboat's wheelhouse. Anne was in a chair nearby. He was shivering uncontrollably, and he was soon bundled in blankets. One of the crew helped him sip a hot cup of coffee laced with whiskey.

"Good for what ails you," the man said.

He turned to Anne. "We made it." She, too, was bundled in

blankets, and someone was giving her coffee.

They were aboard the Confederate gunboat that had been prowling the center of the Appomattox. An officer appeared. "We saw those Yankees chase you into the river and reckoned you might like to be picked up. That water is damn cold."

"We were trying to swim across," Snodgrass tried to explain.

"Might as well try to swim to the moon," the officer said. "Why were those Yankees chasing you?"

Anne spoke up. "We're spies. They were supposed to hang us this morning, but we escaped."

The officer laughed. "This is some catch, a couple of spies! Well, we can take you most of the way into Petersburg, at least as far up the Appomattox as we can navigate. Then we'll put you ashore behind our lines. From Petersburg you can go right to Richmond, if you want."

Anne looked at Snodgrass and smiled through chattering teeth. "I haven't seen Richmond since the war started. I have friends in the city."

"I've been there," Snodgrass said. "It's a fine place. Lots of card games and whiskey for a soldier."

"Then you'll go with me?"

"I reckon I will."

Anne's smile faded. "What about Lucas?"

Snodgrass shook his head and looked away. *To Cole,* he thought, and took a deep drink of the hot, whiskey-laced coffee.

"You look like hell," Colonel Bowers said, stooping through the low doorway of Mulholland's cabin.

"It's been quite a day."

Mulholland had his feet up on a crate and was sitting on another, leaning against the cabin wall. His leg throbbed.

"What happened to your escaped prisoners?"

"You haven't heard?"

"I was down at the trenches, carrying some dispatches. General Grant has called off that big attack he planned for next week. He thought the Rebs might know too much about it."

Mulholland nodded. He had made his report to Grant, and the general had told him as much. Spring wasn't far, Grant had said. A winter attack was risky, especially if the Confederates had been warned. They would wait for better weather to launch a campaign.

To Mulholland's relief, Grant had seemed distracted by other events. He didn't say a word about the whole incident, other than that he was glad the Reb sharpshooter was dead.

After leaving Grant, Mulholland had put Hattie on a steamer for Washington with a letter to his grandmother. She already knew Hattie from Anne's visits and had made a place for Hattie in her household.

He shoved the whiskey bottle at Bowers and took a sip out of his own tin cup. He had been drinking steadily all afternoon. It was the only thing to do after the kind of morning he'd had.

"Stump juice," Bowers said, pouring some into a cup and tasting it. "Virginia's finest."

"Cost me a damn fortune. But I had to have some."

"I know what you mean."

"We lost two men in the fight at the end. Bayliss, too. I shot that Reb sharpshooter."

"It was either that or a rope for him." Bowers hesitated. "What about Miss Clark?"

"She drowned." Mulholland studied the amber liquid in his tin cup. "Anne and the Reb who helped them escape made a run for it and I split off some troopers to go after them. They chased them right into the damn river."

"That water's cold."

Mulholland nodded. "I thought maybe they landed downstream, but the men never found them. Could be the current carried them out. They lost sight of them."

"Maybe they made it."

"The river was too wide there, and the water was too damn cold. They drowned."

Bowers sighed. "I'm sorry, Brendan. I know she was a friend from before the war. I could tell you were sweet on her. You saw her up in Washington, too, didn't you?"

He sipped his whiskey. "I never knew she was a spy."

"Of course not. Better men have been fooled. Besides, you probably weren't the only one she tricked."

"Who would have believed Anne was a spy, much less a Rebel?" Mulholland sighed. "This war has ruined a lot of lives. I'll be damned glad when it's over."

"That's the truth."

Mulholland poured more whiskey into his cup. "Let's get drunk."

Bowers grinned. "That's a fine idea."

Mulholland sat in the warmth cast by the tin stove, sipping whiskey, his leg up on the crate. His leg hurt fiercely after all the activity of the last two days, and he didn't think it would ever be the same. Old veterans of other wars had told him that some wounds never healed. Damp weather, or cold, made them flare up. The pain, he knew, would always remind him of the sharpshooter.

About the Author

David Healey was born in Baltimore and developed an interest in history while growing up on a Maryland farm visited by J.E.B. Stuart's cavalry on the road to Gettysburg in 1863. A graduate of Washington College and the Stonecoast MSA program, he works as a newspaper editor. He has written articles on historical topics for *American History*, *The Washington Times* and *Blue & Gray*. He is the author of three Civil War novels and one nonfiction book about the War of 1812. He lives with his wife and two children along the Chesapeake and Delaware Canal in Cecil County, Maryland.

Visit him online at www.davidhealey.net